D0628715

RICHMOND HILL
PUBLIC LIBRARY

OCT 2 4 2011

RICHMOND GREEN
905-780-0711

BOOK SOLD
NO LONGER R.H.P.L.
PROPERTY

PRAISE FOR *Ni...*

'Genre labels just don't app... ...ur Mark has managed to incorporate so many wonderfully varied ideas and themes into a ...ent and interest that the marketing departm... ...invent a whole new section just for him'   Peter F. Hamilton

'I was reminded of Jack Vance or Gene Wolfe . . . this is a promising start to a series worth pursuing'   *The Times*

'This is a grown-up fantasy that touches on real-life concerns, and this is where fantasy is at its most potent and relevant. Newton is certainly a new talent to watch, and I look forward to the next in the Legends of the Red Sun series'   SpeculativeHorizons.blogspot.com

'*Nights of Villjamur* is a terrific debut, it starts with a bang and keeps on going, building action upon action with terrific pace and plenty surprises before relenting and letting you catch your breath before it starts up again . . . refreshingly deft storytelling from an author who clearly knows how to write and I look forward to the next in the series'   Sci-Fi-London.com

'Mark Charan Newton's *Nights of Villjamur* has established itself in my mind as a contender for Best Fantasy Novel of 2009. Highly, highly recommended'   FantasyBookCritic.blogspot.com

'A great book, which takes old tropes and re-imagines them into something new and memorable . . . Definitely my favourite fantasy of the year so far, in what is a very good year for the genre. This will be a "best of the year" novel, unless I'm much mistaken'   Sffworld.com

'A polished and accomplished debut novel'

TheWertzone.blogspot.com

'While the sun over Villjamur is dying, Mark Charan Newton's star as a writer is burning with a fierce talent'

Stephen Hunt, author of *The Court of the Air*

'A solid, imagination-holding debut. Mark has crafted a layered, memorable tale that confirms his entry into the SFF world with a bang . . . Sure to be one of the top debuts of 2009'

DaveBrendon.wordpress.com

'A remarkable debut, a lush, fully-realised world defined by a writer with a mesmerizing style that evokes some of the greats of fantasy fiction without in any way being derivative. I look forward to following what will undoubtedly be a great career'

Mark Chadbourn

'*Nights of Villjamur* is self-evident in its awesomeness . . . Both broad in scope and sufficiently detailed, *Nights of Villjamur* succeeds – like many of the best modern epic fantasy series – because of its adult themes and shrewd political intrigue . . . Newton's language is beautiful and refreshing; his word choice at times is strikingly unique, experimental and genre-pushing. It's reminiscent of R. Scott Bakker's erudite and poetical prose. On promise alone, Mark Charan Newton may be the best of the new generation of fantasists. Better than Abercrombie, Scott Lynch, Patrick Rothfuss, Brandon Sanderson, and Peter Brett'

BloodoftheMuse.com

'Newton handles his multilayered world and diverse cast of characters with the assurance of an experienced author and balances his fantasy tropes with elements of horror and political commentary in vividly descriptive, compelling prose'

Publishers Weekly (starred review)

PRAISE FOR *CITY OF RUIN*

'Happily *City of Ruin* exceeded the already high expectations that I had, mainly because the author started going quite deeply into the sense of wonder and new weird territory, while keeping enough of the traditional fantasy modes to ground the novel too . . . The novel builds up relentlessly and then in the last hundred pages or so it becomes all "heart-stopping" action . . . With this novel Mr Newton shows that *Nights of Villjamur* was no fluke and he is entering the rank of premier fantasists working today'

FantasyBookCritic.blogspot.com

'*City of Ruin* is far more than a fantasy story. It contains obvious traces of crime, mystery, horror and even a whiff of urban fantasy. You get a lot of action, fair amount of military action, crossing plot lines, intrigues, superstition, betrayal, secrets and surprises. Stunning, awesome, gripping, intriguing, amazing, gorgeous . . . they all apply in this case. But this time I want to be simple and unpretentious: *City of Ruin* is definitely one of the fantasy highlights of 2010'

EdisBookLighthouse.blogspot.com

'Complex and convincing characterization, convincing world-building and increasingly accomplished prose to enjoy. *City of Ruin* is an excellent fantasy novel fusing elements of the New Weird and traditional epic fantasy into a satisfying whole'

TheWertzone.blogspot.com

'A deft melding of murder mystery, gang warfare, corrupt politics and full-blown war . . . a rewarding experience'   *SFX*

'In this second book of the Legends of the Red Sun series, Newton is braver. He mixes the same ingredients he let us taste in *Nights of Villjamur* but his elixir is bolder this time . . . Newton does an excellent job in keeping the reader captivated and surprised, and in creating an unusual setting that is not absurd but that creates an intriguing world full of mysteries and astonishments'
                                       BetweenTwoBooks.blogspot.com

'He has a great eye for detail, knows how to create characters that resonate with the reader and creates scenes with enough action and tension that I was left breathless at times. This is definitely one of my top reads of 2010'
                                       DaveBrendon.wordpress.com

'*City of Ruin* exceeds *Nights of Villjamur* in many ways, a great accomplishment for a sequel. In its own right, *City of Ruin* is a quick, detailed, passionate and virtually unputdownable read'
                                       LECBookReviews.com

CITY OF RUIN

Mark Charan Newton was born in 1981, and holds a degree in Environmental Science. After working in bookselling, he moved into editorial positions at imprints covering film and media tie-in fiction and, later, science fiction and fantasy. He currently lives and works in Nottingham. *City of Ruin* is the second book in the Legends of the Red Sun series, following on from *Nights of Villjamur*. The third, *The Book of Transformations*, will be available in 2011.

For more information and updates, visit his website
www.markcnewton.com

ALSO BY MARK CHARAN NEWTON

Nights of Villjamur

The Book of Transformations

CITY *of* RUIN

Legends of the Red Sun
Book Two

MARK CHARAN NEWTON

TOR

First published in the UK 2010 by Tor
This edition published 2011 by Tor
an imprint of Pan Macmillan, a division of Macmillan Publishers Limited
Pan Macmillan, 20 New Wharf Road, London N1 9RR
Basingstoke and Oxford
Associated companies throughout the world
www.panmacmillan.com

ISBN 978-0-330-46167-2

Copyright © Mark Charan Newton 2010

The right of Mark Charan Newton to be identified as the
author of this work has been asserted by him in accordance
with the Copyright, Designs and Patents Act 1988.

All rights reserved. No part of this publication may be
reproduced, stored in or introduced into a retrieval system, or
transmitted, in any form, or by any means (electronic, mechanical,
photocopying, recording or otherwise) without the prior written
permission of the publisher. Any person who does any unauthorized
act in relation to this publication may be liable to criminal
prosecution and civil claims for damages.

The Macmillan Group has no responsibility for the information provided by
any author websites whose address you obtain from this book ('author websites').
The inclusion of author website addresses in this book does not constitute
an endorsement by or association with us of such sites or the content,
products, advertising or other materials presented on such sites.

1 3 5 7 9 8 6 4 2

A CIP catalogue record for this book is available from
the British Library.

Typeset by SetSystems Ltd, Saffron Walden, Essex
Printed in the UK by CPI Mackays, Chatham ME5 8TD

This book is sold subject to the condition that it shall not,
by way of trade or otherwise, be lent, re-sold, hired out,
or otherwise circulated without the publisher's prior consent
in any form of binding or cover other than that in which
it is published and without a similar condition including this
condition being imposed on the subsequent purchaser.

Visit **www.panmacmillan.com** to read more about all our books
and to buy them. You will also find features, author interviews and
news of any author events, and you can sign up for e-newsletters
so that you're always first to hear about our new releases.

RICHMOND HILL
PUBLIC LIBRARY

OCT 2 4 2011

RICHMOND GREEN
905-780-0711

For my mother, Kamal,
who never let her sons go without.

ACKNOWLEDGEMENTS

A whole heap of people really supported the success of the first book in this series, *Nights of Villjamur*. We live in interesting times for the genre, with the blogosphere really taking off, so I especially wanted to thank several bloggers and reviewers who gave me a wonderful boost by their kind thoughts, coverage and opinion – because that all helped during the writing of this one:

James @ Speculative Horizons, Aidan @ A Dribble of Ink, Pat @ Pat's Fantasy Hotlist in particular. And also Liviu @ Fantasy Book Critic, Larry @ OF Blog of the Fallen, Adam @ The Wertzone, Graeme @ Graeme's Fantasy Book Review, Gav @ Next Read, Mark @ SFF World, Dave Brendon, Adele . . . There are many more I've most likely forgotten, but thanks to you all.

The guys at Team Tor are terrific, but especially Julie Crisp and Chloe Healy, who work far too hard, and have done well to put up with me so far. Julie has helped make this book much better than it was when I sent it to her, as has Peter Lavery. And, as ever, my agent John Jarrold has been a great guide.

'What would your good do if evil did not exist, and what would the earth look like if shadows disappeared from it?'

– Mikhail Bulgakov, *The Master and Margarita*

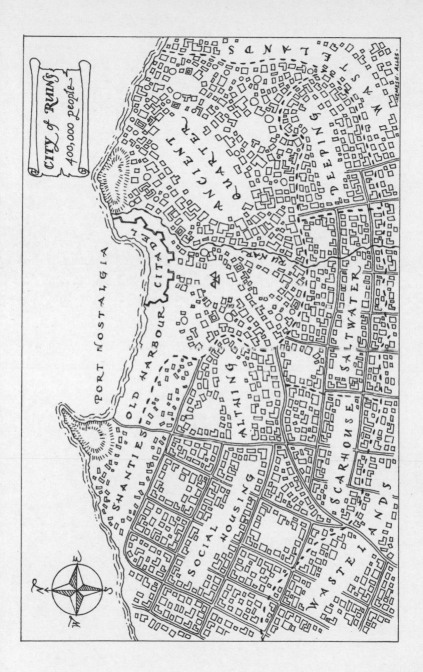

PROLOGUE

It entered the deep night, a spider reaching taller than a soldier. Street by street, the thing retched thick silk out of itself to cross the walls, using the fibrous substance to edge along improbable corners. Two, then four legs, to scale a wall – six, then eight, to get up on to the steps of a watchtower, and it finally located a fine view across the rooftops of Villiren. Fibrous skin tissue trapped pockets of air and, as tidal roars emerged from the distance, the creature exhaled.

A couple walked by, handy-sized enough to slaughter perhaps, their shoes tap-tapping below – but *No, not them, not now*, it reflected – and it slipped down off the edge of a stone stairway to stand horizontally, at a point where observation took on a new perspective. Snow fell sideways, gentle flecks at first, then something more acute, adding to the brooding intensity of the streets.

Within this umbra, the spider loitered.

As people sifted through the avenues and alleyways, it sensed them by an alteration in the chemistry of the air, in minute vibrations, so no matter where they were they couldn't hide. With precision, the spider edged across to a firm overhang constructed from more recent, reliable stone. Webbing drooled again, then the creature lowered itself steadily, suspended by silk alone, twisting like a dancer in the wind. Lanes spread before it, grid-like across a plain of mathematical precision. The frequency of citizens passing below had fallen over the last hour; now only a handful of people remained out to brave the extreme cold.

It could almost sense their fear.

One of them had to be chosen – not too young, not too old. The world collapsed into angles and probabilities as the creature made a controlled spiral to the ground.

Scuttling into the darkness, the spider went in search of fresh meat.

*

That was a shitting scream all right, Haust thought. Unlike a banshee's, this one was cut off so suddenly, it sounded almost as if it had been stolen from someone's throat. Maybe a last gasp for help? His senses were provoked wildly, his fear grew extreme. Pterodettes flapped and squawked eccentrically as they carved circles through the night sky.

Fucking hell, last thing I bloody want on a night patrol. And here was the deal: he should have already been in bed – no, better still, in the officers' mess, necking cheap vodka – but it was all the bloody commander's fault, him and his public-security nonsense. Patrol the streets, maintain a sense of control and authority, reassure the populace, reduce their scepticism regarding the army. At the moment, Haust didn't care if he was a Night Guard, therefore a man with advantageous augmentations – he was freezing his balls off, and no amount of augmentations could stop that.

Torches flared up the underside of snowflakes, conferring upon them the appearance of sparks from a blacksmith, an enhancement the snow didn't need these days, not in an ice age when everyone was sick of it.

Few citizens were loitering at this hour. The last figure he'd seen was a hooded man picking at his teeth assiduously as he ran through the passageways. There was a deviant psychology generated from the regularity of these surrounding buildings, from their sheer modernity. Bland labyrinths. When you turned one corner you thought you had just come from there, and before long you began thinking you might never leave. Buildings in this particular neighbourhood had been constructed without much desire for aesthetics, and he was glad he didn't live here.

Haust had only been a member of the Night Guard for a few months, but already thought himself a hero. Brought in from the Third Dragoons, Wolf Brigade, because of his flair with a bow, he now found himself in the Empire's elite guard deployed far across the Boreal Archipelago, in a city preparing for a war. Tall, blond, handsome – he thought he was invincible. *And why not? After all, being a Night Guard, you practically are.* The albino commander had selected him above others, to fight alongside them. It was a promotion that set his career in stone, gave him recognition as one of the best. When he dreamed at night, voices came and told him that he was a chosen one. *You can't ignore facts like that.*

He pulled his black cloak around him while tromping an exploratory path through the alleyways. He was somewhere about a mile from the Ancient Quarter, towards the centre of the city, which lay beyond the bad hotels and closed bistros. Bone archways from large whales were embedded in the cobbles, totems to the thousands of lost fishermen across the ages, and it was one of the few remaining features that suggested the ancient city had once been something grander. Also in that quarter rose three pairs of massive reptilian Onyx Wings, two hundred feet high and positioned in a triangle about a hundred yards apart on each side.

Another scream, but he couldn't tell where exactly it had come from. *Devil take me, this is a creepy place.* Something moved above his head, maybe one of the garudas? Why was he so scared? He was in the military, for Bohr's sake: a man meant to be at the top of his professional form.

Cats suddenly began to spill into the passageway, two, four, then countless numbers, all pouring through the streets like it was a mouthpiece, their claws tapping stone, occasionally lashing out at each other, before they spread out in exploratory arcs into the distance.

'Anyone there?' he offered.

Only his own voice came back at him, and he experienced something like vertigo – the very fabric of the streets changing in that same moment. He seemed an awfully long way away from a comforting bottle of vodka right now.

Around the next corner he spotted something and moved closer – it was a young body on the stone, severed down the centre, the ribcage split, organs spilling out into the night. Curiously, this body looked as if it had been dead for a while, certainly for longer than the gap in time between now and when Haust had heard the terrible scream. More detail he detected: the wound wasn't clean, and there were loose hairs around the edge of it, fine but firm, and the length of a thumb. To one side lay a butcher's meat cleaver, silvery and bloodied. The public torches exposed steam as the under-city heating system bled warmth into the icy evening air above.

Who'd done this?

A scuffle of boots on stone approached from somewhere behind him, and he immediately unsheathed his sabre. He couldn't see anything yet, so he followed the symmetrical line of the buildings to one side. Stone crumbled from a corner – *Fuck was that?* – but there was still nothing evident. He stood perfectly still to gain the most from his heightened senses. A cat padded down an alley to one side, but a hundred paces away. There was the glint of a broken, discarded sword up ahead. One of the Jorsalir priests was chanting, his voice carried on the breeze from some distance way to the south of the city.

A blow to his head and Haust blacked out . . .

*

The sound of metal woke him eventually, a grim shudder of sharp surfaces being raked across one another, and quickly he discovered that he was lying flat in a dark chamber. For some reason it felt as if it must be situated beneath the city itself, although he couldn't tell why – something about the air, perhaps, or maybe the vaguely domed ceiling that reminded him of a tomb. At the periphery of his vision, light defined the edges and flat surfaces of blades and knives and small swords hanging along the perimeter wall.

A clear voice spoke up suddenly: 'Welcome to my abattoir.'

'The hell are you?' Haust gasped. The man wore a top hat, white shirt, waistcoat, black breeches, the kind of outfit normally bedecking eccentric figures found in underground theatres in Villjamur. Slender, with a thin moustache, and smiling – always smiling. To his right loomed something rather like a spider, but with two almost-human eyes. Now and then it would rear up on its two hind legs, rubbing the other six limbs together, while clicking the lower pair sharply on the stone.

'Me?' replied the man in the hat. 'I just run this little show. I suppose, technically, I'm therefore your killer.'

'But I'm not dead ... Am I?' Another glance around the room, just to make sure – but still, none of the signs might encourage him to believe he was in a safe world any more.

'Give it time, dear boy,' the man said. 'A grammatical amendment: I *will* be your killer. We must be correct on such points! You really did pick the wrong night for a stroll, didn't you?'

Haust felt himself being lifted up, confirming the presence of a rope around his waist – then it occurred to him that the rope wasn't tight, wasn't connected to anything else. As if noting his expression of confusion, the well-dressed man said, 'Oh, it's for hanging you up to drain and cool afterwards. Procedures, procedures, I do tire of them occasionally ... you know how these things work.'

Thin smoke trails took the shape of arms, forming faint outlines of bodies, mere wisps of figures smothering him, touching him, caressing his hands, his neck, his face – in a faintly erotic manner – and he noticed how their eyes were suggested by featureless holes.

'What are they?' Haust was petrified – his body shuddering within the resolute grip of these wraiths.

'You're being lifted by what we call Phonoi,' the man told him. 'Grand creatures, aren't they?'

A whisper emerged from one of the apparitions: 'Shall we dump him now, sir . . . ? Shall we?'

'Sir, what will you have us do with him, sir?' another murmured. 'What now?'

'Shall we break his bones?'

'Shall we rip him first?'

'Spill his offal?'

'Can we?'

He was hauled through the air towards a massive cauldron, with fire licking up its sides, steam skimming across its surface. Haust began to shout again, as the smiling-faced man in the top hat offered him a wave and a bow.

A sudden drop, a desperate scream – and for the second time that night, everything faded to black . . .

ONE

It started with a knock at his door in the middle of the night, then someone urgently whispering his name through the keyhole, a voice he didn't recognize.

'Investigator Jeryd?'

In his still dreamlike state, the words seemed to float towards him like a ghost of sound.

What was going on?

He was in bed with his wife, Marysa, spending his eighth full night in Villiren. Jeryd had only just become used to the late-night noises of the city, the constant hubbub, and people walking by his window at all hours – sounds that played on his mind even when his eyes were closing. Sleep was a precious business, and being in a different bed was like living in a different context. His life felt full of disorder – which was ironic, really, considering that it had now been stripped down to the bare minimum.

He rubbed his hand over his paunch, and absent-mindedly swished his tail back and forth at the tip. *Too damn late in the evening for such a disturbance.* Over a hundred and something years to reflect on, and he couldn't remember the last time his life seemed like this, so constantly up in the air. Until recently his work had always been his life. He had felt safe when representing the Inquisition of Villjamur. He knew what the routines were, what was expected of him. He had substance, a knowledge of where he did and did not fit in, and now without his regular routine, the confidence of his many years was undermined.

The only calibrator of his previous existence was his wife, Marysa. Marriages had their ups and downs, didn't they, but recently they had both rediscovered their love for each other, and that made his existence just fine. In fact, their separation from their home city had brought them even closer together. He couldn't want much else. He glanced instinctively towards Marysa, whose white hair, such a contrast to her tough black skin, now attracted the glare of one of the moons as it slanted through the shutters in strips. Her own tail wafting gently beneath the sheets, the presence of her sleeping form was deeply comforting.

Again came that whisper: 'Investigator Rumex Jeryd!'

'Oh, hang on!'

Now he was more annoyed at his sleep being disturbed, than curious as to the reason someone wanted to speak to him. For a moment he lay there thinking, *If someone calls on you in the middle of the night it's seldom to tell you anything nice. Should I bother seeing who it is?*

Embers were still glowing in the grate, and the dust that had accumulated over the years in the room was pungent. This was only temporary accommodation because, with a war predicted, he didn't know how long he'd stick around here.

'Please, open up.' The voice was calm and firm, one clearly used to issuing orders.

Focus, Jeryd.

He flipped himself out of bed, hanging his legs over the end. Already wrapped up in thick layers, he was wearing outside them an outrageous pair of red night-breeches with hundreds of tiny gold stars stitched into the fabric. Marysa had bought them for him on their way out of Villjamur. She claimed he was too grumpy, that he needed cheering up, that he should smile more often. Vaguely ashamed, the ability to smile almost forgotten, he tiptoed across the room, his heels creaking on the floorboards.

A spider scurried across the floor, then under the cupboard, and he froze. This was Jeryd's secret shame: he feared and hated the creatures, always had since he was a child. They infested him with paralysis and brought him out in a cold sweat. The bulbous shape, their skittering movements – such *disgusting* creatures.

Shuddering, but now very much awake, he crouched to look through the keyhole, but could only see blackness beyond . . .

Then an almost red eye appeared on the other side and stared back at him.

Jeryd jumped back and said, 'Just a moment.' He opened the door.

An albino was standing there, his pale skin glowing white even in this light, so you might easily think him a ghost. A Jamur star was pinned to his breast, conspicuous against the black fabric of his uniform. 'Sele of Jamur, Investigator Jeryd. I'm Commander Lathraea.'

Jeryd recognized the softly spoken officer, one he had known from Villjamur but never met. He was a tall man, with narrow cheeks, a thin nose, and there was the faint whiff of aristocracy about him. But Jeryd had heard he possessed a little grit and know-how, qualities to be admired, attributes he could rely on. He'd also heard stories about how good this man was with a sword, how logical his mind was on a battle-field, how unusually compassionate he was as a leader.

'Sele of Jamur, commander,' he mumbled in response, rubbing his eyes. 'What can I do for you?'

The commander moved aside as Jeryd stepped out into the corridor, pulling the door shut to allow Marysa some quiet. For a moment, the officer eyed Jeryd's breeches with fascination. Why couldn't she have bought him a pair in black or brown, a colour that would blend with the night? *Red with gold stars, indeed.*

The commander continued, 'I put the word about for an investigator, and was told you'd come up recently from Jokull. I'd rather put my trust in someone from any other island than this one.'

Jeryd liked that because it confirmed two suspicions right away. One, the commander was a man who operated on loyalty; and two, Jeryd wasn't the only one to assume this city was full of scumbags.

He replied, 'Well, I'm as paranoid as any man can become these days, so your secrets are safe with me, commander. Though you could also say I'm not exactly welcome back there . . .'

'What did you do to end up here?'

Only piss off the Chancellor – now Emperor – by uncovering corruption at the heart of the Empire. Then went on the run from those who might call me in. Came to the only city in the Empire that takes the law into its own hands, and whose Inquisition is independent of the Villjamur – though it's not meant to be. Therefore found somewhere I could use my official medallion and connections to get work, and not starve during this ice age. All without any questions being asked. These were the things he wanted to say, just to tell anyone to get it off his chest.

Instead he muttered, 'They never liked the fact that I didn't complete my paperwork on time. It turns out that this benighted hole of a city is the best place for me.'

The commander frowned, gave a discreet nod. 'Fair enough.'

'What about you, commander? Not the prettiest town about for you either.'

'No, but it still needs defending. This city faces military threats, and we're here to oversee the defence operation.'

'You surely don't want me to help with that, do you?'

'No. But one of our soldiers has gone missing, a Night Guard named Private Haust. He was tall, thin, blond, blue eyes – typical of the south-west islanders. He'd only been in our unit for a couple of months, and was incredibly proud to be serving here. There's no reason for him to simply leave his post, especially with duties still to be carried out. He'd be thrown out of the army for ignoring them, yet he's been missing for six days now.'

'What took you so long to come here then?'

'We've conducted our own searches for the first couple of days, but our resources are limited – and the local Inquisition claimed they were too busy, then someone mentioned an officer from Jokull in the city, without many cases to deal with. I applied gentle military pressure until we got your name and address.'

For a moment Jeryd wondered how easy it would be for his present location to be given away to some clever sod from Villjamur. If they would even bother to come looking for him, of course.

'And I've heard about other people who have gone missing, too – not just Haust. A surprisingly large number, in fact.'

'They could just be getting the hell out of here because of the Freeze,' Jeryd suggested, while considering his options.

'Not that many without leaving some hint,' the commander argued. 'Most people in this city seem preoccupied with just getting through each day as it comes, rather than trying to escape the ice – or even the threat of war. Besides, where else would they go? No, from all that I've heard, they've simply vanished from their homes.'

Jeryd asked him for the usual details about the missing Private Haust, seeking minor clues that might help out immediately. To his mind, every detail mattered. From what the commander said, it sounded as if this could have been a murder, yet there was not a lot Jeryd could do in a city as unruly as this, with so little to go on. People went missing all the time. From his experience, such disappearances were an all too common mystery.

'This would usually be the sort of thing I'd send some of my men out to investigate,' the commander explained, 'but what with events in the north, and events anticipated in the future, we're all too busy planning and training. I need someone else to trust on this.'

'You're a very suspicious man, I see,' Jeryd said, approvingly.

'I've reason to be. I don't even trust our Chancellor – who's Emperor now, of course. Apologies, I'm still not used to the overthrow of the Jamur lineage.'

'We've something in common there, commander.'

Jeryd remembered all too clearly the events that transpired in Villjamur. The information he himself had uncovered. The replacement of the Jamur family line with a new ruler. The conspiracies of the religious cults. How Urtica had moved from Chancellor to Emperor overnight, by cunningly manipulating facts and words, money and people.

The albino smiled at him and nodded, confirming a shared opinion. Jeryd then decided that they had an agreement; that he would look into this matter first thing in the morning.

As the lithe commander strolled off down the corridor, Jeryd shuffled back to bed in his controversial breeches, put his arm around Marysa, his curves moulding closer into hers, and began to contemplate just how the hell he was going to navigate his way around a city about which he still knew next to nothing.

Two

A roll of thunder, loud enough to have been generated by an invading army, the noise from the auditorium could be heard well in advance of them getting anywhere near it, as Brynd Lathraea and Portreeve Lutto descended into the underworld of Villiren. Down here there were moments of such deep disconnection from ground level that Brynd wondered if he was strolling through some nightmare.

Rank waters trickled across their path as the snow melted under treatment from above, and it began mixing with the sewage and something else he didn't dare name.

'Lutto is aware of the smell,' the Portreeve of Villiren mumbled, 'but in times of crisis, the odour of my fair city – that is to say, the *Empire's* fair city, ha! – is the least of my concerns.' He waddled like a duck through the dark and featureless passageways, arms splayed out either side of his rolls of fat, a candle in one fist, and he continued leading them ever downwards – towards the riotous din. At least Brynd now faced the man's back, so he didn't have to look at his mendacious face, with that strangely hypnotic wedge of moustache. He thought the man grew it just so people wouldn't search his eyes for any residue of truth lurking in whatever he said. Lutto hadn't quite taken the ultimate plunge into full stupidity but, judging from the few conversations they'd shared, there was such potential evident in everything he said. Behind that, however, something else lurked, a vicious and spiteful intelligence that was known on occasion to be tapped. Some whispered that it was actually Lutto's wife, and indeed, how this man could successfully lead a city was beyond Brynd. He'd only been in Villiren for a few weeks, and already he was becoming distinctly annoyed by Lutto's manner, his way of speaking, his way of treating people – of treating Brynd himself.

'How far?' Brynd demanded.

'Such impatience. A soldier, I would have thought, should—'

'How *far*?' Brynd growled.

'Apologies, commander. Not much further, just ten minutes, Lutto promises.'

'You going to tell me sometime why you're bringing me here in civilian clothing?' A basic brown tunic, a dull grey cloak, a wide-brimmed hat pulled down low, and Brynd had even smeared some dirt across his face to disguise his albino colouring.

'Secrecy is essential, with some of these peoples,' was all that the fat man muttered in response, and Brynd was used, by now, to the mysterious and elusive manner in which he spoke. It pissed him off immensely, but there was no getting away without the loaded sentences, the hidden meanings.

And it wasn't as if Brynd wasn't burdened by a few secrets of his own.

This little trip, Lutto had said, could be vital to the defence of the city, and Brynd was keen to examine all opportunities that he had before him. Preparing properly for a likely siege against an unlikely opposition was essential.

This passageway reminded him of those in Villjamur, twisting and dark and apparently purposeless, although these were more recently built, the stone still sharp at the edges where time had not eroded them. Five minutes later and they had reached an even lower level, Brynd could feel it by a gentle shift downwards in the angle of the path. Rats flew across the ground ahead, chasing shadows. The odours of incense became intense, the noise of a crowd somewhere became defined, and Brynd's heart beat a little faster.

'Just about there . . .' Lutto whispered, pointing.

Through two featureless doors, and they were into the auditorium, a wide circle of stone seating stepping down to an arena in the centre, where there was a roped-off square about forty paces along each side. Pillars clearly separated the two rival tiers of spectators chanting and whistling, maybe four or five hundred of them already, and filling up quickly. Dozens of urns raised on pedestals burned violently with some kind of liquid fire, casting a surprisingly strong light, all the way down here beneath the city.

Brynd looked on in disbelief. 'Is this sort of thing legal?'

'You soldiers!' the fat portreeve laughed. 'Always sticklers for the law. Lutto can assure the commander that everything here is permitted under our ancient by-laws.'

Brynd glared at him. 'By-laws, indeed – sounds spurious, that. I'll take a guess that you yourself get a cut of the proceedings taken here?'

'A minor tax, is all.' Lutto smiled. 'We must try to use some of this bad money for good! If I shut it all down, then we would not be able to pay for some essentials, and then Lutto would have to spend all his time chasing stronger and faster men than himself.'

You don't spend much on such services, though, Brynd thought. *I've seen the accounts.*

Enhancing the eldritch ambience of the place, there were perplexing, gelatinous light-sources fixed to spikes or grouped together in small cages, and now and then someone unseen would dowse them in water, whereupon the luminous glow would intensify and flicker and oscillate.

'The lights, what are they?'

'Biolumes,' Lutto replied. 'They are taken from the sea. It is a recent practice, and not something encouraged, for ecological reasons, but it cannot be avoided.' Brynd had never heard of them. Lutto's maw opened to say something else, but then he seemed to think better of it.

As they took their places up at the back, Fat Lutto leaned closer to Brynd, and introduced him to how combat was performed this far north. 'Malum is the man I want you to see, and then you will know why a meeting with him could be of use. He should be coming on very soon.'

'A good fighter then, this Malum?' Brynd enquired.

'He loves the golem fights, so it is said, and who does not? A chance for combatants to prove themselves. Now and then you will see one of the great underground cultists, Gento Dumond, Feltok Dupre, even the old golemist Ninety-Six – and they bring their talents and relics here to the side of a combat ring, such as this, where their misshapen golems transform themselves from stone into fighters. How they then go about it, tearing chunks out of each other and then change state back into stone, and sit calmly to one side – if they managed to survive. My word! Such stagecraft is one thing, but thrice yearly you see the cultists bring in something a little more exotic: weird relic-enhanced animal-hybrids, say. There are times, too, where mortal men have to prove themselves worthy, as aspiring gang leaders. They must step into the arena to face these things . . . these bizarre fuck-ups of cultist obsession. Look, here's one now!' Lutto gestured with one porky hand.

Three figures wearing brown-hooded cloaks were busy pulling something from a hatch over to one side of the ring, where there was a gap in the seats, and as the trapdoor flipped open there arose a cheer, followed instantly by a collective intake of breath.

Out shambled three awkward, grotesque creations, something halfway between a reptile and a man, their skin tinged green with tribal tattoos circling the major muscle groups, and each of them stood a good head taller than any man present.

'What the hell are they?' Brynd demanded in awe. 'Lutto, what are these things?'

'As I say, cultists create these breeds by whim. Delightful, are they not? The sheer inventiveness—'

'Are they legal?'

'Here in Villiren, yes, of course.' The fat man pressed a palm against his chest, shaking his head. 'Very clever, yes. They're made only for fighting here, so it's quite all right. These are the most impressive I've seen in a long time!'

The three reptile men staggered forward in unlikely movements, exaggerated yet reluctant, sharp yet strained. Yanking at the ropes around their necks, they seemed to know that they were destined for the arena. Suddenly one slipped to the ground, as if it had forgotten the motions involved in walking, whereupon a man darted forwards with some metal object, shoved it into the creature's mouth, twisted something, firing off a contained bolt of purple light, before retreating back into the crowd as the amalgam pushed itself off the dusty ground.

Lutto explained, 'Cultist,' and Brynd nodded his understanding. They weren't looking at anything natural here.

Within the minute, the hybrids had all been handed weapons, scimitars and maces, and they began to communicate with each other in some primitive tongue, guttural noises replacing dialogue.

They then moved apart, gripping their weapons, eyeing all around them with purpose. Screams and whistles arose as the creatures shifted into a position they were obviously familiar with, at three corners of the square.

A single word was being passed around, just a whisper at first hidden among all the noise, then something more definite, taking form:

'Ma-lum! Ma-lum!'

'That chanting – what are they saying?' Brynd demanded of Lutto.

'They're asking for their favourite fighter,' Lutto declared. 'The star of our little show!'

'The one you brought me here to see?'

Lutto nodded, his chins wobbling, sweat glistening on his forehead. The crowd's violent incantation was eventually rewarded as a hooded figure emerged at the front of the audience. Two men removed his cloak and underneath the man was bare-chested. *He must be freezing*, Brynd thought, *going about dressed like that with all this ice enveloping the city*. Wearing only a pair of black breeches, he stepped under the rope, entering the square itself, and then Brynd realized he was also wearing a red mask concealing the upper half of his face. In fact, many members of the crowd watching were masked, more so than he had seen above ground. This was a cultural tic of Villiren that he hadn't yet become used to.

Malum took a short blade from one of the attendants: a messer, an armspan long with a single edge tapering to a turned-up tip. It was a weapon of choice for the common man, and perhaps this selection said something about him. Lean and muscled with tattoos flowing around his arms, his flanks, and around the base of his back. Black-haired, a few days of stubble on his face. There was something about his teeth, something distinctly savage, and this man looked as though he knew his way around a dark night like this.

'His name?' Brynd wanted confirmation.

'He is Malum, leader of a gang called the Bloods, and considered the most powerful man in the city's underworld. The Bloods have hundreds, possibly thousands of men in their ranks. Lutto himself has had dealings with him several times – best to get these types on one's side, no? That way Lutto is in control, too.'

Malum took his place in the fourth corner of the square, barely glancing at the three reptilian hybrids that occupied the others. The face painted on his mask looked as if he was contemplating some far-off fury.

Eventually someone rang a bell and a relative hush fell on the crowd. A man called out the rules, so far as they went: anything goes, last man standing wins, no pause for rest. Let it begin.

Another ring of the bell and the crowd roared and Malum was instantly alert. He strode forward, immediately holding his messer blade out ready for action. He took a defensive stance as the three hybrids approached simultaneously, their guttural communication with each other drowned out by the furore amid the audience. For a moment, the green-skinned beasts looked down on him as if to consider their next move. Then one slashed out with a mace, Malum leaned back deftly and another moved in with a sabre. Malum never retaliated, seemed content to roll to one side or the other, and there was something about his manner that said he was reading these creatures, observing how they moved. The third hybrid screeched then lunged at Malum with his scimitar. The human fighter ducked and slammed his blade quickly and methodically into the creature's stomach, then withdrew to the sight of black blood dripping down. The creature stared at it in disbelief, and turned to face its quarry once again. But before it could think further, Malum had raked his messer blade across its throat. It collapsed to one knee, eyes bulging, then fell forward to the ground. The other two hybrids wasted no time in stumbling forward, and brought their weapons crashing down on Malum, who simply spun backwards and out of their way. Using his astonishing speed, he manoeuvred past them, and clipped his blade across the heel of the one with the mace. It screamed, buckled to one knee as blood surged across the dusty ground. The crowd cheered and Malum smiled, holding his sword out to the auditorium. He was enjoying this, was arrogant even as he considered the two creatures again.

The one with the sabre began to slash at him with force in a combination of moves, and Malum seemed to struggle for a moment before he wedged his blade into the creature's flank.

The following slash of the sabre would have brought off his head had he not changed position. There was something disturbing about his speed, which seemed almost *inhuman*. Malum's muscles flexed, tendons bulging, his torso glimmering with sweat and still he grinned.

Brynd couldn't be sure if it was a trick of the light, but it almost looked as if he had fangs.

The creature with the mace was now limping at the perimeter of the ring, and as it presented its back to Malum for a moment, the man sprinted up to it and dug his blade in and along the spine. As he wrenched it down further, the crossbreed collapsed and began to spasm. Another cheer arose, another one down. Malum turned back to regard the last creature, clearly the best fighter of the three.

He ripped into it with all his skill and poise, dazzling all with artistic flourishes to the way he moved. Right then he might as well have been operating in some different dimension of time.

The hybrid received a gash to its arm, then to its flank, then to its face, and it began to wilt like a dying flower as Malum forced it stumbling back over one of its fallen comrades. Finally, Malum severed the hand that held the sabre clean off its arm, and drove his messer blade through its chest. A second or two later, it shuddered into stillness.

Malum stood there, breathing heavily, covered in unnatural shades of blood, then turned to face the cheering crowd and let them know by his stance that his position had been well earned, absorbing impassively the shouts and whistles coming from all around, as if to tell them not to ever question his worth. He even began to lick at the blood spattering him, as if savouring the taste.

Someone shouted, 'Next – you and you,' and two men pushed themselves up from the front row, massive triangular-torsoed figures, eyeing each other in readiness for bare-knuckle combat.

'Interesting,' Lutto declared, 'that no matter how sophisticated a culture we achieve, there is always need to prove how tough people can be, no? So, I assume you'll now wish for me to arrange a meeting, commander? You think he'll be of use?'

Malum had been astonishing and mesmerizing and brutal. His skills were the equal of any soldier that Brynd had encountered for a long time, perhaps surpassing them all. Men like him could prove invaluable when it came to it. There was no point in considering such a question further: he needed all the help he could find.

'I do indeed,' Brynd admitted. 'And if there are other men as able and as talented as that one, I would like to be made aware of them too. They might make the difference between your city surviving or finding itself reduced to rubble.'

'Lutto understands clearly,' the fat portreeve replied, 'and will make the appropriate enquiries.'

THREE

'*My sweeeeetheart is a soldier, as handsome as can be-e-e,*' sang Arletta, stage vixen of Villiren, forty-six years old, broad about the beam, and still making the most of those curves. From the unrevealing sanctuary of his red bauta mask, Malum watched her sashay about the stage in a bulging sparkly size-too-small gown, while fetchingly wrapped in lantern light and candle glow. The guitarist struck another bum chord, and she shot an angry glare at him. '*My daaarrrhling, I'll tell you what toooo dooo.*'

Another night in the Partisans' Club, and it was essential that Malum be seen here right about now. His presence was his alibi, confirming to others that he wasn't responsible for the forthcoming crime.

An unusual spirit of solidarity had come upon the city. Rumours of impending war blossomed, and it seemed in such times that anyone with any money in Villiren just wanted to piss it all away in clubs like this one. He had heard that Arletta was doing a roaring trade, and she now flashed him a smile caked with make-up before bowing to her audience's thunderous applause and whistles. She knew who he was all right, as did most of them in here. Any who wanted to further their careers, or even their lives, that was, and he was fine with this reputation he had built up. The waiter was about to bring Malum his tab until someone spoke a word in the waiter's ear. And there was that 'Oh, him' expression on the waiter's face, and the man retreated back into the shadows behind the bar.

Malum had to go. He removed his mask and placed it on the table ready for JC, who was waiting just behind him and surprisingly sober tonight. The man quickly slid on an identical hat and surtout to Malum's, then put on the red mask as he took the seat just vacated by Malum, at his usual table against the wall near the left of the stage, and conveniently in the half-light.

And Malum slunk away to collect his coat, before he headed outside into the cold.

*

Malum lingered, in the frozen night. Now wearing a white mask, a few paces from the corner of Ru Nár – a little too close to home for comfort, but he had to get this business out of the way. A hundred lanterns and the occasional biolume shifted around the city streets, like the heavens at night swirling around here on the ground. Fiacres were still passing, carrying night-goers to illicit destinations. Two blonde girls in cloaks walked by, laughing, bottles clinking, heels clacking, a sight so typical of this area in Villiren. A red-haired woman shuffled in his direction, heavily pregnant, then stumbled and dropped her bag to the cobbles. She obviously couldn't afford to buy a new coat to accommodate her condition so her belly ballooned beneath her present one, forcing it to part. He wondered what babies thought, cocooned in all that sticky warmth? *Does this one have any instinct of the hell it's about to be born into?*

He stepped forward – thinking *Sod it if my cover's blown* – to help her collect her scattered cuts of meat from the ground. At first she might have thought he was there to rob her, but then she murmured a grateful 'Thank you' as he handed her back the possessions. As they exchanged quick glances, Malum could smell the deep scent of her . . . her *blood*.

He hadn't felt like this for so long because he could usually

23

control the urge. Immediately he turned aside and the pregnant woman continued on her way.

He had to get back in the *zone*, that certain mental space he needed to inhabit – in order to do what he was about to do.

It was one of dozens of public squares in Villiren, but one of the few districts to forgo the monotony of incessant redevelopment of the city. Amazing how quickly things had changed all around, he contemplated; how the wooden houses had inexorably given way to stone. Money from the mining industries fed the prosperity of the smiths of the city, propagating an urban expansion so speedy that if you sat on a street corner long enough they'd build a shop around you.

Check the knives: one in his boot, one up his sleeve, slick messer blades, the kind of gear he needed to get this job done. Scarf around his mouth, a heavy surtout keeping out the fine mist of sleet, tricorne hat pulled down and a white mask to cover the upper half of his face. With his heart pounding, he could almost taste his own anxiety.

Forward yet again. A few traders were still here, some frying food, or selling thick clothing, or jugs, pots, plates. He noticed a kid he thought he himself had sold a pirated relic to, and was surprised to see he was still alive. Inevitably a few youths were milling around with nothing better to do, such was the way of things around here. Never anything sufficient to occupy them despite the hundreds of distractions on offer, the hundreds of market stalls during the daytime, the eclectic mix of peoples, the nightly entertainments. No, they just seemed to want to lounge around.

A rectangle of light signified a doorway, his destination, the shadow of a man standing inside, bulky in his heavy coat. As soon as their vision connected, they knew each other, though they also knew not to show it. Malum slipped him a few silver Lordils, and went inside, downstairs to the relative warmth, where musky smells added to the sudden claustrophobia.

These jobs did not get any easier, but this was one he felt he had to do himself.

*

Tindar Lesalt managed a few bordellos around Villiren's smarter areas, limited though they were. He ran a few scams, too, not a great deal more than gambling operations, and these latter didn't bother Malum much. You could find him, if you could get near him, every other night, in the basement rooms of a bordello that provided women trafficked from the local tribes – and that disgusted Malum rather more. These women had been ripped from their native communities and forced to open their legs to business men and gang members who would drink imported vodka, fuck the women on offer, talk about fucking them, and laugh together about the good old times.

Malum was certainly not one of *those customers*, they were simply not his kind, and he reckoned they gave the gangs a bad name. Some people suggested that Tindar ran a side operation that involved cultists augmenting human bodies for extortionate amounts of cash. The more esoteric buzz concerned people being fitted with animal parts, that it was Empire-sponsored, and that communities of such adaptations currently persisted across the archipelago. Malum could believe it – he'd seen artificially messed-up examples from time to time, including cases much more severe than the hybrid beasts he often fought underground. There were remote villages on Dockull and Maour, outside of Empire territory, where such half- and quarter-breeds manage to frighten even themselves as they shambled with alien movements from shack to shack.

These dubious activities were just a selection of things that Tindar got up to, but they weren't the main reason Malum was going to kill him.

*

Three doors along the corridor, and the last on the left. Noises coming from the other side: exalted chitter-chatter, squeals of laughter. Malum headed straight in, sliding himself sideways through the doorway. Old masked men sat playing cards under the light of a green biolume. Other clients drank at a bar where a dodgy cultist was busy trying to persuade punters to buy into a relic, conning people into losing limbs or even their lives to his broken magic. Malum walked halfway across the room, as if to sit down at an empty table, then paused. Over to one side there were dogs set to fighting in cages: gargantuan breeds crossed with gheels or something else, some with two heads and massive fangs – which seemed to substantiate all those outlandish rumours. Money passed hand quickly in the shadows, quicker even than in the city above. *Down here it just evaporates.* Glances were towards him, some of them familiar, others he had never seen.

There, over there. Two fully clothed, red-haired hookers were practically straddling a wealthy-looking muscular man, Tindar himself, who was slumped in the corner, wearing brown breeches and nothing but the very finest of waistcoats. He regarded Malum with a smile that might or might not have signified that he knew who he was. For a moment there was an absolute silence in the room.

Malum called off the poor girls, giving a gesture they would understand, which sent them running to the bar. He shook the messer blade from his sleeve. Rage bared his teeth so that his fangs became prominent – *control yourself, control yourself* – and meanwhile the man tried to retreat back into his chair, nearly spilling himself onto the floor. 'Fuck you doing?' he spluttered.

Malum raked the messer across his victim's chest, a wide cut from hip to shoulder; blood blossomed invitingly in its trail – but he wouldn't be drinking this, not the blood of this bastard. He raked another line diagonally to scribe an X across his entire torso.

Tindar's eyes bulged as he feebly gripped his opening gut.

A skinny, handsome man in all black, maybe the victim's son, leapt forwards yelling, 'Get him!' to the others. Malum swiped twice, hissing, bearing his fangs, further tracing fine wounds on the assailant with his blade. He grabbed the man's wrist and head-butted him savagely, drawing blood from above one eye. Then Malum embedded his messer in his open mouth, snapped it back sharply so that he crumpled to the floor with a permanent scream on his face.

Malum prepared to run for it, but no one else got up to stop him.

Others made out they hadn't witnessed this; they focused instead on the fighting dogs or the cards or just their drinks, shifting uneasily in the dull lighting. Only the girls showed any concern on their faces.

Back up the stairs, then back out into the cold, almost slipping on the ice, quickly around two corners – and Malum was clear.

Hand against a wall, he threw the mask clattering across the streets. He inhaled deeply, and then slumped forward with his head resting against cold stone. Everything inside him was pounding with adrenalin.

He put a hand to his mouth and felt his fangs, as if trying to push them back inside with his thumbs, thus denying that he was half-something else rather than human. When the rage set in he could become uncontrollable – and that made him a danger even to himself. He suffered torments from being a half-vampyr but could always just about restrain his darker urges. For years a state of human normality was something he had craved. After a kill like this one, when he assessed his state of mind, all he could think about was being *normal*.

Malum headed with purpose back towards his home, littering an alleyway with the distinctive scarf and hat. *I've three thousand men to do my bidding, but there are certain things you have to do yourself.*

Tindar had dared to boast to members of the Bloods about running a child-abuse racket – dozens of innocent lives ruined, young minds subjected to the cruel perversions of influential citizens. And that was why Malum had needed to kill Tindar himself.

*

Malum nodded curtly to two shaven-headed ex-military men, hired guards without uniforms, brutish-looking and efficient.

'Sir.' They eyed him carefully, then the surrounding streets. Always wary, just as Malum had trained them, because there would always be someone who wanted him dead.

'Night.' Malum emitted a barely mumbled reply, the words drying up in his throat because he was still hungover from the recent kill. He was certainly relieved to be back on Ru Una, a wealthy street at the further end of the Ancient Quarter under the moon-cast shadow of one of the great Onyx Wings.

He hoped she wouldn't ask questions, not tonight.

A large, whitewashed building now presented itself to him. Home. It was practically a palace by Villiren standards – the real ones had been demolished decades ago by property developers with no sense of the city's heritage. Sometimes he even felt like an aristocrat: he had his own private militia in the Bloods, men and women who would do anything for him, no questions asked – and commanded more loyalty than any landowner could ever hope for. Money flowed through his hands daily, and he was married to a smart, talented and beautiful woman.

But things weren't what they used to be.

He entered and, sighing deeply, he shook off his cloak. Pain shot up his legs as he hauled himself up the staircase. He slumped into a burgundy-upholstered chair in a large room on the second floor, studying his luxurious home with casual pride. Two tall vases glittered in the moonlight slanting through the skylight. He'd bought them some years back, when the Bloods had reached five hundred members. The ornaments themselves were said to be from the time of King Hallan Helfen, the man who had completed the initial construction of Villjamur eleven thousand years ago, before the series of emperors began. He was the first ruler to sign a treaty with the cultists, so as to stop their warring, and it was even suggested that some relic technology had been used in the construction of the vases.

Truth be told, Malum didn't give a fuck about that. They just looked nice with the rest of his house. And who said crime didn't pay? He had been hoping for some antiques from the Shalafar era, forty thousand years back – just to say he had some. Something to indicate *I am better than you*. Máthema items were even harder to come by, but that never stopped him looking.

He poured some Black Heart rum into a crystal glass, and used the respite to contemplate the coming days. There were rumours that the street gangs had been invited to liaise with the Night Guard about providing help with the expected war. There was talk of good money, too, not just bribes, but the sort of cash that would see most of his guys eating well for years to come. Payments in Jamúns, no less. And via the portreeve, it transpired that private companies had expressed an interest in hiring Malum's expertise to deal with masses of their employees. *That could get messy.*

'I *thought* I heard you come in.'

Beami was standing in the doorway to their bedroom, cocooned in thick blankets like some giant woollen insect. She shouldn't need to do that, and it annoyed him, because he had paid a great deal of money for the finest craftsmen in the city to install a new firegrain system in their house. Her sleek, boldly fringed hair shimmered even in the poor lighting, which also did wonderful things to the angles of her face. Her eyes absorbed darkness, shadows pooled against her collarbone, under a softly rounded nose, fully defined lips. He adored her.

Do I?

She was his sole reason for being *normal,* a reason for him to at least try. Beami was smart and tall and good-looking. *So I should feel something, shouldn't I? I should and yes I want to.*

Beami sighed, 'What're you doing up at this hour? Or was there a combat this evening?'

'Yeah,' he lied. The fight was last night; tonight had been business.

'You never invite me along these days.'

'You never ask.'

Discreetly, and with great thoughtfulness, he had managed to keep his dealings largely to himself. She knew about the fights he engaged in for sport – it would have been impossible to avoid her noticing the occasional scars. But it seemed important to him to keep these aspects of his life compartmentalized, as a crucial factor in making his daily existence as normal as possible. He could not hope to explain his needs.

'I won though,' he declared.

'What a champion,' Beami yawned. Her habitual sarcasm was once something he admired, but these days he hated her dismissive attitude towards him. Funny how the little things you like at the beginning often become the things you ultimately abhor. 'You coming to bed?'

As if to highlight the ensuing silence, the heating system wheezed like an old man dying of pneumonia, indicating firegrain caught up in the piping somewhere. *Cheap shitting hack workmen.* The whole house suddenly shuddered like a living thing.

'I'm just unwinding. I'll be there in a moment.'

Beami gave him a forced smile, then uncoupled her gaze from his face. It took her a while to say it: 'You want to try again tonight?'

'Maybe.'

She left him then, with only his rum and costly possessions

for comfort. The last time he'd tried ... hadn't ended well. Their attempts never did.

And afterwards I get overcome by rage, and try so hard to transform in front of her ...

It took him a while to get out of the chair, through laziness, tiredness, whatever. Then painfully slow strides to the bedroom. And there she was, lying in that huge bed, looking so small amidst all those coverlets and blankets, her hair spread out across the pillows. Boots off first, then clothes off, he climbed in next to her, the sounds of the city muffled in the background.

Warmth and soft skin.

He pressed against her, wondering if she was still awake or not, and when Beami turned towards him, the dread hit him, like it always did. Kisses didn't do much for him, though she tried – along his neck, his jawline, and she made those noises, the ones she thought he liked to hear, little groans to indicate he might be satisfying her, as if to rebuild his confidence. Her hands skimmed across his bare skin.

Nothing, no sensation.

He made efforts too; he did not simply lie there. He felt for the heat of her stomach, tentatively explored her wetness. As he moved his mouth across her neck he resisted the urge to bite. He concentrated on the kinds of things he imagined he should be feeling. This went on for a while, duplicating gesture after gesture, and when she finally touched his cock he held his breath in anticipation ...

Nothing. No reaction.

Time became less abstract and more relevant, and this added pressure to react pushed him over the edge. Rage had been flaring beneath the surface, and he didn't want to express it, but he did ... 'Just leave me the fuck alone.'

And he shoved her aside, and turned over; he felt if he didn't see her, it wouldn't happen. He was now seething with anger, wanted to strike out at anything ... But he held back, somehow. It wasn't that easy, but he managed not to *turn* in front of her.

And he lay there, in the darkest of nights, unable to get an erection, wondering about something he dared not mention in public, not even to her. A question that couldn't be said out loud to any of his gang, because it came loaded with shame and embarrassment.

Am I even a man any more?

FOUR

Private Lupus Bel of the Night Guard informed Brynd that Villiren today was a world away from the one he remembered, and given the current rate of development and saturation with building projects, Brynd could well understand the lad's childhood memories being different.

Under those interminable flat roofs, throughout the dreary crowded streets, men and women sought escape from reality in increasingly diverse ways. It never used to be like this, Lupus assured him. People kept hearing terrifying stories that flooded in from neighbouring islands, embellished as they passed from mouth to mouth. So what else was there to do but drink and party themselves into oblivion?

Secret drinking joints and burlesque clubs were springing up and closing down daily, moving around the city as if planned by stealth. If you had a fetish, you had a place to go. New music too, styles based around the Villjamur standards, but taken down smoother and more intricate routes, gentle minor chords and variants, a little extra beat. Despite the chill, girls would sit barefoot by fires, drinking cold lager. Teens risked injury in suicidal horse races along black-iced streets. Lift the lid on this city and you might never guess Villiren was almost under siege, a city with nothing else in mind except to wait for a war. There was an illicit fatalism about the place, a generation about to be lost to something.

In public places, Brynd had raged about his findings. Weeks

had passed since the Night Guard had first encountered the enemy approaching across the ice. The military had travelled halfway across the Empire in order to investigate reported killings on Tineag'l, the island due north of Villiren, and there they had discovered what amounted to a genocide. An island's population, all but wiped out – people butchered on the spot, or taken from their homes, leaving only blood-trails through the main thoroughfares or signs of futile skirmishes while attempting to resist. Only the elderly and children had been left – well, their bodies, at least, with bones half removed and the flesh discarded. In crowded halls Brynd had told the people of Villiren of these shocking events, while they listened dumbstruck. Still, no one seemed to have any real concept what the city was in for.

*

Brynd had been here for several weeks but still didn't know what to make of Villiren.

Empty of dramatic spires and bridges, when compared to his time spent in Villjamur, the cityscape now seemed vacant. Everything to be found over a mile away from the Ancient Quarter appeared flat and hastily built. More and more blocks were being constructed, their dull featureless facades set atop gothic foundations, and they seemed to proliferate at an alarming rate.

Another surprise to him was the heating system. Lutto had ensured that a network of firegrain pipes was constructed over the previous few years, admittedly with a little help from cultist technology. Channels of warmth were pumped like blood under the streets, through underground networks, through steaming pipes and up through the floors of houses in the wealthier neighbourhoods. Meanwhile outside, passage-ways and even main thoroughfares were doused by Cultist Water, a version of seawater primed with enhanced salinity, which was enough to keep the ice off for weeks at a time.

The garudas had now arrived, though only a few of them, who swept in investigative arcs to the north, along the fringes of Tineag'l, over the ice sheets that had almost bridged the islands; and sometimes pterodettes would coast lazily in their trails. These bird-soldiers never ceased to amaze: tall, and elegant yet surreal. When they flew in low one could see their dull armour, their feathers, in clearer detail, even the powerful muscles beneath their massive wings. Two or three times a day, Brynd would see the flash of *Brenna* devices, those explosive relics the cultists had devised to ensure the surrounding waters remained free of ice, so no enemy could traverse it on foot.

And now what? An endless wait, it seemed, as he discovered and observed further the idiosyncrasies of this strange city.

*

With Lupus in tow, Brynd was parading down from the citadel's battlements, heading towards the markets that lay between the district of Althing and the Ancient Quarter, where those Onyx Wings dominated the city skyline. From here the older styles of building could be seen: the original city, a mishmash of cylindrical towers and domes. This area was surrounded by a sea of flat roofing, only interrupted now and then by a large warehouse or a windmill.

Traders hastily erected stalls in the irens in the early morning, tying strips of coloured rags to indicate their territory, red or blue or green. Awnings were flipped into place and signs hoisted inscribed with esoteric symbols, in scripts of Jamur-tribal hybrid languages. Citizens themselves were hybrids, cross-breeds of the inhabitants of all islands of the Archipelago. But there were still some who clung to their island ways: Jokulites exhibiting awkward restraint and tentativeness at being this far east; Folkens behaving with spurious machismo or indifference. And derived from all cultures were thieves stealing the wares of others, seemingly nonchalant as they went about their business, of deftly pocketing whatever they could.

Villiren, rather than Villjamur, was the real commercial centre of the Empire. Metals came south from Tineag'l, meaning they were the first to get hold of the ore. Conspicuous qualities of goods therefore were manufactured here and distributed around the Jamur Empire, mainly to Villjamur, a city distant enough to never see completely what was going on here. Consumer items were branded according to the fashion they were made. Fabrics were woven in unique ways, specific colours, alloys that resonated at a given pitch, then sold on in the cities as desirable commodities. Branding, in fact.

Whether or not they were distracted by such a plenitude of trinkets, Brynd couldn't tell, but it seemed that the people here didn't care too much about the ice, let alone the threat of war. But that was the way of things: people concerned themselves with the small details rather than prophetic events.

This was no prison city: indeed what really made the difference was the absence of encircling walls, no sense of confinement. Buildings sprawled ever southwards, to dissolve gradually into farmland or forests. No tent city of refugees camped outside, like Villjamur. Nevertheless Brynd guessed they were probably crammed inside the community somewhere, hidden away within the large housing blocks, but well away from what was left of the old city.

Some of the traders had lit stoves so that passers-by would loiter around them for warmth and, given time, perhaps be tempted to buy something. Everywhere around them there was snow, on the roofs, on upturned crates, lining the walls of houses. People, garbed in furs and a few wearing masks, rooted through the stalls for the freshest catch of fish, and there always seemed to be a surprising amount of meat on

36

display, given the city's circumstance, which was another thing Brynd couldn't fathom.

A small cluster of figures caught Brynd's eye.

The three of them were huddled next to a corner, examining something on the ground, while other citizens milled around them heading towards the iren or on their way towards the old harbour.

As the two soldiers now approached them, one looked up and saluted. She was a tall and lanky woman with a permanent expression of surprise etched on her face by age. Nevertheless pleasant-looking, she wore a tweed cloak with a muddied hem, and a fine-tailored tunic underneath, of the type of cut you just didn't see much any more. Under one arm was a battered old book, bound in brown leather.

She greeted Brynd. 'Sele of Jamur, sir!'

The other two looked up abruptly from their business. One man was chubby, with a moustache, a flat cap, and a serious look on his face; the other completely bald, stocky and savage-looking. Both wore layers of brown tweed, and neither of them reacted in the slightest to Brynd's unusual appearance, his albino skin, his red-rimmed eyes – as so many other people did.

'Sele of the day,' flat cap hailed, an older variation on the usual Empire greeting, and his voice was heavily accented from some place Brynd didn't recognize.

'Sele of Jamur. Can I check what the three of you are doing?' Brynd enquired.

The tall woman, clearly the leader of the group, stepped forward with an earnest smile. 'A little examination of old ley lines, dear sir.' Her voice was bass with age, and loaded with cheap charm. A quick gesture on her part steered Brynd's gaze towards a small tripod at the base of the wall, presumably a relic to judge by the metallic shimmer and the dials. At the top of it rested some kind of graded instrument, aimed at the faintest glow of red sun visible behind the clouds. These were cultists, surely.

'Nothing illegal, this?' Brynd asked, glancing towards Lupus. The private had his bow already slung across his shoulder, but he didn't think there would be need of it. These people seemed innocent enough.

'D'you hear that, Abaris?' She turned to flat cap, then back with her face creasing in smiles.

'Pah! Illegal, he says,' Abaris replied. 'Nah, nothing of the sort, lad. We're merely exploring some technology of the Ancients, ley lines and the like. Bit of lore stretches across this island – you know, myths and whatnot. All in all, we were rather hoping we could be of some use, given that the city might soon be having a few problems, like.'

The bald man remained utterly silent.

'We're from the Order of the Grey Hairs, sah!' Abaris confirmed. 'Last remaining cultists of various minor sects. United in the fact that, well ... um, the rest of our lot are dead, more or less. Us old things is all that's left. And now at your service!'

Brynd and Lupus stared at one another, and the young private raised his eyebrows, stifling a smile.

'Do you reckon you can be of any use in the coming war?' Brynd asked. 'Can you hold a solid weapon well enough? There might be call for that, as we need everyone we can get.'

'Weapons have never been of much use to us, I confess,' the tall woman observed. 'But, we're not aiming on burning ourselves on a funeral pyre just yet, oh no. Here's our card, then. We've digs on the other side of the Ancient Quarter – so we're never far, should you need our assistance.'

'Very good.' Brynd smiled, placing the card in his pocket without really looking at it. 'Well, carry on. We may indeed need your help yet.'

Brynd shook his head and turned away, the three elderly cultists gazing back at them in a line as the soldiers departed.

The two Night Guards resumed their patrols of Villiren, pondering if they could actually be of any use. Cultists were notoriously unreliable, unless they came from among those who had links with Imperial networks, and even those they did occasionally work with couldn't really be trusted. These three in particular seemed like crazies. His plans were best founded on solid facts and good probabilities – so, unless they could manufacture military weaponry of some kind, you couldn't hope to build a strategy around them.

*

Giant trilobites the size of dogs clicked along the streets, investigating scraps of food. They would lurch back and forth from people's paths, antennae waving in the air, giving some mild screech of alarm, before finding some dark doorway in which to disappear. You didn't get these creatures much further south than this, and he had missed their eccentric presence. Nearby hung a rack of their shell casings, ready to be sold as decorative armour to people with more money than sense.

Brynd had stressed to Lupus just how important it was to be seen in the city, to be visible at a time like this. People smiled at them, old men patted their backs, young boys watched in awe on seeing the finest of the Empire's soldiers here to offer support. They had to represent stability, show the citizens that everything would be all right – even if it wasn't. But everyone here seemed full of calm, and whenever he asked them about the ice, they simply shrugged.

One trader summed it up: 'Everyone's got problems, in't they, commander?'

*

'You can buy all sorts of junk here,' Brynd observed, indicating exotic pots, ornaments, chalcedony necklaces, paduasoy scarves. In their craftwork he could discern a mixture of cultural influences, from the tribes of other islands – maybe Folke, Blortath, even Varltung – to ancient designs of the

Shalafar civilization, the Máthema who had been obsessed with mathematical precision.

Brushing a hand through his white hair, Brynd said, 'Odd place, this. I mean, we're near the seafront, where the streets are older, so you'd think there'd be some air of history at least . . .'

Lupus turned sharply, peering through the crowds.

'Trouble?' Brynd asked, his hand casually dropping on the hilt of his sabre.

'No,' Lupus panted. 'Nothing.'

'Didn't look like nothing judging by your reaction,' Brynd muttered. 'Don't want another Haust situation here, do we? Can do without *you* going missing, of all people. We'll be needing our best archer in the weeks to come.'

Days had passed since Private Haust had disappeared, another reason the soldiers were exploring this neighbour-hood. Even if the Inquisition were working on the case, it was still worth keeping an eye out, because there might be some remains to discover, a boot, a strip of ripped material, some-one who'd spoken to the victim before he vanished.

Eventually Lupus replied, 'Was nothing, really. I just thought I saw someone I recognized . . . Apologies, sir. Let's continue.'

Brynd could see patches of alien stonework now and then, the city betraying its age, a wall maybe that was out of place, buildings that denied the surroundings their coherency. Brynd was constantly assessing the layout of the streets, the vantage points, closed-off zones, those regions which were solid, and those that would eventually crumble. They'd been doing this survey for weeks, in preparation for war. The enemy was reported to be gathering in significant numbers on the island opposite, gearing up for a seaborne invasion. Combat would be here in a city if the surveillance was right, not on a battle-field like they were all trained for.

'Lupus Bel.'

Brynd looked up curiously; the young soldier seemed to recognize the voice even before he saw her. A tall woman was standing there – though a fraction shorter than Lupus himself. She was wrapped in a brown fur coat, thick boots, her sleek black hair hanging loose under a severe fringe.

Brynd watched him, curious. Years collapsed in Lupus's face.

'Beami,' Lupus spluttered. 'I thought I'd seen you. I knew it.'

'Me, too, I . . .'

'I mean I know you used to live here, but not now. I just caught a glimpse.'

'Yeah, I saw you,' the dark-haired woman replied. 'That's why I came back.'

Brynd could see Lupus was searching his mind for something suitable to say, but was disorientated, a soldier with no clue of his current location.

'You might as well smile,' Beami said. 'I've not changed that much, have I?'

'Sorry.' Lupus broke into a genuine laugh. 'How long's it been?'

'Six . . . seven years.' She touched his arm, a gesture made from instinct rather than thought, from the habit of being close to him. She eyed his black uniform, the neat stitching, then stroked the star on his breast. 'You've done well, I see. You always wanted to be one of the Night Guard.'

'And you? How . . . are you?'

'Good. I'm, uh, married now, but I'm good,' Beami replied. 'Still working with relics . . . you know me.'

'Are you happy? I mean . . . sorry, I meant I *hope* you're happy.'

Brynd coughed into his fist. Enough of this chat, they were on duty now.

Lupus glanced at him sheepishly. 'Where are my manners? Bea, this is Commander Brynd Lathraea, Commander of the Night Guard.'

'Oh, my.' Beami examined the commander. 'The leader of the Jamur military. The mysterious albino. I've heard a lot about you.'

'Nothing bad, I hope,' Brynd smiled. 'Sele of Jamur, miss.'

'Sele of Jamur, commander.' Her voice possessed a slight hesitancy; the usual reaction whenever anyone's gaze met his red pupils for the first time.

'Commander, this is Beami Del. We knew each other a few years ago – when I was sixteen.'

'Nice to meet a friend of the private,' Brynd said. 'One of the finest soldiers I've worked with, this one. Youngest member of the Night Guard as well.'

Tense smiles were exchanged between them as local people sailed past around them. Some stopped to contemplate these well-dressed men in their black uniforms, standing talking to this beautiful woman. Time seemed to shudder to a standstill.

'We need to order some meat,' Brynd reminded Lupus eventually, 'for the troops. It seems a mastodon's been brought down, not far off, so I want to put an order in for sufficient cuts to be delivered. I know we have our own supplies already, but we'll be needing to build up strength.'

'Right you are, sir,' Lupus agreed, still observing Beami.

– Faces turned to the sky.

A garuda flew in low, flashes of brown and white and red, creating a downdraught that rattled the canvas awnings of the stalls, then it headed straight out to sea, in skies empty of buildings, before it arced upwards – towards Tineag'l and into the grey.

'If you're staying somewhere in the city,' Beami said, 'you'll find me on a street in the Ancient Quarter called the Ru Una. Visit me there. I'm free the day after tomorrow, so we should catch up, if you can find the free time.'

'I'm not sure of our itinerary . . . commander?'

'I'll be in meetings all day, and there's no training scheduled,' Brynd replied. 'Feel free to take a few hours off. Things are just a waiting game at the moment.'

Lupus looked at her again, a new eagerness in his expression. 'The day after tomorrow, then?'

'It's right by the Onyx Wings, the whitewashed house with the red door.' She made a move as if to kiss him, but glanced away, thinking better of it. As she walked past him she breathed into his ear, 'I've missed you.'

Brynd read it on her lips and it seemed like it hurt her to say it. She moved on through the crowds, soon lost in their mass.

FIVE

Cities were much the same wherever you went in the Archipelago. Jeryd saw the same types of inhabitants no matter who built the buildings or where they were constructed. There were the down-and-outs, the drunkards, people reacting to them in the same way, with disgust. There were always people who wanted things, and those who could and who couldn't have them. But you might also see a little happiness contained in the smile of a child, and everyone liked that.

In addition to his night breeches, Marysa had bought Jeryd a new hat, a broad-brimmed affair that kept catching in the wind, but it offered him a little style, and he felt that it added an air of authority to his demeanour – a touch of class, perhaps. For this new rumel investigator from Villjamur, there were, after all, people to impress.

So, a new city, and a new start.

Before he left Villjamur he had spoken with a couple of people he could trust high up in the ranks of the Inquisition, in order to request immediate transfer from the island via boat. Except the boat couldn't make it through the ice sheets so he'd had to travel on a particularly dense and stubborn horse. And while Marysa's horse was fine, Jeryd's had gone lame halfway along the coastal track, so it had taken two days to find replacement transport, and then he managed to get lost somewhere on the way.

By the time he and Marysa were nearing Villiren, Jeryd

was, understandably, thoroughly pissed off. Much of the journey on land had been through tundra; nothing but snow and frozen grassland, long bird calls shrilling across enormous skies, rapid blood-red sunsets, ice-cold winds that rolled in from the seas with venomous impetus. Layers of grey clouds constantly overlapping on themselves, intensifying but never delivering – such, it seemed, was the way of things around here.

But being this far north was the only way Jeryd could guarantee that he would not be hunted down for his recent investigations in Villjamur, and in Villiren there was a shortage of good men working for the Inquisition.

His new chambers were buried deep in the Ancient Quarter. He was surprised how well the Inquisition lived in Villiren, but too cynical not to assume that they resorted to a little extortion to fund their lifestyles. His office was a simple stone room with a desk, a couple of chairs, a bench and a fire, also equipped with a few books on the Jamur legal system arranged tastefully on a shelf. And mostly *unused*, he had noticed when he arrived. Through a slot in a wall he could see the ridge of one of the giant grandiloquent Onyx Wings close up, looming there as if some primordial creature was permanently readying itself for flight. Snow was constantly falling behind it, from grey skies onto slick roofs.

As soon as he sat down in the chair, placing his hat on the desk, there was a knock at the door. *Typical annoyance.* But maybe this would be the aide that Jeryd had requested several days ago to help him find his way around the city. He needed to get to know the neighbourhood itself – he didn't know how long he'd be stuck here, but it didn't hurt to fit in. If he was going to clean up a few streets and thus impress his superiors, it was essential he acquired some local knowledge.

With a colossal sigh he stood to open the door.

A young woman stood there, with tied-back black hair, a high forehead, a slender pale face and dark lips – something about her that spoke of islands other than the Boreal Archipelago. She couldn't have been any more than thirty years old, and her petite frame was smothered in brown cloak and a plain heavy skirt. She was pretty, he realized, not that he was much into such soft human skins. Behind her, an investigator in a mask came strolling down the corridor. Those masks gave Jeryd the creeps.

'Sele of Jamur, miss. How can I help you?'

'Sele of Jamur, investigator,' she declared, the pitch of her voice surprisingly deep. 'It's not how you can help me, but rather how I can help you. I'm your new aide, sir.'

A female aide in the Inquisition? Jeryd wasn't sure about this at all. He couldn't remember any specific ruling, but the arena of the Inquisition had always been male-dominated. Not that he was against female staff in the least, but in the Inquisition such things were usually a matter of tradition, for better or worse.

'If you were expecting a man, I understand your surprise – but I've been good at my job so far. They tell me you're from Villjamur, that you're a brilliant investigator, and that you do not accept bribes . . . and I wanted to learn from the best.'

There was no reason why such flattery should be anything other than that to be expected from the young or naive. If only she knew how out of touch he felt, and how he simply could not understand the mechanisms of the world any more. Hell, he could barely understand himself any longer. 'Come in, please, take a seat.'

'Thank you.' Walking past him, she graced him with a whiff of gentle perfume, a little vanilla musk. Her steps were lively, although slightly halting, as if she was recovering from a limp.

He first asked her for her name.

'Nanzi.'

'That's a beautiful and unusual name. As you know I'm Investigator Rumex Jeryd – just arrived in the city. Worked in the Villjamur Inquisition for a hundred and eighty years, and have seen a lot in that time.' It was growing on him fast, the idea that someone wanted to learn from him. It brought a new consistency to daily proceedings and he soon forgot his reservations about her being a *her*.

'The good investigator,' he continued, 'does not merely stand still. He never accepts what he learns to be absolute and final. Same with anything else in life. Those who are more prepared for change generally get on, while those who don't . . . they're forgotten quickly, left to rot.'

She nodded, took out a small notepad, began detailing what he said. This went on for a quarter of an hour, these introductory notes, a little wisdom to kick things off, things that might or might not be of direct help but needed to be stated anyway, if only for him to articulate them for himself.

Jeryd was beginning to like Nanzi more and more. He told her about his first possible case in his new city, about the albino who'd come to his door in the middle of the night whispering his name. She offered no opinion.

Jeryd said, 'I'll need, most of all, someone to show me around the city. You know this place well?'

'I've been here a few years now,' she admitted, 'but in that time I've come to know nearly every passageway, every stall, every cobble, every cobweb.'

'Wouldn't you rather get out of here with the coming fighting?' Jeryd felt a sudden curiosity about why people were in Villiren at all.

'Where else would we all go?' she asked. 'No one is going to take their chances out in the wilderness, in this weather. None of the other major cities are likely to let anyone in, so all people here have is *this* place. It might not be pretty here, but there is a great sense of belonging, a sense of purpose, even. And with that comes pride. It's long been a city of immigrants – from all over these eastern islands. I, myself, am not from here, and I have no family left, so this city is a haven for people like me, who needed to rebuild themselves.'

Jeryd contemplated her words. Maybe he had been quick to judge the city, too quick to think it lacked soul. As he had said himself moments earlier, those who were more prepared for change generally got on better.

*

As they made their way onto the streets heading towards the citadel and the barracks, Jeryd asked Nanzi more about her background, discovering how she had previously travelled around the Archipelago, even found a partner and settled down. Nanzi continued to walk with that distinctive limp, and it made Jeryd speculate on how she might have acquired such an impediment.

'Were you injured in the line of duty?'

A pause, a distant gaze. 'An accident, years ago. It still pains me, if I'm honest, but I'm *much* better off now than before. Working here is good – not too physically demanding, and I get out and about. That takes my mind off my own problems, which are nothing in comparison with some of the things we see here in Villiren.'

'A noble sentiment. How long have you worked for the Inquisition?'

'Not very long. But, given my accident, I realized how life is short – and I wanted to do some good by serving the city. I want to help wherever I can, to do the right thing for humanity. The Inquisition here is not as efficient or as good-intentioned as I would like – so I try very hard to make a small difference.'

'The good investigator,' Jeryd declared, 'is always motivated by positive goals. In the end, when people start to argue over intricacies of the law, all you have is your integrity to fall back on.'

'Things are rather relaxed in the Inquisition here,' she observed, 'too much so. Perhaps crimes go unsolved, some not even investigated. The Freeze has changed our priorities to more administrative matters. Many cases still need sorting out. The rumel who work here as investigators are just not interested any more. With the war coming, many such cases simply have had to be overlooked. Burglaries are never talked about, rapes never followed up – women, I find, are particularly hard done by in the culture here – but in some tribal communities you hear of worse. I do what I can in difficult circumstances. And then there are all those missing people ...'

'People vanish all the time,' he remarked. 'The good investigator knows that. He has to start off at the source of information, because if people want to disappear hard enough, they will manage to do so. It's easy enough never to be seen again. Your source will quickly give you a hint as to whether you are wasting your time. A good investigator cannot afford to waste his time.'

'Or hers.'

'Whose?' Jeryd said, momentarily puzzled.

'Cannot waste his or *her* time.'

'Right,' he conceded.

'Anyway,' she continued. 'That is why I was excited when I heard that an investigator from Villjamur was heading our way. I hope to learn from your experiences there, but I do not know why you left such a prestigious place just to come here.'

'Sometimes we haven't got the choice, Nanzi, because things get decided for you.' *And this dive was the only place I could get to work in, simply because of their casual attitude to the Empire's laws.*

*

As they made their way to the barracks, along those rigidly aligned streets of the city, now and then she would stop to introduce Jeryd to a trader, or a tavern owner, which was something he appreciated, being so keen to become a familiar face with the locals. He adopted a friendly tone towards them, and they chatted back readily. One woman who was running a textile shop even offered nervously to pay him a bribe, as if

49

he was involved in a street gang. *A protection racket, perhaps?* Nanzi had implied such shenanigans went on, but were the Inquisition involved too?

The final approach presented them with a glorious view encompassing numerous shades of white and grey, where the city met the sea met the skies. Accumulating force between the cliffs bordering the harbour, icy winds assaulted the Citadel violently. Jeryd had to keep a tight grip on his new hat. Nanzi led him up the final stairway to the vast Citadel directly at the front of the city, a decrepit and fortress-residence facing the sea. He couldn't believe how massive it was, getting on for twenty storeys high. Many different shades of rock had been used in its construction – from the speckled texture of granite to the smoothness of sandstone. Despite its vast, towering facades, crowded with spiked crenellations, the light mist of drizzle and gentle fog seemed to lend it an ethereal, almost otherworldly quality. Access was gained by several wide, shallow-stepped staircases, and the thin rectangles of lantern-illuminated windows were ranged regularly along each side. This was a place where you felt you wanted to be on the inside, certainly, and Fat Lutto, the portreeve of Villiren, lived here, as did the Night Guard, who had made it their head-quarters. Other contingents of soldiers were arriving daily, though housed on levels lower down, but most were still gathered in camps to the south of the city.

*

Now this was impressive: a room surfaced all over with obsidian. The same reddish volcanic glass also lined some of the main chambers in a dazzling display of craftsmanship. Sure, some of the rooms and corridors he'd passed through were pretty deteriorated, with old stone that was falling apart like in Villjamur, but now and again there'd be some fancy section of wall with gemstones pressed into the surface, in an ostentatious display of tastelessness. He liked this, nevertheless: it was so bad it was good.

50

When they finally met the commander, Jeryd was delighted to recognize the thunderous old Dawnir creature, Jurro, who he'd met before in Villjamur. The beast loomed a few feet taller than Jeryd, his exposed body thick with brown hair, his modesty concealed only by a mere loincloth. Set in a narrow, goat-like head, over a pair of arm-length tusks that peeled back his gums, two large black eyes stared down unblinkingly at his visitor. To call him intimidating was an understatement, but Jeryd wasn't worried by this creature who was carrying a pile of books tall enough to crush the average man.

'Ah the rumel investigator!' Jurro rumbled. 'What brings you here?'

'Sele of Jamur—'

'Urtica. It's apparently the Sele of Urtica now,' Brynd corrected, smiling to himself.

'Sele of Urtica,' Jeryd continued reluctantly. Then to Jurro: 'How come you're all the way out here? I thought you were rotting away in that room of yours back in Villjamur.'

Jurro set the books on the floor – a stack of leather-bound tomes that reached as high as Jeryd's shoulder. 'On the contrary, the kind commander there permitted me to stretch my legs at long last, so I have ventured to this city with them. I have since seen many things, though few of them what I hoped for. Alas, still no clue as to my origins. So I assume you're here for the coming war?'

'Not exactly. I'm actually here pursuing the case of a missing soldier. Still got a fondness for the books, I see.'

'I have been soaking up information for so long now it seems easier to read than to breathe. Though, this time the commander here has set me to work.'

Standing close by, Brynd cleared his throat. 'I sent some men to the libraries throughout the city – which here are small and scattered institutions – so Jurro might be provided with some bestiaries, or records that might enlighten us as to what the enemy might be. I have myself looked through several volumes of xenopathology, but there are few cladistical similarities with those infernal creatures.' He waved to the pile of books. 'He has been a great help already,' Brynd continued. 'Jurro, might I spend some time alone with the investigator?'

'Why of course. I have many pages here to digest.' Jurro reached down for the load of books and hunched his way out through the doorway.

Jeryd gave a sideways glance at the commander. 'Strange customer, that one.'

'It isn't easy being the only one of your kind.'

*

Jeryd was introduced to a few of the Night Guard, those superior troops, as he wanted to build a profile of them. Any one of these men might have been responsible for Haust's disappearance.

First there was Mikill, a slender man in his late twenties, with long brown hair. The commander explained he was a supreme swordsman, having joined the Dragoons when he was fifteen, and had become a sergeant by the time he was eighteen. Apparently he didn't have much of an appetite for drink, so was constantly mocked for that by the others; but he was a considerable ladies' man, apparently, much to the envy of the older men. Brug was a veteran in his mid-forties, heavily muscled and with a close-shaven head and numerous tattoos. Unlike his younger colleagues, he was a bit of a wine-lover with an appreciation for paintings. Jeryd learned that he had lost his wife twenty years ago and hadn't wed since. Jeryd took an instant liking to the next man, Smoke, a mature, expert horseman who spent more time looking after the animals than socializing. With tanned skin and short-cropped hair showing streaks of grey, he was a descendant of the tribes, and considered best of all with an axe. Quiet and reflective, he stared back at Jeryd gently, contemplating his questions, and answering carefully in a whispery tone. Very different was Syn, in his mid-thirties, who could well have been a psychopath judging by the look in his eye. Although usually quiet, the commander revealed that he was extremely violent and efficient in combat. In fact everyone was secretly wary of him, since Syn was thought to have been involved in a wholesale massacre of Empire-friendly tribesmen about fifteen years ago. As a result, no one seemed that close to him, and Jeryd made a particular note of this individual.

He met a couple of other men briefly, Bondi and Haal, but they soon had to go back to their training. Meanwhile, other soldiers in black jogged by, conversing in loud voices that followed them along the corridor. Jeryd couldn't help but feel a little disappointed at the sight – these men were legendary with their cultist enhancements – providing greater strength and superior skills – but they still seemed like very ordinary people.

*

Later, in the same obsidian room as before, Jeryd, Nanzi and Brynd sat in discussion as a massive fireplace generated a much-needed warmth. As they began to discuss the Haust case, Jeryd asked Nanzi to note down any minor details. After having talked to some of his men, Brynd confirmed that the private had disappeared during night-time while on regular patrol. At that point, the albino reaffirmed that numerous other people in the city had similarly gone missing. Jeryd made a mental note to study all the reports back at the Inquisition headquarters.

At Jeryd's request to see Private Haust's quarters, the commander led them over to the dormitories. The rest of the regiment were on training exercises, and the place was empty: a long, narrow room that housed five soldiers, as well as Haust himself. Sparse and oppressively neat, Jeryd could tell from this one room that the life of a soldier would never have been right for him. Haust's bed had been left untouched, the sheets folded down immaculately. A few sheets of paper were rested tidily on the side table – a letter from his partner, another one from his brother, a hand-sketched portrait of an attractive young lady and, resting on it, a woman's bracelet.

'Everything's exactly as he left it, I believe,' the commander said.

Jeryd regarded Haust's meagre possessions. 'These from his lover at home?' he enquired.

'Yes, his wife, back in Villjamur. They'd been married quite a while for such a young couple, but Haust, like a few other soldiers, would go out and play with the local girls.'

'Not the most trustworthy of gentlemen then?' Nanzi sneered.

'I'd trust him covering my back with a sword, if that's what you mean.' Brynd glanced meaningfully at Jeryd then at her, and Jeryd weighed up the scenario in his mind. 'They can get up to whatever they want in the evenings, the men, so long as they're not participating in a military engagement.'

Jeryd nodded.

'But he sent most of his wages home to her, so that she lived well, in one of the upper-level apartments,' Brynd continued. 'Her letters kept him going – that's what keeps a lot of these men going, in fact.'

'Yourself included?'

A smile. 'I don't like to complicate matters too much.'

'Very wise,' Jeryd murmured. 'So he'd left his precious personal items here. I reckon we can rule out the notion that he's just run away.'

Commander Brynd Lathraea quickly followed Jeryd's logic, and nodded solemnly. 'Someone's taken a Night Guard soldier? That seems most unlikely. This unit contains the most efficient warriors in the Boreal Archipelago. You don't just *take* one of them against his will.'

Jeryd wasn't so sure about this military bravado right now. 'I think we can safely assume that if Haust has been abducted or murdered, our suspect is likely to be a little on the tough side himself.'

*

Jeryd and Nanzi accepted drinks in the officers' mess, while Brynd was called away briefly. After he returned, the conversation turned to the mysterious enemy with hard shells and claws.

'This is partially classified, of course,' Brynd said, 'although I will be shortly making some public announcements. Not even the Inquisition know the full details just yet.'

'Understood,' Jeryd said.

'Okun,' Brynd declared. 'That's what they've been called, based on the old language upon which Jamur itself was constructed. It comes from the word *ókunnr*, meaning unknown or alien.'

'You mean you don't actually know what the hell they are,' Jeryd observed dryly.

'You might say that.' The commander's gaze settled on some deep distance. 'Tineag'l has suffered a genocide at the hands of these Okun. Mass culls were involved – whole towns and villages simply cleared out. Over a hundred thousand people have gone missing, and the rest were slaughtered. I was out there with a band of my soldiers on an investigative mission that turned into a rescue operation. It wasn't a pretty sight, finding the corpses, seeing the trails of blood all across the snow. People were just taken from the safety of their own homes.' Brynd shook his head. 'As for what did this – these new creatures? Well, I suspect they arrived by crossing the ice sheets – but where from originally, I'm afraid I cannot be more specific. One garuda scout reported getting sight of some sort of gateway up in the far north, but that claim needs re-examining. It sounds ridiculous, but they're like crustaceans, and stand taller than any normal man. From what we've witnessed, they're vicious fighters, totally ruthless, and they're massing on the southern shores of the gulf waiting to launch a raid over here. Although I hesitate to ever label an entire race as evil ... I mean, we're just judging them from one perspective, seeing only the threatening aspects of an alien species armed and on a mission of conquest. They ought not to be defined simply by their appearance – although there are many in our world who would.'

'Talk to me about racism,' muttered Jeryd, contemplating this inherent understanding between an albino and a rumel.

'We've two prisoners in our possession, which I've not yet had dissected because they're still breathing though unconscious. I hope to learn more from them, perhaps detect some weakness in their structure. It's probably best you see them, too?'

'Sure.'

There followed a swift walk through security checks – Brynd waved them both on through, the guards snapping smartly back to attention. A brief nod to a couple more standing by a metal door, and it was swiftly opened.

The holding cell beyond was lined with metal sheeting, with a stone-tile floor and a barred window that seemed to suck the cold air right through it. The room was utterly vacant apart from the two creatures, and Jeryd could scarcely believe what he was seeing. Nanzi gasped and pressed herself back against the wall, putting as much distance between herself and the strange creatures as possible.

A new race. A new species. It seemed *unbelievable*, but here they were in all their exo-skeletal glory.

'I'm not sure how their physiognomy can be described in any clearer way than giant black crustaceans,' Brynd remarked, strolling casually around one of their resting forms. 'Seven foot tall, they're almost insectile, with a head, thorax, abdomen, and glistening textured shell. Also noteworthy is that an acidic scent lingers around them consistently.'

Right now the two Okun lay hunched up and lifeless, in

some sort of dormant state. Their equivalent to ankles were bound firmly by metal chains.

'Are these ... things likely to attack Villiren soon?' Jeryd enquired, staring at the Okun.

The commander's brow scrunched up as he considered Jeryd's question. 'I honestly couldn't tell you. We understand so very little about their culture, their tactics, or even their motives. Whatever they want with us, whatever they kill our people for, it's nothing that registers with my understanding.'

'You paint a pretty picture, commander,' Jeryd said.

'It's all relative I suppose,' Nanzi announced suddenly. Jeryd turned with interest for what advice his new aide might offer. 'I mean, one man's murderer is another's freedom fighter, so they say. But the thing is, we all look at it from a given point of view, don't we, and so evil really is evil – and at the same time isn't at all.'

She was certainly articulate, if the concept a little abstract. Wasn't afraid to have something to say, this one. Jeryd found himself liking her more and more. He stared down once again at the dormant killers, contemplating what rage they might soon enough produce.

Six

The spider crossed a line of silk woven above a busy night-iren, bobbing up and down as it skittered across to the other side. A festival was going on below, in the marketplace, with men and women in furs and masks acting out a legend of the yellow sun. As they pranced around firelight brandishing sticks and biolumes in time to the drums, the spider mounted the opposite rooftop and skimmed down the near flank of the building.

It banked over one of the numerous drainage channels that penetrated the city like a network of thick veins. Many of them were littered with waste and scrap metal, and appeared no more than slivers of apocalyptic landscapes. Every night the city's poor would scavenge them for the chance of survival, and for a moment it considered selecting one of them . . . but no, they were too poor, too undernourished.

Only healthy, lean cuts will do.

Besides, they weren't on the list that Doctor Voland had been given.

Through the streets again and up onto the metal railings running along outside one building. *Tap-tap-tap* up to the top, and soon it had a perfect view of the windows opposite, squares of light signifying ordinary people's lives.

Red lanterns glowed inside two of the nearest rooms, with fires roaring in their grates in the background. In one of them, an old woman was reclining in a chair with a book laid to one side of her. In another on the floor above, a blonde woman in underwear was staring out of the window, her blue mask pressed up against the glass. She seemed to be peering directly at the spider, but it knew it was too dark to be seen, for the creature had the advantage of the night. A bald man with a pencil-thin moustache approached her, slapped her behind and she giggled. She removed her mask, turned and kissed him, who then took off his shirt to reveal a skinny frame.

The spider seethed at the indignity of the woman's behaviour. This man was one of the union leaders – he was therefore on the list. The lantern sputtered out as the couple merged into the darkness of the room behind – and the spider waited.

*

As Larkin kissed the nape of her neck she realized she didn't really care about her husband any more. That sorry loser was nothing compared with her visitor. She had watched as Larkin, eloquent and passionate, had earlier that day called for strike action from the fishermen and stevedores. The portreeve had reduced both their pay and their prices in order to help fund the war effort, so he said, but everyone knew this was just an excuse to worsen the conditions of the workforce. Her husband, the dickhead, had walked away from the meeting, insisting that he wanted to work, and the rest of them could fuck off. She hated his lack of commitment to the movement, and his small-town opinions. She now felt a faint thrill at the fact that Larkin was so popular with the ladies – yet he had chosen her.

She'd be rid of her husband by the morning.

She kissed her way down Larkin's lithe body, unbuckling him, basking in the warmth of the fire to one side. Breeches slid off slowly, then his socks, and she slowly teased him to arousal, then finally wrapped her mouth around his expectant cock. As her hair fell forward to cover this act of intimacy, he groaned the way most men did, but did not push her head down so she was forced to gag. He seemed almost grateful for her skills – and why not? She knew how to give good head.

Something rattled at the window and she paused for a moment, but now heard only the sound of the festivities taking place two streets away. *Must be the snow*, she decided.

Bang.

She flinched at the sudden noise.

'Don't worry,' Larkin reassured her, running a hand tenderly through her hair. 'It's only a firework.' His eyes were so sensitive, so big and blue. She turned her attention to him once again, prolonging the moment, while enjoying the sense of his mounting excitement. His breathing started to quicken and . . .

Bang.

'What the—?' Everything seemed to happen so slowly: the ceiling collapsed and debris clattered around the room, then a monstrous beast descended through the continuing rain of plaster, and pinned them to the bed as the rubble smothered the fire.

It can't be . . .

A monstrous spider loomed above them.

'Dear Bohr, no!' she screamed, and found her hands were pinned tight by a couple of its massive hairy legs, and she was now pushed flat on top of Larkin. 'Get off me, please, no!' And the eyes – those horrible, countless eyes – were staring back at her, and Larkin began to shudder and whimper underneath her and something warm covered the bed. He had pissed himself.

Fireworks continued to explode outside, the shouts of enjoyment drowning out her own screams.

The monster gurgitated something from its mouth and silk began to fill her throat. She gagged – and fainted away.

*

Commander, I'm about to embark upon the reconnaissance journey, Flight Lieutenant Gybson signed by making complex shapes between his finger, palm and thumb. *Are there any territories you wish me to explore?*

As Commander Lathraea addressed the garuda, the bird-soldier standing a foot taller than himself, his vision swept across the brown and white plumage visible beneath the bronze breastplate. Touches of red tingeing the soldier's facial features reminded him of tribal warpaint. Two arms protruding beneath those mighty wings were a reminder of something vaguely human that Brynd could never quite comprehend. They never spoke much about themselves, these bird people, so all he knew of them essentially came from journals, reports, a bunch of statistics and strategies. *Who* they were exactly, he suspected he'd never know. Personality was so difficult to ascertain without being able to decipher the subtleties of a facial expression, the nuance of their voice.

'I'll check the maps.' A few stops to the other side of the chamber brought him to a large desk, where he picked out a map of Tineag'l – one of the more up-to-date ones commissioned two years ago for tax purposes – and brought it over to the table. 'If you could investigate the channel running directly north from here, keeping the sun always behind you, then we can judge more accurately the depth and level of enemy forces. We know there's little sign of them along the coast itself, yet they're constantly massing on that opposite shore. Nothing more than a two-hour flight should be necessary. I'd like to get more of an impression of the potential longevity of their assault, when it arrives.' And how many of his own soldiers he could anticipate dying.

Very good, sir. Gybson exited the room towards the viewing platform, and mounted a merlon.

Brynd moved to a viewing hatch encased in the wall. A flick of wing obscured the red sun for a moment, as the garuda leapt off the side in a sudden freefall, before catching the wind and pushing a little higher to catch a thermal.

*

Days like this were what flying was all about: rare, clear weather on all sides, with nothing that threatened snow. There were few days like this one, when he could make out the horizon so exactly, when he could feel a sudden thrill. Winds raced underneath his spread feathers.

It wasn't an ideal life, all the same. Gybson had family back on Kullrún, in the garuda caves on the north-western coast. Two chicks to see fed well, another egg in the nest. The money was good, being employed in the Empire's service, so they could afford a good life compared with their garuda kin. The last time he was on leave, his youngest had only just begun to fly: it had been a sprawling, messy attempt that led to Gybson having to swoop down in order to stop the little fellow splitting his head on the rocks below.

Talking to some of the other lads in the air force about his homeland always brought a vague nostalgia for the good old days when he just wanted to explore the skies, climb higher, travel further. And enjoy endless summers – when there *were* summers, of course. But he had been one of the garudas selected at an early age for military service, so those expansive days of soaring through infinite skies were soon over.

The harbour below was crammed with the old refugee vessels, making it difficult for the fishermen to navigate any of the channels exiting Port Nostalgia. All along Y'iren's north-ern coast, military stations and warning beacons had been spaced at regular intervals, in case an invasion fleet should bank and alight some distance away from Villiren itself. Dragoon soldiers held these positions, just visible in their black, green and brown uniforms, operating in small patrol groups of threes and fours.

A flight heading directly north for any considerable distance was uncommon. Gybson's usual missions involved patrolling the coast indefinitely, to observe if there were any marked variants in the progress of ice, if a passage could still be cut across it, and then to watch out for any attempted enemy crossings by boat, or if these Okun could traverse the water by other means.

Eventually having reached sight of Tineag'l, he glided along some distance above where the shoreline proper began, over ice sheets extending towards the mainland beyond. Nothing ever seemed to change along these shores: abandoned villages, the trails of blood faded into white, sometimes a lone cart.

Then he'd fly higher, safer, with grim knowledge of what came next.

Another quarter of an hour, and there they were, these Okun, their black armour a stark contrast against the dazzling snow. Their numbers had proliferated, a good three thousand in this first community – a tentscape with tendrils of smoke drifting above. Red-skinned rumel rode on horseback between them, apparently in command of this freak-show army. They had already cleared Tineag'l and wiped out every town and village across the island.

And yet thousands still approached, a thin line in the distance now, like a deep scar cleaving the landscape. The best part of ten thousand gathered within an hour's reach of the southern shore – the nearest crossing point to Villiren.

By an adjustment of focus, he could see broadswords and maces, arrows and axes and spears. This was an army preparing for siege.

Further north still, the garuda headed across tundra and blue-hazed hills, mountains and gorges, across frozen lakes and rivers and snow-filled mining basins. The land was otherwise void of its population.

This was already known to the military. Local people had been systematically cleared, only the very young or very old being left behind, and even then only their carcasses – the bones tentatively stripped out of the bodies, then rejected.

Evidence of this was occasionally provided by bloodstained banks of snow bordering empty villages or mining towns, and the garuda's sensitive vision could pick out how the remaining people had been left, their bodies broken into awkward shapes, and then preserved by the cold. The irony of people being themselves mined on this mining island was not lost on him.

Now and then were seen pockets of the new race, these alien creatures, out scouting in small troops. Sometimes they would be accompanied by a rumel rider, steering his horse in the middle of their group, or narrowly ahead.

Theories had evolved quickly about why the rumel had been seen amongst them, but Commander Lathraea didn't want this inflammatory information released to the public. Humans and rumels had been living alongside each other for millennia now – two bipedal creatures that shared a similar culture, but that symbiosis could crumble from time to time – racial tensions had always existed.

But since humans would always find ways to react in a new set of circumstances, to somehow take control of such uncertainty, he now feared a backlash against the rumel living in their midst.

*

This was as far north as the garuda dared go, for the muscles along his spine were beginning to indicate painful frissons of strain. Wind pushed more violently at his side, undermining his attempts at stability, his plumage ruffling thickly. It had taken him many hours to fly just this far, and the geography of the icescape had meanwhile begun to change. Contours of landscape fell flat as he cruised over level ice sheets.

But, at the farthest end of his vision, he could see something glow.

He adjusted his altitude, descending as he drifted landwards.

Unbelievably, a doorway existed in the fabric of the air

itself, about the height of a two-storey building. Pale purple was constantly emitted, darker lines within denoting some kind of grid beyond, as if this manifestation was carved from mathematics. The very air around it vibrated – though that was something that the garuda gauged no human would be able to sense, therefore he would have trouble describing it to the commander. He banked into a circle, staying high enough not to be easily seen, icy wind rippling steadily underneath his hovering torso.

Gathered around the astonishing doorway were several regiments of this new race, rumel leaders riding among them on horseback. Now and then something could be seen amid the purple light, a shimmering silhouette barely noticeable against the sheer brightness; then out of this a single figure would march, becoming more definable against the surrounding snow, sometimes one of the Okun, sometimes a rumel. Where were they coming from and where were they going to next—?

An arrow was suddenly launched from below, and Gybson swerved just in time to see it clip the tip of his wing. Another came after it, but wasn't so close, rising and then falling from the sky, like a dying bird.

He knew when to quit.

Hauling back and up, Flight Lieutenant Gybson retreated to the sanctuary of altitude, and retreated back to base to report.

SEVEN

Some people would see Villiren as a division of alleys and sections – determined by lines drawn on a map. Technically there was the Ancient Quarter, nestling under the long shadows cast by the Onyx Wings. North of that rose the Citadel, the imposing edifice where Malum was now headed. Saltwater and the Deeping lay just a few streets to the south, both districts dominated by the Screams. Further out on the opposite side of the wings there was Althing, and then Scarhouse south of that, a quarter where many decent traders lived. And beyond that, tucked just behind Port Nostalgia, with its harbour-front hotels that the Freeze had closed down, lay the Shanties, a district where the fishermen and stevedores lived, largely in poverty. And finally the various shades of the city, known collectively as the Wastelands – though they hadn't been wasteland for thirty, maybe forty years at least. Multicultural niches had been established there, various pockets of exiles creating their own sense of belonging, like the Folke quarter or the Jokull district – unofficial names that meant little to the city's developers. Beyond that again was the dark Abies-strewn Wych-Forest, a place that was eaten into constantly by the urban crawl outwards. And raising a peak within the foliage was the Spoil Tower – a pile of refuse so high it had become the highest point locally, harvested eagerly by gulls and the homeless.

Villiren was broken up into distinctive patches of territory, undrawn lines running across unnamed streets. Which you either dare not cross or else you were obliged to defend. This territorialism gave Malum and his gang a sense of belonging and, as in most major cities across the Boreal Archipelago, there was an underground complex of tunnels and excavated caverns for them to hide out in.

In fact, Malum did most of his work out of part of this basement network. In Villiren, you needed to ascertain the way down there from someone who trusted you. Then, a sidestep out of sight, followed by a downward journey from a certain corner of the Ancient Quarter. Such passageways were scored right through the heart of the city, guarded well by cloaked figures who knew their way around a blade.

Sporting three-day stubble, under his black surtout he wore a thick woollen tunic with the hood drawn up and his red bauta mask in place. A messer blade at his hip, he took the steps two at a time.

Eventually he came to the heart of the complex that was the Villiren underground. A gangland zone, a no-man's-land, the place was constantly lit by a string of lanterns and biolumes, long passageways connecting cavernous dust-filled spaces in which the ancient houses were barely still standing, faded posters nailed to their doors. These stone facades remained only because the authorities were too scared to come down here and rip them apart.

Voices came to him through the hubbub as a few masked men nodded in his direction, or even stood up to give him vague acknowledgement. Others turned back to their tables, their faces anonymous behind their masks.

This place was a sort of decrepit tavern extending into a former marketplace, and had become a hang-out for mainly the two largest street gangs in Villiren – the Screams and his own, the Bloods. You could buy yourself the best of anything down here. Blades and drugs, ultra-strong alcohol and women, as well as decent cuts of reindeer and seal, or the more nutritious types of seaweed, for variety.

Three of his youngest recruits, none of them older than twelve, stood giggling over a crate of porno-golems. 'Put those fucking things down!' Malum shouted. 'They're not for you. Get out of here.'

He cuffed one lad around the ears and the three scampered off. Sighing, he realized his work here was endless.

Two of his men sauntered over to him, JC and Duka. The young red-headed brothers had been there from the beginning, when his business activities had turned to the darker side of life. Always ready to hand when he needed men to call in credit or clear up debts, they'd become his surrogate family early on, turning from callow boys into men he could trust. More to the point, they too had been *bitten*.

JC and Duka were now in their late twenties, and equally tall, but JC always wore a black mask while Duka wore none. They could almost have been twins, otherwise, but JC had tribal-motif tattoos all over his neck and chest, and possessed the most ferocious blue eyes, while his brother's were green. JC therefore looked the tougher of the two, but in reality he was more mellow, even slightly spiritual, and this helped to disguise his alcoholism. The brothers had been through a lot together – turf wars and smuggling and suffering bad drug trips, and they treated Malum like a wiser, older brother. They came from a vast family and Malum had always been welcome at their table after he was first bitten – they helped to set him straight again.

He now greeted them both in hand-slang, fingers and palms crossing according to the old code.

JC spoke first: 'Malum, how's it going? Thought you was working with those soldiers.'

'Not until midday,' Malum growled. 'I was hoping to meet up with Dannan first. Seen him anywhere around?' The man he spoke of was the bastard son of a banshee, a man who consequently called himself a banHe.

'Not seen him,' Duka confessed, burying his hands back in his pockets.

'Anything important?' JC slurred, and Malum could detect an alcoholic glaze in his eyes.

'Some union activity we need to interrupt. And I just wanted to make sure we're in agreement before we go to meet the soldiers.'

Duka muttered, 'None of us give a damn about what those soldiers are up to.'

'We might not have a choice in the end, and that's what I'm afraid of. Don't even know what it is they're fighting. They suspect trouble's on its way here so who knows what they'll want from us.'

'Hey, will you need us all to fight too?' Duka said.

Malum wasn't a military man, and he had no concern about the Empire. His own turf was all he cared about. 'Forget about it for now.'

'Right,' JC muttered. 'Hey, last night we got ourselves a crate of pirated relics off a dealer who said he'd just been to Ysla.'

'Where's he now?' Malum asked.

'Dead,' JC replied, as Duka disappeared down one of the nearby passageways. 'We dumped him in the harbour last night with his coat pockets full of masonry.'

'You drink him first?' Members of his gang had a habit of draining their victims before Malum himself could get to question them.

'Nah, he smelled of bad blood – cultist-tainted or something.'

Malum grunted a laugh. 'Are the relics any good? I don't want any of us killing ourselves for no good reason.'

'We ain't tested them yet.' JC glanced behind him, where Duka reappeared lugging a small chest. With a grunt he dumped the box at Malum's feet, and then looked up at him expectantly.

Malum rummaged carefully among the collection of odd-shaped metallic devices.

Customers were always stupid enough to buy pirated relics. They sought the dream device, the object that could improve their lives. Punters were even prepared to kill themselves – literally – for the chance to own some magic. Markets in the city thrived on ordinary people being selfish, and for the last ten years his gang had thrived on exploiting such weaknesses, making money through whatever nefarious means he could contrive.

'You did good, guys.' Malum lightly punched Duka in the arm. 'Even if they don't work, we can still get a decent price for them.'

*

Two hours later, Malum sat coolly across the table from the albino commander, only being here out of curiosity rather than any sense of duty. They were gathered in the obsidian chamber, with its view across the sea towards Tineag'l. In the distance, a garuda was curving through the air. Up on the walls cressets of burning oil were spaced at regular intervals between hunting trophies: gheel heads glaring down on proceedings, their triple-forked tongues hanging out as if hungrily.

The albino commander gave a slight smile that betrayed his need for Malum to play nicely ... while Malum vaguely wondered if albino blood tasted any different from that of normal humans. The commander's pallid features seemed to provide the most subtle of masks, but for Malum his expressions were clear to interpret: here was a man looking to bargain.

Two Night Guard soldiers, blond and black-haired, stood at the back with arms folded, behind their commander as if to enforce his air of authority. Another half a dozen of them sat on benches around the edge of the room, in carefully informal postures. Malum read this as a signal for everyone to stay relaxed.

Dannan had arrived late, obviously deciding to saunter here at his own leisurely pace – either that, or too messed-up on drugs to notice what the time was. With harsh and angular features, the pale banHe deported himself with surprising neatness and elegance. Malum loved to test him occasionally to see if it was all an act, but the banHe always stayed true. Malum had once caught him engaged in some occult ritual centring on a bowl of blood, three naked women, various body organs, and an old book of rituals he assumed were cultist. And close members of his gang suggested that they'd witnessed the banHe getting stabbed, manically and repeatedly, but there was little or no sign of wounding afterwards, and at the time of the attack, Dannan had simply laughed it off. The banHe was here now representing the Screams, a guild with a thousand men in its ranks. Usually these gangs comprised a dozen men at the top, and everyone else working for them, but Malum's group was much larger, as was Dannan's, yet these two were the only leaders present.

Lutto, the portreeve of Villiren, suddenly blundered through the door still wrapped in a thick green cloak, and clutching a sheaf of papers under one arm. There was something comically duck-like about his gait, and his cheeks were flushed; and despite the chill there was a constant, sweaty glow to this panjandrum's demeanour.

'Sele of Jamur, Commander Brynd! Dannan and Malum, my greetings, gentlemen.'

The albino greeted him formally, correcting 'Jamur' to 'Urtica'. Each of the gang leaders gave a disinterested nod.

'You gang types,' Lutto chuckled, as he squeezed himself into a chair next to the commander, and then spilled his papers across the table. 'Will you not remove your mask for this meeting?' Lutto asked, as he cleared them up.

'No,' Malum snapped. 'Just tell us why're we here?'

'Ah, straight to business,' Lutto announced. 'A man after my own heart!'

'Leave me out of your heart,' Malum growled. 'Or are you into fucking men these days, you queer?'

Malum then noticed a flicker of darkness cross the albino's face. *That was strange*, Malum thought. The commander certainly didn't like that comment, he could tell. He was a weird-looking man, with those devilish eyes and that angular face, but something in his expression definitely tightened. *Very odd . . .*

The albino hurried on with the meeting. 'I called you gentlemen here because . . . very simply, we need your assistance. Lutto here reliably informs me that you each control a large number of citizens – a few thousand, so I believe.'

Dannan broke his hush. 'What of it?' His voice sounded mildly feminine.

'If I may just give you a summary of our latest intelligence?' The commander glanced warily between his two visitors. It was clear that the man regretted having to be so polite to a couple of thugs.

What the commander then described was both enlightening and alarming. He confirmed the rumours they had heard of the extent of genocide on Tineag'l, whole towns and villages wiped from the map, creatures called Okun currently crossing the ice sheets. The commander certainly presented the gang leaders with something to think about.

As drinks were eventually fetched, the commander's tone softened into something more relaxed. Anticipation still hung in the air, however.

'Now, I'm not expecting you to want to help us out of the goodness of your hearts,' the albino continued. 'You're tough men, primarily interested in your own affairs, I understand that.'

'We've got morals, commander,' Malum snapped. 'Our world isn't black and white.'

'So you will help?'

'Never said that.'

Whispering, the commander leaned over to Lutto, who nodded, his cheeks wobbling. 'Lutto here has agreed to open some of the city's vaults for a payment to you, to be refunded to the citizens by Villjamur at a later date. But the point is we'd be hiring your services, should we need you. I cannot be sure when, as for the moment we're just . . . waiting.'

So nothing was resolved; no conclusion was reached. Both Dannan and Malum agreed they would consider the situation in principle. Did they want to be employed by the Empire? Would they become just another unit of irregular soldiers?

The only firm outcome for Malum was that he ordered one of his men to shadow the commander from a distance. Whether it was just his ultra-pale skin, he didn't know, but there was something really weird about him.

*

Under a sleet-filled sky, in an area of the city currently blocked off for renovation, Malum and the banHe had words.

The banHe smoked his roll-up nervously, as if paranoid, though there were always a couple of his thugs loitering nearby, their boots crunching on the vacant rubble-patch. This place used to be an educational establishment until the rents got too high, but now it was marked out for being turned into a larger apartment block. At the moment, it made a good place to meet: there were no places to hide a crossbow, not even enough cover behind which someone could crouch with a blade.

'What is it, Malum?' the banHe enquired, an almost musical quality to his voice.

'Portreeve says there's going to be a massive march of strikers heading through the northern districts – protests from stevedores on the docks, support from the smaller merchants, that sort of thing.'

'What they angry about?'

'Dangerous working conditions mainly.'

'Why ain't they taking it up with their employers? What's Lutto got to do with it? It's a free market, right?'

Malum smirked. 'C'mon, you know better than that, Dannan. Private companies in this city means no one takes responsibility for things like deaths occurring at work – mainly from hypothermia at the moment. No one wants to work shit jobs for shit money in the ice, especially when they're dying all round, but their employers say shut up or they'll just ship in cheaper workers from off-island. Even talk of slaves coming in to work for next to nothing, though Lutto told me that he's uncomfortable with that – might spoil his image back in Villjamur. Not even the Inquisition can get involved, in case it sends out a bad signal – that there isn't much democracy here. Got to create the illusion of freedom just to placate the rest of the masses.'

'So what's Lutto want us to do then? Kill a load of innocent protestors?'

'Kind of – but from within. Business leaders have asked politicians to help them out as times are tough, and they don't need this kind of unrest. They fired a hundred men for organizing action just a few weeks ago – illegally, according to what laws we do have – but soon things are going to get out of hand. And the portreeve doesn't want it either. He's offered special tariffs and subsidies and tax relief to businesses to keep them here in Villiren – part of that *free market* thing, I'm sure! – and this unrest just interferes with his grand plans for development. So Lutto comes to us, as usual, to help out. Treats us like business leaders because we do what we do well. There's a lot of money up for grabs, here, same as the Scarhouse Massacre two years back.'

The banHe made wide eyes at him.

'Exactly,' Malum said. 'We didn't have to do another job of the kind for a long while after that. So we're meant to join the protests and kick up a bloodstorm inside the movement. Claim that unions are nothing but violent thugs, good for no one. Not only does it get rid of the key troublemakers who stop private industries from fattening up their wallets, but it means others won't want to get involved with unions. Less solidarity, you see. People just get on with their work. This is all part of Lutto's long strategy, his campaign for free democracy.'

'What, so *stopping* people from having any control over their lives and their work conditions is a *free* democracy now? Who changed the fucking definitions?'

'Welcome to Villiren, Dannan. Anyway, they get to vote, right?'

'Between two or three men who are indistinguishable from one another. Anyway, Lutto always wins because he's got the most money – and our support, too.'

'Yeah, I know all this shit.'

'You seem to know a lot,' the banHe remarked, genuinely impressed.

'Just because I'm a thug doesn't mean I don't read any books. But, anyway, we're part of this now – so can I guarantee him some of your men for the job, too?'

Dannan sighed deeply and contemplated a response. 'How many *you* got involved?'

''Bout a hundred, but there'll be best part of a thousand protesting.'

'I'll throw in a hundred as well. Enough yeah?'

'Should do it. I'll send on the details to you on time and location. We already got a couple of men undercover with the unions at the moment.'

The banHe nodded and inhaled on his roll-up and continued looking around him.

Malum walked away with the intention of fading into the cityscape.

EIGHT

'Shit.' Beami pressed her head into her hands. Then, through strands of dark hair, she regarded the mess lying on her desk. Hybridization: the dangerous art of combining relics – also her area of expertise – and if she had tried to activate this particular blend she might have blown herself to pieces. That was because two copper sections of a charged *Foroum* relic didn't want to fit into this theoretical structure. A hundred different pieces of metal were scattered across the desk, so she scooped them all up and shoved them in a box waiting to one side. Leaning back in her leather chair, she groaned despondently. The Nantuk Development Company would have to wait another few months for its demolition device, which she hoped would be able to age stone so rapidly that it would become instant dust. In a room full of traders and government officials – even the portreeve himself – she had announced this as an improvement on what she'd developed before, and as representing by far the safest stage in the evolution of remedial work. They could, she promised, clear unsafe buildings within a day. Lutto's eyes had lit up and he spoke of a tempting subsidy.

But today's shoddy results had aged her a good few years. The bloody theory was there, all the equations blazed across the bits of vellum pinned on her wall like the graffiti of intelligence. So why wouldn't it work?

Stupid fermions. Stupid eigenvalues. Stupid ancient mathematics.

A lantern faded out, leaving her with just the other one, which hung against the far wall. Books and papers were littered everywhere, many of them irrelevant to her efforts, and some of them not really legal – but this was Villiren after all. Jars of elements and compounds, boxes of metals known or unidentified, the room was a spoil heap of junk to the untrained eye; but to her it offered a haven for relative independence.

Then, in the relative darkness, she contemplated seeing *him* again. She needed to get out: the thought of Lupus was a distraction.

This girl needed to talk.

How long was it now?

*

Away from her work, her social circle consisted of poets and libertines, artists and illegal priests, and those who wanted in on the scene. Their distractions were music and ad hoc plays, discussion and intense debate going on until the small hours, even though she never made it to such gatherings as often as she liked. All in all, it seemed unusual company for a cultist – a woman dedicated to technology – but she hoped she would find some of them in the Symbolist, a glittering little bistro crammed with wine bottles and candles and polished wood.

It was early morning, and perhaps some of them might still be hanging about from the evening before, hungover enough to sit still and listen to what she had to say. Deep in the Ancient Quarter, where the buildings leaned against each other for support, the entire mood of the city changed. This was a bohemian district, a place of distinct character, of an alien dignity. Of domes and spires and the Onyx Wings. Incense drifted from open fires beside which tribal prophets preached their doctrines openly. Rumel and humans mixed equally amongst the esoteric wares on display.

The Symbolist was deceptively small, a whitewashed building that looked out on an impoverished iren. As she approached, someone recognized her, an old man wearing faded garments, and with a distant look in his eyes.

Clasping both hands before her, he said, 'Please, you are a cultist, aren't you?'

'What's it to you?' Beami replied, sick of receiving this sort of attention.

'Please, save us from the imminent dangers. There are stories of war and terror—'

'Look, just piss off, all right? We're not your saviours. Stop trying to worship us.'

The old man collapsed to his knees and bowed obsequiously before her. How many times did people need telling? Beami just wanted to get on with her own life, not be venerated like some fake priest. She hurried on past him.

Inside the bistro, in a far corner, was Rymble, the short, skinny poet with annoyingly well-kept blond hair – and those wild shirts. Today's was a garish, orange flower pattern. Sprawled across a table, he sat up on her entrance, and called out jokingly from beneath his green half-mask. 'Beami! You miserable bitch! I bet you've not even got me some arum weed. I was going to immortalize you in a poem, but, alas, I shall refrain, and instead give that honour to a better-looking woman.'

'Your words are shit,' she replied. 'Perhaps try shutting up more often?'

'You'd only want to fuck me if I remained silent.'

'Your voice is a contraceptive, then?'

The same routine as usual, and all harmless. It was well known that Rymble was too afraid of catching syphilis to actually sleep with anyone; and they had grown so close that she had begun to appreciate his more elaborate and competitive insults. She loved him really.

Coffee was already being served for the morning shift, with fried flat-breads and kippers. This place never closed. Two young couples sat together by the entrance, hangers-on who looked inquisitively and hopefully at the art scene gathered here.

Suddenly it occurred to Beami that she didn't know what she was doing here. She had desperately wanted to speak to someone, anyone, and was now disappointed at the small crowd available. Today there was only really Rymble she knew well – until Zizi entered just then from the back, wearing her fur coat and high-heeled boots. Even in her fifties, Zizi was still one of the most glamorous women Beami had ever known. She'd made her name on the stage, still used her stage name, in fact. Her milieu was both theatre and choreography, and she was responsible for several dances that had become popular throughout the Boreal Archipelago. Then she gave up that passion for the love of her husband, a rich banker from Villjamur – who, after marriage, promptly left her for a younger woman. Zizi, lovelorn and with a shattered heart, never danced again. Beami considered herself as strongminded as Zizi though, and it worried her to know that someone like her could give up a career for love. She never wanted to use her sexuality in order to get on in this patriarchy; she wanted to earn her place, and so Zizi's story always saddened her.

Knowing each other's moods so well, Zizi took one look at the expression on Beami's face, and the brunette woman immediately suggested they sit down and talk. While Rymble slumped into a slumber, Beami informed her friend in rapid whispers that Lupus was back.

A startled expression came over Zizi's face, then she said jokingly, 'Honey, you're far too pretty to be a one-man woman.'

'I'm not like that,' Beami snapped.

'Easy, darling.'

'Sorry. I'm just not that kind of woman. I know Malum and I have had some problems—'

'Problems? You bloody hate the man.'

'That's not true.'

'Well *we* all do. He's so weird, so sinister.'

'He's not. You just don't know him like I do.' On more than one occasion, the others had encouraged her to leave Malum, and one night Rymble had even kindly offered to venture into their house and stab him – then immortalize the act with poetry.

More seriously, Zizi continued, 'Look, I know you have your problems, but you either walk away from Malum now or you stay with him.'

Beami's mind was drifting.

'These situations can become increasingly dreadful if . . .' Zizi's expression softened as her intensely green eyes focused on something deep within her. 'Hang on. Why are you here? You didn't come all the way just to get some advice – especially if you'll be seeing him shortly.'

After a moment of reflection, Beami finally confessed, 'Perfume. I want to find one particular scent I liked to use. It was one Lupus adored me wearing. That sounds stupid, I know.'

Zizi grasped her hand. 'It says you've made up your mind already. But I say never let a man stop you – I say it all the time. I never knew Lupus, but don't give up everything for him. Don't let your passion for him ruin your life.'

'He's not that type of man. I'm already involved with one of those.'

'Well, there's your answer.'

'Lupus is . . . something else.'

Zizi's gaze softened. 'Tell me about him.'

Beami's mind drifted back through time. 'One night I went up to the bar just as they were closing, spoke his name when I shouldn't have known it, gave him the wildest smile – then tripped, spilt my drink all over the floor, and started laughing.'

'Smooth,' Zizi remarked.

'He used to clear tables and serve drinks at what was once considered the smartest bar in Villiren – although that's not saying much. It's not there now; it's long gone. All that's left is what's in my head – echoes of a younger life, of simpler times.'

'You're hardly that old. Just you wait until you get to *my* age. Then things can be as simple as you want them to be. So, you went to his bar?'

'Well, I went in from time to time with a few of the girls, an ambitious young cultist with a taste for bad wine.'

'Some things don't change,' Zizi smiled.

'No, I guess not. I suspected he had developed feelings for me, you know, aside from the usual lingering glances, holding mine for as long as possible. I would then chat to some other man who approached me, sometimes looking at Lupus, sometimes not. Love feeds upon jealousy – that's what he himself told me once. Working in taverns, he said, you see that behaviour so much. Anyway, he picked me up off the floor, gave me a large mug of water and waited for me to sober up. He had such lovely eyes – just like a wolf.'

'Honey, that sounds wonderfully romantic. You got pissed and he mopped you up.'

'Shut up, Zizi! It was good, you know – it was fun. And we did nice stuff – lots of it. Before the Freeze, you could walk for miles out into the grassland, and the forests. We'd take a canvas tent and spend the summer evenings wrapped up in each other's arms. We'd go to the lakes further inland, away from everyone, and catch a fish, start a fire. I'd set traps for hares and sometimes I'd use his arrows to bring down a deer. I love this island, Y'iren. You can feel like you're the only people alive. We'd have sex four times a day.'

'Stop it. You're making me jealous now. I need some drink, and I don't care if it's too early.' Zizi stood up and ordered the young waiter to bring some whisky for her coffee. Once she had settled again, she waved a finger at Beami to get her to continue. 'This revelation is the closest I've got to love in a year.'

'Well, I was older than him by two years. He was so laid back, and I guess that's why we worked. I sometimes needed someone to boss around, and he couldn't be bothered ever to decide on matters. I wanted someone to air my frustrations to, and he liked to hear them.'

'What happened in the end?' Zizi asked. 'It all sounds too good to be true, yet the pair of you didn't last.'

'The army,' Beami explained. 'He wanted to be a Night Guard and I wanted to stay here, to work. It's so rare for any woman in the Empire to make something special of herself, and devoting my time to relics seemed a way around that for me. I didn't want to give that occupation up for anyone. We started to argue loudly, and we did those little things where people try to make each other jealous – when you try to make the other *want* you more. He promised he'd write often, great sprawling letters they were at first, and then they turned into simple updates. Pretty soon I never heard from him again.'

'Now that,' Rymble announced, suddenly wide awake and feeling gregarious, 'breaks my fucking heart. I'd scribble you a poem if you wouldn't wipe your arse on it.' He played with the gold ribbons dangling from his half-mask.

'Your poems are not even good enough for that basic function, you disgusting cretin,' Zizi declared, which made Beami laugh.

*

Like using a relic to carve a pathway back to your past.

This was it, the rarest of opportunities, a chance that most people didn't enjoy. Beami couldn't remember when she had last felt like this: the angst burning inside her, the worry about how she looked, whether her breath was fresh, wondering now if her new perfume was too strong, too obvious. Wondering if he would still think the same about her, after all these years. The mirror had become like some tool through which she began to deconstruct herself, noticing all the changes that age had brought. But she was still young. It wasn't as if an aeon had passed between them seeing each other.

In her best outfit, comprising of two layers of dark-red dress with a black shawl, a look that had lasted well in Villiren for a couple of years now, she waited. Waited for *him*.

Beami took a look around the furnishings of her room. Everything was expensive: decorative mahogany, not from this island, elaborate rugs and drapes, decorated in patterns from unheard-of tribes, ornaments that may or may not have had names, a crystal console table. Here was quality acting as an expression of her husband's wealth, yet she did not care for them at all. A deeper emotion had disabled the impact of these items on her life.

What am I thinking, asking him here?

The heating system spluttered again, firegrain stalling somewhere in the pipes. Snow skidded across the windows, distracting her attention, and she went to one, to regard the city beyond. The people of the city were still out and about, wrapped in furs, some selling biolumes, traders heading to the irens, carts and fiacres grinding to and fro along the main thoroughfares.

What if Malum returns unexpectedly . . . ?

Malum was out, but this was still their marital home, and his property. Then again, why was she being so paranoid? It wasn't as if she was actually in the throes of an affair, was she, by just standing here in preparation for exploring the emotions of her past, feelings that she hadn't analysed for a number of years, also ones she had tried to forget. But she couldn't deny that it felt good, to allow this sense of nervousness to get the better of her. To feel such intensity again – to feel *something* again. It was like a game, and she felt she could almost burst with anticipation.

Was she being merely licentious? She hoped not.

A knock at the door.

She froze, then realized it would need to be answered by herself. She headed downstairs and with deep breaths opened the door to one of Malum's hired men.

''Scuse me, madam,' the thug grumbled, broad-shouldered and shaven-headed, wrapped in a thick cloak. 'Someone from the military to see you. Says he's from the Night Guard.'

'Yes, that's OK ... I was expecting him. It's to do with my research on defence methods.' She should have known these men would be here first. What if they then told Malum? She didn't want to arouse his suspicions, so she had to act calmly.

'Fine.' The man gestured to one side.

Within moments, Lupus stood there, puzzlement evident on his face as he stepped around the thug's hulking figure. He was dressed in his Night Guard uniform, utterly black save for subtle patterns in the sewing and the gold star of the Empire on his breast. How he'd matured, she realized.

She let him in and closed the door. 'Please, come to the study area, and let's continue our business there.' Her voice was loud enough for the thug at the door to hear, and she could tell from Lupus's expression that he understood her need for secrecy.

'Lead on.' Lupus gestured eccentrically, playing along.

Beami's heart thumped as they headed down the corridor, entering the basement room in which she pursued her explorations of cultist technology.

She lit three lanterns, knowing their location by instinct rather than touch, but nearly knocked one over in her flustered excitement. To a stranger this workroom must look like a junkyard, a litter of curious devices that would mean very little to the layman. But she had organized and investigated much of this over the years, made notes, tested, then tested some more, all the time wondering if she might thus unlock some

84

device the elder races had set, and if, as a result, this was how she might die.

She moved her *Brotna* relic – a great lumbering metal cone with wires sprouting from the top end – to one side.

'What's that?' he asked.

'A project I'm working on for the masons and architects,' she explained, wondering why they were wasting time talking about her work. She told him how she had found a way to reduce stone to dust, and how the project had now received sponsorship from the city developers. As she spoke, she found her mouth turning dry, her nerves increasingly getting the better of her.

All the time she was examining him: he looked more athletic than she remembered.

Lupus turned his face this way and that, inquisitively, to where papers covered the walls: diagrams, sketches, a profusion of arcane symbols that she barely understood herself. His profile, too, had become more hardened, better defined.

He finally turned to face her. 'Quite the fire hazard, this place.'

Before she could give herself the opportunity to respond, she was kissing him, thrusting him back against the wall, and no sooner doing so than pulling away, flummoxed by her own actions.

'What was that for?' he asked, smiling.

'I don't know.' Pacing the room and running her hands through her hair and feeling her pulse accelerating. 'I don't know.'

'I missed all that,' he said. 'And your scent, I haven't smelled it in years.'

Lupus had such big eyes, and a world of empathy lay within them. He was always the only one who could make her melt with a glance. He took her hands in his own. 'I have never – not once – stopped thinking about you.'

Perhaps the ice age and the coming war made her want to live for the moment, but she could not really help herself any longer. A host of memories returned through his touches: because she remembered the diligence with which he would attend to her desires, kisses in her preferred zones, his hands exploring her for her own pleasure as much as his – ever a mutual enjoyment.

It felt like they could now just continue from where they had left off years ago, and she made no objection when he pushed aside her clothing, her cloak falling first to the ground, and she abandoned herself to sensation. She was entirely a victim of her own cravings. His hands moved down to her sides, and she grabbed his wrists at first to push him away, but then realized she was instead holding him there, in place.

'Let's go somewhere else,' she suggested.

'Why?' Lupus asked.

'I'm scared someone will come back.' This was her livelihood on the line, her life, her home, her marriage – her whole world.

Underneath her desk was stored the scinan *Heimr* relic. She extended it into a knee-high tripod, then set it on the ground, manipulated a dial the way only she knew how, understanding its sensitivities, and twisted the tiny ball on the top.

'Get over here,' she instructed.

She grasped his hand, touched the ball again, and she felt her skin—

—s–t–r–e–t – c – h, tingle then normalize—

*

—and there was a blanket sheet of purple light glowing around their vision ... before they stepped forward into the meadow.

When she turned back to him, Lupus was shading his eyes against the powerful sunshine. His hair was golden in this light, in a scene that seemed locked permanently in some summer afternoon. Heat shimmered around them.

'What the hell ... ?' He shambled, dumbstruck, in a quick

circle, searching the landscape and the horizons, exactly the way she had done herself the first time. 'Where the hell . . . ?'

They were at the bottom of a shallow valley, meadowland sloping down to a river, deciduous trees clustered to the left, a hawk calling overhead. Orchid flowers seasoned the grass with colour, insects zipping from plant to plant. Sedges and, near the borders of the trees, quercus and fraxinus, with ferns crowding below in bold shadows. A pungency generated from the water, amid the humidity of vegetation, plants offering themselves to the air – so unlike anything on Y'iren. And it was so hot, a temperature she would never experience in Villiren; under a bold blue sky, and the *yellow* sun that dominated it.

She had imagined this situation, never quite believing it would be possible, to bring him here, to her secret place.

'How did you do that?' he asked, looking down at the tripod as if it would explain. He turned in a full circle yet again, taking in the landscape, the low-lying hills. 'Where . . . where are we?'

She explained how they weren't in their normal time, maybe not even in the Boreal Archipelago itself. On countless occasions she had come here alone, to spend a few hours exploring, researching, making sketches and notes and reference maps, but had never yet met another human or rumel. There was a small garuda community, out to the south coast bordering this place, some hours' walk away, but they weren't all that sociable.

No one else knew of this secret world, not even Malum. This was her *hidden* zone.

Lupus appeared in awe of her ability to carve a path through empty space. It wasn't anything she considered particularly skilful, just the result of dedicated study. All it entailed was manipulating the relic technology that the elder races had created all those aeons ago. This was not essentially *her* doing, nor was anything else relic-based; and that was something she hated about other cultists, their assumed arrogance at possessing this knowledge. All they did was monopolize the relics, and had been doing so for thousands of years.

'So this is where you get your tan,' Lupus observed. 'I wondered what kept you looking so nice and brown.'

She laughed, then threw her arms around him again, safe in the knowledge that now they could not be discovered. They knelt together in the humid grass, and kissed passionately, with the deep sunlight warming her back and all her troubles out of sight. This was pure escapism, a fantasy – hiding from her sense of guilt.

Avoiding the cold realities waiting in Villiren, she didn't want to think about a future or even a past. She desired only to taste his skin, as she undressed him, and he undressed her. Clothes soon heaped beside them, he noticed a silver tribal necklace she still wore – the one he'd placed around her neck all those years ago. He kissed it first, then her collarbone, then her chest. He moved across her bare skin with familiarity, like a hunting wolf. She let him push her back and ease her legs apart, and in the alien heat of this hidden world they escaped into the rediscovery of each other's bodies.

*

Later she showed him more of this world of hers, aware of some vague symbolism in the gesture. It wasn't so easy, however, to do this, to permit him back into her life.

Did she still love Malum? That wasn't a simple question. She had affection for him, but she didn't like being with him any more, and certainly she didn't care for his absolute rages where he could almost turn into a monster. When did he ask her about progress in her work any more? The last time was probably their conversation about golems, but when she admitted it wasn't her area of expertise, he had lost all interest. The time she was now spending with Lupus replaced months, even years, of Malum's empty substitute for conversation. How had she and Malum drifted apart? When was the moment that he ceased to provide for any of her emotional needs?

Beami and Lupus talked of the gap that had developed in their understanding of each other, the missing years of shared acquaintances, the onslaught of the Freeze – the slow ice age that had now taken a grip of the Boreal Archipelago and how it was changing their lives and the lives of others all around them. More than anything else, she felt the impending ice had forced a sense of urgency for things to happen. Perhaps this was in the back of her mind when she reopened herself to Lupus.

She possessed some undetermined fear that Malum would hurt her if he discovered what was going on, but while she and Lupus were here, in this otherworld, they were quite safe and she knew they would return to the Boreal Archipelago at the precise instant they had left it.

There was an aching perfection to the landscape, now that they were a part of it. Light began to add new textures to the surroundings, refracting off each substance – grass, water, tree – as if the landscape itself possessed some ethereal quality. Newer creatures passed by, their body shapes seeming unlikely – four-legged oddities that shifted along under a diamond-shaped spine, and pink fist-sized insects with choppy patterns of flight.

Now and then a garuda would skim past just above the ground, its downdraught rippling through the sedges. She had tried communicating with them before, through voice and sign, but they never responded, perhaps not recognizing the Jamur shapes she made, or perhaps merely ignoring her as, impassive, they soared ever upward.

There were some ruins of a civilization around them which she did not recognize. Structures that were dense and elaborate, mixing unusual shapes and materials. Monuments that were crippled by time; vines and lichen had long ago begun reclaiming them, wiping out any cultural residue carved into the stone. For some time the two of them hesitated on coloured tiles that blended effortlessly with grass, as they peered through a window arch towards the vista beyond.

The deep sense of long-past time was humbling.

*

Beami told her lover of the names she had assigned to certain places there, simple names so that she had something easy with which to familiarize herself over the year or so she had been visiting the hidden world. Lupus wanted to name something there after himself, teased her until she gave way by re-titling some ugly fish in his honour.

Silences in their conversation were not in any way awkward – much was revealed in them by the tender gesture of a hand, a searching look. They sat in the shade of a salix tree, its graceful weeping form astir in the wind. Still she could not get over the unaccustomed warmth.

The discussion of their intervening lives continued until they met up with the present. As soon as he mentioned the coming war, and the perilous situation that the city faced, the mood blackened. He told her of his duty as a Night Guard soldier, the honour, the pride and commitment entailed, even described the ritual of enhancement he had received as a new recruit. When he told her of the cultist-doctored fluids involved he could provide little explanation of the process, only the surge of pain running through his body, the rapid recovery times from injuries thereafter. He lay on her shoulder when he told her of the recent attacks on Tineag'l, describing as best he could the bizarre alien race that they had fought against.

'Aren't you afraid that you might die?' she asked, concerned.

He gave a wry smile that could have meant anything. 'I'm a Night Guard. I'm an enhanced soldier. I'm one of the best fighters amongst them. Yes, I might die – we all might – but I therefore stand a better chance of survival than most of our soldiers. And if I'm killed it will be while protecting others – that's what I trained for, that's who I am. I'm used to the idea of my own death.'

To her silence he said, 'I don't expect you to understand, but you've got to accept it.'

She was increasingly afraid of losing him to the army once again. They talked thus for hours, might have gone on for days as if that didn't matter. Eventually, both felt they should return. Guilt had ultimately caught up with them.

*

After producing the *Heimr*, she closed her eyes to sense the subtle drifts in current beneath the surface of its metal. When they both reappeared together back in her study the coldness of the room hit them, causing both to gasp as if they'd risen from underwater.

'The exact same moment as when we left,' she assured him, as he looked around incredulously. 'You should maybe go now. I don't want him to find out.'

'Of course,' he said, then kissed her softly on the lips, passion having given way to a tenderness she knew she would soon miss.

She showed him to the door, provided him with some spurious documents to make his visit look semi-official, so that there wouldn't be any reason for Malum's men to worry. From an upstairs window she watched Lupus depart without looking back, striding with purpose through the snow, heading back into the city.

After he had gone, there was a concentrated stillness throughout the house.

NINE

A new city required finding a new place in which to drink. Jeryd had always enjoyed his favourite bistros in Villjamur, where he could sit with his notebook and sip some flavoured tea, whilst poring over cases and watching the world go by. As he crossed the irens, he noticed there was still a surprising amount of food in this city – he had assumed that the ice age would mean a lack of fresh meat. Certainly, at home, agricultural industry had all but collapsed, and only those wealthy enough to employ cultist assistance could supply meat. Yet, all around this city, there were chefs who could consistently rustle up a quality meal, using all sorts of rich fusions of old tribal origins as well as contemporary recipes and subtle, Villjamur-style concoctions.

On his quest to establish for himself a brand-new routine, he was struck by just how long he had spent in the Inquisition, nearly one hundred and eighty years, not a day of it ever the same. He wondered if they did things differently in this community.

The Ancient Quarter offered the most interesting-looking bistros, some were baroque structures lurking in the shadows of the Wings. He entered one, a warm if not overpowering place with red and white chequered floors and some wealthy-looking customers. Incense burners stood on the counter, behind which two young blonde girls hovered idly, one with arms folded, the other slowly wiping a plate. It was a large room, with little natural light, and the shiny wooden tables reflected the flickering candles that rested on top. About ten customers in all were sitting in there, the average number you saw in any bistro anywhere in the world, at this time of the morning. They all stared hard at Jeryd, mainly men, and in those not wearing masks, their eyes were cold and distant. He had heard rumours of such hostility towards his kind from another rumel back in the Inquisition.

'Morning.' Jeryd slung his outer garments on a chair by a corner table, then took off his hat.

They were certainly not a particularly friendly bunch, this lot, but he didn't know whether this was normal behaviour in a city so far north.

'Morning.' Eventually, a grey-bearded man with tiny eyes spoke to him. 'Rumel, I see?'

'You see right,' Jeryd muttered in response, then to one of the serving girls, 'Black tea and a pastry, please.'

'We don't get many rumels visiting this place,' grey beard remarked coldly.

'That right?' Jeryd lowered himself onto the chair with a groan. *Still not getting any younger.*

Grey beard stood up, and his companion, a blue-masked woman wrapped in a matching cloak, looked away, probably embarrassed. 'Not sure you understand me, friend.'

Jeryd stared back at him, conscious now of his coarse dark skin, of his tail, of his glossy black eyes. He hadn't dealt with any of this kind of shit for a long, long time. 'You'll have to forgive me.' He undid the top buttons on his jerkin to reveal his Inquisition medallion, featuring its iconic angular image of a crucible. 'Investigator Rumex Jeryd, pleased to meet you. New to the city, you see, so I'm not yet sure which of these places are full of bastards – or not. I'm still finding my way around.'

'Oh,' grey beard replied, backtracking desperately. 'Well . . . I can see . . .'

'All you can see is a rumel, right? I understand. And if you don't like that, you can just wait half an hour until I've finished one of these delicious pastries, or I can haul your arse into a cell overnight, where you might or might not get beaten unconscious by one of the inmates. Now, then – is that enough to impress your fancy woman, *friend*?'

The waitress brought over Jeryd's order, just then, with a cheeky smile on her face that said she was enjoying the show. He winked at her.

Grey beard sat back down, to commence a terse and angry argument with his female companion. Sure rumels constituted a minority across the Archipelago, so Jeryd had had to deal with racism before, a while ago, but Villjamur was enlightened now, so he just didn't expect to encounter it in any major city elsewhere. At home they'd closed down the last humans-only tavern before he was even born. Perhaps things really *were* different, this far north.

As he chomped into his pastry – a wonderfully sweet creation with honey bleeding from the middle – and sipped his tea, he found the mood in the room becoming much more amicable.

*

Arriving at his desk by eight each morning, he found his groove quickly, getting some of the good tea available, then chatting to the few enthusiastic Inquisition staff, and getting stuck into things. They began to respect him – and he knew it. It wasn't tough to work out why, because Jeryd seemed the only one to actually care about solving crimes – a fact that somewhat surprised himself.

He asked for some unsolved crimes, and files soon piled up on his desk.

He scanned the papers for anything that might help with the Haust case. There were the usual cases you got in any big city: theft, rape, assault, murder. Yet more people had been reported as missing recently, though no one had found the time to pursue the fact. There'd also been an interesting increase in the number of porno golems being distributed – cultists were manufacturing these doll-women via gangs as an alternative for the desperate males of Villiren, so that prostitutes would not die of pneumonia from having to stand outside in the chilling temperatures. Jeryd was sickened, though not surprised, when someone hinted that this trade might have been sanctioned by the portreeve, and the Inquisition were advised to ignore the seedy industry.

The previous evening's murders: there had been four reports of dead bodies found with puncture wounds in the neck, the corpses shrivelled, but they had never gone missing for long – and were usually found round the back of whichever tavern they'd been drinking in the night before – and no one was too surprised at them ending up dead. Anyway, such cases tended to be allocated to a special department within the Inquisition, and passed out of Jeryd's hands after that.

An hour later, after skimming over all the cases, Jeryd found himself seated at a meeting table with three of his superiors, all grey-skinned rumel much older than himself, and who seemed drunk even before midday.

He briefed them on the new case, to ensure that he could pursue it legitimately, and found they put up no objections. No one else in the Inquisition seemed all that bothered about what he was doing, which both annoyed and gratified him. No distractions, no one pushing administrative duties his way, no one tying him up in red tape.

*

Jeryd began the process of interviewing all those who had reported missing persons. He went about things in a thoroughly organized manner, touring the streets with Nanzi, the girl proving as diligent as ever in her assistance.

Jeryd liked her. She brought some much-needed stability and an enquiring mind to their partnership. She also brought him tea regularly. She kept fuel for the fire well stocked. She organized his notes, fetched in a map – he didn't even have to ask for it. On top of helping him she saw to the needs of the women and children who thronged the lobby of the Inquisition headquarters, reporting sickening deeds of one kind or another. Good aides were hard to come by.

As they plodded through the streets they soon found that those who had vanished from the streets of Villiren were a varied range of individuals. Jeryd had numerous bereaved families to interview, but he was especially keen on locating any similarities to the disappearance of the missing Night Guard soldier. By concentrating on that, the probabilities of discovering him or what had happened to him were greater.

Some of the houses in the city showed evidence of extreme poverty; hastily built constructions with no flair for design. People were crowded into cuboid rooms that adjoined exactly similar rooms – in buildings run up because they were claimed to be the future in modernity and clean living. This was progress, Lutto had declared, as he pocketed their rent money, but somewhere over the course of the years the soul of the entire street had died.

Thus he persevered: family after family, door after door, face after face.

Jeryd knew, without understanding how, that some of the missing were never going to be found again. He saw the homes that they'd vanished from, and there was something about these decrepit places that suggested they were probably better off now, wherever they were.

Jeryd was surveying lives that no one in authority had ever bothered to check on. Lives that had capsized years ago: women who looked constantly on the verge of tears, men beyond desperation, young girls holding younger girls he hoped weren't their own, the elderly afflicted with diseases he didn't know how to describe. Forgotten people rotting inside their homes, conscious that they were not wanted in the city proper. Jeryd knew he could have been the first investigator to ask these families about the person who had vanished from their existence. Mothers who had lost their eldest children, on whom they depended. Husbands who had lost their wives of thirty years. Families of children with no parents.

You will find them, won't you? You will help us?

Many said they couldn't find a job, yet couldn't survive out in the ice. Some claimed the portreeve had crippled or bribed the unions, and encouraged such an influx of cheap tribal labour that it meant they were paid next to nothing. Some described how he had issued regular pamphlets declaring that benefits had to be limited to pay for the cost of mounting a defence against the threat of attack from the north – which was merely a variation on earlier years when he said the money was needed to fund preparations against terror attacks from the tribes of Varltung. Thus Lutto created an air of danger to keep these people in their place.

If these families knew that a war was imminent, they didn't show it.

How can you destroy people who are already broken?

But he and Nanzi found out one crucially interesting fact: those who had disappeared in larger numbers were the citizens with better-quality jobs – traders and tavern owners and smiths. Jeryd was frustrated with how the Inquisition could have overlooked such reports.

They strode from the houses back to the Inquisition headquarters in the ambience of the falling snow.

'It's not a pretty picture, is it?' Jeryd's mood had been so contemplative, he had momentarily forgotten Nanzi was next to him. He supposed today's task had not been easy on her.

'I had no idea how bad things were in this city,' she confessed. 'It doesn't look like we can do much for them though, does it?'

'The good investigator', Jeryd replied, 'always has choices

before him, even when it seems there are none. He instinctively knows what's right. He knows he has the option to do *something*.'

'Sounds as if you're the only good investigator left,' Nanzi remarked.

'I feel like I'm holding the fort all by myself.'

*

Another long day till his legs ached and sentences were drying up in his throat. After Nanzi departed for the night, he sat and contemplated the day's findings in his chamber, a cup of tea in one hand, a biscuit in the other.

Patterns materialized.

Give or take half an hour's walk, the majority of disappearances had taken place between the Ancient Quarter and the seafront, or concentrated in Deeping, around the Citadel and the barracks.

Jeryd brooded on these facts, as if tuning in to their importance.

What was special about the types of citizens who resided there? He had to also consider whether they had been murdered by some careful killer operating stealthily, or if perhaps prosperous men and women were walking out on their families because of the threat of war.

The red sun having set early this far north, he deliberated the subject for some time while in darkness.

*

Another whisper, someone calling out a name, one that wasn't his. Night-time now, and once more Jeryd was lying in his bed. His gold-starred red breeches hung on the back of a chair as if mocking him. He'd been reading a history book he found on the shelf, the kind of dry information he needed to take his mind off things.

Marysa had kept herself busy by hunting for all the libraries. Not one central depository, they were spread across the city in small bohemian enclaves, some no more than front rooms or attic spaces. Her current area of research involved antique architecture. The Boreal Archipelago was littered with the remains of structures of dubious purpose, edifices that had been reduced to nothing more than crippled aesthetics, though there was little of the old stuff to be found in Villiren. She hoped to find herself employment from history tuition, but few people seemed interested.

And tonight she had recently returned from one of her first classes in some obscure technique of personal combat. Garish advertising leaflets constantly made their way around the city, promising methods of safety amidst the gang violence. He himself could never keep up with them: there was always a new technique to be learned: a punch or a jab that would defeat all others.

The ultimate fighting moves! The killer system! Women, defend yourselves against gang tyranny!

Currently she was out of the room making them some more tea, when suddenly he heard a voice that might or might not have been merely the wind; he couldn't be certain.

The second time, it spoke a name, for sure.

When he opened the window to investigate, the area outside was quiet. No one walked the narrow, lacklustre streets. Was it possible he was being spied upon?

TEN

Malum was enjoying a card game with JC and a choleric trader called Gall, who was bleeding Sota and Lordil coins across the table. Malum didn't need the money, just liked to win, although sometimes he wished that these types didn't let their fear of him get in the way of a good game. Gall did a little work for the Black Eyed Dog mineral franchise, and some said that he dealt in slaves, though Malum had never seen much evidence of that.

There was a glass of blood to one side, from which he took a swig, savouring the metallic taste. Down here, none of this gang made any effort to hide what they were. In one corner of the room, watching the door, was Múndi, a tribal kid no older than ten who'd become orphaned after the rest of his tribe was slaughtered by Imperial soldiers. He normally sauntered around with a spurious arrogance, carrying his machete with casual ease.

Múndi stepped aside as two of the youngest recruits came clambering in to the rear of the dimly lit bar, and Malum studied the two youths from behind his mask. They were both blond: Jodil the chunky one, while Din was skinny. Fourteen and fifteen years old respectively, they wore thigh-length leather coats and the same brand of paduasoy hooded jumper that Malum had bought for them on their initiation. Annoyingly, they kept wearing crude home-made fangs to blend in with the fully ordained members of the Bloods, but Malum didn't discourage their enthusiasm.

They now seemed nervous, each shifting his weight from foot to foot, hands buried deep in their pockets. He liked the kids. There was a deep sense of loyalty in them, which derived from the fact that they'd both lost their fathers to the sea and didn't have much else in the way of family. They had drifted, he had caught them and nurtured them. A lot of young recruits came to him that way.

Malum slung down his cards as JC stood to berate the two for disrupting the game.

Malum placed a hand on his shoulder. 'Leave it, it's fine.' He gestured for JC to sit back down again in his seat. Then, to the kids, 'What's wrong?'

Jodil, the thickset one, spoke through the pauses in his breathing. 'We lost Deeb. We was down by the boneyard. To keep watch to see if any of those dicks from the Screams was being brought in there this morning after that fight. Then Deeb tried it on with these two weird old men. And . . . And . . .'

'Slow down.' Malum moved over to them both and placed a paternal arm around each shoulder. 'Sit, and speak a little more clearly.' Soothing tones, close body contact: the things these young street-warriors most needed right now. Malum glared at the fat trader until the man picked up what was left of his coins and slunk out of the bar. The young Bloods took their seats.

'Now' – Malum leaned forward across the table, his arms folded, seeking eye contact – 'what happened to Deeb?'

'Dead,' Din murmured.

'He's gotta be,' Jodil agreed.

Malum pondered their body language. 'You don't seem convinced.'

'Those two old men,' Jodil continued, 'they was fucking

around with these graves. There was one that was already open.'

'Criminal's grave?' JC offered.

'They all are at the boneyard,' Malum grunted. Anyone who broke the law was buried, not burned, so that their souls remained trapped within the city: an imprisonment during the afterlife.

'Whatever,' Jodil continued. 'Deeb went over to see what was going on and he started calling them all sorts of names.'

'Why?'

'You know what he's like. He's a dick. Gives them all this attitude.'

'The men, what did they do? Did you get a good look?'

'One was bald,' Din said, 'but we didn't get a proper look at the other. They was wearing too many layers – all dark shades.'

'And what did they do with Deeb?'

'They grabbed him by the neck, snapped it just like that, and threw him in the grave.'

Malum gestured for them to go on.

'Then there was a flash of something. Cultists, we reckoned at the time. Then Deeb was lifted up out of the grave by three of the things that was already in them.'

'What, the corpses?'

The youths both nodded.

'What were you two doing at the time?'

'We shouted something but we couldn't move. It's as if there was some sort of wall between us. We swear we tried to get to him. We tried to throw rocks over it, but only a few managed to get near them. Even that small crossbow of mine wouldn't shatter it.'

Malum nodded. 'Then what happened?'

'Deeb looked dead. He shouldn't have been able to move. His neck was broken and his head was hanging at an angle. His eyes was closed, too. The things to one side of him were really decayed. They looked like melted men with their skin peeling off. The three of them came towards us and that's when we legged it back here and didn't stop. We could hear them men laughing at us as we left the boneyard.'

Everyone waited for Malum's next words to fill the painful silence, but no one made eye contact.

He had heard about these sorts of situations before, but they tended to amount to just rumours, fanciful stories designed to intimidate others, yet he'd recently heard about something similar happening on Jokull, with dead people walking across the tundra, but that was too far away to concern him.

Knowing what it was likely to have been, he eventually declared, 'Cultist necromancers. That's what they sound like. In the boneyard, raising the dead, killing one of our gang members.'

'What shall we do?' asked the skinny youth, hunching his shoulders, retreating into himself. 'Could go back again, see if they return?'

Malum stood up, stretched his legs. 'The Bloods, we're family remember. If one of us goes down, I go down with him. We respect and support each other. But dealing with necromancers, well . . . that's something way out of what we normally have to contend with.'

None of them would be equipped to fight people like that. He had a pact with a few cultists, a deal arranged to make their lives more comfortable in exchange for a little help, but he didn't think that they were worth wasting on a power his own guys wouldn't be able to comprehend. Necromancers were rare even in the weird and fucked-up world of cultists. His decision now would be to do nothing, but he would promote these youths up a level for at least trying to fight off a necromancer to help their already dead friend.

ELEVEN

'Lady Rika, you want to say a little prayer, or something?' Randur muttered. 'Might make the snow stop.'

He gazed out across the treeless plain, at a stolen glimpse of sunlight – at skies turning the colour of a rusted sword, providing the only distraction from the same bleakness they had travelled through for so long now. Pterodettes circled terns that circled pterodettes in avoidance manoeuvres. In such vast open skies there was nowhere to hide.

'From the sound of your voice,' Rika said, 'I assume you are having some fun at my expense, Randur.' Her black cloak rippled in the breeze, revealing an ornate medallion attached to the robe underneath, a reminder of the wealth she and her sister were once used to.

'Not much, if I'm honest,' Randur replied, catching a wry smile from Denlin.

Randur leaned on his sword as they sheltered from the constant snow under the porch of an old farmhouse. The building hadn't been lived in for years, but it was *somewhere*. Psychologically, points like this were essential havens on their map. Thirty days now, and most of them spent icy wet. Thirty days on the run from Villjamur.

They were fugitives, no less; he'd stolen these girls from certain death and angered an entire empire in the process, and to say he was now feeling paranoid was an understatement. On a rickety boat that lurched and lunged amid choppy waters, they'd skimmed north along the coast of Jokull, under nothing but empty skies and sea spray. They avoided ice sheets near Kullrún, then travelled south with mordantly cold winds chasing behind them, before landing with more luck than skill on the east coast of Folke the previous night.

Yet they were barely at the halfway point of their route. Villiren, a city located at the end of the next island north, was their target destination – though it seemed a world away.

Still, at least we're out of the fucking freezing water.

Folke: Randur's homeland. He knew it well, so was aware of the dangers to be encountered anywhere away from the major towns. Looking out across a snow-blasted landscape, with nothing ahead but biting wind, with only a few provisions and having not seen another person in days, the success of their journey seemed improbable at best. Patches of exposed land near the coast were so inhospitable that only moss and lichen could survive, but the territory itself was familiar enough to provide him with reassurance on a deep level that he wasn't really aware of.

Denlin briefed their companions, now that they were further inland. The old man's age and experience were useful out here, but Denlin now seemed to have an opinion on *everything*. 'Girls from a fancy background who have lost everything – money, family and whatever. You two are nobodies, now, right? What are you?'

'Nobodies,' they mumbled, sounding as if they had been berated for some petty misdemeanour, not fighting for survival in a deleterious landscape. Both were garbed in featureless brown furs, hoods flipped up for protection, travelling bags at their feet. Rika's once-elegant hair was now lank and dishevelled, leaving black tendrils clinging to her face. Unlike Randur's partner Eir – her hair was shorter, scruffier, her face more gently rounded than Rika's, but otherwise almost identical in appearance. This similarity gave Randur some concern – that he might make some inappropriate suggestion to the wrong sister, maybe slap the wrong behind. And get his face slapped back. Two times he had come close, two times he caught a fine detail at the last moment in time to make him stop.

'Because if you're *somebody*, you get your arse kicked,' Denlin declared. 'No, you get the crap thieved from your arse.'

'Does he have to be so crude?' Eir asked.

'It grows on you,' Randur grunted.

'Seen a lot, lad. I'm a man of the world, me.' Denlin faced him with this new-found authority, and this sense of command added a little dignity to his age-sagged face. His forest-green cloak, ex-military, was annoyingly clean, probably an old soldier's habit. When Randur had first met the old man, he could barely keep himself clean, could barely gather together enough money to buy himself a meal in the rancid taverns of Villjamur. Randur no longer hated being the best dressed, even out in the middle of nowhere, under these big island skies.

'This ain't the time to be nice and kind,' Denlin said. 'You got to speak the language of the wild.'

A movement in the distance.

'Well, using that same language,' Randur interrupted him, 'how do you say "There's a caravan of militants over there, and they're heading our way"?'

The old man turned to observe the approaching group. 'Good point, lad. Bugger.'

A horse-drawn caravan crested the hill, with a red symbol painted on its side: a crude image of an eagle on fire. Randur knew it to signify one of the rebel groups that cropped up now and then across the Empire, a crew of rascals that he'd encountered once before on Folke. They called for freedom from Jamur power, and refused to pay their taxes, but still managed to defile the good name of anarchism. You would hear about them cruising from town to town, seducing girls who were impressed with their half-baked philosophies stolen from others, more thrilled at outraging their elders' feelings than engaging in revolutionary activities. These young men liked to challenge others to fights, but it was only machismo, nothing more than posturing in taverns.

'Two horses at the front, one at the back, one to the side of the caravan and, more importantly, four armed men in ragged cloaks, all carrying big, fuck-off swords,' Randur observed. 'Reckon they're selling flowers?'

'You think we can take them, Rand?' Eir fingered a gold necklace, one of the few trinkets he'd rescued from the city. She had certainly grown in confidence since he had tutored her in swordsmanship back in Villjamur. Randur liked her new attitude – he longed to get a moment alone with her so they could explore their developing feelings. Truth be told he was gagging for it, but with her god-blighted sister and Denlin always hanging around, that wasn't possible.

'Wouldn't recommend it,' Denlin suggested. 'You two fancy yourselves something rotten since Villjamur. Think you're heroes after that display on the walls. Well, things is different, out here.'

'I would hope we can stay away from more violence,' Rika interrupted. 'Astrid, I've seen enough of it.' She lowered her head, as some kind of Jorsalir prayer began to form on her lips. The girl had spent years on Southfjords studying the Jorsalir religion under the guidance of a priestess of the god-dess Astrid. It annoyed Randur, the way she'd turn to religion at times like this, when they needed no divine-intervention shit.

'Lass speaks some sense,' Denlin agreed. 'No violence is needed, no cause for alarm. Better let me handle this.'

Denlin sauntered gingerly over to meet the approaching crew, a right bunch of Neanderthals judging by the look of them. When he was fifty paces away, after Denlin's initial greeting, Randur couldn't hear a word. The old man began to make all manner of gestures, pointing this way and that, laughing appropriately, hand on hips, and it was reassuring to see some of the other men lighten up and begin to smile themselves.

The momentum of the day changed in an exchange of glances.

One of them aimed a crossbow and shot Denlin through the eye and blood flamed across the snow. The old man crumpled backwards, while the gang looked on nonchalantly.

Rika gasped.

'Get inside the farmhouse *now*,' Randur urged. 'Eir, if I fail, look after your sister. I don't think this lot will be kind to her.'

Indignation contorted Eir's face – she wanted to stay here to prove herself, he well knew, and she might yet have her chance, but he suspected she wasn't up to killing again, not yet, despite her best intentions of being a hero. Eir opened the farmhouse door and, with a final glance back, ushered Rika inside.

Fucking hell, Randur thought. *Denlin . . .*

Saying prayers didn't seem like such a bad idea any more.

Tuning out all his emotions, he focused on the task at hand, tugged aside his black cloak and gripped his sword handle with an edge of anticipation. Randur approached them with slow, measured strides, hoping not to be shot to pieces before he even reached them. He was aching to get away from here, trying desperately not to look at the dead corpse of his friend. Snow compacted underfoot, and the wind calmed, leaving an eerie ambience that protracted the walk towards them indefinitely.

'A little unnecessary that, wasn't it?' Randur called out to the man sitting at the front of the caravan, an obese and swarthy figure in a brown cloak. Crumbs and stains were spattered down his front, and in one hand he held a bladder of wine. *Probably pissed.*

'Military,' the man grunted casually. He shrugged and held up his free arm. 'Wore the cloak, so he had to go, didn't he?'

Two other men manoeuvred their horses. Once the man at the rear was in place, they were surrounding Randur entirely. He just glared at the leader, suppressing his emotions. 'He wasn't in the army, not any more. He was retired for years and had only the other day fought against Jamur troops.'

'We don't like them Jamur soldiers, new or old, plain and simple. Far too many on this island at the moment. Basically, you gotta badge of the Empire, you int no friend of ours. We kill anything to do with the Empire. You got anything to do with them?'

'Have I fuck,' Randur lied. 'Anyway, he wasn't a real soldier. He stole that cloak to keep warm. Just trying to show off.'

'Not what he told us,' the fat man replied, sitting up with difficulty, 'when we asked him.'

At least Randur couldn't yet hear the click of a bolt being loaded. 'He was merely an old man who liked to impress.'

'He *failed* to impress me then. So, about the rest of you – what are you doing here? Them juicy-looking bitches made their way inside, they a good fuck or what?'

'That is no one's concern.' Rage swelled within him, but Randur reined back his reactions. Instead he fed them some lines about how he and his companions also hated the Empire, that they had been taxed until they could no longer afford the lease on their lands, and how they now owned nothing, not a Drakar ... and finally that the girls were both diseased and really weren't wasting anyone's time over.

'You look like you got cash by your fancy clothes.'

Randur snapped, 'Do you think we'd be all the bloody way out here, in the middle of fuck knows where, if we had any money?'

'Got a point,' the fat man grunted.

Something happened in the glances again.

Randur dived to his right, rolling under the shot of a crossbow, then intentionally spooked one of the horses so it backed into the other, and in the ensuing chaos he pulled both their shouting riders to the ground. One, two, he slashed the men's throats, then plunged behind the caravan, underneath it and through to the other side. There, Randur caught the final horseman by surprise, slammed his head into the wooden side of the carriage twice so hard that it splintered, and shoved his sword through the man's gaping mouth.

Up onto the carriage, then Randur hauled the fat man to the ground – the momentum increased by his target's excessive weight.

Randur aimed his sword point between the man's eyes.

'Don't you kill me!' he spluttered, as a dark stain of urine bloomed at his crotch.

'Right, you fat bastard,' Randur grabbed a clump of greasy hair, 'give me one reason to believe that the world would not be a better place without you.'

'I . . . I . . .'

'Sorry. You've *failed* to impress me.' Randur stood up, and ran the near edge of his blade across the man's throat.

He let him bleed slowly into the snow, lying on his back, his legs quivering. The horses merely stood there, their breath clouding the air.

Randur walked over to Denlin's body, crouched down to cradle the old man's head, staring at the gaping wound in his friend's face. The snow all around was polluted with blood that spread out in vast stains highlighting the carnage.

He then went back to the farmhouse, headed straight across to the far end of one empty room, slumped in the corner, and slung his sword clattering across the floor. 'Well, we've got ourselves some well-behaved horses, some food, and a fat pile of coin,' he announced. 'That's progress.'

He rubbed at his face vigorously, felt an absurd urge to weep – from the continuing pressures, the tension, the relief of not dying, he wasn't sure why.

No glory here, no get-the-girl.

Rika and Eir shuffled out from the dimness of the interior,

clearly hesitant as to how to begin a conversation after that display. Randur could see pity in Eir's face. He couldn't be sure if she was appalled at his brutality or not, if she even witnessed it. She should be used to it, though, after seeing the butchery that occurred when he liberated her in Villjamur.

Rika said, 'Did you really have to kill them?'

Closing his eyes, he breathed out slowly, then to Eir he said, 'Not very grateful, this one, is she?'

'Is Denlin . . . ?' Eir began.

'Dead. Very much so.' Randur slid his knees up against his chest, and Eir crouched next to him, her hand resting on his arm, but he looked right past her, out through the open door, and across the scene where his friend had been dispatched so casually. He began to shiver.

*

Under a blood-red sky, Rika offered to perform burial rites for Denlin. Randur didn't know what to say to her offer, and merely grunted some form of approval. Praying was what she did, generally, other than being dull company and seeming ungrateful for her rescue. Well, not exactly ungrateful, but hoping for everything to be accomplished with religious purity. Saving the day couldn't be achieved so cleanly.

Bugger that. She could freeze her arse off out here on her own, and see how long she'd last. Essentially, it dawned on him, he was here solely for Eir, doing whatever she wanted to do, and he was fine with that. It gave him some direction, a sense of purpose. Being back on Folke for the first time in months, he felt the urge to ride across the island to Ule, where his mother lived, to check if she was all right. He knew that when you couldn't see the future, people tended to gaze longingly towards the past. So he now considered travelling to that town on the south coast where he'd grown up. Learned to dance there, learned to fight under the local skills, *Vitassi*, an expertise that had given him the advantage so many times.

From hunks of wood wrenched from the farmhouse walls,

they constructed a pyre on which to burn Denlin's body, so as to carry his spirit away to the higher realm. Having wrapped him carefully in cloth, the fire was then ignited. The flames burgeoned up the timber pile, and gnawed into the old man's corpse, till the fire spat sparks right across the evening sky.

As he listened to Rika's soothing incantations, they seemed to touch him on some deeper level he was unaware of. Randur hadn't had much time for religion in his past. Too busy chasing girls around the villages, too busy dancing in fire-lit shadows. There were too many pleasures on offer in life, surely, to become occupied with stilling your natural urges, and contemplating what came next. Especially in Villjamur, where he'd travelled pretending to be someone he wasn't, there were even more ways to be distracted.

Yet he had to admit that Rika's vaguely melodic prayers were luring him in some ethereal way. 'What are you chanting about? Must admit, I've not much of a clue about your Jorsalir stuff.'

A look of happiness fashioned itself in her face. 'When the two gods, Bohr and Astrid, male and female, created this world, they created other ones too. Different worlds, some parallel, but many on higher and lower plains of existence. Gods and half-gods engaged in petty combats, there at the top of existence. Godhood is a good life, supposedly, but they are never satisfied, and always competing. There are even ghost realms occupying that layer on top of ours, Randur – prisons for those trapped in some harsh memory. Which is why being in this present realm, despite its joys and hardships, *because* of its joys and hardships, is ideal for spiritual development.'

He grunted at that point, though not exactly disapproving. 'What about Denlin?' Randur asked. 'Where's he going to end up, then? One of these other realms?'

'Yes, and my prayers are intended to help him reach a *good* realm.'

Did it matter any more? Denlin was dead, just dead.

Eir and Rika stepped back into the farmhouse for the night, leaving Randur alone outside to brood, staring into the flames. Denlin had helped him so much – by selling on the jewels that Randur had seduced from the grasp of rich old ladies, and thus brought in a lot of money for the two of them. They'd become colleagues of sorts, and a firm bond had developed from the need for each other's presence.

Somewhere in the dark distance, a wolf called, the creature heightening Randur's sudden sense of isolation from the world.

Thank you, you old bugger.

TWELVE

'Commander Lathraea, my son, please – come forward.'

Again, there had been that initial reaction he was used to – the realization that he was albino, that he was someone different. White-robed and reeking of musk, the old priest tilted the back of his hand upwards. Brynd removed his wax cape, folded it to one side, walked forward and knelt to kiss the offered hand. There were far too many gold rings on those aged fingers for his liking.

'A Night Guard soldier in my church,' the priest rasped. His face was lightly pockmarked, his eyes sharp. 'That is indeed an honour. And the famed albino, too . . .'

The church was more like a cathedral, really. It was filled with those ornate decorations that Brynd couldn't stand. Why did Bohr and Astrid, the creator gods, those epitomes male and female . . . why did they need such excessive finery? It suggested that these priests and priestesses extorted a lot of money from their followers merely to spend on ornate fripperies. Candelabras and crest mirrors and console tables of such craftsmanship. A thick red carpet bisected the cavernous stone-built room, wooden benches ranged on either side of it, where men and women of the city would come and pray segregated in their allotted areas.

'Priest Pias, the honour is mine,' Brynd lied. He stood up to face the old man directly. Thick wrinkles in the priest's face contradicted the air of a peaceful existence. His nose was bird-like, over lips that were unusually small.

'How can I be of help to you?' Pias's voice was commanding in the stillness of the large chamber. They walked side by side to one of the front benches, where the priest gestured for the commander to sit down.

Light leaked from the hundreds of candles in the vast space, creating a warmth and peace that seemed unnaturally potent. Incense burned at the rear, sandalwood, the flakes of smoke catching the light.

'I'm here to ask a favour,' Brynd said. 'You already know of our current crisis, so I won't bore you with the details.'

'Indeed,' Pias sighed. 'This is a grave matter, isn't it? And how are you coping?'

Brynd related the grim information in its true and honest form. 'I wonder how long we can survive against such a scale of attack. We've decided to request the presence of a lot of cultists to aid us in preparation—'

'That way lies insanity, commander. Cultists are untrustworthy and unsavoury individuals.'

Brynd knew how much the church disapproved of cultists, but he'd not been aware of this degree of vitriol. Saying nothing, he waited for the priest to go on.

'They mess with the universe on unethical levels. Of course, Bohr would not approve of their techniques, but they continually perpetuate lies regarding the functioning of this world, commander. You'd do well not to listen to their seductive suggestions.'

'These are desperate times, I'm afraid. I'm even having to seek the support of some of the street gangs.'

'Really?' The priest licked his fingers to slick down some errant strands of thin grey hair. 'I would not think that such criminals are much use to anyone.'

'Admittedly, but these are unusual times. Those street men

are tough, and they might find some way to redeem themselves . . . in the eyes of Bohr and Astrid.'

'This is true.' Priest Pias gave a philosophical shrug.

'But what I'm after,' Brynd said, 'what I need is some guidance. You deliver some enthusiastic sermons here, so they say.'

'Ah, it has been known, yes. I am passionate about our Jorsalir teachings.' The priest smiled. 'But how could this be of any help to a military man?'

'Inspiration, essentially. I wondered if there are any references in the scriptures to ways of fighting for great causes. Because if the intelligence brought to my attention is correct, we're dealing here with great evil. You might even say something *otherworldly*.'

'A military man wishes for spiritual guidance against the forces of evil?' Pias could hardly contain his amusement.

Smug fucker, Brynd thought. 'Not precisely, Priest Pias. But are there such references in the scriptures?'

'Yes, of course. Although it is not as black and white as one might think. Well, the teachings of . . . the Hunter Saint in particular. His sermons suggested that Bohr and Astrid have demanded such action of our citizens in the past. To protect the realms of yore, in our vast, vast history. Many scholars suggest that inactivity on the part of previous civilizations – the Shalafars in particular – in the names of our creators, led to their eradication. "Because of Bohr's great mercy to us I appeal to you: offer yourselves as a living sacrifice to Bohr, dedicated to His service and pleasing to Him. This is the true worship that you should offer."'

'I've no wish for our people to be eradicated.' Brynd's gaze was met by the priest's.

'Nor have I.'

'Here's how things stand,' Brynd continued. 'If our suspicions are correct, this city will most likely fall unless every man and woman wholeheartedly fights for its survival. My soldiers will do all we can to stop them, but I fear the worst. This . . .' – he sought the word again, for emphasis, no matter how inaccurate it was to how he really felt – '. . . *evil*. This evil will stop at nothing, so I want the people to be willing to fight for their homes – for their very survival. If not that, then for some greater spiritual cause. Perhaps for a rebirth in a new realm, something beyond their present everyday existence. They need' – he hated to use the words – 'hope and faith.'

'You refer to the intervention of Bohr and Astrid?' the priest offered.

'I do.' Brynd despised how low he was having to stoop. People did what they did because they believed in it or else, at a very basic level, believed it would make them happier. Motivations were simple affairs, and he needed to rouse the citizens of Villiren to fight for something greater than themselves. 'It might also reduce our reliance on external bodies . . . such as cultists and the like . . .'

Priest Pias leaned back on the bench and stretched his arm out to one side. For a moment there was perfect stillness in the room.

'Are you yourself a religious man, commander?' Priest Pias asked.

'I have my moments.' Another lie. How could he connect to a belief system that helped outlaw what he was in secret?

'I shall contemplate your words, commander,' the priest said. 'If some great evil, as you say, is coming to this city then I hear your concerns. I shall talk to some of the other priests, and see what they come up with regarding our scriptures. For a greater good, as you say.'

'For a greater good,' Brynd echoed.

*

A cold night, again, as horses belted through the dark, their hooves slipping on ice. Two fiacres clattered by, the riders barely looking his way. Thugs loitered wherever streets intersected, converging in the language of the streets, that queer

Jamur-tribal hybrid. Amongst these nocturnal scenes, he wondered vaguely what had happened to Private Haust, the young blond man who had disappeared.

Brynd was wearing civilian clothing, thick cotton layers, of an earthy brown colour, a hood so that he could hide his face as he walked, so he would blend into Villiren, even, as on the night that saw the underground fights, using a paste to darken his exposed skin, to hide the fact he was albino. Nothing he could do about his red-tinted eyes though, so he had decided to wear a full-face gnaga mask.

Constant stress was crippling him and the logistics of the military operation were overwhelming. Night after night, the other soldiers could unwind in taverns all across the city while he imprisoned himself with charts and reports, saw to the needs of thousands of others who remained ignorant of how he was serving them. He had slept maybe eight hours only over the last three nights.

Well, not this evening. Tonight he sought relief.

After exploring a few tip-offs, he was striding towards a certain featureless building, with a facade that could be found in any city throughout the Boreal Archipelago. Anonymous-looking. There were two men standing behind the door leading to his destination, big guys with daggers ready at hand. Behind them lay a dark corridor. A few discreet words were exchanged, tentative and searching sentences, then they let him in.

The first room was lit by just two cressets, on opposite walls, and a couple of tea-light candles set on each of the tables. *Always the same, these places.* Dark enough for the hypocrites to escape into their fantasies without ever being caught – which annoyed Brynd, since these might be the very same men ready to label others as being 'abnormal'.

Bender, queer, faggot.

Words loaded with a pain that burned inside his head. In his darker moments he could hardly blame them – there were times he could hardly tolerate himself. But such words were spoken every day with a casual thoughtlessness, often issuing from the mouths of those he worked with and trusted.

How could the world be so consciously loathing of such a natural emotion, merely on the word of some very old text? Other cultures, Brynd was certain, would not forbid such desires.

Shirt-lifter, mincer, fairy.

Was he a weak man? Was he weak for wanting sex, wanting *to pay* for sex? No. It was safer that way, a transaction which would secure his anonymity.

From behind a doorway, music drifted into the main bar. He poked his head in briefly, saw a violin player and a man clutching a small drum belting out a few folk rhythms, could smell the intense aroma of arum weed and spilt vodka. There were a few candles at the far end, nothing in between but shadows gliding through the darkness. His heart rate picked up, matched the intensity of the drumming. Sudden nervousness kicked in, and for a moment he considered walking out again, back to the barracks, ignoring this side of him like he had so often before.

In a fake accent, he asked someone nearby where he could go to pay for it. Directions were issued, gestures barely discernible in the dimness. He felt his way around the corridors until he reached where he hoped to be. A moment later, he'd chosen his man, one with oil glistening on his skin, slightly perfumed with patchouli, a scent aiming to relax him.

'Don't worry if this is your first time.'

'It's not.' Brynd tried not to laugh. How much cock had he sucked by now? He couldn't remember. He threw the man some Sota coins – and didn't even look at how many.

They found a room shrouded in darkness, with a decent enough bed, and everything proceeded by touch. Brynd liked that, his vision removed, it meant his other senses were heightened. Liked the feeling of not having to make decisions, of following someone else's orders. The man tried to remove Brynd's mask but a firm grip on his thick wrist thwarted the gesture. Instead, Brynd tilted it slightly to one side, and kissed him ... and his primitive instincts dispelled that inert, empty sensation he felt with a complete stranger, because this was now a body at least, another man, more than he'd known in a while: meat and tongue and cock. This one was thuggish and direct, and Brynd tenderly explored the thick ridges of muscle moving against him, the thick arms around his waist. *Fuck, that feels so, so good ...* Brynd turned, reaching behind his body, and eased the man's dick out of his breeches and wanked him until he was hard.

'You have protection I take it?' Brynd asked. A few movements to one side, and the man-whore was safe. *A trustworthy establishment, at least.* He made sure some oil from the man's torso acted as lubrication and, as he leant forwards on his knuckles, he purged his mind of thoughts.

*

Brynd departed with no attempt at conversation, no goodbyes, just headed back out through the confusing dark corridors – smacking straight into the cold night air of Villiren, back into his normal life. A quick fuck to relieve the built-up stress – or replace it with guilt, whatever.

As he left, he couldn't help but think he was being followed. Maybe it was his paranoia. These streets could do that to you, but still ...

Was there actually someone there?

In the shadows?

THIRTEEN

Another row with Beami, another bad start to the evening. All she ever did was spend her time with those stupid relics, tinkering away at them, trying to make some money. Like they needed any more of that – she wouldn't listen to him though, just wanted to do her own thing. Those kind of interests didn't seem to matter at the start – back before the ice, she'd loved the stability he allowed her, his wild edge, his passion and exuberance. And tonight came another pointless discussion on the state of their marriage before he stormed out.

Right there and then, he wanted to go out and sleep with some other woman, and aside from the obvious repercussions, here was the real bite: that was just the kind of thinking that had got him into this mess. Years ago that was all he ever did, floating from woman to woman, uncommitted and angry, and just for a moment he anchored on one. He had that intense fling with an alcoholic chain-smoker . . . what was her name? It didn't matter. He used to let her strike him. That was before he discovered she was in a constant state of anger because of repressing her urges for *vampyrism*.

Ultimately, it was a disease he caught from a cheap fuck. Those were his low days. While he was wasted on drugs, he'd asked her to bite him – he'd pleaded with her and, despite her refusals, she had eventually capitulated. Her fangs appeared and she plunged them into his neck – but because of so much alcohol in her blood and too many substances in his own, something went wrong. There was some failure in transmission.

And he wasn't infected properly.

That woman left him the next day and he never saw her again. Whatever had caused his vampyrism was only passed on at half strength, so he didn't possess a full-time urge to drink blood. His rage increased in intensity, his muscles hardened over a single week, his ageing process slowed – but it never felt complete, and now neither did he. It was as if his life, from that point, became one endless longing for something more. When his gang brethren begged to become infected with his bite, they too received this diluted strain, they too became only half vampyr.

It took him a while to become accustomed to his new body, and he had sought help from a witch, who assiduously treated his wounds in exchange for a large fee. Vampyrs were not immortal, she had warned, and they were susceptible to many other ways of dying ... That, she concluded, was why they were so rare.

This was no fairy tale, then, nothing to romanticize. He was a violent monster.

*

Through the second-floor doorway, Malum glanced southwards across the roofscape. Lights glistened intermittently, showing him a glimpse of a city residence, of someone's life conducted within. Moonlight would steal a moment to expose some silhouetted figure leaping from building to building, on a mission he could only guess at.

Malum sat straddling a chair, gripping the backrest, clenching his jaw against the pain. He had insisted on the door being left open to let in blasts of icy winds – even so, sweat lined his forehead. An arum-weed roll-up burned in one hand, and he took a drag whenever the stinging became too much. At times like this he was grateful that his mask covered only the upper half of his face.

An old man wearing a white gown and with a steady hand was applying a woodblock design to Malum's naked back, adding layer upon layer of black ink to his exposed skin, then scraping with chisels or gouges. Pain pulsed through his body, before it was dulled by whatever it was within his body that rendered him not fully human.

The man painfully grafted art under Malum's skin: symbols, decorations, every line of tattoo loaded with meaning and intent. He was assiduous in his scraping. Jars of pungent, coloured ink covered the table to one side. The artist's slippers shuffled constantly on the tiled floor. Diagrams of designs papered the walls, fluttering in the wind.

Malum took another drag of the roll-up, flicked ash to the floor.

This time he had requested a tribal dragon, a fearsome representation of non-Empire deities, building on an elaboration of designs that crept from the base of his spine up to his shoulder blades.

'Hey, Malum, you got a moment? I got some news.'

Malum looked up as one of his scouts approached him from behind.

'Sure. Go on, speak. He can't hear you. He's deaf.' Malum tilted his head to indicate the old artist. 'Move round the front so I can see you.'

The scout moved into view, by the open doorway. It was one of the older, skinnier men in his service.

'Well, what have you got?' Malum inhaled some more arum weed.

'It's about the soldier,' the scout said. 'The leader.'

'The commander?'

'Yeah,' the scout said, and smirked. 'You gonna love this. I followed him like you said. And you was right.'

'And what was I right about?'

'The soldier was seen going into one of them places where men buy men. For . . . you know, sex.'

Malum contemplated this information for a long moment. His instinct had proven right and, well . . . it just wouldn't do. There was no way he was going to allow his men to fight for someone like *that* now, was there? It just wasn't right. Malum then considered how he could arrange to confront the albino about his despicable activities.

*

Malum didn't bother going to bed much. Instead he slumped in a chair, reading or smoking, or contemplating the bottom of his glass of vodka. Beami had been playing with her relics all night anyway, and recently it seemed easier if their lives didn't cross paths. *Fine with me.*

No, he needed to be up particularly early this morning, the day of the strike. His tattoo had begun to heal quickly and form a scab – such were the beneficial side effects of being what he was: *unnatural.* He stretched himself, to induce a more alert state, then began checking his gear – three short blades, one messer, a knuckleduster – not much but he was skilled enough with his fists and with his fangs should he need them. A different mask for today: dark blue, like all those belonging to the Bloods would be wearing. Brown leather coat, thick boots.

A quick breakfast and he was out the door. The skies had cleared and the sun was purpling the day. This would be a crisp morning. Sometimes it seemed as if this ice age wasn't natural, as if it could somehow be the amalgamation of a thousand cultists trying their best to reduce the entire land to freezing temperatures. You'd get the occasional breeze that promised spring, but that was soon beaten back by another more chilling.

Hands in his pockets, he strode towards the arranged meeting point, by the corner of the iren on the border of

Althing and Saltwater. The strike would be heading down from Port Nostalgia towards the Onyx Wings, which was an impressive distance, and would take them past some of the wealthiest zones of Villiren. Past the houses of wealthy businessmen.

Fifty or so of his men were already gathered, in their dark-blue masks. A lot of the strikers would be wearing masks too: no one wanted to be recognized by the authorities while causing political trouble. As individuals they could suffer, so united they would make their stand – and such unification would now be their downfall.

Malum gave the instructions. They'd blend in with the strike movement, by now a large crowd, and pretend they were part of the protest. Lutto had given instructions for soldiers from the Regiment of Foot to guard much of the rich property nearby, so lesser ranks of the Inquisition had been delegated here. Tensions existed though because the military were trying to get the citizens on Lutto's side, so he had ordered them not to attack civilians. Therefore only the gangs could perpetrate violence. Dannan's crew turned up too, black-masked and keeping to themselves. Pretty soon everyone had massed, and they knew exactly what they would be doing and where to go.

*

Slipping across the border of Althing and through much of the social housing, they headed north to the Shanties: where the strike action was scheduled to start.

Rumels and humans, workers of the ocean, of deep and open-cast pits, metal-smiths and construction workers and stevedores, there were much more than the predicted thousand here. At least four thousand were crammed in between the back of the cheap terraces and the industrial warehouses, and they were angry and loud and organized, young men mainly, because poverty didn't allow them the chance of ageing.

'Fuck Ferryby's,' some chanted. And 'Broun Merchants kills workers!'

Painted signs were brandished aloft, demanding improved wages and better protection and rights – for an end to the employment of slaves, lowering their wages. There were declarations of the numbers who had died during the last ten days at their workplaces. Some proclaimed that cultists were using their magic in order to be rid of regular labour.

This busy industrial zone had ground to a halt.

Red sunlight streamed across the seething masses like a premonition of the spilled blood Malum had planned. A nod directed across Malum's own ranks and the Bloods and the Screams proceeded to merge with the strikers' procession, flowing in gradually then dispersing.

Bodies crammed tightly, there wasn't much room for fighting in this mass. Someone blew a conch and several announcements were called just out of earshot. The noise level altered as the crowd began to march. There was a strangely positive mood: most participants seemed peaceful, seemed to have found their purpose here. They drifted on past the stench of the fish warehouses, stepping across the fresh marine brine that washed constantly over the cobbles. Surrounding structures became taller and narrower, displaying a little more elegance in their design. Malum shoved himself towards the edge of the ranks, eyeing the soldiers drawn up to one side, standing neatly, in sparse rows, shields locked.

Not yet . . . Not until the Citadel is in sight.

The crowd chanted slogans at the soldiers and the Inquisition. They called them abusive names for not being on their side, for not supporting the ordinary people who had to forge a living in this hellhole. Malum didn't give a shit what they said: he just did whatever was needed to collect a fat pile of coin.

There it was, the Citadel itself, the massive structure that stamped its authority on Villiren. Malum moved swiftly into action, and began pushing and shoving those around him.

'Hey, watch it, cunt!'

'Fuck you doin'?'

Malum ignored them. Instead he pointed out anonymous faces declaring loudly that the Inquisition had infiltrated the crowd. Paranoia exploded across the packed street. Malum drew his messer blade, and the woman next to him shrieked at the sight of it. Another man drew his own blade defensively and, at closer than arm's length, Malum struck the other weapon aside, punched him in the neck, and cut his stomach open. The stricken man collapsed to the ground as the movement of feet continued surging over his back. Another fell, then another. Just across the way Malum could see one of the Screams intensifying the violence. He was through the throng, hacking away at spines randomly.

The crowed turned on itself. People began striking out at their own brethren. Nearly everyone nearby was holding some sort of crude weapon – he saw strips of chain and cheap swords, iron bars and broken bottles. They had come ready to fight but probably had not expected it to start within, and suddenly all those masks guaranteeing anonymity and solidarity didn't seem like such a good idea. No one knew who to strike out at. Their target became *anyone*.

The soldiers meanwhile remained impassive ranged along the sides of the streets, as the strike procession turned into a bloodbath. Malum got down to serious work: carving out at the most violent-looking individuals or those holding up placards or those shouting slogans the loudest. He ripped his blade through throats, sliced open guts, stamped skulls into the cobbles, all the time feeling the pressure of his fangs, and his animal instincts liberating themselves.

He moved freely, slicing up the crowd – stopped to lift a young child out of the way – before continuing with his butchery. One giant of a man grabbed Malum's collar and hauled him up, so Malum turned his head and sank his fangs into the attacker's wrist. As the giant dropped Malum with a roar of insults, he stabbed his blade upwards into the man's neck, who tumbled down to the ground in a spray of blood.

Malum wiped his mouth.

A good number of people had been injured or killed by the time he spotted at least five of his gang members. That was the sign: once they could see a handful of each other, they should get out of there, quick.

To avoiding the risk of becoming identifiable, Malum slunk out of the crowd and into one of the side streets, putting his blade away. Hand up against the wall, he panted heavily. Within a few moments, another of his gang had joined him, then one of the Screams jogged by.

People were fleeing the scene in panic, running past, covered with bloody injuries. The clamour of the strike movement had all but gone, and what remained was the murmur of those participants left in shock. Soldiers shifted past the end of the alley, starting back and forth across the main street.

Malum gathered what there were of his gang and set off back into the city.

Their work here was done.

FOURTEEN

Jeryd was reminded that it was Nanzi's day off – not by her absence, but by the chaos of paperwork in his office. Amid this mess, he spent the first hour of the morning in deep contemplation. Actually that wasn't quite true. The first half-hour he spent enjoying a luxurious breakfast, hungry after his attempts at starting a diet the previous day, which he had regretted immediately as hunger pangs stabbed through his stomach.

After perusing the reports of the previous night's crimes, he stared at the large map of the city he had pinned to the wall, noting all the marks he'd made to indicate where disappearances had taken place over recent months. Then following the lines and notation, he decided to investigate those urban areas physically. He picked up his cloak and his broad-brimmed hat.

Just as he was leaving, one of his colleagues, a young and rather lazy grey-skinned rumel called Yorjey, entered and dropped a letter on his desk. Yorjey seemed to him typical of the Inquisition members here in Villiren, more concerned with his social networking rather than with getting any serious work done.

'What's this?' Jeryd indicated the letter, ever sceptical of official documents.

'An invite,' Yorjey replied. 'A number of top-level officers get entertained at the Citadel at Portreeve Lutto's request, every now and then. And what with you being a seasoned professional from Villjamur, you're considered top-level. It'd be a good idea to go, sir, get your face seen around, you know? You need to loosen up a bit, Rumex. People say there's a war coming, you might as well enjoy yourself like the rest of the city.'

Like the rest of you sorry excuses for investigators.

That last sentence summed up the whole attitude of the Inquisition here in Villiren. Jeryd gave a paper-thin smile as the grey-skinned rumel strode out of the room. Then he wondered if he really should perhaps socialize with the others a bit more, thus forging acquaintanceships, making friends as potential future allies if there was indeed any future for this city. Would he be sucked into the easygoing lifestyle these other investigators favoured?

*

A bright day – tall skies, the red sun slouching through its southerly arc. Streets were being cleared of ice and snow by cultist-treated water. Occasionally he might see the underground piping cough up plumes of steam into the air, the firegrain doing its work to keep people warm. Jeryd marvelled at this, and wondered why such systems couldn't have been used in Villjamur. *Bureaucracy, for one thing. A lack of decent leadership under a mad Emperor, then his poor daughter who was set up to replace him, then that bastard Urtica who deposed and imprisoned her.* No doubt Urtica was thoroughly enjoying the perks of his new-found position. How long would it be, Jeryd thought, until the name of the Empire officially changed – even out this far. The only alteration so far was that an order had gone out for new government stationery with new lettering. 'The Urtican Empire,' he muttered, the words bitter on his lips. It was probably used as a mantra in Villjamur.

He had to adjust dramatically to his new life here: this was a hedonistic city, a more liberal society, one without the tight laws of Villjamur. Now and then he'd come upon a shop that sold items he didn't agree with, some kind of new drug he didn't approve of, or someone used a phrase involving far too much vulgarity. People here tended not to queue for things in an orderly fashion. People pushed past him rudely. Women were too forward for his tastes. Hookers loitered in doorways, calling over to him with half a smile, half something else entirely, almost suggesting an exhaustion at the lifestyle they led.

Having memorized the wall map, he walked up and down the various areas where people had gone missing in the largest numbers. What was unique about this neighbourhood? Why were people being targeted *here*? To the south lay the Ancient Quarter, the Onyx Wings almost silhouetted against the lowering sun. To the north stood the barracks and Citadel, their ramparts bold against the horizon. He tipped his hat to two old rumel ladies who seemed to be admiring him, smiling gently in his direction.

It was generally the middle- and upper-class zones that had lost most residents, although what had surprised Jeryd was how a significant number of the others who were missing had held high-profile roles in the local labour movements or were known for their political activism. Among miners and stevedores and tradesmen, it was those most active in defending labour laws who had vanished. That wasn't much to go on, and he was cynical about government methods at the best of times, but he had to look for trends wherever he could.

Irens cropped up all over the place, using any corner they could find. From cooking equipment to clothing, it seemed you could find anything on the stalls scattered about here. Jeryd made his way through one of the larger markets.

'What animals do these come from?' Jeryd innocently asked one meat trader, a slender, bearded man who constantly rubbed his hands together.

He responded with a shrug at first. 'Got all sorts, mate. What y'after?'

'I'm just browsing for the moment,' Jeryd replied.

Temptation plagued him. *A good steak goes a long way in satisfying an investigator.*

Once he had cleared the huddle of irens, the city became quieter.

So, once more: why were people disappearing from relatively prosperous streets? Was it simply because the poorer districts didn't bother reporting their losses, or was there something shared by these people that made them targets?

He made a note to make enquiries in the Wasteland district, a loosely applied name that covered the endless shacks and crudely constructed shelters spreading to the south of the main city.

An external stairway led up to the top of a range of houses, whereby you could walk for some distance along the outer edge of the roofs overlooking the districts of Scarhouse, Saltwater and Deeping, which were to the north of the wasteland, but where the old southern boundaries of the city were to be found. Jeryd decided to go up, if only to discover what the view offered. His ascent wasn't particularly dignified, since the stone steps were very slippery. Luckily, a handrail stopped him from falling off in complete embarrassment, and he gripped it like a drunk holding on to a friend.

He sighed with relief as he reached the top. From up here he could see more of the roofline and many of the defined landmarks: squarish Jorsalir churches, multi-storey tenement blocks and, on the other side, over towards the Ancient Quarter, columns of smoke indicating street vendors busy cooking, and a clutch of mixed architectural styles displaying history heaped up on itself. Rising up amidst this cityscape were several vast and blandly built towers. As he studied them he was exposed to the wind and had to hold on tightly to his hat to stop it from being gusted across the city.

What was he looking for exactly?

Suddenly something caught his eye.

Along the walkway where two streets intersected, something web-like seemed to be dripping from the handrail. He approached it cautiously; the stuff looked utterly alien to him. White gloop drooped thickly, like frayed rope, from one surface to another. It was everywhere around. He took a small, blunt blade from his boot, then prodded at it. Opaque and viscous, and with a confusing texture, it was firmly attached to the metal rail. What the hell creature could produce something like this?

Jeryd thought immediately of cultists, as he so often did when he found no rational answer for something. He twirled the viscous substance on the blade, spinning it, lengthening it, testing it for consistency. It was nothing he knew of, and why would cultists devise something like this? He took a handkerchief from his pocket, smeared a thick globule of the gunk inside it, then placed it back in his pocket. There was nothing else around to arouse much thought; one or two smashed masks lying further down the walkway, but they could be found everywhere in the city.

*

Jeryd spent his lunchtime chatting with the commander, eating a seafood platter that was very agreeable, while the albino spoke intensely of troop movements, of statistics and probabilities. The two voiced their dislike of the eerie-looking masks that people in Villiren hid behind. What was that nonsense all about? They were seated in the canteen of the Citadel barracks, a dreary granite building that rang with the boisterous laughter of soldiers.

Jeryd was impressed that Brynd, despite his seniority, saw fit to sit there with his subordinates. *Says a lot about a man, a gesture like that.* Jeryd watched him eat with precision and fine etiquette, so much so that he was almost scared to continue eating himself, in case he spilt sauce down his dark robes. Every now and then, he couldn't help but be held captive by those burning eyes.

'I'm no closer to finding Private Haust, I have to admit,' Jeryd muttered eventually. 'Finding just one man in a city as large and as chaotic as this one isn't going to be simple. The fact that he had no friends outside the military makes things worse – because that leaves us very short on leads to explore. But I have since confirmed there have been a lot of other disappearances, just like you said. An extraordinary amount, in fact.'

'You seem somewhat surprised, investigator,' the commander drawled.

'I am, to be honest.'

'Could it be fear of the war?'

'Nah, I thought that,' Jeryd replied. 'But folk are safer here than out in the wilds during the Freeze. Plus, they don't seem to care much – haven't you noticed?'

'I have actually. I've found, by and large, that people focus on what's in front of them, rather than the big picture. And, with this severe weather, I don't blame them. Any other thoughts?'

'Well, I don't know why it should be the case, but most of the missing have vanished – that's if they're reported at all – from between the Scarhouse area and the Ancient Quarter, also around the Citadel, Althing, Shanties and the Old Harbour.'

'The wealthiest areas, more or less,' Brynd observed.

'Right,' Jeryd agreed. 'Now don't you find that all a tad strange?'

'Could be, investigator. So what are *your* thoughts?'

Jeryd paused to finish a mouthful of crab. *Damn this is tasty*. 'Well, I've a couple of theories. It could just be that the poor don't bother reporting their missing people. And these aren't murders, either, as we've got too few corpses to support that suggestion. Deaths, otherwise – well they're mainly gang-related affairs. No, these are people being taken straight off the streets, in my opinion, and then completely vanishing.' He waved his fork as he voiced his thoughts. 'Could be that the wealthier ones are simply being kidnapped.'

'Being held to ransom, you mean? There's plenty of money around,' Brynd observed. 'Half the city has been thriving here in recent years, what with Lutto's expansion policies. Some people are much better off than ten years ago. Many less so.'

'Exactly. Except we've got no evidence of demands for ransom, no contact so far from whoever's snatching all these people.'

'So how many, precisely, are we talking about?'

'Four hundred and eighty-five reported so far in the last six or seven months – and that's just *reported*.' Jeryd nodded at Brynd's reaction of surprise. 'Yeah, that's a lot, isn't it? Doesn't take into account anyone missing who lived alone, those who didn't have any friends, things like that. People vanish all the time for any number of reasons. And this doesn't fit with any conventional theories about criminals that I've come across. They'd almost certainly die out there, on the ice.'

'They certainly would,' Brynd agreed.

'So,' Jeryd said, fancying a change of subject, 'you any closer to knowing when the fighting will begin, or what the rest of the city'll be doing?'

'Goes no further,' Brynd warned, and Jeryd nodded. 'Enemy units are gathering on the opposite shore in frightening numbers – reaching tens of thousands at the moment. They mass like a swarm of insects, and I've witnessed their capabilities for violence first-hand. Meanwhile, our own army is spread too thin. I'm calling in as many Dragoon regiments as we can get – the Fourteenth, Sixteenth just came in, and we soon expect more of the Regiment of Foot. Garudas are constantly on patrol, or dropping Brenna devices to serve as ice-breakers – anything to stop the enemy simply walking across the ice to us. And although the city is well prepared for evacuation through its numerous escape tunnels, the mass of people themselves . . . they will have to fight. Could do with some of the gangs agreeing to join us, too, but they're reluctant to help anyone other than themselves. It's likely to be an occasion where every man will count. You think you yourself can be a soldier when the time comes?' Brynd finished, with a dry smile.

It wouldn't be the first time Jeryd had put his life on the line for the greater good. 'When duty calls,' he sighed.

*

If Jeryd needed any further guidance along the path to total disillusionment with the world at large, that evening provided it.

As a treat, he took Marysa to the Citadel's masked ball, a more glamorous affair than he had thought could be staged given the Freeze and the forthcoming war. There must have been a hundred people fluttering around each other in the hall, a strangely opulent place with eclectic decorations derived from every corner of the Empire.

People milled about dressed in their finery, clutching delicate glasses. Everyone wore fancy eye-masks, with gold trim and ribbons in dozens of striking colours. The whole atmosphere seemed so unnaturally decadent to Jeryd: this was an ice age, for Bohr's sake, and a war was looming around the corner. Women were necking wine or vodka copiously, men admiring them. How could they party like this, appearing all so carefree? Lute players sat up on a stage in the corner, harmonizing their chords, though Jeryd thought them worse than the city buskers he'd seen earlier in the day.

Marysa was more than happy for this opportunity to meet new people and within a few minutes she was off mingling with other guests. How was it she could just go off and chat to strangers like that? It wasn't his own style. He could speak to people, of course, but not in casual situations like this. Usually he needed a dead body at hand to prompt him into conversation.

A couple of the young Inquisition rumel had gone off chasing after a couple of pretty rumel girls, grey skins, and all big eyes. Within moments, each of them had succeeded in kissing one of the girls in turn.

I'm more out of touch with things than I realized, Jeryd decided, mildly envious of them.

Still, at least without Marysa at his side, he could sneak a few of these delicious-looking nibbles. *Diet, my arse.* And if he was going to be miserable and not talk to anyone, he might as well wander around and listen in, to get a flavour of Villiren, maybe pick up on a little gossip, perhaps even fill in some information gaps. He badly needed to learn more about the city.

Jeryd circled the entire room a few times, loitering while pretending to sample dishes. The wine was far too sweet for his liking, but he drank it anyway. Jeryd was a skilled eaves-dropper and so, through snippets of conversation, Villiren's history gradually came alive.

Portreeve Lutto had been elected for a third term after the success of his expansionist economic policies, namely trading with as many of the other islands in the Empire as possible, and thereby turning Villiren into a centre of negotiations. People said that Lutto had delivered economic growth consistently since new deposits of ores had been discovered. The previous portreeves, Fell and Gryph, had never capitalized on the minerals coming from Tineag'l. Apparently there had been several assassination attempts on Lutto's life, but none were successful.

Lutto's wife was the plump Lady Oylga, daughter of the largest estate owner on the island of Y'iren. Depending on who Jeryd listened to, Lutto either had numerous whores visiting his private chambers, especially rumels for those hard-skin kicks – or else he was having an affair with a star of the local theatres, called Felina Fetrix, spending exuberant amounts of taxpayers' money entertaining her and buying her jewels.

Jeryd listened with great interest as two guests, wearing plush masks and robes with matching gold features, had a heated debate at a corner table.

'The poor are no longer as poor as they once were, dear boy,' declared one man, an ill-favoured fellow with a moustache. Even the eyes of his mask sloped downwards, giving him a permanently sinister expression. 'At least that is on average. Admittedly, yes, there does exist a few – namely the bigger landowners – who are benefiting most, but that's for the best. Meanwhile, you and I—'

'Fucksake man,' the other shouted, slamming his hand on the table, rattling cutlery. 'Look at this place! Look at it. We're pissing away money on wine and food and dancing while not two streets away a family makes do with a bowl of oats that must last them a week.'

'You're drunk again, you soft sod. Think of the success of our city and have some more whisky.'

Jeryd shook his head in weariness. How many of these rich kids would ever deign to pick up a sword once the war began?

A scream—

It came from near one of the exits, a woman's voice. A murmur of dismay rippled across the room towards Jeryd.

He pushed his way through the throng, stepping this way and that, saying 'Excuse me, pardon me' as he squirmed under flickering candelabras and between chinking glasses to investigate, his instinct to investigate aroused. The cold air from the open doorway hit him refreshingly hard, and there stood a woman in a thick green dress and cloak, her hair pinned up ornamentally. She was sobbing into her partner's robed shoulder, and both their masks lay discarded on the floor.

'Investigator Rumex Jeryd, of Villiren Inquisition. What's going on here?' Jeryd reached beneath his garments to find the medallion, and clumsily displayed it.

The woman's partner, tall and handsome in his black attire,

simply shrugged. 'I don't know what the hell's wrong with her. I just turned my back for a moment and . . .'

The woman, who wasn't far off being just a girl, gestured towards the balcony, and Jeryd stepped outside, as a crowd gathered behind him. The starlight was obscured in patches by cloud, but you could see the harbour, an arc whose rim was defined by street fires and lantern light showing people sifting through the streets, and dogs barking above a wind that seemed to groan as it passed through the city.

And there it was, close to where he was standing, the same substance he'd discovered earlier that same day, a thick white mass dripping from the edge of the parapet up to the roof behind, slick and web-like. A few tables and chairs were laid out, and those nearest were covered in this mucus-like gloop.

He turned back to the woman, whose head was still angled away from him, and then he noted her bracelets and coloured nails, more brash than anything he remembered from Villjamur.

'Did you see what did this?' Jeryd pointed to the gloop.

She shook her head, and mumbled, 'No, but something big was moving out there. I knew it as soon I came out for some fresh air. I felt as if I was being *watched*. Then . . .' – a sharp inhalation of air as she choked back on her sobs – 'then that white stuff just appeared from nowhere.'

'How much have you had to drink?'

'Hardly anything!' she snapped. 'Don't you believe me? I know what I saw, all right, I'm not fucking pissed.'

'My apologies,' Jeryd said. 'I meant nothing by it. I'm simply trying to build a picture of what happened. Please, you said you didn't *see* anything.'

'I could *feel* it. Something was watching me, as if waiting. I turned around and this stuff just materialized right by my shoulder – right there, look, as it is now. I may have heard some shuffling of stones, but I don't know if that was because of anything else.'

Jeryd nodded nervously, believing what she said, and stepped over to draw a blade from his boot. He prodded tentatively at the mysterious substance. He knew in his heart that this was the same stuff he'd encountered earlier. He contemplated what kind of creature could produce something like this, and in such quantities.

Finally he faced the guests huddled in the doorway and for a moment wondered morosely how he'd ended up in a situation so absurd, with a bunch of pissed-up rich nobodies staring at him as if expecting some answers.

He said, 'All right, back to your drinks now. There's nothing more to see out here.'

FIFTEEN

They were stupid to leave the entrance unlocked, it thought.

The spider squeezed through the doorway, six of its legs gripping the frame, and eased its body soundlessly into the house. Light from both moons poured in behind it, and it could see its own shadow stretching ahead across the floor.

This was a wealthy family, it instantly decided. Aromas still lingered in the air from some hours ago, so it could sense the quality of their food and realized they were well fed. Voland would approve of such high-quality pickings. It struggled to make out the patterns on the wall hangings in this dim light, struggled to make out anything but tiny vibrations in the air. It was essential, though, that this business be conducted at night, as its services to Doctor Voland must remain unseen.

It made its way up the stairs with a liquid grace, the hairs on its legs guiding it to the second and then the final floor. Behind the third door to the right – the texture of the air had changed there. That was where bodies lay asleep.

Meat.

In stealth it crept along the corridor and, on reaching the third door, extended one leg to the handle, willing for a minor transformation – and, ripping painlessly through its tarsus and claw, a hand appeared. Hands could sometimes be much more useful than claws, and the door opened effortlessly. There they were, the entire family, amassed in one bed for warmth, two parents, two young children, all in deep slumber. They were quite unaware that they were about to become prey.

It scuttled sideways, flanking the room.

Then, straddling the length of bed, the spider loomed above them, half wishing it could just use its venom to dispatch them with ease. But Voland would say no to this, that it contaminated the end product. It now located the father – always going for the biggest threat first – a thickset man with red hair, snoring. Using a hand and claw together to tilt his head upwards, the spider then prised open his mouth with the gentleness of a lover's touch.

The man's eyes shuddered open and he gasped 'What the devil—?' But the spider spat inert fibre into his mouth, suffocating him quickly, all the time checking for any change in vibration among the others. The spider flipped the victim off the bed while the others remained silent, then pounced on him again, suffocating him with more of its spittle, while pinning him to the floor with two legs. The man's eyes bulged in silent alarm, and then in recognition.

Next, came the mother. She lay on the other side of the bed, so it levered itself back up, its abdomen hovering over the bodies of both children. Again it manoeuvred the victim, held her head back, mouth open, spat and suffocated her. Surprisingly easy this one, and the body was placed next to her husband.

Then the spider contemplated the children, a boy and a girl.

The pair lay in a peaceful embrace, as it peeled back the sheets to analyse their tiny bodies. They couldn't be more than five or six years old, and their flesh was tender but scrawny, with little accretion of fat or muscles. Voland had always maintained that children were worthless: they provided poor cuts of meat.

Stepping backwards, two legs at a time, the spider bound the two parent bodies together with silk. Then dragged their corpses downstairs, thoroughly cocooned in fibre, out through the open door, and into the ice-scarred night.

*

As Jeryd reminisced about the previous night's activities, while snacking on some breaded crabmeat he'd just purchased from a grubby street vendor, something else caught his attention.

There were two crates wobbling dangerously on a horse-drawn cart, and he watched with fascination as both finally fell off. Frightened by the racket, the horse bolted, charging through the wide streets of the Althing district. No one seemed in a hurry to stop it as it disappeared north into the sea fog that had rolled in overnight. Jeryd pushed down his hat to sit firmer on his head and advanced towards the two men who were busy retrieving the spilled contents of the crates.

'What've you boys got in there?' Jeryd asked them.

The two men glared at him suspiciously, and stood in front of the crates, to block his view. They were both redheads, and the one on the left had tattoos covering his neck. 'Fuck you want to know for?' said one, and the other folded his arms belligerently.

'Oh, I'm just a curious investigator.' Jeryd pulled out his medallion. 'You know how the Inquisition likes to gather a few facts now and then.' *Well, this one does at least.* Glances were exchanged, an uneasy change of expression at the law's presence. For a while neither said anything.

'How much?' one of them finally asked.

'How much for what?' Jeryd grunted.

'How much you want to, uh, go away, like? You know – and we know – the policy.'

This attempt at bribery only made Jeryd more determined to find out what was contained in the crate. 'I'm afraid I'm not like the other guys. I only want an answer. What's in there?'

The young men conferred in whispers. 'Meat,' the one with tattoos explained. 'We're taking it from the slaughterhouse to the irens. Boss's orders.' Then he added, 'And our boss is Malum, leader of the Bloods, someone who don't take kindly to having his men hassled by the Inquisition. You know what I mean?'

Jeryd knew what they meant. Malum was the most influential man in the underworld. A violent sociopath by all accounts. Jeryd had been hearing far too much about this man since his arrival in Villiren. His name was whispered every other day in the Inquisition headquarters, more in awe and fear than otherwise. This individual had myth wrapped around him so tightly that Jeryd wondered how he could even breathe.

He glowered at them both, then at the leaked bits of offal that had slipped onto the cobbles, then back at their street-warrior faces. 'I don't need paying to go away,' Jeryd declared. 'As I said, I'm not like the others – if you understand what I mean.'

*

Jeryd had to pass the gaol cells in the Inquisition headquarters in order to get to his office. Despite the fact that crimes were rarely investigated properly, it seemed that prisoners were still being herded in daily, all types, including many that did not look like typical prisoners. Jeryd made enquiries.

'Just between you and me, right,' one of the aides confided, a short, skinny individual with a mop of blond hair, 'we arrest such people as get in the way of Lutto's progress. You know, he wants a street cleared to let the army pass through, and people disagree and protest, he calls it a crime, and suddenly we've got our cells filled. He wants traditional traders disposed of to make space for more profitable ones – ones that can offer cheaper goods. When the politicians clear 'em out, it makes for a free market. But you know how it is, some folk don't like change, and want to kick up a fuss, don't they? And space is precious here, you see. City's got to make money, like. And those miners who lost their jobs and started getting violent during their protests . . . well, they came straight in here too.

Meanwhile we got murderers running much of the show out on the streets. As for being a criminal – well, I s'pose it's all a matter of perspective, right? Anyway, just doing my job, like, so don't you complain to me about it. And this stays between you and me, all right – not worth my job, this.'

Jeryd was growing more and more disillusioned with this city as each day passed, and as he entered his office was inhabiting a deeply reflective state.

Nanzi was already waiting for him.

'Morning, Nanzi.' Jeryd placed his hat on the desk and slumped into his chair with a thundering sigh.

'Good morning, investigator,' Nanzi said. 'Would you like something to drink?'

'No thanks, I had a big breakfast on the way here.' He rubbed his face to make himself more alert. 'Now, it transpires we have some leads.'

'Clues?'

'Yeah, from the Citadel party. I found an interesting and unusual substance there. I'm slowly becoming convinced it's a step in the right direction.'

'What kind of substance?' she demanded coolly.

'No idea yet. I've already given a similar sample to the commander to analyse yesterday – he has a cultist working with him who might know something about it. I'm not sure if it's linked to the disappearances.'

'Investigator Jeryd, you seem to take these cases so seriously. It is an admirable quality, but do you not need some time off? You must have a personal life that needs attending to. I can follow things up with the commander and give you some relief.'

'Yeah, you could be right, lass. I do take it seriously.' He didn't have the heart to explain just how much he felt he owed to life. He was devoted to his wife, and his conscience was dedicated to seeing that there was a little good put back into the world.

How could he explain to her that he was transferring his secret guilt to every single action in his life? That incident with his wife back in Villjamur had changed him. He had tried hard to put it to the back of his mind, but the after-effects were still there, asking questions of him.

He once thought that the only way to cope with the dark events in his life was by helping other people, but maybe that was wrong: maybe he was running away from them instead, viewing their world from the other side of his desk, resisting his problems with a medallion and a thousand hunches and a wrap-around theory.

'I'm not sure what I'd do with any time off. Spend it with my wife, most likely going on some trip, but there's sod-all places to visit in this ice age anyway, and we do go out regularly in the evenings. No, all I have is my work – and I'm determined to find out why so many damn people keep vanishing from these streets.'

'It seems a most impossible case,' Nanzi declared. 'There are easier crimes we could solve, ones where we could put criminals in gaol and make some progress. There's the trade in pirated relics ... another man lost his arm yesterday, one of the lucky ones. Just before you arrived in the city, a child set one off in an iren, killing three other people besides himself, and injuring dozens.'

'It is indeed a tragedy,' Jeryd agreed. 'But a good investigator refuses to give in even when it seems nothing can be done. Sometimes there will be a clue, the tiniest discovery that'll give you massive consequences. I don't know. It just seems so odd that I know so little about this case – and such a lack of control makes me feel uneasy.'

Nanzi smiled softly at him. 'When will we see the commander again? I'm interested in hearing what news he has affecting the city.'

'You and me both, lass.'

Sixteen

The main island of Folke certainly wasn't how Randur re-membered it. There should have been carts full of something or other trawling back and forth through the day, farmland communities trading with one another, people travelling be-tween villages, but instead there was nothing.

In between the open vistas was the familiar sight of forests, providing some shelter from the elements – abies or betula trees – but there was now something that suggested the people who worked the land were seldom here any longer, either having died from the cold or moved on to more temperate regions.

And Randur himself had changed since he'd left here for Villjamur. He'd grown used to throwing sweet lines of chat at the women in the Imperial Residence, the soft sheets and subtle lighting and gold-trimmed furnishings. Warmth and good food and decadent surroundings. It had very nearly corrupted him, turned him into something he despised and, if he was honest, it was difficult for him to now cope with the harshness of life on the road: finding his own food, trying desperately not to allow water to seep into his boots.

Eir, on the other hand, had blossomed in the absence of her former power. It was as if the strictures of Villjamur had stopped her from feeling truly free. She dressed more like a boy these days, which was ironic considering the comments Randur used to get from others about dressing like a girl.

She'd become tougher and more resilient. The realities of life out here had very quickly shaved away the accoutrements of her former wealthy existence. She had developed the ability to fight and showed it with confidence.

The enforced celibacy of being out on the road was not for him. Rika had already killed the mood more than once when he thought he'd stolen a rare moment alone with Eir. The Empress would have wandered off on some solitary contemplation, braving the cold like a she-bear – *even when you meditate, you can tune the cold out*, she would declare – and then he'd lie down in some shelter, Eir in his arms, groping under her clothing, feeling the warmth and ... Then Rika would step back into view, after her soliloquy to the heavens, and his arms would snap back to his side.

A man can only take so much.

The territory of Folke was a collection of three islands, comprising one major land mass, and two sparse little outcrops in the sea to the south, Folke Mikill and Folke Smár. Apparently communities of banshees lived on one of those islands, the only group of them outside of Villjamur, and people said they lived deliberately alone, away from other human or rumel, so they could remain in peace, since on their own they would not have to announce so many deaths. But how could a group of women survive so long without producing children to keep the line going, without it dying out? Randur had often fantasized about what it would be like to be the only male there ...

Eir nudged him in the ribs, as if telepathically channelling his thoughts. From behind him, on horseback, she pointed across the line of forest towards a collection of rooftops appearing in the distance.

They were travelling along the western shore. To their left the sea, choppy again today, met with a murky grey horizon; to their right extended a forest, arcing gently towards a low range of hills. Having not seen a soul for days, this promise

148

of human contact was mildly unsettling, a sudden reminder
that they weren't the only people around.

'Drekka,' Randur muttered through his smile of recognition. 'Gets its name from the old word for *drink*. Used to be
considered a bit of a party town. I've been there once or twice,
though not from this route.'

'Can we stay somewhere here for the night?' Eir asked.

'I would've thought so,' Randur replied. 'Agricultural town,
mainly, but does a bit of trade doubling as a port. A few
travellers pass through, but I'm not sure how things are with
the Freeze.'

*

It was a town where dreams lay down to die. Places like this
didn't much like change, their nature going against the funda-
mental laws of development or decay. The further you went
from the largest towns, notably Ule, the further you moved
from anything approaching cosmopolitan. In Randur's memory he'd only been there a few times, all during his late teens;
there had been super-strength local vodka, and local women
who were not shy in the least. Each time he had visited he'd
sworn never to return. But there was always a girl, wasn't
there, some reason to make that extra effort, to ride across
the island in search of sensual fulfilment.

The cultural centre lay just where two straight thoroughfares met. Here, the taverns conducted a roaring trade, serving
up equal measures of gambling and debauchery. A haven for
card sharps to work their route around the various settlements. He wondered vaguely if rooms would be available at
the Bitches Brew inn, one of the quieter places in the town,
just off the main street.

An iren to one side sold mainly farming equipment, where
a few men shambled around checking out the wares. The
former dust road running between the buildings was now
muddied snow. The buildings themselves were a mix of dark

stone and even darker wood, at the most three floors high, but always well spaced out because there was plenty of room. Smoke dribbled upwards from most of the chimneys and, amid a sea of thatched and slate roofing, the wooden spire of a Jorsalir church poked tentatively above the townscape.

They rode into town, tied up their horses, and started hunting for accommodation.

*

Cheap lunches were being served at the Bitches Brew, a dreary place with four solid woodstoves and walls littered with old farming equipment now relegated to the status of decoration: sieves, forks, bushels, crooks, potato dibbers. Three men sat in companionable silence over to one side, while two old women played cards right next to the bar. Randur approached the landlord, a slender man in his fifties with a scar across the top of his head. He regarded Randur with startlingly blue eyes.

'Afternoon,' Randur greeted him, while Rika and Eir remained motionless by the door. 'Me and the girls are passing through and need a room for the night. You got any?'

'Might have. You got coin?'

'Enough.'

'You got a room then, lad. So what you lot drinking?'

Half-turning to Eir and Rika, he said, 'I'll have half an ale and the girls—'

'Kapp Brimir!' It was a high-pitched voice, and certainly not a happy one. Randur shot the room a furtive glance. Who knew his real name?

'Kapp! I know it's you.' A girl burst out from the kitchen, a brunette with big eyes and a big scowl. She marched right up to him then slapped him across the face.

'Ow!' he spluttered.

'You think you can just walk off and leave me after that one night we had? You promised you'd take me with you to Villjamur. You and all your lines – it was just to get into bed with me, wasn't it? You boys just want to have your fun and vanish into the night. Ha! Well I'm not having any of that.'

Randur backed off slightly, palmed the air to calm her down. This performance wasn't exactly *not* attracting too much attention. 'I . . . I—'

Another slap, this time on the other cheek, nearly knocking him over, a cloud of flour following the arc of her hand.

'I bet you can't even remember my name.'

This was true.

And just how the hell was he supposed to recall every girl he'd slept with? *No, concentrate.* He glanced back towards Eir, who stood glaring at him with her arms folded, before looking away.

Bugger . . . Randur, this is not looking good.

Back to face the girl – what *was* her name? 'I meant to tell you . . . I was called off on an emergency. My sword skills were urgently required.'

'And yet still the lies pour forth from his rancid mouth!' She reached out again towards him.

As Randur flinched, closing his eyes, she tipped the ale he had ordered over his head before marching off to the kitchen. He peered sheepishly around the bar, the liquid dripping off his face.

'Hope you're going to pay for that drink, lad,' the landlord grunted. 'Isn't a charity I'm running here. That'll be a hundred Drakar.'

*

The room contained four small beds, two on either side of the room. A dreary brown carpet was peeling away from the floor, and save for half a dozen unlit candles, there wasn't much else. A far cry from the glamour of the Imperial Residence that he was used to, but he reminded himself that this was better than camping outdoors.

While he stared out of the window, across a back garden filled with barrels, Rika remarked, 'She called you Kapp?'

'You what?' he replied.

'Kapp? I thought your name was Randur Estevu. So which one is it?'

'My name is not really Randur.' He glanced to Eir, who already knew the story. With a thin smile, she nodded, a gesture that said, *Go on*.

'You've been rather coy about your past so far,' Rika said. 'With good reason, it seems.'

He'd been careful not to show himself as more than a simple island boy who came fresh to the city. There was no need for Rika to have known, no need to make things complicated, but now was the time to relieve himself of his lies.

'I came into Villjamur with papers stolen from a dead man. The real Randur was a young man the same age as me, and when he was found murdered at the docks my dodgy uncle from Y'iren managed to get hold of the documents allowing this Randur into Villjamur. Kapp was my true name, but I took his identity, became Randur. I had plans to fulfil. I wanted to speak to the great cultists of the city – I needed their help in saving my mother's life. But that's another story, one I'm not going to repeat now. Was this deception such a bad thing?'

Details about his sleeping with dozens of rich women then stealing their jewellery to fund these great cultists would, perhaps, be better left unsaid right now.

'So, there you have it. I'm really called Kapp,' he declared, resignedly. 'But Randur or Kapp, I still saved your arse.'

Rika was looking out of the window, as snow began to fill the grey afternoon skies. 'That is true, and your motives were pure – even if your actions weren't quite what I would approve of. Kapp, you say? A better name, I think. Randur does sound a little *sleazy*.'

'What, that's it?' Randur asked. 'No big lectures on morality, on what a fool I've been and that my sorry rear is going to burn in some hell realm for a thousand years?'

Rika laughed then, for the first time, and he couldn't decide if he had been thoroughly stupid in something he'd said. 'That's just it, Kapp. My religion isn't all that complicated at times. Your motivation was a positive one. How else can we judge someone?'

'I thought you had, like, a million rules about what we're not supposed to do.'

'There are some in place, admittedly, but they're to aid our spiritual practice, not pass judgement. Yes, there are some priests who have interpreted aspects of our belief in what I consider a negative way, but really all we are – any of us – is the sum of our actions. Do I really come across as so ... condemnatory?'

'Just a little ... you know, preachy,' he muttered. Then, 'No offence, lady.'

'I suppose I've been through a lot, returning to Villjamur and then ... leaving again so abruptly. We have all been through quite an ordeal.'

'Whatever,' Randur said, forgetting, as he often did, the importance of the woman before him. In truth Rika couldn't have had it easy – she'd been torn from her spiritual retreat to be thrust into the seat of power controlling millions of lives across the Jamur Empire, only to be manipulated by councillors close to her and falsely charged with plotting the destruction of thousands of her own citizens.

'Look, we can either sit and be miserable, or cheer up,' he continued. 'I'm going downstairs to get some food. Who's with me?'

Both girls stood up immediately.

*

They took precaution with their disguises, Rika and Eir slouching as effectively as girls of royal birth could manage, in the rear of the darkened tavern. Randur's narrow sword was always ready by his side. Cards flipping, a glass being settled back on a table, a ticking clock: these were the only sounds for much of the afternoon. Things picked up a little come the evening, they way they always did, people with little money coming to spend it, wasting their daily wage on social investments that could barely show useful returns.

Young women came in now and then, displaying different looks and levels of attractiveness. They would sit at the bar waiting to be bought drinks, and men inevitably approached, older, rough agricultural types, some like the cliché he'd imagined, yet some surprisingly well spoken. And he wondered, again and again: *Is this all there is for these people?*

His life had changed so completely. Doing *something* now seemed to matter.

The three of them made relaxed and innocent conversation, the kind that could occur anywhere at all, anywhere in time. Eir had found a niche for herself in teasing Randur lightly, while Rika asked him about his upbringing here on Folke. For one of the most loftily placed people he had ever known, she certainly showed a deep interest in other people.

In that dark corner they all became closer.

Then under the light of the lanterns throughout the rest of the tavern, a man came shambling inside, wrapped in a wax-covered cape and wearing ridiculously colourful breeches. He even had a frilly black shirt that would have been at home in Randur's own wardrobe. Although naturally slender, he carried the paunch of a man whose drinking habit had finally caught up with him, protruding under a grubby complexion, with a broad jaw smothered in greying stubble.

It couldn't be.

'Drink, by thunder, sir!' the man called out across the bar, before wiping his nose on his sleeve. 'How's a man to quench his thirst in such a Bohr-forsaken hellhole.'

This much was obvious: it wouldn't be this man's first drink of the day. He swayed as he reached hesitantly in his pockets for some coins, then slapped them on the counter. He leaned forwards, slowly counted three, then shoved them over. 'Lager – a pint thereof, barman.'

'You're back, then,' the landlord grunted. 'Didn't think this place was good enough for you, after all that crap you warbled last night. What was it you said? As welcoming as a nun's cunt, I believe.'

'I spout such rubbish most nights, sir, unless you'd forgotten.'

Noticing his reaction, Eir nudged Randur in the ribs. 'What is it?'

'I think I know him,' Randur mumbled. He stood up, brushing his hair back behind his ears. Randur called out a name across the bar room.

'Munio Porthamis.'

The man was about to take his first sip, then paused. An expression slid across his face, something that suggested he was not at ease being known as anything other than the drunken stranger. Was there comfort to be found in the anonymous role he had carved for himself?

He continued with his drink, choosing to ignore the interruption.

Randur strutted over to the man's side, ignoring any glances from others in the room. To hell with keeping a low profile. 'Munio Porthamis. So, this is the glory you aspired to, is it? This what all the money was intended for?'

'Don't know who you mean, stranger.' The man resolutely faced the bar.

Randur could see the old rapier carried by his side still, beneath the man's thick cloak. 'Rule one of *Vitassi*,' Randur said. '"One perceives everything and nothing, and that way one can identify everyone and everything in the world."'

A deep intake of breath and the figure glanced sideways at Randur. His thick, dirty thumbs rubbed the tankard. Munio's eyes could not belie his identity. The old man's soul was still in there, still as sharp as ever. 'I know you, kid?'

Randur drew his sword slowly, in a non-threatening manner, aware of the numerous sets of eyes fixed on him now that the metal caught the light of the lanterns. A hush descended. Randur used the tip of his sword to tap on Munio's old rapier, still resting in its sheath, the ornate gold trimmings on the hilt looking more degraded than he remembered. 'I think we should talk with these.'

'I speak a fine language with it,' Munio muttered. 'Too fine a tongue for anyone to barter with.'

'I suspect I can correct your grammar, these days,' Randur replied.

Munio slid back his stool, flipped his cloak to the ground, and in a heartbeat his sword was in his hand. There was nothing about his manner that betrayed his earlier lack of coordination.

'Randur!' Eir cried, and he turned back to her briefly: 'It's all right, really.'

The two men began to circle slowly, leaning back and forth to judge each other, and he remembered exactly how Munio would react: a flash of blade striking down to his left. The rest of the ritual, Randur knew by heart. He countered, parried, then worked a series of moves to drive the old man back towards the bar. For a moment, Munio smiled.

His sword clattered to the floor, and the older man moved away to pick up his drink.

After three thick gulps, he said, 'By thunder, Kapp Brimir, you've grown. And you still haven't cut your hair.'

'You've grown yourself,' Randur replied, indicating Munio's stomach. He wasn't sure how he felt to see his old teacher like this, already drunk in a bar in the middle of nowhere.

A place where dreams lay down to die . . .

'I can still fight, even in my state,' Munio stated.

'What, pissed?'

'Indeed, yes, some say I fight better like this. But I see you're still wearing those ridiculous fancy outfits.' He indicated Randur's black shirt with wide sleeves, his tight breeches and heeled boots of polished, Villjamur-branded leather.

'I'm not as well-heeled as I would like.' Randur smiled, leaning on the bar beside him. 'And where do you think I learned to dress in such a way? Always dress like you don't know how to fight, you advised me. That way it's easier to slap them around the room.'

'I *did* say that.' Munio rubbed his chin. 'Full of nonsense back then, wasn't I?'

'You want to join us?' Randur indicated with his chin where Eir and Rika sat at the corner table.

'Is one woman not enough, Kapp Brimir? You were always more interested in chasing after the girls, if I remember.'

'Not all the time. I stayed around for your lessons.'

'Only because I forced you. I tell you that you've a gift, and you ignore me. I clip you round the ear, and you stay and listen. Simple, really.'

From the age of four until fourteen, Randur attended the private lessons given by Munio Porthamis. Because of his unusual skills, his mother never had to pay – and she could never afford to. In that plain room overlooking the river, on a bare wooden floor they would spend hours working through postures and manoeuvres and techniques. Blisters came and went. Two days a week at first, then more, in between learning the dance variations. Until one night, for evening training, Munio never turned up, and a letter arrived the week after, declaring that, due to an inheritance from his uncle, he would no longer be available to teach. Randur had never forgotten sitting on that wooden floor staring out of the window at the sky, wondering how someone could abandon him just for money.

'Come, I'll accept your invitation. But I warn you I'm not much company these days.' Munio straightened up, put a palm on each of Randur's cheeks. 'Let me look at you. Still a handsome lad, though you look as though you need feeding. And get your hair cut, boy. How's anyone supposed to fight wearing long black locks like that?'

*

Randur gave his two companions false introductions. Later, as Munio was up buying another bottle of wine, he apologized to the girls, but he didn't think Munio paid much attention to the political climate of Villjamur, which seemed to allay their concerns.

'You might be something important in a great city like that,' Randur said, 'but the Council Atrium is so far removed from these people that they can't fathom any of the decisions affecting their lives. Policies get formulated and accepted elsewhere – out here issues are so local.'

'You would say, then,' Rika asked, 'that these people distrust a central government?'

'How can anyone in Villjamur understand the needs of someone living out here? That's why Munio won't even know who you are.'

The old swordmaster returned, 'I'll admit these wines aren't as good as my own cellar, but they'll do. Besides, on your third bottle, you can barely taste that much anyway.' He put down a bottle of red and after a moment's consideration, in which the conversation happened in glances, he filled their glasses. 'My boy Kapp tells me you're city girls from Villjamur. So how did two Jokull lovelies end up this far from home?'

'We need to visit someone in Villiren,' Rika declared.

'My dear lady,' Munio said, 'it has been too long, too long, since I have heard such a pleasantly spoken woman as yourself. In my day, I would work with many a landowner, and there would nearly always be some well-spoken lady present. Many took a shine to me. Back then.'

Rika glanced at Randur. 'He taught you more than just swordfighting, I see.'

158

'*Vitassi*', Munio observed, 'is not merely swordfighting. It is a way of life. Now, ladies, Kapp, are you staying in this absolute dive of a tavern?'

'We are,' Eir said.

'This is no place for such refined women as yourselves. Come, I have a small manse less than an hour away. We will go there instead and there will be splendours the likes of which you have never seen!'

I seriously doubt that, Randur thought.

*

'It is, admittedly, in a state that needs a little attention.' Munio paced the main hall, lighting coloured lanterns on the tables and sideboards. From gloom to glow to gaudy, they could soon see everything. The exterior was as grand as any small-estate residence, but the design not as pleasing as it might have been. This was no military fortification, that much was certain, but no raiding army could want much from it. There was something of the classical in its symmetry, although no pillars, no nature-inspired flourishes in the stonework.

'I'm not sure how old it is,' Munio whispered, 'but when I bought it I had it refurbished. Many Villiren-branded weaves make up those carpets and tapestries. Wall hangings to rival anything you'd see in Villjamur. But I have neglected to keep things clean.' He leaned towards Rika, a look of optimism in his gaze. 'It is such a chore when one lives on one's own. I have, unfortunately, no wife or servants to assist me.'

Perhaps there had once been sumptuous decoration in this double-cube room. Tapestries were now saturated with mould, and the carpet's pattern suffocated under dust. Paintings were smeared with smoke, the unknown faces within having faded to ghostly apparitions. Ornaments that Randur couldn't ident-ify, silver-coloured and clunky, sat gauchely on the mantel-piece and on the side tables, as if they had been collected by whim. Most of the furniture was made from the same dark wood, quercus, and everything needed a good polish. Leather chairs were arranged neatly enough by the fireplace, at which Munio was now working to introduce some warmth into the room.

'I have several bedrooms upstairs,' Munio offered optimistically. 'I do hope you think it suitable to stay.'

'I'm sure we will,' Rika agreed. 'Very kind of you to invite us.' She turned to Eir and Randur questioningly.

'Yes, it is,' Eir replied. 'Thank you.'

What does the old bugger want? Randur wondered. *It's not like him to be so altruistic.*

*

In the middle of the night Randur lay awake, on a bed in the centre of the 'suite' they occupied, an uncared-for corner of the manse. Eir huddled next to Rika in a double cot near the window, through which nothing but darkness could be seen, no distant lights to suggest a town or a village. Wind raked constantly against the glass. A candle glowed in one corner.

Sleep didn't come. His mind continuously sifted through his memories, contorting them into obscure forms and references. He grunted a laugh: his old sword tutor, a ruined drunk. How things had changed. Munio was no longer someone who bullied him, who pushed him around.

With a glance at the girls, Randur rose to his feet and left the room. Cautiously, he shuffled downstairs in the pitch-black, one hand against the wall for navigation. Because the rest of the manse was so dark, a glow from one of the rooms was immediately obvious.

Randur nudged the door further, the hinges groaning. There, next to one of the leather settees, stood Munio, and he was sobbing.

'What's wrong?' Randur headed over to the old man, his words muted by the vastness of the decaying room.

'Oh, Kapp.' The silhouette of his swordmaster shambled towards him, past the light of the one candle that was left burning. 'Kapp . . .'

He could smell the alcohol even from this distance, his sense of smell being pretty much all he had to go on. Randur approached and paused before him. 'Why the hell are you crying?'

'I wasn't,' he blubbered.

'Yes, you were, I could hear you.'

Silence, then Munio shuffled back to his chair, and collapsed into it with a grunt. 'Join me, won't you?'

Randur searched for the best way there, now and then kicking against tables or footstools by accident. He located the settee only by bumping into the arms of it with his thigh, then he sat down beside Munio, though some distance from the alcoholic fumes. 'You've been drinking all night long?'

A contemplative sigh. 'Indeed I have, young man.'

'Why on earth have you become like this?' Randur said. 'You'd once have clipped me round the ear just for hinting at such a lack of discipline. What the hell's happened to you?'

'I came here and I was rich. I had no need for anything any more. I no longer even had to try.'

'So you just gave up then,' Randur said. 'Just like that.'

'You have never found yourself in a position where so much money comes into your possession in one go,' Munio mumbled. 'It ruined me – quite simple, really. I have no excuses.'

'When I saw you in the bar, I wanted to hit you at first.'

'You would have been well within your rights to do so. Nothing more than I deserve.'

'How could you just abandon your students?' Randur demanded, annoyed and yet sympathetic to Munio's resigned attitude to his failure.

'I taught you all I could. You no longer required my services – not in the end.' Then, 'So, this Rika lady,' Munio continued, his tone spuriously optimistic. 'Is she wedded? Some strapping lad waiting for her? You think a gentleman of my age stands any chance with such a refined individual?'

'No, it's not that,' Randur sighed. 'She's not really, uh, in the market for that kind of thing.' Being here in the manse, Randur felt he could trust the old man a little more. So he decided to reveal a little about who the girls really were.

Munio merely gaped at him for a long moment. 'Empress?'

'Well, not any more. But shush now.' Randur glanced around sheepishly. He whispered a few more of the basic details. 'So that is why you can't hope to get together with someone like her.'

'Destined to be alone. Oh, my life is such a mess . . .'

'Why not talk more about it?' Randur offered.

'Talk! You can tell that a woman raised you. Talk, indeed, as if talk could make me better. Whatever happened to just shutting up and getting on with life? You want to talk, let me tell you this: I once was something, Kapp. And moments of my life are now only memories – if even that. I'm nothing. You will be one day, a nothing just like me. You're filled with the hopeless optimism that blesses youth, but which then taunts middle age. We will all of us fade, like this world of ours will. Cultures come and go, and nothing remains of them. So what else is there to do but drink?'

'Don't be so bloody miserable,' Randur snapped at him. 'People are dying in this world for less that you have – I've seen them pleading outside the gates of Villjamur, no food or opportunities. Refugees crammed up against the wall, pressing into it almost, fading in the ice. And here you are, wasting your life and money and talent because you're running away from the real world. By the look of it, you've been running away from it ever since you could afford to pay for this drinking habit of yours.' Randur stood up. 'I'm going back to bed. Company's better up there.'

SEVENTEEN

'It's as if you're composed from a different fabric than before. I don't know what to make of your mannerisms any more, your tentative gestures and insecurities. Could you even be the same person as you were some years ago?'

How could she answer that?

Physically things were good, they always had been. Opening up was something she would never consider with Malum, and slowly, slowly she was beginning to remember. To learn again.

'Where's your confidence gone? Where're your nuances for mocking me, like I loved so long ago?'

He mellows me . . . 'I need time. Sometimes I feel stressed thinking about such things.'

Again they came to that world with no name. Earlier in the day, they had discovered a beach, and in his eagerness he declared it for himself.

'Lupus Beach is a suitable name for a beautiful place,' he laughed, then changed the subject, as if aware of her sudden unease.

There came an urge, later, to map this place, this other realm, and maybe it was his soldier's mind demanding to analyse everything, to apply a systematic logic to her world. She discouraged him at first, explaining that the place seemed to change slightly with time. No matter how much of this world she saw, each new visit would bring variants – different species of trees, or water carving fractionally different paths for the rivers.

'You just can't apply logic,' she insisted, watching him frown, 'to a place that doesn't obey any logic.'

His explorations didn't stop there: he moved onwards to the curves and blemishes of her body, tasting her skin, which perspired in this heat. The tide came in to drench their half-discarded clothing, her dark hair was left wet, and sand clung to their damp and sweaty bodies.

*

A stove-hot meadow now, the two of them lying in the grass, bright orchids, a flock of some bird species she had never seen before cutting through the sky in a V-formation, their calls utterly alien. Something that had a hexagonal spine and six legs rotated peculiarly along the grassland to drink from the river, and it seemed impossible to Lupus that such a creature could exist.

Because he didn't know where or what this place was, it presented itself as artificial. It was a world without context. A world frozen, ironically and practically, in time. Beami wondered what would happen if they remained here permanently, but there was very little around for her to measure herself against. It was simply a world to escape into, a world in which they could conduct their affair without being discovered.

Lupus noticed a cluster of bruises across Beami's back, and the narrow scoring across her shoulder. Shuddering gently, she let him run his fingers along them. Softly.

'I can do something, you know,' he offered. 'Have a word or two with the lads.'

'You can do *nothing*, Lupus.'

'Makes me angry.'

'And you think I'm not angry, too? Leave it alone. I give as good as I get.'

'I'm sorry. I'm just a fool who thinks he can solve all your problems.'

Mellowing, she realized he only meant well. This conversation was almost impossible to start on. 'He gets angry, but I'm not some meek woman. He's hit me, yes, but once I even used a relic to stop him, and he didn't even notice.'

A garuda came in, one of the local, feral ones, with different colouring from those found in the Boreal Archipelago, their plumages brighter and, of course, with no armour at all. It swooped in about forty paces from them, skimmed the tip of the grasses, its head craning in their direction, then banked away towards the deep blue.

She said, 'It's all because he hasn't been able to have sex for some time.'

'How do you mean?'

'He . . .' she searched for the right words. 'He's impotent, and he hates to talk about it. For us women, that's acceptable, isn't it? We can talk openly about how we *feel* – well, most of us can. But all he can say is that he doesn't feel like a man any more – the rest of it he says with his rage. Maybe that's why he leads such a dark life. I don't know half of what he gets up to any more. I used to be attracted to the element of danger – you know what I'm like – but I know it's not *me*. I'm not some dumb, weak-willed heiress who can't even wipe her own rear. *It isn't me*. It's only important to him to be able to . . . *fuck*. Let's say it – that's what it is, isn't it?' After dwelling on this thought for a moment, she faced him again. 'I've craved you for so long, you know.'

'Merely glad to be of assistance,' Lupus replied. His smile diffused the tension. 'And my rates are very reasonable these days.'

'You became a man-whore while you were in the army, did you? All those lonely soldiers away from home . . .'

'You'd love it there, all those men . . .'

'Hell, yes,' she said.

'Pervert.'

'Dickhead,' she said.

They kissed.

The first signs of dusk, a change in temperature, a shift in wind and the smells of vegetation gaining in intensity. The wolf came again, delighting Lupus. He leapt up as soon as he saw its face peering from within a cluster of sedges – two curious eyes.

'Hey,' he called out gently. He walked towards it wearing only the trousers of his uniform, carrying some of the meat they'd brought earlier. He crouched, offered the meat, while the animal cautiously approached. At first it just sniffed, twisting its head this way and that. Then with a quick nip, it plucked the meat from his grasp and withdrew into the sedges.

Lupus merely laughed, then returned to Beami.

'You two are a bit like each other,' she observed.

'How d'you mean?'

'A brief appearance, take the good stuff, then disappear again.'

'That's not fair. I need to get back to the barracks for training and strategy. I'd take you with me, if you wanted. You only have to say the word . . . but you're married.'

'It's just not easy,' Beami sighed. 'He works so hard and provides us with that magnificent home, amazing food. I can't say he *doesn't* love me exactly. He just gets angry, but sometimes I think he'll change, that I can help him change. This was what I was like, Lupus, until *you* came along. You've *ruined* everything.'

Beami began to cry into his shoulder, a gentle relief so it seemed, letting out the pressure of her situation, of her lack of control.

*

Later in this otherworld, night fell – and it seemed even more sudden with that fantastical yellow sun.

They lay on long grass throughout the balmy evening, staring up at the skies, while a warm wind came from the coast, and the trees had begun releasing perfume into the evening, smells he had never before known. Beami lay with her head on Lupus's chest, and his compound bow and quiver lay just to his right side, within easy reach. They watched the stars for some time, and it felt to her as if there was only the one moon here, the larger and brighter one. Sure it might look a bit out of alignment, but still . . .

'We should probably sleep here, tonight,' Beami suggested. 'If we return to the same moment in time in Villiren, then we'd need to appear fresh and not tired else people might suspect there was something up with us both.'

For a moment he thought a comet flashed at the periphery of his vision.

'The star formations,' he whispered, 'they're more or less the same as when we're back in the city, aren't they? Perhaps they're out of sync a little.'

'I've not noticed,' Beami replied. 'I've not spent too many evenings out here on my own.'

Perhaps it was a soldier's obsession for these things but, after studying the stars further, he became convinced of their location. 'We're actually in Villiren. This is still the same place. We're just at a different point in time.'

Beami said nothing for a moment, then, 'That makes sense. The topography has been reasonably identical and we're near the coast still. There are those higher cliffs sheltering the natural harbour, just like in the city. How far back in time do you think we are?'

Their conversation continued in such speculation until Lupus drifted into sleep, leaving Beami to regard the stars serenely.

*

She didn't know how long she had been staring upwards when a block of the sky began to change texture. The wind altered fractionally, calming a little, then the stars in one quadrant became obscured by some massive translucent presence. In a precise shape looming above, a huge oblong the

167

size of a small town, the stars became hazy, almost vibrating, and then were blocked entirely by something that was darker, more textured. Wind gathered momentum, the trees in the distance fizzing, and birds burst cover, startled. Beami's heart beat rapidly, but she was too stunned to wake Lupus. She merely stared dumbly upwards.

An utter silence fell as the presence loitered in the sky above some distance from the ground. How far away it was, she couldn't be sure, but for a moment it did appear to be a town of sorts, because it reminded her of the windows seen nightly in the city.

And hardly had this entity appeared when it disintegrated into nothingness, leaving the starscape exactly as before. She eased herself away from Lupus's sleeping form, and for the next quarter of an hour she paced the nearby meadow, all the time craning her neck upwards waiting for the shape to return.

*

Their affair was locked safely in another place, another time, another dimension entirely. But now they were back in her house, *in Malum's house*, the guilt came storming into her mind, like a raid on her senses.

Lupus tried to nuzzle against her neck, offering a comfort too far. With the tips of her fingers she traced the crispness of his uniform. He was so organized and neat for such a laid-back personality, so well groomed. *The army must have taught him this discipline*, she decided.

Suddenly Beami pushed him away and said, 'Not here, not while we're so exposed.'

She couldn't even meet his eyes. Over his shoulder she could see the snow descending outside the window, nothing like as harsh as it had been, but still a constant reminder of the troubles everyone in this city faced.

'What's wrong now?' he growled.

How could he not understand, despite all that she'd already said? 'Don't you even care if we get caught?'

'Not really, no.'

'Well, I do, OK. It's *my* life that could be ruined.'

'*I* could be your life, Bea. *Me alone.* Once I'm finished here in the city, I'll quit the army.'

'You're already married to it. With me you're cheating on your marriage too.'

'I'll quit, just after—'

'The war, I know,' she interrupted. 'After the war in which nearly everyone in this city might die. Do you think I want to give up everything just for the promise of a man who might be killed at any moment? Can you even begin to understand the consequences of that?'

'Why say all this now? We've talked about this before.' Lupus placed a hand on her shoulder, but she shrugged it off.

Why did you join the army in the first place? she wanted to say. *Why do you still have to be a soldier, the second time you invade my life?*

Footsteps approaching outside. Her heart missed a beat as she shoved him away, whispering, 'Malum.' Lupus nodded his comprehension, moving further from her.

The door opened and in stepped her husband, a hessian sack in one hand, his gaze settling on them from within the darkness of his raised hood.

Beami felt as if her whole life was about to implode.

Lupus saluted him. 'Sele of Jamur, sir.'

Malum stood there in his mask – something she once regarded with awe, but now found ridiculous. Still in the doorway, he was assessing the situation he had walked into.

'What're you doing here, soldier?' Malum growled.

Lupus's voice maintained a perfect calm. 'I'm visiting as many of the establishments around the Ancient Quarter as possible, briefing them on the potential hazards that may soon arise. There may be a possibility for rehousing, should you consider it safer.'

'The hell we will,' he grunted; then to Beami, 'This man hassling you?'

'It's no trouble. I understand what a soldier must do – for the good of the city.'

'Whatever.'

Lupus then addressed Malum again. 'Do I recognize you, sir?'

'I doubt it.'

'Sir, madam, good day.' Lupus nodded to them both. He left Beami alone with her husband.

She tried to remain looking utterly calm.

'Fucking soldiers.' Malum closed the door. 'Think just because this city's under threat they can get away with anything.'

'Do you think we've anything to be worried about?' Beami tried to meet his gaze, as if showing she had nothing to hide.

He pushed back his hood, placed the sack on the floor. 'Nothing at all. You're safe here with me, right?'

'Right. What's in the sack?'

'Thought we deserved a decent meal tonight . . .'

'That's very kind.' It pained her even more to see how he was making an effort to be nice to her. Seeing him like this it . . . just made her want to at least try. Was she mad for risking herself in this situation? Surely she should take some control of her emotions.

She was a cultist, after all! She was meant to be this powerful woman who could utilize ancient technology, and here she was being so . . . *pathetic.* This was not her. This was not who she was.

*

Malum and Beami ate their food between stifled conversation. At least this was better than another row – something they had recently become expert in. They began arguments that referred to older arguments. There was immediate context in the delivered insults, which inferred moments from the past.

There were words used that brought to mind rooms and events, distant images from their increasingly broken relationship.

Tonight he was trying so hard to put aside his machismo, his posturing, his elaborate and competitive boasting. For once his mask was in some other room. In moments like this she could see her husband as she remembered him when they had first met: him articulate and genuine, but from herself: brief responses, mixed with pangs of dread. Eventually his gaze travelled across her body, as if she was some prize he couldn't win.

In a pause during the meal, she noticed him sip from a vial when he thought she wasn't looking. *Some concoction brewed by that witch?*

Matters moved on to the semi-darkness of the bedroom, where he began his ritualistic attempt at making love – while guilt ravaged her – his body silhouetted against coloured lanterns. 'I reckon I can do it tonight,' he breathed in her ear.

He removed her clothing in the usual fashion – nothing new here – first lifting her outer garments off quickly, then getting down to her underwear. He kissed her neck: stubble on her skin. Her own guilt and his predictability soon removed any sense of excitement.

She closed her eyes and thought of Lupus.

Eighteen

'Fucker's gay?' JC said.

'No shit,' Duka added.

It was snowing as the three of them stood hunched together in Port Nostalgia. The light from the two moons fell brokenly across the sea, as Malum focused on the tips of the waves, searching them for anything unnatural. He'd only recently returned from dropping off a bribe to members of the Inquisition to cover up after the boys had discarded some blood-drained corpses rather too recklessly, and he still had plenty of work ahead. Running the underground city was no luxury: it was hard graft, and he had to do most of the dog-work himself.

Dusk, and the streets were calmed after a full day's trading – even the buildings seemed to be breathing a sigh of relief. The city was easing itself into night.

It always amazed Malum how – given the ice age – so much product could still be traded. Horses cantered through the emptying streets, and somewhere, as always, a firegrain pipe coughed streams of vapour into the icy air that plagued Villiren like a thousand ghosts.

'So what we gonna do about it?' JC shuffled from foot to foot to keep warm, both hands buried in the pockets of his hooded coat. Malum watched him and wondered if he was drunk again. The man always seemed to hide it so well – his inability to get through a day without touching the stuff. He'd been losing his fitness, and his freckled cheeks had puffed out of late. Malum might need to have a word with him sooner or later, even threaten him with expulsion if he didn't get his shit together.

'We can't have a queer running things. You think we should tell other people? That is, Lutto and the likes?'

'I suspect there's not much point in that.' Malum had not wanted to tell them about this discovery because he knew how revulsion would take over and come to the forefront of their minds. These were men who reacted to one thing at a time and, now the union issues were out of the way, and they had the cash in their pockets, they were free to concentrate on issues of a more personal nature.

'Who the fuck would believe us, anyway?' he went on. 'Just be our word against his. No, I'm going to confront him about it, the albino, and we'll see what he has to say. Prove himself that he's a real man, not one of . . .' Malum shook his head. 'If he thinks I'm going to get the street gangs on board now, he's got another think coming. If his army can't fight their own stupid wars, then fine. We'll just use the escape tunnels like everyone else.'

'We should rough him up,' Duka said. 'Beat him to death, like. I mean, it's sick what he does, ain't it?'

Malum reaffirmed again that it was. He himself was disgusted that this could occur so high up in the military. It was certainly not what men did, was it, to stick their dicks into other men. He didn't have much regard for the Jorsalir church, but they had established some codes of conduct that were certainly worth sticking to. So, yeah, maybe he should teach that commander a lesson, to show him what a *real man* was like. 'Leave it with me.'

At that moment something shattered the surface of the water and glided up onto the dockside with an unlikely grace. Another followed, then another. Slender, and with a dark skin tone, the arriving figures shambled along the docks, their movements at first improbable.

'Merpeople are here,' he announced to the others.

'Fucking freak me out they do,' Duka grumbled.

Several more figures emerged from the background, and began hauling up crates onto the quayside. One approached Malum, and he strode forward to meet it. 'Evening,' Malum began.

Indigo skin stretched taut over thick musculature, thick gills splicing each side of his ribcage, the merman's feet were webbed, and his hair resembled kelp or bladderwrack more than anything mammalian. He towered over Malum, dripping salt water. These were hybrids, beings that cultists had begun working on centuries ago, or else had grown from some ancient interbreeding, depending on what book you read. They lived mainly in the sea, sometimes staying the night in beach shacks on isolated shores or lurking in protected caves.

But for Malum they plummeted regularly to the pitch-black bathy-regions in search of biolumes. He had struck a deal with them long ago, to hunt for these biological light sources in exchange for guaranteed protection of their coastal dwellings, and supplying them with the types of land food they were addicted to, but could rarely stay above water long enough to gather for themselves.

'Greetings, trader.' The merman's speech, when it eventually came, was awkward and strained, yet still fundamentally human. It gaped at Malum like he was a curiosity, examining the under edges of his mask, trying to read him.

'What've you got for me tonight?' Malum asked.

'A good haul. You wish to see?'

Malum followed him towards the other merpeople. A shorter female had already opened a crate with her nails, and from it a soft glow issued. Amid the brine, shapes of deep-sea creatures flipped and drifted and gave out light. The other merpeople crowded around him, and he felt uncomfortable, still after all these years, with how alien they appeared.

'You were right, these are good,' Malum confessed. 'This should keep Coumby's company happy for a while.' Such specimens were in high demand in the richer districts, even deep into an ice age where people seemed to prefer firelight for the added warmth. You had a biolume, you were showing off your wealth. It was a spurious market in which Malum supplied the merchants, since they daren't deal with the merpeople themselves. These invertebrate biolumes could then be sold on to the superior street traders, or even to the elaborate high-end stores in the Ancient Quarter, depending on the type of specimen in question.

He whistled for JC and Duka to bring over a small box containing basic foodstuff and some sharp blades, and the two men displayed it before the gathered merpeople like a sacrificial offering.

The aquatic people loomed over the contents, eagerly investigating what they'd been brought. They looked up, one by one, seeming happy enough, and nodding their approval.

'Farewell, tradesman,' said the first one. They moved away, carrying their exchange load. Eventually they slunk back into the sea in neat bursts, until there was simply no sign of them.

*

Later, Malum went looking for the banHe, Dannan. He found him ensconced in his plush apartment that overlooked the harbour. Outside, as darkness began to dominate the sky, the streets subtly changed their texture. Dirtied workers or traders faded into their grim houses, before manifesting in the taverns with pocketfuls of cash, and no future to prepare for. A line of bars rimmed the harbour, all pretty much the same in their style and clientele, the latter merely intent on getting drunk and forgetting about the state of their city. Mention anything about forthcoming war and you were likely to attract a fist in your gut. You'd see more such violence along these parts, the cobbled waterfront that arced around a cluster of boats that the refugees from Tineag'l had abandoned. Fishing vessels could no longer manoeuvre so easily, to the detriment of the food stocks.

Malum heard a moaning come from the upstairs room, like some enharmonic lament. He glanced up at the latticed window, where a lantern could be seen burning on the sill. *What the hell is the damn freak up to?*

Although he'd never admit it openly, and even barely to himself, Malum was disturbed by Dannan. He'd never seen the witch-women of Villjamur, the banshees, but it seemed odd that they would shriek instinctively to herald a death. How could they sense that someone was about to die? It all seemed so unlikely. So if Dannan was a male version – something no one had previously heard about – did he not feel the same urge to scream? Did he have some strange powers? Malum's own vampyrism seemed a more real tic, something he had normalized and controlled.

Dannan was simply a freak.

The door opened and Malum turned back to face it. 'I need to see the banHe,' he announced.

One of Dannan's gang, the Screams – a short, thin guy with black hair and stubble and a drooping white mask – peered back at him from the doorway. 'Why d'you wanna see him?'

'It's urgent. Tell him it's about the commander of the army, about that meeting we had.'

'Wait here.' The door closed.

Malum shifted in the cold once again and it seemed far too long until the door reopened. They searched him first for weapons, he handed over a messer blade, then he was beckoned in.

Escorted by three men in cloaks and masks, Malum hurried through the building, up a set of stairs sporting an ornate handrail. Lantern light exposed red fabric and furniture, bathing the interior in shades of blood. He had to admit that some of the decor was tasteful, if a little garish, with bold, gold-rimmed portraits of figures that seemed to hail from another world. One painting in particular was central to the room, depicting a figure with its back to a waterfront, holding its head in both hands, its mouth wide open in a scream, with textures of colour swirling all around into a deep orange sky. As if representing a state of existential angst, this painting seemed to come from another age entirely.

Once upstairs, Malum was directed into yet another room. Dannan was seated by the window, slumped, as if drunk, in a chair that was more of a throne, and the same shade of red was everywhere, in the fabrics, the paintings, the lantern-shades. In his hand was a silver comb that he raked assiduously through his long hair. The smell of musk and something sweeter peeled away in smoky wafts from the incense burning on a metal plate in one corner. The men who escorted Malum dropped back to the edge of the room, in a manner that suggested they weren't at all comfortable being here. Malum was beginning to feel that way himself.

Hunched, with her knees drawn up to her chin, a young woman was sipping cautiously from a bottle. She regarded him with a distant look in her eyes, then laughed to herself. She wore a dark outfit, with unfashionable ruffs and frills of lace, and her face held so much make-up that her skin was practically white like an albino's. Whether or not she was the current girl in Dannan's favour, he couldn't tell, but Malum entertained vague thoughts about what it would be like sleeping with her. And then he realized it would be the same with any woman these days. Frustrating.

Dannan groaned, catching Malum's attention. He was clothed minimally in black breeches and what appeared to be a suede jacket with a hood pulled up from underneath. The angles of his face were prominent, and now and then his eyes would close as if he was in pain.

'You all right?' Malum enquired, more wanting to say

something than a question posed out of politeness. He raised an eyebrow at this strange performance.

Again a groan, and Dannan lurched forward suddenly, in a posture that suggested he was going to vomit, but nothing came out of his open mouth. The silver comb skidded across towards the visitor. The banHe tried to cough, and strangely there ensued an intense silence, as if the room itself had become mute. Only then did Malum notice how sharp the banHe's teeth appeared, and his second realization was that there was almost a smile on the other's face, as if he was enjoying his pain.

'Fine . . . thank you.' Dannan almost coughed the words.

Malum turned to the other men. 'Does he need water?'

'I'm fine.' Dannan's posture became a little more refined, and he leaned over towards the window, peered out left and right across the harbour. Then back at Malum, tiny red veins crisscrossing his eyes. 'Someone's dead, is all.'

'What do you mean?' Malum said.

'Out there.' He flicked his head in a gesture towards the window. 'Someone just died.'

'The fuck do you know this? Is that why you weren't at the strike?'

Dannan glared at him violently. His eyes never seemed to maintain any consistency in colour, and the more you looked at them the less you could define them. 'I just fucking know, OK. You got my men for the strike – you never asked for me.'

'That's true.' Malum didn't actually know whether or not the banHe had been there – they were all wearing masks, and he was just guessing now – but the man's weird response to death certainly made Malum doubt his commitment to normal gang activities.

'You haven't got any arum weed on you, have you? I'm all out.'

'No.' Malum bent down to pick up the comb, noting its meticulous craftsmanship. He tossed it back casually. 'I came to see you about the albino commander, and that meeting we had. When he was wanting our gangs to help him.'

'What of it?' Dannan again ran the comb once through a clump of hair by his ear then laid it on the windowsill delicately with his long, spindly fingers.

'The commander is gay – he likes to fuck other men,' Malum revealed. 'I don't know about you, but I'm not going to have my lot working on the side of someone like that, if you know what I mean. My men fight for real men.'

'Gay, you say?' Dannan replied, slowly regaining his composure. 'What d'you think we should do? More to the point, what's in it for my lot? My tastes ain't exactly mainstream.'

'Dignity, honour, doing the right thing is what matters,' Malum suggested. To him it was totally unnatural for a man to perform those acts with another man. Malum felt he had something to convey to the commander. 'Look, I need to know if you've made a decision yet – if you lot were thinking of helping him out. When this war comes to the city, I mean.'

'We was thinking about it. Maybe we'll need to fight just to keep what turf we've got here already. I mean, war's nothing more than a big fucking turf fight, ain't that right?'

Malum grunted a laugh. 'Well, I guess so, yes. Look, we get on, our lot, you and me. We're similar – we're both *not natural*. We work together from time to time, dealing with the unions and shit. I want to teach this commander a lesson. I want to go back in there, tell him to shove his war, and I reckon I should get him set on. Fucking hate soldiers anyway, so I mean . . . you know, get him beaten up – made an example of. And, what's more, we need to put on another display like this, cos I've got traders moaning at me all the time, wanting relief from paying their protection taxes, the precious little darlings. No, I think one of these exhibitions of force can serve us well.'

'And how're you going to get the commander into our hands?'

'Oh, I don't know. But people in this city need to know that he sleeps with men.'

'Maybe we could get some cash out of him?' Dannan suggested. 'Blackmail. Some of my good men for backup and then we go halves.'

'That's a good idea. We can get a lot of cash out of someone that high up in the military. We can just pick a stupid number, and he'll do his best to keep his secrets safe. But then we should beat him to death on the streets once we take his money.'

Dannan ogled the girl in the corner for a moment, who seemed to be heading further towards uncharted territory inside her own head. 'Sure. You take control of this one, and let me know when you need my help.'

'And are your lot intending to fight in the war?'

Dannan paused thoughtfully, his gaze fixed on the girl transforming into something predatory. 'Not for the likes of him, no. If shit happens on a large scale, I'll ship out down south, maybe try another island. Getting too damn cold up this way, anyway.'

*

Satisfied that he had the banHe's street gang on his side, or at least not against him, Malum strode towards the barracks, through the streets, past the drunks and the whores and the addicts, then past the partygoers and the couples walking arm-in-arm, onwards through the nondescript streets of the city. It had snowed, then that stopped, and the evening now had a sense of calm about it, despite the hubbub audible from some of the more lively districts.

He approached two soldiers standing at the entrance arch framing a massive quercus wood door set into one of the older stone walls surviving in Villiren. The men were wearing crimson uniforms under their dull metal body armour, and massive sheathed sabres hung from their hips. They chatted idly, unprofessionally, rubbing their hands and shifting their weight from foot to foot to stamp out the chill.

He declared, 'I would like to see your commander.'

The guards laughed. 'Yeah, right,' one said, a chubby man with deep-set eyes and bad skin. 'He don't just see anyone unarranged.'

Bugger. Malum should have realized he couldn't just walk in there, not at this time of night. 'I'm Malum, of the Bloods,' he explained.

'Don't care who you are, mate,' the other stated. 'We need to be expecting you.'

'Fucksake, I've already met him before. Look, can you at least pass a message to him?'

The guards conferred. 'Go on then.'

Malum continued. 'Tell him that Malum of the Bloods has come to a decision about helping the commander out with the impending war. And tell him that his preferences *as to men* has been noted, and frowned upon. Make sure you get that *men* bit, though. I'll be waiting outside the Victory Hole tavern at sunset tomorrow. He can meet me there if he wants to keep his rep intact.'

And with that, Malum turned and merged again with the cold Villiren evening.

NINETEEN

Wax cape bundled around his shoulders, Brynd marched through the dreary streets of Villiren back towards the Citadel. Another failed meeting with some of the self-appointed district representatives. When would they realize that if no one would help by joining the citizen militias, then they would have no houses left in which to take sanctuary?

Featureless stone facades lined a narrow iren, which seemed much poorer than many of the others. There wasn't a lot for sale either – cheap incense, pots and pans and blades rusted by months of bad weather. Traders scowled at him from under decrepit canopies. Some bore wooden signs supporting the unions, or cursing some of the larger corporations – Broun Merchants or Ferryby's or Coumby's. Brynd learned that companies or individuals rented out space at the larger irens, taking in return a slice of the profits, but the traders couldn't do anything about it – that was where everyone went to buy their goods, and Lutto himself had passed the relevant legislation in the first place.

Up ahead three figures, huddled on the ground, gaped up at his approach.

'Commander Lathraea!' the woman spluttered. She hastily handed a book she had been carrying the last time to one of the others, then made her way over. It was those same old cultists dressed in tweed. The woman herself was nearly as tall as him, but the other two – one with a moustache and the other bald – continued studying some of the designs they had made on the flagstones, weird script and cipher marked with chalk. They kept gesturing to each other erratically.

'Yes, it's uh . . .'

'Bellis! Of the Order of the Grey Hairs, at your service. Sir, have you found any use for us yet? We're still as active as any of those reckless young cultists who keep blowing themselves up. Years of expertise, you see.'

This bunch seemed mad and untrustworthy, and he had better things to be doing right now. And he could smell alcohol on her breath. 'As of yet,' he said, 'the planning has been concentrated on less esoteric methods, I'm afraid.'

'Oh well, we'll be about if you need us. A shame really, as we can offer quite a bit, but if you insist on using those silly conventional methods then you go ahead, young man.' She gave him a kind of salute, and he wasn't sure if she was mocking him or not.

He gave a cautious smile and continued past.

*

Red sunlight streamed across the table in Brynd's small study overlooking the harbour. Seagulls and pterodettes screamed outside his window, circling the skies endlessly. Charts and maps papered all four walls of this room, lines of potential strategy marked on them in various colours. Bold lines slashed across them like wounds. He'd been studying the streets for real, as well as these sketches, calculating the flow of troops needed in response to flows of attack. Probabilities of access and of restrictions: these were tight streets, and bottlenecks could prove a weapon or a curse, depending on the situation. Such variables he had committed to memory on the spot, then written down instructions to be fed to other officers.

According to garuda reports, the most likely method of attack would be a sea landing directly into Villiren's harbour – since the enemy was lining up directly opposite. Punctuating the shoreline for miles in either direction, he'd stationed small units to keep watch.

A knock on the open door and Brynd glanced up.

Nelum Valore stood before him, a lieutenant of the Night Guard. One of Brynd's closest comrades, they'd long served alongside each other and in the field, getting to know each other by instinct. His wide-muscled figure suggested someone who relied upon his strength to get by, but Brynd had instead come to value the man's ferocious intelligence, his keen eye for logic, his knack of looking through the gaps in the world he confronted. Nelum's swarthy figure seemed to add to the mysterious aura he gave off whenever he retreated into his mind during deep contemplation. In such uncertain times Brynd felt that Nelum should be ranked at the top of any command structures.

'Sir, the Okun.'

'What about them?'

The Okun had been captured on Tineag'l several weeks ago, in a small-scale skirmish that had led to the death of his friend and comrade, Apium, but ever since they had been in Villiren, they had proved unresponsive, locked away in darkness while remaining seemingly dormant.

'They're up and alert now.'

'How did they wake?' Brynd asked.

'They were moved into a different cell yesterday,' Nelum replied. 'One with more light. They'd been showing marginal reaction to torchlight, so we suggested they might have preferences. And guess what? They appeared to react after being exposed to daylight, slowly coming to life. They even began to bleed again from their wounds. They're still locked up now, the two of them.'

'Right, I'll come.' Brynd grabbed his sabre and followed the lieutenant from the room.

*

Brynd entered the metal-lined holding cell, with Nelum and guards stepping in behind him. He pulled his sabre free, uncertain of what might happen – fearful, if he was honest, because he had no idea what to expect.

They were still lying there, on the floor, massive and alien. Both creatures' flesh pulsated under their shells, slick juices seeping out of their skin, the black fluid pooling near his feet. The stench of them was rancid and more intense than ever.

Two pairs of eyes opened and he lurched backwards.

In that instant, Nelum and the guards were gripping their swords in readiness, but Brynd cautioned them to hold back. The Okun would most likely feel threatened in a new world, imprisoned like this, and they could prove more dangerous if undue pressure was applied to them.

Nelum leaned over towards Brynd and he asked earnestly, 'Your thoughts, commander?'

'Your guess is as good as mine. They're definitely alive, which is good. As long as they're alive we can examine them, and study them, for points of weakness to exploit in combat. Surely this must be our best chance of understanding the enemy? I mean to say, if a victory is possible, it might come from such a careful study. And perhaps they can offer more clues as to the nature of Earth – it's clear we're learning more and more about the Boreal Archipelago as time goes on. Apparently they came through some gate, from some other world. So much clearly exists that we don't understand.'

'Other worlds . . . perhaps, perhaps.' Nelum nodded, looking down as his mind began to sift for a theory. 'But I'd suggest they're closer to us, to our world that is, than we first thought. We know they're bipedal and – look – they have two compound eyes, and a structure much like other life forms that can be found on most shores under the same red sun as ourselves. Hypothetically, in another world with other landscapes and alternative biological systems, one would expect selection pressures to have forced greater differences. Morphologically, say, three eyes or legs. The interesting thing, if this is not the case . . . well, it means that the world they came from has once shared similarities or ancestries to our own. We share similar evolutionary traits, and therefore we share a history.'

'Our roots are the same,' Brynd whispered, in awe of his lieutenant's theory.

Nelum nodded, not removing his gaze from the creatures.

There lay, somewhere in the coming weeks, a solution, although more questions were growing exponentially before them. Brynd could only just about get his head around the facts – he was not a man who had devoted much of his life to detailed academic pursuits, unlike Nelum. These Okun creatures had at some stage shared a past with humans and rumel. So was it possible that they could now share a world? Brynd contemplated his lieutenant. If anything happened to Brynd himself during the coming conflict, then he would want that mind, that man Nelum, to take full charge of anything remotely tactical.

'It would perhaps be useful if we could visit these gates, the ones they purportedly came through.'

'We can't because . . . ?' Nelum asked.

'Surrounded by enemy troops. You've seen the garuda reports, I think. Huge numbers currently pouring across Tineag'l. The journey there would be too reckless, especially since we'd have to cut right through their invasion force.'

'So we must just sit and wait for them to attack – either us or a city further up the coast, who knows,' Nelum said, not a question, just a statement of what they both realized. Theirs was a waiting game. 'Bohr, we might die before we find out what it all means.'

One of the Okun suddenly began to cackle. Brynd crouched to take a better look at it. There was a mouthpiece, a jaw resembling that of a rabid dog, equipped with several incisor teeth that glinted metallically.

Brynd glanced askew at Nelum. 'Is it trying to *talk*?'

'Well, I think it might be – who would have thought it? Now, what do you suppose it's aiming to say precisely?'

The sounds it made were more like staccato coughs than anything resembling a voice, and even though he listened for a while, Brynd knew any communication was unlikely.

'If only we had some way of knowing what the hell it was going on about,' Brynd said.

'You know, I suppose there's always Jurro...' Nelum offered.

'Could be worth a go.'

*

The Dawnir progressed thunderously through the hallway leading to the small cell which housed the Okun. He was already so excited! How often had any new creatures come to his attention? Possibly never – or, at least, not after the discovery of his own existence in the Boreal Archipelago. Thousands of years spent trying to find a memory of his own, yet he was once so fresh to this world that he might have been a baby. He needed to learn a language from scratch – and had now mastered over fifty of them.

He had been told he was found wandering through the tundra outside of Villjamur, and assumed to be some kind of prophet at first, then even a god of the creator race, the Dawnir. And when everyone finally realized he knew nothing of the world, that he could give them nothing, they lost interest in him, such was life. He had been kept as an imprisoned guest of the Council ever since, and they had been reluctant to let him outside, for his own good, in case disaffected types hailed him as a religious leader.

Rotting away in his chambers, he had all his books, and had made the most of them, turning nearly every printed page available in a quest to discover who he was and where he came from. The recent opportunity to leave his dark retreat inside the Imperial residence of Balmacara had been a godsend. And now the opportunity to investigate a new-found race . . . well, that was something to be utterly delighted about. For the first time in centuries had come an opportunity to discover his own origins, for if these shell-creatures came from somewhere else, some other world entirely, then they might bring with them pertinent information.

Information was his life. There might now be some answers.

He had to hunch to fit into the room, but still very nearly caught his tusks in the door frame. More than once he had scraped them in these cramped stone shells of his new home. He brushed a hand across his thick body fur as a cobweb smothered his ear, then he lowered his head to focus on Brynd, dominating much of the available space.

'Commander Brynd Lathraea and Lieutenant Nelum Valore. A pleasure, no? I hear our little *malacostraca* friends are no longer slumbering like cherubs?'

'Sele of Jamur, Jurro,' the commander greeted him, apparently amused, as so often, by the words issuing from Jurro's lips. The Dawnir estimated Brynd highly. He was a sound man, a philosopher as well as a warrior – just as much a warrior, even. The two had conversed during many years in his forgotten chamber in Villjamur.

'Let's show you these things, then.'

Jurro felt the gaze of a few Night Guard soldiers fixed on him, as they stood aside to let him through. They always moved so quickly, these humans, as if there was an urgency to all their actions.

It was not easy being the only one of a kind. Even these two Okun outnumbered his own race at the moment. Brynd soon brought him up to speed on their analysis of the situation. They led him over to the Okun, the two creatures now quivering perceptibly on the tiled floor.

They froze as soon as they registered the presence of the Dawnir in the room. Then, as one, both the creatures shambled to something resembling a standing position, though awkwardly, in such an unlikely connection of movements. Together they fell to their knees, as if in the presence of some Jorsalir priest.

The commander turned to his lieutenant. 'Well, they've never behaved like that before.'

'Intriguing,' Jurro mumbled, then crouched until he was at eye-level with the humans surrounding him. These Okun were unyielding as they were inspected by the Dawnir. They began clicking again, something quite incoherent at first, and then he began to understand the noises they made on some level. Not understand perhaps, merely recognize? After all, he had been cursed or blessed with spending all those centuries reading the texts within the confines of his chamber in Villjamur. The knowledge he had accumulated was only useful once he was out here, in the real world. It was a relief, finally, that he might serve some function other than as a curiosity.

'You comprehend these sounds?' the albino commander enquired.

Jurro turned to face the humans in the room. They all seemed to him the same at first, and it was only the commander's red eyes that singled him out. 'I know only that they are asking me for my forgiveness or pardon. Something along those lines, I believe. Yet, I don't understand quite how I know that. Such random knowledge! I might have read it in a text, you see. Or I have learned it at some other earlier time. I cannot quite tell. How can we trust memory, when it is not accurately documented, when it is perhaps only the shadow of something I remember. My mental vaults have grown vast.'

There were no expressions evident on their faces that he

could recognize, nothing to give away their emotion as the expressions of humans or rumel so often did – so easy to read, and childlike. These Okun were something altogether different. It was truly baffling!

'I think I sense it, rather than know it, but they see me as some threat. Yes, that is so. They know who I am!' The realization almost stung him, he was so used to appearing as nothing but a myth to those he encountered.

'Or *what* you are,' Brynd suggested. 'Do you suppose there are more of your kind where they come from? And that, in that other place, whoever your kind are actually frighten them?'

Jurro muttered, 'It may well be.'

He knew for sure that he must ascertain more about them. Although their communication was one way, this was the first time in his long life where he had the opportunity to find out who he was. For so long he had remained an enigma not only to the officials of Villjamur but, more importantly, to himself. He had watched the lives of countless rulers and the general populace come and go, had watched the ice encroaching in recent times. None of it mattered to him, because the pattern just repeated itself: humans and rumel alike making the same mistakes for decade after decade. He himself aged hardly at all, and for all that time he had wanted to know his origins.

'I must, of course, discover from whence these two little specimens came,' Jurro announced.

The albino studied him with empathy. He had always been unusually smart, Jurro reflected, this pale thing. 'I understand,' the commander replied. 'You think their invasion force might let you through its ranks?'

Jurro held out his hands to either side, and shrugged. 'I may need assistance, but before I leave I want to interrogate them as thoroughly as possible. I understand a great deal about forms of language. Perhaps I could gain crucial intelligence.'

'That would be deeply helpful,' the commander agreed.

'Although if you want to leave here you might have to progress on your own. We have to commit all of our numbers to protecting the city.'

Jurro acquiesced, studying the Okun once more. They had risen to their feet again, still focusing their eyes on him, still unmoving apart from their mouthpieces. 'They seem to fear me greatly, so I doubt very much that their kind will offer me much in the way of hindrance. I shall make plans, and I will need some maps, and your advice, commander, on the routes to follow to find the location of these so-called gates through which these little fellows crawled. And I will need you to allow me some time with them in a cell so that I can press for information.'

With that, he departed.

Twenty

The Dawnir squeezed through the narrow metal door and lumbered into the cell to engage with the Okun again. The creatures scrambled away from him, thrusting their backs against the stone wall, feet skidding on the floor. Jurro motioned, in whatever forms he thought appropriate, for them to settle, but it wasn't much use. Fear had possessed them, made them nervous and volatile. He set two lanterns on the floor, as a guard slammed the door behind him, leaving him utterly alone with this new species. No chairs in the room, no tables, nothing civilized here, only bare stone surfaces and a vacant space between them and himself. But they shared a tension, something indefinable.

How could he unlock the secrets intervening between their languages?

Ceasing their twitching, their gaze – or what he took to be their gaze – settled upon him. Bulbous eyes, glossy shells, all those alien features – he was almost frightened of their otherworldly qualities, but knew better than to mistake those for inherent evilness. People were not good or evil simply because of their physiognomy.

A thousand variants in ancient languages, he sifted through all the dialects he knew, while for long, breathless minutes they did nothing but glare at him: 'Hello.' Then 'Greetings.' 'Peace.' 'Friend.'

A guard came to check on him every few minutes, but

witnessed nothing of any interest. Jurro might have to accept that he could not acquire any intelligence for the pale commander, though the thought of returning empty-handed disappointed him. Eventually he tried responding to them in their own fashion, producing a series of surreal guttural clicks from the back of his throat. That finally made them sit up again, their motions coordinated. He could barely form a sentence, obviously missing key elements, but it might be enough to engage them. They stood up suddenly as the guard came to the door once more.

'Are you OK?'

'Fine,' Jurro replied, waving the intrusion away dismissively.

Further progress, then, by resorting only to further clicks. His heart thumped as the creatures began to sound off in return. He finally began to believe he could understand their reactions. There was something almost recognizable there, as if a corner of his memory had been unlocked.

Who ... are you? he thought they were saying. *Why you here? How?*

It was impossible to answer them properly, not because of a language barrier but because he couldn't even answer those questions himself.

You shouldn't be able to come through here.

Only we know how.

Their next word struck him hard when they addressed him as: *Child.* How could he be a child when he was thousands of years old? Had he, too, slipped through from some other plane of existence? There were books of theory on the subject, concerning the eleven dimensions through which reality could operate.

Suddenly one of the Okun moved nearer to him, began circling him, the other eventually following. They shambled with an awkward gait, feet scraping across the stone floors, yet their movements were synchronized. Throat sounds were emitted, bass and guttural and threatening.

Jurro rotated slowly, twisting his massive torso round to observe them, all the time throwing further attempts at communication towards them.

They had become suddenly unresponsive.

Simultaneously they lunged at him, collapsing him to the ground first as, in the periphery of his vision, he saw a guard come to the cell door. A pain such as he had never felt before surged suddenly through his body. The Okun stabbed their claws into his chest and began ripping him apart, shredding skin and fur, while smashing his head against the floor. How could he have been so stupid? He saw his own blood seep across the cell floor before he faded into blackness, wondering, philosophically, if this was finally true freedom coming his way . . .

*

Brynd was in the midst of planning training schedules when he was called urgently to the cells, all the time the accompanying soldier muttering something about the Dawnir and two dead guards. Brynd urged him to be clearer, but it wasn't much help. They sprinted towards the cells, the other man now breathless, Brynd with his sabre in his hand. Then the soldier gestured to the grille in the door.

Brynd peeked in between the bars, then lurched back in disgust. 'Shit . . .'

Jurro had been slaughtered, his carcass strewn across the cell. His entrails were exposed, the slick organs scattered around the room, his hide slopped to one side like a soggy rug. Thick, dark blood flooded half the floor. It was obvious from the other remains that two of the guards had been savaged as they tried to escape towards the door, their arms left outstretched, and all that was recognizable of the rest of the corpses was their faces.

'I slammed the door so the things couldn't escape,' the soldier muttered, still in a state of shock at having witnessed such savagery. His hand was shuddering by his side. 'I didn't seal them in to die, I swear on the Emperor. They were dead men by the time I managed to get the door closed to keep those . . . those monsters in.'

Brynd sheathed his sword, rested his hand on the man's thick shoulder and tried to make strong eye contact. 'You did well to prevent their escape.' *Soothe him, for the sake of his sanity.* 'Who knows how much damage they would have done otherwise.'

A few minutes later, the guard had finally calmed, and Brynd turned his attention to the Okun, who huddled in a corner of the cell, up against the wall, almost dormant once again.

'Fetch slop buckets and bring a few other men with you,' Brynd ordered.

As the guard's footsteps echoed down the corridor, Brynd slammed his hand against the metal bars in rage. One of the Okun looked up, curious, but lowered its head once again.

He was fucking stupid to have let Jurro in alone, despite the Dawnir's insistence that he would be fine. This was no dignified way for anyone to go, was hardly a fitting death for such an exotic figure. He would have the Okun killed and their bodies given to the cultists to dissect.

*

That evening the Night Guard, along with dozens of Dragoons, lined up along the perimeter of a small quadrangle inside the Citadel, as they prepared to burn the Dawnir's body on a towering pyre.

Brynd was particularly keen on giving Jurro a respectful send-off. The creature had barely been known by most people in Villjamur, but the two of them had shared many a conversation and discussed philosophy over drinks, whenever Brynd was not away on various expeditions. It was a curious friendship, between the beast and the albino, but they shared a bond over the fact that they both felt isolated because of what they were.

A Jorsalir priest rattled out a sermon and mumbled a few prayers, then someone played a funeral hymn on an accordion. Melancholy notes wafted across the courtyard as a torch was lowered to the base of the pyre, then flames took shape and billowed upwards. Green-blue smoke sizzled free from the creature's corpse, before dissipating up into the black sky, while the remnants bubbled and spat as the fire ripped into the fat. Presently there would be nothing left of this ancient creature.

When everyone fell away to retire for the night, Nelum approached the commander as he stood on the rampart overlooking the remains of the pyre.

'Sir, did he ever obtain any information from those things?'

Brynd shook his head. 'No.'

Nelum sighed. 'For the love of Bohr, he was just about our only hope of understanding what they might be.'

'You think this is a good time, at Jurro's funeral, to get annoyed with the lack of progress on that front?'

Nelum muttered something that might or might not have been an insult.

'Did you say something?' Brynd pressed.

'Nothing, sir.'

'You'd do well to remember your position.'

'Meaning?'

'I keep the Night Guard as a close family, and I've kept you close to my side recently, but that shouldn't mean we confuse our positions in the regiment. I hope I'm clear on the matter.'

'Indeed, commander,' Nelum snapped, his lips thinned as if suppressing a biting retort. 'My apologies.'

TWENTY-ONE

For the men and women of the Seventh and Ninth Dragoons, the day commenced in a sombre mood, and didn't much improve from there. These soldiers had landed on the coast of Folke four days ago, after returning from a failed invasion of the Varltung nation, where thousands of comrades had died under the ice sheets as they attempted to claim another island. All in the name of the Empire and empire building. The official story was that the tribal nations had gathered along the edge of the ice sheets and rained arrows down on those drowning in the frozen waters. But some suggested there were no enemies in situ, that this was merely to provide reason for the Emperor to launch a much larger and more brutal invasion.

A mild sleet seemed to make the air above Villiren rattle, with grey skies smothering every point of the compass. The Dragoons were now lined up to attention, forming precise rows in the colossal quadrangular courtyard of the Citadel, framed by the wide granite arches and pillars. Awaiting further instructions they stood in silence, soggy, muddied, still mourning the dead.

Brynd remembered reading the great poets from an era when the sun was stronger – translations that had survived collapsed civilizations and forgotten languages, rhetoric and drama that injected glory into the legends of war. Bitterly he wondered if many of those writers had actually stood in the front line of any battle.

*

The troops began moving directly into the city, first in their tens and then in their thousands. Many empty structures in Port Nostalgia needed to be taken over in the name of defence. Citizens looked on in misery as the soldiers shuffled into their positions. This was an invasion of their normality – and the mood of the city changed perceptibly. The mere presence of the military seemed to augur death and decay.

Days of rigorous training continued in camps scattered to the south of the city, in Wych-Forest, manoeuvres practised in accordance with Brynd's detailed instructions, based on military traditions and his own theories. Such staged combat scared the richer districts into holding late-night meetings where landowners would protest. Seafront shop and bar staff pleaded for the army not to take over their homes, as if not realizing how important the front line of the city would be in staging a defence.

Did people ever see beyond their own everyday lives? And why should they, Brynd reflected, when it seemed enough to just stay alive in these harsh conditions?

Extra food had been imported through military protected networks, to prevent prices from soaring in the city proper, but he was careful, too, not to fix prices, because such artificial lowering could lead to severe shortages later on.

But there was always food, strangely. Good cuts of meat were imported from massive agricultural settlements beyond the suburbs, which Brynd had never known existed. Portreeve Lutto had indeed prepared his city well, and no matter how grossly he acted, no matter how much of a buffoon the man appeared, there was clearly an active, useful mind in that bloated head.

Brynd had recently been impressed by a shield design employed by many of the local tribesmen, and which had subsequently entered the culture of Villiren. It was called a hoplon or an aspis, depending on who you spoke to, and was crafted to a circular design that Brynd deemed more efficient than the longer traditional variety. So the city's armouries went into mass production, and he ordered a different type of helm to be manufactured at the same time, one allowing a much greater range of vision, completely without unnecessary adornments – just a simple, skull-gripping design.

And day in, day out, Priest Pias's sermons delivered throughout the Jorsalir churches had proved potent in driving home a message Brynd otherwise did not care for: religious propaganda. Leaflets were simultaneously scattered around the city, carrying the same message:

> *I beseech you all – join hands with the soldiers now prepared to lay down their lives so that we & our children may continue to walk our streets as free citizens. Opportunity to guarantee your soul's salvation is to be found currently at the Citadel, where you can sign up & collect sacred weaponry from the heroic soldiers who have always protected this Empire & have fought off the devilry of the repugnant, unevolved races for thousands of years. Their glory can be yours, too, with the opportunity to fight hand in hand with them. The future of our city lies in YOUR hands. Either you are with US or you are with this new race of invaders. Think not of this life but of the FUTURE & I promise you safe passage to the hereafter.*
>
> Priest Pias, Arch Pater of the Church of the Jorsalir

Later still: there was to be the initiation of a new recruit to the Night Guard, whose addition would bring the total back to twenty, the minimum figure acceptable in Brynd's mind. Being selected to join the elite regiment was the highest attainment a soldier could hope for. It signified someone possessing extraordinary skills in close-quarter combat, but also a supreme degree of physical fitness, outstanding tactical judgement, and the ability to endure extreme mental and physical torture. Once the potential recruit had been accepted, only then did the real hardships begin.

Night Guard soldiers were expected to undergo enhancement.

Tiendi was stripped down to her breeches and vest top in a stone-tiled chamber at the lowest level of the Citadel. She was due to become the first female Night Guard to be ordained for years – there were simply not that many women in the army who could physically reach the required levels. Having risen to sergeant within six years, Tiendi was long overdue for this promotion: during four campaigns on the southern islands, she'd proved extremely proficient with the sword, diligent out in the field, and had saved the lives of no small number of her comrades. And she was only twenty-seven. She would retain her rank, although it was meaningless since, with the exception of Brynd, all Night Guard were considered equal.

Blavat, the cultist who had accompanied the soldiers from Villjamur, was busy working in a corner of the room with two or three of the standard relics she needed for the procedure. Brynd had seen it performed so often now – had seen it done to himself, of course – but he was certainly not a cultist, and did not understand how the devices worked. He had brought with him a few vials of the precious fluids for the necessary injections.

The impending ritual followed an antiquated tradition, involving a stylized liaison between cultists from the Order of the Dawnir and the senior military official, which went back several hundred years. It went back so far, in fact, that no one really knew how it had all started, but it had succeeded in binding the Empire to one of the major cultist orders.

Tiendi was beckoned to lie down on a thick stone table positioned in the centre of the room, while all her comrades-to-be stood around her in a circle, watching. A few cressets burned steadily, casting enough light on the procedure, but not so much as to make the scene seem eerier than it should have been. She was strapped down, the muscles of her pale, lean body tensing, and her chin-length blonde hair bunched up to one side.

Blavat's gaze was utterly focused as she assembled her bits of equipment around the new recruit, cautiously adjusting some settings, deciphering the technology. Two metal plates were attached to Tiendi's forehead, whilst a brass syringe was poised just above the base of her neck. Blavat deftly flicked the switch on a cylinder resting behind Tiendi's head.

Then she was injected.

Tiendi screamed and clenched her fists, saliva appearing in a thin line across her cheek. Her body flared into a network of purple, as if a luminous web clung to her skin, forcing a surreal display of veins and arteries. The soldier tried to reach up to her face, but her arms were restricted by the straps, biceps bulging under the strain, and all the time Blavat stared nonchalantly at the spasming body of the young woman before her. Brynd watched with concern – this was not always a procedure without casualties.

Once Tiendi's screams died away, once her throes had diminished, she was unbound. She rolled off the table, collapsed sweating onto the ground and begun hugging her own body, scrunching up her eyes to hold in the tears. Gradually, the trauma wore off, and she began to gape around the room as if discovering the view for the first time.

Brynd knew what was happening, that she was becoming accustomed to the enhanced vision, more perceptive of details in both shadow and highlight, of colours at the limits of the spectrum – seeing the entire world so much more clearly.

He smiled as the rest of the Night Guard swarmed around Tiendi, patting her on the back and genially welcoming her into their elite brigade.

Twenty-Two

Randur slapped down a mug on the table next to the settee. Munio woke and immediately gaped at the flames. They were roaring away in the fireplace, the spare logs neatly stacked to one side, even the mantel thoroughly cleaned. Randur had transformed this part of the manse into something almost habitable.

'Ah,' Randur remarked. 'I see the princess awakes from her slumber.'

'The hell hour is this?'

'Late afternoon, nearly time for dinner.'

Munio pushed himself to test his feet, swaying gently as he came to terms with the new day.

'Is that baking bread I can smell?'

'Yep.' Munio probably couldn't remember the last time he had smelled such a heavenly aroma. To be honest, neither could Randur.

Munio leant over to pick up his mug of tea from the side table. 'This will not do. The day must begin with something a little stronger.'

'You're a total pisshead – and that's why your life's such a mess.'

Randur shuffled through into the kitchen, where he found Eir intent on working through some *Vitassi* moves with a ladle. He humoured her, as they clattered around the room.

'No, no,' Munio called out to her from the doorway. 'Eir, your left foot is all over the place.'

She whispered something to Randur, then made to leave the room.

'Don't go on my account,' Munio yelled after her.

'I'm just going for a walk with my sister. You two need to catch up.'

'Is she around somewhere – Rika?' Munio struggled to contain his eagerness.

'Later,' Randur declared, then gave a nod to Eir, and she left.

The two men said nothing for some time, and Munio began ambling around the kitchen with a sense of purpose.

'You won't find any more drink,' Randur said.

Munio glared at him. 'And just who is this young parvenu who comes storming in from the past to invade my house like this?'

He slumped onto a stool at the table.

Randur ignored the tantrum and, slicing some warm bread, buttered it and slid the plate across to him.

'Why're you all here anyway?' Munio asked.

'Because you invited us, you miserable sod,' Randur replied. He grabbed a mug of something hot and sat down opposite.

'You've done all right, lad.'

'Is that a compliment?'

Munio grunted a laugh. 'The petulant child still exists, inside this glossy exterior. So how did you get away from this shithole of an island and come to meet the likes of those two posh lasses?'

'I managed to steal a name from a dead man who was meant to be sword and dance tutor to Lady Eir. Originally I was there to get a cultist to help my poor mother, but I found cultists only helped themselves. My world then took something of a drastic turn and my priorities changed. Eir's sister was due to become Empress. Then the man who's probably now Emperor set them up for a crime of treason, and I helped get Eir and Rika out of the city. We're now on the run to Villiren – since Rika's got a plan, which is more than the rest of us have.'

'*Bohrsakes*, child. Can't believe you didn't tell me this at first.'

Randur shrugged.

'Well, makes no difference to those of us way out here who runs the Empire. And so having the burden of such responsibility – is it eating away yet?'

'People can change,' Randur replied. 'And I'm not who I used to be. I can choose to be different if I want.'

'People never really change,' Munio declared, a statement of intent regarding his alcoholism, perhaps.

'Look, there's likely to be a big price on our heads, and that level of bounty can change a man's thinking.'

'A big price, for just you lot? You would've thought the Council had better things to be worrying about than a couple of kids.'

'Money's no problem to that man, Urtica – he'll have a regiment or two spreading out across the Empire. Don't forget, we're fugitives. I have to keep looking over my shoulder, but I never let my concern show to the girls – I prefer to carry that burden myself. So we're on our way north, to Villiren, to meet the commander there, and we'll leave here as soon as we feel up to it.'

'Why bother?' Munio asked.

'Rika wants to be able to clear her name – strangely, she actually wants to serve her people, to help them. She reckons the commander of the military – you must have heard of the legendary albino? – can help her out. Seems he brought her to Villjamur in the first place. We're focused on that as our objective, and it's all we're living for at the moment.'

'Long journey you have in mind.'

'I think you should come with us. In fact, I want you to.' Sudden, thrusting words.

Munio glanced at him in disbelief. 'At *my* age?'

'We could do with the extra protection. Also I only half remember the routes north from this part of the island, so your assistance in getting there would be bloody useful. You reckon you'd be up to it?'

'Pah, I'm too old. People like me never change, like I said.'

Randur didn't buy that. Like he deployed his sword strokes over the years, Munio had more than likely repeated the habits of his misery until he knew, by heart, how to shun the real world.

Randur pressed him further, more persuasive blows. 'I know you've talked about money, or lack of, but when you're on the road with us you won't have to worry about that. Maybe we can catch up a bit, because there are so many years to talk about. I used to respect you so much, old friend. After all I didn't have a father, and . . .' Randur trailed off, as if expecting Munio to say what he then said.

'Well, I never had a son.' With these words Munio disarmed himself, let his guard down, and no longer had anything to parry Randur with.

A pause, and Randur said, 'Or at least none that you knew about, you filthy old scrote. So you'll join us, will you?'

'I'll think about it.'

The two of them laughed and Munio looked much the better for it.

'Maybe it would do me good to get on the road again. What has my life here consisted of but sauntering around drunk and alone amid clouds of dust motes?'

Eir entered the room again and said, 'She's now busy meditating.'

Munio blurted out, 'Young Eir! This one here has been telling me all about the pair of you.'

'What kind of things?' She eyed Randur with suspicion, as he shuffled over to her side.

'Nothing bad.'

As the old man drew a sword, she turned sharply.

'Lad says you've been keen to learn the ways of *Vitassi*,' Munio said. 'Shall we now see if he was as lazy a teacher as he was once a student.'

'Rand, would you like to fetch my sword?' she said coldly.

'What, am I your servant now?' He stomped off but returned moments later with the same thin blade she had used to cut her way out of Villjamur.

She grabbed it and turned to face Munio, who said, 'Let's have a look at you.'

His blade darted aggressively towards her torso, and for the next few minutes her sword was slapped around the kitchen by a master of the technique. Every time she made a strike, he seemed to predict what she was intending. He barked out corrective instructions, but when he eventually started singing, she lost her poise completely, slipping over, her sword clattering at Randur's feet. He handed it back to her with a grin, knowing that if he said anything, he'd earn one of those glares she did so well.

'And that', Munio declared, 'is why you should not be distracted by anything I say while I'm advancing. You must hear only your sword-stroke. You listen to me when we finish.'

'The enemy aren't exactly going to be advising me in combat, are they?' Eir muttered breathlessly.

'That depends', Munio replied, 'on whether you know exactly who your enemy is. Well the three of you obviously need my assistance, and I admit that it feels rather good to be non-sedentary again. So I will agree to join you. Anyway, there is not a hope in hell you'll scramble your way north through all those forests without someone like me to guide you.'

Randur leapt across and slapped Munio on the back. 'Knew you wouldn't be able to resist.'

'Indeed,' Munio said primly. 'But I have some business in town this afternoon, so we may leave tomorrow morning.'

Twenty-Three

'Individual from the Bloods – claimed he was their leader. Decision to be made on bolstering troop numbers. Said something about your preferences in men? Possibly staffing arrangements. Details of locations overleaf.'

Brynd had received the message earlier that day, telling him to meet the gang leader, Malum, outside the Victory Hole tavern at sunset. For a long time afterwards he held the piece of paper in his hands, staring into the distance.

At the specified time, he was loitering in the freezing cold by the quayside. The streets were again being treated with solution to flush away any remaining ice while the dreary evening skies filled with yet more snow. Lights from the bars could be seen tracing an arc along the rim of the harbour, but out towards the north, where the invasion would originate, there was nothing but darkness. The Victory Hole itself was becoming increasingly rowdy as traders and fishermen began lining up against the bar to talk shop in the half-light. Men, for the most part, shuffled past him huddled from the cold, many of them not wanting to make eye contact with a soldier, as if he was a bad omen. Brynd was fine with that.

Soon a hooded man with stubble shuffled up to Brynd. Expensive cut of clothing, thick grey woollen top, flashily tailored boots, the red mask: he could tell it was Malum.

'I got your message,' Brynd said.

'I see you got a flair for stating the obvious, albino.'

'You've reached a decision about your men helping the city in the coming war?' Brynd asked.

'I have. Neither the Bloods nor the Screams will join in this charade.'

Come on, you selfish fucker. 'You realize that the city may fall because of such a decision? Because of such cowardice?'

'Speak to me about cowardice?'

'The fall of Villiren would be the start of something darker across the entire Archipelago. We've already lost one island, and one by one they'll all fall. And if people just stand back it'll happen a lot sooner.'

'Problem is,' Malum declared, 'that none of us wants to fight alongside a man like you.'

'A soldier of the Empire?'

'Someone who's not *right*. Not natural.'

'Not sure I follow you, sir.'

Malum then explained about having the commander tracked, about him being spotted seeking out the company of other men for a fuck – about having that male prostitute located, and a confession made in front of witnesses, before the man was executed with a crossbow bolt through the skull.

This conversation was so surreal that Brynd's heart rate tripled in an instant. As word by word followed, he retreated further into himself, panicking that his secret should be exposed in such a careless manner – to this thug of all people. Even if it was only one man's word against another, that signed confession might destroy his career.

As Brynd's hand moved to his sword, Malum snarled, 'Fuck you think you're doing? Reckon you can kill me here, you can think again. I've fifty men waiting within sight, and if you make a move they'll hunt you down despite how fancy a fighter you think yourself. Anyway, with that confession released publicly, we'd ruin you and your whole fucking army.'

It might have been a bluff, all of this, but as Brynd's military mind reduced the situation to probabilities and chances, he realized quickly that the odds were not in his favour. 'What do you want?' he growled.

'Now you're talking,' Malum whispered, in a more accommodating tone. 'You'll provide me with several thousand Jamúns. Say, enough to buy most of the city? A different city, of course, since this one might not even be here in a few weeks.'

'Why threaten the one man offering a hope of defending this place? I could save hundreds of thousands of lives.'

Tough to tell behind that mask, but it seemed the thug appeared to consider this question for a while.

Brynd listened to the boats tapping against one another in the wind, providing an endless, gentle drumbeat that could drive a man insane.

'I'm a *real* man,' Malum grunted finally, 'someone the likes of *you* just wouldn't understand.' He gave some curt instructions about where to leave the money, warning him to come alone or else. With a final sneer, he then faded into fog.

Brynd felt a perfect stillness surrounding him. His world had just imploded.

*

Brynd poked his head into the officers' quarters where several of his own men were slumped in chairs, either reading or playing cards at a table under a large map of the city. 'A word, lieutenant, if you wouldn't mind.'

'Of course, commander.' Nelum set down his book, glanced at the others, who smirked as if he was in trouble. Someone joked, 'Lavatory cleaning for the lieutenant,' and the others laughed.

He bounded to his feet to follow Brynd.

Every footstep was loud, every breath clear and sharp as they moved along a corridor of the Citadel, heading outside to one of the walkways positioned behind the long crenellated battlement.

Late in the evening, and both moons were concealed by

cloud. Only a few guards from the Dragoons were stationed up here, long-range archers with precise vision, the green and brown of their uniforms barely noticeable in this dim light. They saluted as the Night Guard soldiers passed them, curt and respectful, before returning their focus to the northern horizon.

Eventually Brynd and Nelum paused by a turret at the eastern edge of the Citadel, staring into the black distance. Taverns down below were emptying, with drunken songs and harmless screams from women.

'Make of this information what you will, lieutenant,' Brynd announced.

'Go on.' Nelum's expression was sincere, and Brynd waited as long as he could.

'Is everything all right, commander?'

He told him what had happened in succinct nuggets of information, being as discreet as he could, but ultimately coming clean about one fact: he was being blackmailed over a rumour that could corrupt everything they were working towards.

'I see the predicament,' Nelum said. 'Can I enquire as to the nature of this rumour?'

The question lingered in the air.

Brynd said, 'His accusations are of a personal nature.'

'Which are?'

'Suggestions of my affiliations with – I don't need to tell you it's utter rubbish of course – other men. Personally I suspect it's merely an excuse for his gang not to fight along-side us.' He gave a confident laugh. 'But the problem is how to deal with things should such lies destabilize all we've been working towards. The guy is phenomenally well connected, and controls a large number of men.'

Nelum's face remained expressionless, until Brynd could no longer bear to look at him. Rubbing his hands for warmth, he strolled a few paces away.

Eventually, his lieutenant spoke tentatively. 'Such things . . . well, they happen in the armies, don't they? I mean to say, that men bed with men when they're abroad, so I've heard . . . Nothing is ever said of it the next day.'

'I know that, you know that – nearly every soldier who's been signed up for more than a year knows that it happens,' Brynd growled, glaring at Nelum.

Nelum's silence was intense.

'These rumours are serious, enough to destroy the good name of the Night Guard, and that could rupture all our plans and defences.'

The lieutenant remained utterly expressionless, his breath clouding before his face. 'It has not happened yet, has it? I say we take this man out.'

Brynd said, 'He told me there are others who know about it, and that if he disappears, someone else will spread the false news.'

'The fellow might be bluffing.'

'But what do *you* think about it?' Brynd turned to face him again, eager to gauge a reaction. It seemed important for any kind of response. 'I know you're a man with a passion for the Jorsalir teachings that don't exactly welcome such doings. I need to ensure these lies don't get out.'

'None of my business what a soldier does in his or her spare time.' Brisk tones, bitter feelings – all suggesting that he knew Brynd was lying. 'You're known as one of the ablest fighters in the service, and we all have to persevere despite whatever has been impugned.'

Brynd's control snapped and he slammed his lieutenant against the wall, glaring. Nelum didn't flinch. The two soldiers were assessing each other, waiting for the other's next move. 'They are rumours, OK? I told you only because I valued your fucking advice.'

The sloshing of the water down in the harbour seemed to bring Brynd back to his senses. He released his grip, muttering an apology, and rested his hands on the parapet, facing the coast.

'Indeed. We should therefore prepare ourselves for different scenarios,' Nelum continued, ignoring the incident, 'but I think we should counter by circulating rumours of our own that there's a move afoot to smear the honour of senior soldiers. We could suggest that it comes from enemy agents working for the invasion force, in order to weaken our defences.'

'Good thinking. I don't want to let this business interfere with our plans. Fucking hell, I've a city to save.'

'*You've* a city to save?'

Things were happening in the gaps between their sentences. '*We've*,' Brynd corrected himself quickly. 'You think I should face Malum. If anything then happens to me, then I want you to take my place. I'll want you to succeed me as commander of the Empire's armies. I can assemble the appropriate documentation, but how would you feel about such a role?'

Shit, did he say all that now simply to obscure his guilt, to win the man over? Brynd's mind began bubbling with paranoia.

'Sir ... of course,' Nelum breathed. For a moment this normally verbose individual couldn't seem to find words. 'It's overwhelming, and an honour ... but you're still here, still the most senior officer outside of Villjamur.'

And don't you forget it. 'Thank you for your time, lieutenant.'

*

'Oh, sure, totally fuck that. We'll just take the money and kill him, right?' Malum grunted. 'I mean, simple plans are always the most effective.'

JC laughed aloud, then the others – ten in all of the Bloods – joined in. There was a clashing of tankards, and then the spirit of the night subsided into low-level conversations.

Slouching on the chair in the corner of the tavern, Malum sharpened his messer blade on an oiled whetstone, while others began to make jokes in the dim candlelight. They were all going to be there, all ready to butcher the commander if he did not come up with the cash.

Butcher him, even if he did.

TWENTY-FOUR

Marysa threw punch after punch, weaving to and fro to avoid the approaching sweep of his arm, bending back and kicking in all the right postures. Then she stepped aside as the next student shuffled forwards to engage with the master, a bald and tightly muscled human with an expression of relentless serenity.

In a large, torch-lit, minimally furnished chamber with pine-wood floors and heated by two woodstoves, the ten students in crimson garb were working through the offence techniques characteristic to Berja, a dark martial art based on tribal combat. The leaflets had promised increased physical fitness as well as expertise in self-defence and both had come in spades. She had already passed the first two levels in twenty days, though there were another ten still to go.

There was only one other rumel attending. The rest of the students were all humans of various ages. They were all here to practise self-defence due to increasing fear of a war. Or fear of the street gangs. Actually, she didn't really know precisely why they were here, since no one ever spoke during their session, except the master. And even then, his comments remained terse.

Her progress on to level three was to be rewarded by training in bladecraft.

The master produced a short messer, and handed it over to her first, she having proved the best student. Marysa was utterly thrilled with the recognition, and she was rewarded with a moment's rest while he again led two of the poorer students through the more simple techniques.

She sat cross-legged on the floor and half-heartedly watched the demonstrations in progress.

Well, this certainly made a change. Up till now she'd only ever excelled in academic work. Back in Villjamur she had specialized in antiquarian artefacts and architecture, more recently studying the preservation of ancient buildings. So far Villiren had proved disappointing, having cleared away most of its interesting structures in order to replace them with soulless, hastily constructed monstrosities. Only the Ancient Quarter and a little of Port Nostalgia still proved fascinating.

But she couldn't find a job – unemployment being high, which seemed odd for a city that shamelessly proclaimed its wealth. There were more beggars here than she had ever seen before, and living in such squalid conditions. Fortunately, she had some savings with her, though most of them were being spent on these lessons. Still, it seemed, at last, that it was all worthwhile. She was more confident. Her body seemed more agile than it had ever been – which was more than she could say for Rumex, letting himself go to pot the way he was doing. She was beginning to feel ... sexually attractive, for the first time in a long while, and although she would never cheat on her husband, that seemed to matter. Just to feel good about herself.

The master beckoned her forwards and challenged her with his messer blade. She didn't know what to do at first, and was more than a little apprehensive at using a real weapon, but he began barking orders at her, telling her to extend or retreat her arm, to move backwards or forwards.

'Not like that!' he would snap.

After ten minutes or so, she began to get a feel for the blade in her palm, growing familiar with its weight and how it moved through the air. In between his attacks he would stand by her side and correct her posture. Their blades soon clashed effectively. His constant instructions improved her techniques and, when it came to her turn again, after watching some of the others, she gave him as good as she got.

After class, he smiled at her. He had never smiled.

'Marysa,' he whispered, and continued in a voice of extreme precision. 'You may keep this blade.'

'Really?' she managed, a little breathless after her rigorous training.

He bowed as he handed it to her the second time. 'You have earned it. I only wish you could have been my student years ago – starting as a young rumel. I might have seen you become a master by this time.'

'Thank you, master.' Marysa returned his formal bow and accepted the weapon. Eventually he faded into his back room, behind the wooden slats and the paper lanterns.

She examined the blade in more detail, noting the beautiful simplicity based on no era she knew of. Just simple steel, with a varnished wooden handle.

Marysa owned her very first weapon.

*

Jeryd wanted a steak that night, and to hell with his diet. He was all this way away from home comforts, investigating crimes that were apparently unsolvable no matter how assiduously he applied himself, and most of all he now wanted to spend the evening with his wife, who he was beginning to miss more and more. As the months slipped by, since he had risked his life in Villjamur, he was becoming ever more the philosopher. On his deathbed, would he be wishing he'd spent more time at work or would he be regretting lost days with Marysa, either way a nostalgia for the never-was?

Exactly. So tonight he would share a steak dinner, perhaps with a bottle of some cheeky little northern vintage, conversing with the woman he loved, then maybe with his personal appetites satisfied, he might be able to work on the crimes of the city more effectively. With that plan in mind, he set out along the streets on a quest for meat and wine.

By its presence alone, the military had slowly crushed the spirit of Villiren, that was certain. Where, only a few weeks back, people had seemed sanguine in the face of an almost-certain war, the company of so many soldiers sifting through the lanes and among the populace brought a feeling of an occupied city. Locals were largely welcoming, but the sight of precision weaponry displayed in an open, brazen fashion was unsettling.

The soldiers had not been buying much in the way of provisions from the markets, relying instead on their own supply routes, so thankfully prices weren't being forced too high.

Activity in the irens carried on as normal. Some were already starting to take down the strips of coloured cloth denoting zones, wares, individual flair. Biolumes arranged in brine-filled trays continued to provide no end of curiosity for Jeryd – they had never had anything like them back in Villjamur. One stall offered an array of masks, in different shapes and colours and materials, and for a moment he even considered buying one to see what the fad for wearing them was all about.

He came to one of the meat sellers, a portly man speaking in an exotic dialect, that Jeryd decided was a bastardization of Tineag'l and Y'iren grafted on a Jamur framework.

'I'm after some steaks,' Jeryd announced to him across the now sparse selection of fish and crustaceans. Hanging from the top of the overhead frame were two large trilobites, about two armspans in length, twisting this way and that in the wind.

'Steak? We got steak. What animal you wanting?'

Jeryd shrugged. 'I don't know. You any beef steaks – pork chops, even?'

The man's eyes settled on Jeryd for a moment, then he

nodded, shifted to one side of his stall to retrieve something. When he returned, on the flat of his palm sat two fat, juicy steaks. 'Just the thing,' Jeryd confirmed, reaching into his pocket for a Lordil. 'Keep the change.'

The trader growled his appreciation after he inspected the coin, then he wrapped the steaks in paper and passed them across to Jeryd, who tucked them under one arm and continued on his way to buy some wine.

*

Later, with candles giving their shoddy apartment an aura of nostalgia, he thought he might make the dinner a success. It wasn't ideal, this place, but with some good lighting and incense it could become rather romantic. *You can make the most of any situation*, Jeryd reflected, *when you seek to instil a little romance. The good investigator is always up for any challenge* ... He'd even bought a biolume just for the hell of it, and the creature oozed gelatinously in a glass jar like a weird living lamp.

He realized that he was even beginning to get attached to the place, and perhaps, with a little effort, he and Marysa might make love like they used to in the old times. Their relationship wasn't quite as perfect as it used to be back in the day, some hundred and fifty-odd years ago, but since they'd repaired things between them a few months previously, they were at least considerably more intimate. They were starting to read the little gestures again, to hold eye contact a little longer. Gentle touches across the other's cheek or ones directed against the side of the neck. Their relationship was being rebuilt in the little details, which made nights like this all the more important.

In rolled-up shirtsleeves, his tail extended well out of the way for fear of splashing it with hot oil, Investigator Rumex Jeryd set about the task of making dinner for two. Marysa had begun to hum a tune in the other room while she stoked the fire, a song he couldn't recognize, but it felt as if they'd begun dating all over again. Her body was becoming noticeably better toned with her martial-arts training, and she was now confident, said she could handle herself in any physical confrontation, a claim that left her open to his innuendo. Though it also helped make him more conscious of his own expanding paunch.

Who'd have thought an old coot like me could still feel like a kid falling in love at this age . . .

He unwrapped the steaks and laid them sizzling in the hot pan. He turned to unhook some dried rosemary, which wasn't as cheap as it should have been.

Damn rip-off traders.

Within a minute, something began smelling bad.

He lifted the pan away from the stove immediately, and examined the steaks with his investigator's eye.

Marysa popped her head around the doorway. 'They're not done already, are they? You only just put them on!'

Jeryd gave a bitter laugh. 'Something's not right with these.'

She approached him, laid a hand on his shoulder, her perfume a pleasant contrast to the smell emanating from the pan. She said, 'Has the meat gone off?'

'No, I bought these steaks earlier, didn't I, and they looked fresh to me. I mean, they weren't dried out or anything.' It then struck him that the smell reminded him of something – and not something from a wholesome source.

'It can't be . . .'

'What?' Marysa demanded.

'No, it just can't be.'

'What?' she repeated, now irritated. 'What do you think it is, Rumex?'

Jeryd placed the pan very carefully on the table, and closely scrutinized the contents. 'I remember a similar smell from funeral pyres . . . which suggests this meat is either human or rumel. I can't be sure though – perhaps it's just some unusual breed of livestock.'

Marysa squealed in shock. 'That's vile, it can't be hominid.'

'Well, I don't know.' Jeryd put the pan aside. 'But in the morning, I'm going to find out where the hell the trader got this from. As I've often said, the good investigator always follows his nose.'

TWENTY-FIVE

Streets were cold and narrow. The doorways of the stores were empty, apart from drunks or the insane hopeless.

Brynd was intoxicated by his own nervousness. He carried none of the money Malum had asked for and he had come without telling the others. This was something he had to do alone. So what if he died; the prospect of death seemed to lessen the pressure of having to protect this city, the pressure of being what he was in a world that hated such beings.

Brynd sauntered into an empty iren site two streets away from the Victory Hole tavern, a vast cobbled courtyard with three-storey buildings built up along each side, with only one or two windows showing lantern light. There was a chill to the air and he paused for some time, listening to the sound of his own breath.

Someone hailed him by rank, the sudden sound resonating within the enclosed space. Malum was leaning against the wall over in one corner, arms folded, face hidden behind a mask. 'You got my money, commander?'

Flakes of snow were beginning to fall with a steady dignity.

'I'll tell you what I have: I have fuck all for you.'

Malum showed no sign of agitation. 'Then why're you here? Got yourself a death wish?'

'I'm here to clear my name, to prove myself more of a *man* than the likes of you, who don't understand the concept of fighting on behalf of other people. Remember, cowardice takes many forms.'

'Cunt,' Malum grunted. Something changed in his tone then, some bitterness surfacing. Brynd could only see his mouth, how it had tightened. Malum whispered something into the darkness behind him. With his booted heel he pushed himself away from the wall, and strutted into the centre of the empty courtyard.

'I bet you've probably not come alone, either,' Brynd taunted, 'too scared even to take on someone you consider beneath you. Shows how much of a man you aren't. Confirms everything I've been hearing about you and—'

'You've heard of my reputation?' Malum suggested. 'People fear me with good reason.'

'I've seen you fight,' Brynd admitted, remembering the man's performance in the underground. 'You act tough, but it's sloppy technique, and I'm willing to take that on. Tell you what, if I beat you – you get your men fighting for the city. Besides, your little plan won't work – we're already dealing with any rumours about me you'll spread. You're not the only one with influence here.'

'Too much talking,' Malum grunted.

Shadows against the wall: more thugs arriving. Brynd could smell arum weed, hear the shuffle of boots as they filed in.

'You and me, or are you going to get your gang alongside you?'

'They won't fight as long as it's just you and me.'

A messer blade was shaken free from Malum's sleeve, and just then his teeth seemed to alter strangely – two prominent fangs – now snarling from beneath his mask. Lunging forward, the man swiped the blade sideways across Brynd's face, but he ducked, grabbed Malum's arm, held it away, gave him a sound thump in the stomach with his free hand. Malum hardly reacted, merely absorbing the powerful blow. They separated and Brynd drew his sabre, twice as long as Malum's weapon.

'Hey, catch.' A voice from the shadow, followed by a hurled sword. Malum caught it, and just then several torches were lit. Fifty or so of Malum's men were leaning against the perimeter of the empty iren site, their faces hidden by hoods or masks. Eyes glimmered in the torchlight, and Brynd noticed how they all possessed unnatural fangs.

Brynd lunged forward following a modern technique he'd been working on, leading into the flank so that he was in control of the sequence. He swung for Malum's ribs, then his shoulder, aiming to kick his legs away from under him, but the thug was too nimble, too clever, backing off at angles. Controlled moves from studied routines, swift and relentless. But Brynd slipped on the cobbles, then realized he was on the defensive.

Malum became remorseless, slicing in at all degrees, a fusion of random styles to make the most of what he could snatch from the situation. The man was even trying to bite him – here was rage, nothing but pure, undisciplined rage.

Their frenzied movements clattered across the confines of the courtyard. Malum made a lengthy slice, and Brynd jumped up to avoid his legs being taken out. Then as he landed he brought his heel to Malum's thigh, pushing him backwards.

Whistles and cheers at the periphery of his mind, the calls of encouragement from the gang members, Malum's name yelled on all sides, and it spurred the thug on – his fury becoming more apparent in every thrust, retreat, thrust. Their swords rang out, metal skidding, till a sudden flick of a blade caught Brynd's jaw and he stumbled backwards. Malum paused for breath. Blood had been drawn, but the wound healed in an instant. Brynd wiped it off with his sleeve.

He could see the reaction by Malum's open mouth. 'That's right, I'm enhanced. Or didn't you know that? Still want to carry on?'

While the animal-thug stood gaping, Brynd moved in once again, aiming for his neck. Again defended, again turned into an attack, but Brynd then forced Malum into a set of moves. Suddenly Malum twisted his ankle on the slick cobbles, stumbling and dropping his sword. Brynd kicked the weapon away, glaring.

'Finish it, queer,' Malum grunted.

For a moment Brynd considered that, but threw his own sword away to one side. There were certain things he had to prove now. 'We fight with fists. Or are you scared you'll get aroused by close contact with a man?'

'Fuck you.' Malum lunged towards him and knocked him to the ground. Brynd smacked his head on the stone, but he immediately recovered, concentrating on the fight. He kneed Malum violently in the chest sending him sliding sideways. Brynd was already standing ready as the other shifted to his feet, and kicked him in the ribs, but Malum grabbed his foot, and sent them both tumbling. Malum leapt sideways but he was wearying by now and Brynd suddenly pinned him to the ground, then punched him hard in the face twice. 'I'll let you live if you get your men to fight!' He couldn't stop eyeing the man's fangs.

Brynd paused for a response.

Malum's face was scored badly across his lip. 'Fuck. You. Queer.'

Brynd lost control, punching Malum in the face repeatedly, but Malum merely laughed. *Was the fucker insane?*

An arrow shot suddenly across in front of Brynd's face, inches away, and skidded away across the cobbles. It was only then that he noticed the man's gang advancing—

– Then men on the opposite side of the iren, Night Guard soldiers, ten of them, running over to Brynd's side. Lupus was there, hauling Brynd away from the gang leader, who was struggling to his feet. 'You keep behaving like that, and you're a thug just like them. You understand, commander?'

'What?'

'We're here to protect people of the Empire, not kill them.

You are not here to exchange blows with a thug. *You are a Night Guard soldier.*'

'I'm no hero, private. That much is clear.' Heaving breaths. 'What are you doing here?'

'Heard you were in a spot of bother, sir.'

Brynd watched dumbly as his men formed a protective wall against the gang, tried not to feel sentimental as he realized how his men were standing by him.

Malum shambled back into the midst of his gang members, wiping his broken mouth. Like two opposing tribes, the Night Guard and gang stared at each other across the courtyard.

A bell rang abruptly, from the Citadel. Brynd instantly knew what it meant.

Ignoring Malum, he turned to lead his troops back towards the barracks, at a run through the freezing night-streets of the city. More soldiers appeared, Dragoons, about twenty of them, and they were sprinting toward the docks.

Brynd located their commanding officer and demanded a report.

'Small attack unit, sir – a boat heading for Port Nostalgia. No more than ten of them aboard.'

'The Okun?'

'Aye, sir.'

They scythed a path through the bitter chill, along the dark streets, preparing weaponry. Brynd realized he himself wasn't armed properly.

The Night Guard soldiers didn't refer to prior events, though Nelum was now here, leading the group.

Shouts began arising from the district of Shanties, and from Port Nostalgia. The snow abated. Two minutes later, they rounded a corner and were presented with a view of the docks, where a unit of soldiers was already engaged in combat. Thankfully the light of one of the moons broke free of the clouds, and they could see what they were dealing with.

Men were screaming and dying. The last soldiers fell, and only two Okun were left standing, moonlight glinting off their shell-armour and dark claw-blades.

Lupus nocked an arrow, fired it into the neck of one creature where he knew there was no protection. As it collapsed twitching to the ground, he did the same with the other, but this time missed. He tried again but clipped the top of its well-protected head.

Brynd ordered a walled attack. Three privates of the Night Guard formed a line and advanced forwards with locked shields, the commander just behind. The surviving creature made that clicking sound, sparing in its movements until finally provoked into defence, lashing out with its claw-blades.

A soldier collapsed screaming, but the other two – including the newly promoted Tiendi – managed to force the creature back, then hack it down. A moment later Brynd himself stepped forward to assess the situation. The fallen soldier was severely injured in his shoulder, a deep wound that would take time to recover from, even an enhanced Night Guard.

Offshore hovered a boat carrying what looked like several rumel and possibly another Okun, and it was retreating, slowly moving away from the vessels packing the harbour. A swing around a rock and it was gone.

Brynd assessed the situation: twenty-three dead soldiers. Two civilian casualties. Ten dead Okun.

Scouts had returned reporting no sign of further attacks, so he ordered a garuda to patrol the shore in confirmation. He demanded dense patrolling of the area from now on, and for garudas to find that missing boat.

Brynd turned to his soldiers. 'This was a feint. I think they wanted to observe our response. They've little knowledge of us, like we've little knowledge of them.'

'They were happy to sacrifice ten of their own then,' Nelum agreed. 'Annoyingly they left no survivors to inform us about their fighting methods or reveal how they got here without being seen. And why use a boat? I would have thought if they were basically crustacean-based then . . .'

'Perhaps their body armour is too heavy,' Brynd suggested, suddenly aware of how cold it was becoming. Dragoons and Night Guard milled around in the aftermath, clearing bodies from the harbour, then loading them on carts. More civilians had gathered, but were held back by Dragoons, and one woman wearing a headscarf started wailing loudly as she realized her husband had been killed.

There may well be a lot more grieving widows soon.

Brynd turned and sought out Lupus, who was busy helping with the removal of the Okun. 'Private, a quick word.'

'Sir.'

They stood away from the hubbub, under the shelter of a boarded-up rope store. 'I wanted to give you my personal thanks for what you did earlier.'

Lupus nodded. 'I hope you didn't object to being followed – Nelum saw you leave and just wanted to check you were safe, what with the disappearances.'

'Did he now? Well we discovered tonight that it's a fine line between being a soldier and being a thug. We must keep disciplined, and you two kept me that way. You both have my deepest thanks for your act.'

'I would rather you killed the bastard, of course,' Lupus replied. 'Sir, I heard those accusations in the iren . . . the things he said . . .'

Had Nelum said anything? 'I was only taunting him. You have to rise above these things, and find mental weaknesses in their armour. He was deeply unstable. I think it was because of my skin-tone, originally. People often take umbrage to my whiteness.'

'Sir, even if those things were true, I want you to know . . . I'd still follow your command.'

'Such open-mindedness is admirable, private. But not necessary in this case.'

Lupus fell back in line with the others, who waited for the next command. Up above, the second moon came out, and both Bohr and Astrid offered their illumination of damaged Port Nostalgia. Brynd was acutely aware that this was only the beginning.

Twenty-Six

As he headed for the church, Nelum noticed Private Lupus shuffle away from the barracks with his face half hidden under his hood.

'Out late tonight, private?'

'Lieutenant, I, uh . . . I'm heading out on a quick patrol . . . Well, actually it's personal business – and the commander sanctioned it.'

Nelum nodded and watched the private continue on his way through the snow-filled streets. The number of patrols had increased recently, equipped with hand-held bells to warn against further attacks.

Nelum had known Lupus for a few years, and reckoned he seemed rather disturbed of late. Rumour had it that he was seeing some woman, an old flame living in the city, and Nelum didn't mind that, so long as it didn't interfere with his professional work. Though it seemed a damn silly time to be having an affair: what was the point of falling in love, in a city that might soon be doomed?

He hailed a fiacre that rattled across much of Villiren, before he continued on foot. He passed two homeless men smothered in blankets inside a doorway. Then an entire family huddled around a fire blazing in a metal drum. When they asked him for spare change he could only walk on.

The church dominated the surrounding streets here. Old architecture loomed, imposing a sense of history on the city.

Its mullions and transoms were some of the finest he'd ever seen, and its enormous lancet-shaped windows were awe-inspiring. He marvelled at its glory. Above the finely sculpted entrance to the Jorsalir church was a parvise with a light burning inside, warm and inviting, and he headed towards it.

A moment later Nelum stood inside the entrance, smelling the history beyond. He studied by candlelight the massive murals that covered the walls with faded colours and shapes. He placed a Sota coin in the box labelled 'Offerings'.

Everything here was familiar, a trigger to his memories. He remembered walking through similarly ornate chambers to reach the libraries in the vast private academies in Villjamur. In all those years after his mother died, bringing him into this world, his father frequently urged him to become an academic, that he should train with the eschatologists or genethlialogists. In that strict Jorsalir household, it was even mooted that he join the priesthood, and more than once the young student received a curt slap for scoffing at the notion. The irony that his father had been a failed priest in his youth was not lost on Nelum during those times, and he could forgive the man for taking his anger out on his own lost opportunities. But Nelum had shunned all that, eventually shunned the money his father was ready to throw at him to study. Instead he chose to enlist as a soldier.

Despite those painful memories, being here brought him a sense of relief, rejoicing that there could be such beauty in this city. History was present in these walls, deep within the Ancient Quarter. Images of the founder gods, Bohr and Astrid, two of the ancient Dawnir race two hundred thousand years ago, their names now attributed to the two moons. Representations of the rumel wars, fifty millennia later, before even humans existed. Depictions of the Máthema and Azimuth civilizations, from over thirty thousand years ago, two immense kingdoms that possessed everything, that worshipped mathematics and had technology far superior to that of the present day, only to be brought to their knees by crop failures and war – a harsh warning against excessive reliance on technology. And finally the Jamur Empire, now known as the Urtican Empire, a tradition of greatness of which he himself was a part. He was proud of that fact – everyone was in the Night Guard.

And here was his dilemma: that the commander of the Night Guard, the most senior military figure, was someone whose lifestyle troubled the prestigious qualities becoming to the Empire, and its most sacred doctrines.

Nelum remembered the whispered conversations of the past. There had always been rumours from soldier to soldier matching the one Brynd had told him. People had seen him go to this place or that over the years – never a direct sighting, of course, but he had thought he could ignore it. The man fought well, led well; these things weren't important for a while. Some spoke of a man back in Villjamur who Brynd would visit some evenings, but if the Night Guard could contain the problem then their name would not be tarnished. Only thing was, the rumours were feral.

Without saying so, earlier Brynd had confirmed Nelum's suspicions about him. It was there in his mannerisms, in his awkward gestures and his strained voice, and now Nelum could no longer overlook the problem. Nelum only wanted to do the right thing, but no solutions came to mind. He badly needed advice.

'Lieutenant.'

Priest Pias met him as agreed, offering a hand. Nelum kissed it. The mere presence of the learned prelate was calming.

'Priest Pias,' he whispered across the aged knuckles, 'I seek your counsel.'

'Rise, my boy,' the priest replied. 'Follow me.'

*

They drank tea in what seemed like a golden room: candlesticks, portrait frames, gold leafing on the chairs and plates – everything shimmered with wealth. So many times he had felt the same in Villjamur, even when, as a young child not knowing better, he was reluctant to go to church. Once again he felt spellbound by the beauty and the incense and the arcane texts.

When Priest Pias asked Nelum about his visit, the lieutenant told him about the allegations regarding his commander.

The old priest nodded gravely, a rhythm of deep contemplation. 'That is, of course, a major sin in the eyes of the Jorsalir church.'

'I understand, sir. The problem is that he is working wholeheartedly to unite people of this city into strengthening their defences, and he is training the local soldiers expertly. He aims to save this fringe of the Empire from falling into . . . From whatever evils lie beyond.'

'Yes, I am quite aware of his intentions. He has already come here asking my help.'

'Sir, I'm not sure I see the church's role in any of this.'

'Of course not.' A smile. 'Which means the old methods work! As the Empire evolved, it couldn't simply rely on the whip hand any more to persuade subjects to behave in acceptable ways. One doesn't build a policy of imperialism unless one is *seen* to be fair. There is democracy now, they would cry. There exists the illusion that they had a say in political affairs. So to control people's minds they needed other means of persuasion. Including the Jorsalir church.'

Nelum was aghast at this blatant manipulation of people's spiritual beliefs.

'Do not lose your faith, my dear lieutenant. This is not to question the ultimate word of Bohr. Our synergy with the Empire has allowed our church to flourish over thousands of years. It is a symbiosis that serves everyone's interests, and that's why we remain so close – a link that helps keep cultists at bay too.'

The gold glitter in the room was suddenly overbearing, refracting the candlelight too harshly into Nelum's eyes. 'I was never aware of such a depth of rivalries between the cultists and the church. Granted I have spent many of my years in active service.'

'We try not to make it all that public, but it is no secret that the church disdains those who propagate false histories – cultists especially.'

'I had no idea . . .'

'The threat of schisms exists. We currently have one developing on the more southerly islands, a sect led by a priest called Ulryk is promising to be quite the danger . . .' The old priest paused and composed himself – *has he said more than he should have done?* 'But let us now consider dangers closer to home: the nocturnal habits of the albino commander.'

'Indeed, sir,' Nelum agreed. 'So, what do you suggest?'

The priest stared into deep space for a long moment before he began to quote. '"So Bohr let them go ahead to do whatever shameful things they desired. As a result, they did vile things with each other's bodies. So they worshipped the things Bohr made but not Bohr himself, and Bohr left them to their shameful desires. Men committed shameful abominations with other men and suffered within themselves the penalty they fully deserved. Bohr abandoned them to their evil minds and let them do things that should not be done. Their lives became full of many kinds of wickedness, sin, greed, hate, envy, murder, fighting, deception, malicious behaviour, and gossip. They are haters of Bohr, insolent, proud, and boastful."'

The scripture was vaguely familiar to Nelum.

Priest Pias continued. 'In our texts it is stated clearly that such acts are intrinsically wrong and against nature. The punishment according to the law of the Empire and to our own scriptures is execution of the guilty. Given his public position the exposure of your commander could bring shame and humiliation on your regiment, and on the army in general. Indeed, the whole structure of governance might be affected.'

'Surely you'd be able to manipulate the ill effects?'

Judging by the curl of his lip the priest seemed to like that remark. 'I appreciate the difficulties. We need his skills in the coming crisis – I understand. We must think of the citizens. So for now, let him help us, but presently we should dispose of him. Meanwhile, do keep me informed.'

Nelum bid his farewell to the priest, kissing the old man's fingers before retreating outside into the cold, then a hard slog through heavy snow, past the homeless and on to his next destination, wondering when might be an appropriate time for him to engineer the fate of his commanding officer.

*

'I'm seeking a man called Malum,' Nelum explained to the barman, dropping a couple of coins on the counter. The tavern was dingy, a real spit-and-sawdust joint, with currently barely a customer in it. Two old men sat in companionable silence at the far end of the room, which stank of stale beer.

The return glance the barman gave him said he either knew Malum or at least knew of him. He slung down his cloth and leaned over the bar. He glanced to either side before grunting some directions, then he leaned back and said sourly, 'That's all I'm telling you.'

Nelum nodded, thanked the man, and headed out into the street, where he hailed a fiacre. But when he mentioned the location, the driver refused to take him there directly, only to somewhere close by.

'That's fine,' Nelum agreed, wondering at the mystery surrounding this gang leader.

It was a bone-rattling ride across the cobbles of the city in a once-plush carriage, whose dignity had long since faded. Snow brushed against the window as Nelum became lost in his own thoughts. He still tortured himself about what he must do, weighed up what the priest had said and what he himself felt was right.

The fiacre came to a halt and he turned to pay the driver, before regarding his surroundings. As the carriage sped away, he decided this area was not all that bad. Buildings were much the same wherever you went in this city, but this was a comparatively clean area, with a wide plaza, and a concentration of decent shops. A cold wind stung his cheeks as he moved on, studying his surroundings, following the route outlined by the barman.

Three doors along from one intersection, he knocked loudly on a door positioned between what looked like a shop selling erotic garments and another selling knives. The door opened and a scruffy youth demanded, 'Fuck you want?'

'I need to see a man called Malum.'

'Well, he don't fucking want to see you.'

Another voice from behind, 'Get away from there, kid. Who is it?' A red-haired man shambled up to the door, with his shirt unbuttoned. 'Yeah?'

'It's urgent that I see Malum. I've got money.'

'Sure you have.' The redhead looked him up and down. 'Looks like you're a soldier.'

'Can you ask him, please?'

A lingering pause, then the man stepped away, leaving the vicious-looking kid to watch over him. Nelum decided to wait, uncertain what was going on, but eventually he was beckoned inside.

Two minutes later he found himself sitting at a table surrounded by gang members deep underground. They watched him suspiciously, as a man with a red mask sat down opposite.

'Boys said you were asking for me,' grunted the man, whose mask was some hideous tribal item, giving him an additionally sinister edge. The outer rim of a bruise could be discerned just underneath it.

'That's right. I understand that you received some information regarding the commander of our armies.'

'Fuck should I help a soldier?'

Nelum felt frustrated at his ridiculous arrogance. 'I understand you suspect the albino has certain . . . preferences.'

'He fucks men, you mean?'

'Is it true?'

'Come on now, soldier. I'm not giving information without getting some back. You all fucked off to some conflict last night – why were those warning bells ringing? What does it mean for this city?'

Nelum hesitated for a moment, then revealed the details about the skirmish. 'Ultimately, last night's incident means there'll be an increased military presence out on the streets. So. Is it true about our commander?'

'Course it fucking is. We got a confession from the man-whore who bedded him. Got two of my lads following your albino. Saw what he got up to, more or less.'

Nelum had half hoped that he would hear otherwise. 'Why should I trust what you say?'

'Should I care?' Malum replied. 'I've no business with you anyway. I gain nothing out of telling lies. I want that albino dead – and, for sure, the gangs won't fight for a pervert like him. Think about it: why would he come alone to fight last night if he was innocent?'

Nelum nodded, absorbing the information, scanning the sentences for logic, then reached into one of his pockets. He retrieved a purse of coins, dropped it on the table. 'For your help,' he explained.

'I'll take it.' Malum slid his chair back. 'But it's not much to me. I've got more money than you could even begin to imagine.'

Twenty-Seven

'No refunds!' the trader insisted, holding up his palms towards the descending snow. The skies had turned a dull grey, and Jeryd's mood wasn't any more colourful.

'I'm not after a refund,' Jeryd said firmly, 'I just want to know where you got this meat from.'

'No say.' The trader frowned.

Jeryd sighed as a fiacre rattled along behind him. He loosened his collar, to display the medallion of the Inquisition, making sure it was clear for the trader to see. 'Investigator Rumex Jeryd of Villiren Inquisition. Now, will you tell me where you damn well got your meat from? Or do you want carting off to spend the rest of the week pissing into a bucket in the corner of some gaol cell?'

'I can't tell you. I . . . scared.'

Jeryd frowned. *What the hell is he scared of?* 'I'm not sure I follow you.'

'No say.' The man's eyes were wide; now and then he'd flick sideways glances towards the neighbouring alleyway as if he was being watched.

'If you're frightened, we can protect you,' Jeryd offered. 'The Inquisition will stop anyone from harming you as an informant.'

'Very good.' The trader gave a hollow laugh. 'You think Inquisition tough, yeah? Not so tough as him. Not as scary.'

Jeryd grabbed him by the scruff of the neck and pulled him

close to his face. 'If you don't give me a name, I'm going to haul you in for selling strange meat, so don't fuck with me.' He pushed him away.

The trader scribbled something down on a piece of paper, before he backed off, palming the air helplessly, and disappeared down an alleyway, abandoning his stall.

Jeryd read the note he had been given. It said simply 'Malum'.

*

He had some paperwork to catch up with, and Nanzi was already waiting with his morning tea – a gesture he couldn't get enough of. She was bundled up in various dreary shades of brown, a cardigan overlaying a shirt, and one of those long woollen skirts she always wore.

When she enquired as to his romantic night in, he merely shrugged it off.

'I'm not the romantic type,' he lied, knowing his entire existence seemed a futile attempt to peel back the layers of his own sense of nostalgia.

'Tell me,' he asked her, 'is there any gang leader the street traders are particularly afraid of?'

'I've heard things . . .' She glanced across to the door, as if checking it was closed. 'There's talk in there, occasionally . . .' She tilted her head, indicating the rest of the Inquisition. 'Some of the gangs keep good control over a lot of things going on in the city, let's put it that way. I don't know any specific details, but if payments were being made by the gangs to the Inquisition, to turn a blind eye to some of their more violent activities, it would not surprise me. But sometimes it is better not to ask about names in this organization – that would be heavily frowned upon, but I myself refuse to be caught up in such matters.'

'Glad to hear it,' he observed. 'The good investigator always keeps well away from the temptations of such underhand dealings.' He wasn't at all surprised to learn that this sort of thing went on in a city as unruly as Villiren. The only question for someone like Jeryd, who increasingly convinced himself that his position here was only temporary, was how deep it all went. If the gangs were too strongly linked to the government, there would be no point trying to clean things up. He was, after all, attempting to lie fairly low, just in case any of his recent dealings in Villjamur came back to haunt him.

'Is there any particular reason you need to find out more about these gangs?'

'I came across some bad meat,' Jeryd replied finally. 'Bought some steaks of questionable origin from a trader who wouldn't open up. Probably nothing in it, but I just want value for money. This'll be pursued in my free time of course – everything done by the book.'

'Do you have a lead?' Nanzi asked cautiously.

'I've got a name. Malum.'

'King of the underworld,' Nanzi whispered in awe.

'So I've heard. I'm guessing there's more than a few people in this institution prepared to turn a blind eye to such kings of the underworld. A little detective work is in order.'

*

Jeryd and Nanzi spent the rest of the day chasing rumours.

From bar to bistro to subterranean dens, they found themselves being passed among some of the most brutal-looking characters in the underworld. Gang types: Jeryd knew the look of them all right, the things they were saying to each other through their glances. It helped to have Nanzi with him – they displayed a little more restraint while she was alongside him.

Jeryd made sure that word got around that the Inquisition wanted to talk to Malum. The trail of leads seemed endless, but towards the end of that day Jeryd and Nanzi were provided with a firm address by a scruffy young kid with bad teeth. Not just an address – an address and a booth number.

Strange . . .

The kid insisted, 'Come alone. Lose the woman.' Then he scuttled off into the crowded iren.

Nanzi guided Jeryd through the snow to a back alley somewhere in Scarhouse, then she left him, as requested, alone and without another word. He was grateful for her tactful attitude.

A wooden board hung decrepitly above an iron door, a garishly coloured sign reading 'Peep Show'.

A knock on the door and a hatch slammed open. 'Fuck you want? We ain't open.'

'I'm looking for Malum. I was invited here.' Jeryd glanced furtively behind him as the snow began again, always coming and going in bursts. A fiacre clattered by and Jeryd pulled down his hat; this was no place for him to be seen outside, in a strange city or not.

'You the investigator?' the voice slurred back.

'Investigator Jeryd, yeah.'

The door clunked open and he was beckoned into the darkness by a grubby-looking dark-haired guy barely out of his teens.

'I'm looking for booth three, apparently.' Jeryd held up a slip of paper to the young man, who proceeded to ignore it completely.

The dark corridor smelled vaguely of stale incense. He could feel the enveloping damp. *This place reminds me of an Inquisition gaol.* Voices drifted towards him from rooms out of sight; conversations stuttering to a halt as they walked past. Now and then he heard a groan or two, then strange guttural noises he couldn't recognize.

'In there.' The young man gestured to one side.

'Thanks.' Jeryd now faced a narrow wooden door with the number three carved into it, and stepped inside, closing the door behind him.

A wooden stool had been placed before what looked like a large window; only blackness was apparent beyond. A bucket, some towels, there was very little else, just the bare cold stone. Jeryd shuffled towards the stool and peered at the darkened glass, his pulse quickening in the silence.

The tension mounted as he continued staring into the weird window, but he couldn't discern a thing. He tapped it with his knuckle – this was thick stuff.

Light suddenly sparked and flared on the other side of the glass – where he now noticed a figure sitting slumped in a chair, wearing a stylish long coat, and a mask, half-concealing short brown hair. Lingerie and chains were draped over a meat hook to one side, and three or four silver-framed mirrors leaned against the walls, presenting this well-clad figure from unusual angles.

'Investigator Jeryd,' the man said. 'I hear you've been asking for my name. Got a lot of people asking after me recently – clearly, I'm a popular guy.'

'Yeah, that's correct. You're Malum then?' Jeryd couldn't figure out a way around the glass, which was set deep into the stone. A tiny metal hatch to one side seemed designed for dropping in coins.

'I am indeed. And there's no way in, Jeryd,' Malum replied coolly. 'There's no point looking. They're specially designed by cultists for safety.'

'Safety for who?' Jeryd asked.

'Right now, your own – but mostly for my women.'

'Do they normally just sit there?'

'They strip behind the glass for money, and lonely men gagging for excitement drop a coin in that hatch to the side.'

'And the men . . . ?'

'Watch,' Malum replied, 'or masturbate. There's no sex, the women are protected. Everyone's happy.'

'How come I couldn't see you until you turned that lantern on?'

'Cultist glass – it's good stuff. I got a lot of contacts.' His tone changed. 'Get to business: why were you asking for me by name?'

'Someone gave me your details in connection with some bad meat I was sold.'

Malum laughed. 'That it? Just meat?'

'I've reason to believe that there is meat of questionable origin being circulated in this city. The trader said you helped put it about. All I want to know is where that meat is coming from.'

'You got guts, coming here, asking for this.'

'Either that, but quite possibly because I'm stupid.'

Malum grunted a laugh. 'I like you, investigator. Look, people are beginning to ask those kind of questions, and I don't like to have my name associated with such triviality. Tell you what, you leave me the fuck alone if I give you a name and an address?'

Jeryd could see through the tough-guy talk, but didn't want to anger him. 'Agreed.'

'Voland. That's who we get it from. I've done some business with him recently – other than distribution – and to be honest, I'm not happy with what he provides. He's known to me as the niche-maker, among other things, and he's let me down over poor equipment that just stopped on the job. I'm more than happy to see trouble go his way, by way of the Inquisition. So you see I'm not unreasonable.'

'What did he do?'

'You ask a lot of questions.'

'That's what I get paid for – not that you can call it much.'

'People have niches – and remember, I've got a permit from the portreeve for this establishment. Look in booth seven on your way out, and you can see some of Voland's work. I'll put the light on and activate the glass. And never ask for my name again – otherwise I can't vouch for your safety.'

Light faded to black, then something clicked inside the

hatch to one side. Jeryd opened the little drawer and picked up a piece of paper with an address written on it. 'Thanks,' Jeryd said, though he didn't know if Malum was even there any more.

Voland ... a strange name.

Pocketing the note, Jeryd got up and exited the room. He lit a match to navigate the corridor and found booth seven at the far end. He twisted the handle and the door slipped back smoothly. Behind the display area, a soft light shone down from above, illuminating a vibrant, crimson-walled area. Jeryd approached thinking about niches and what that might mean, when he spotted the woman's body on the floor.

No, not a woman.

A ... *thing.*

Jeryd pressed his hands against the glass to steady himself, his stomach churning at the sight. Garbed only in white lingerie, the woman-creature possessed the legs of some animal, like a horse – though he couldn't tell precisely. Hunched in a foetal position, on closer inspection her entire body possessed the texture of fine fur, splattered with blood, a trail of which issued from her mouth. A horn protruded from her forehead, like in some mythical beast, while blood-stained blonde hair tumbled across the floor. And all of this – all of this mess – was highlighted by three other mirrors allowing a full view of the vileness on display.

What the hell was this Voland producing? What kind of person ... what kind of city permits this stuff? Who would even pay to see this?

Niche-maker.

Jeryd ran to a bucket in one corner of the booth and promptly vomited.

Twenty-Eight

Dead forest after dead forest, and littered with snow: it was a landscape on constant repeat. Anything deciduous had long been killed off, and only various evergreen species persisted, banking up steep slopes into the dark distance. The horses helped them trudge northwards through the thick woodlands of Folke, the beasts insouciant of the hostile environment, just plodding along, showing fright at nothing.

Randur felt as if the four of them were now quite alone, despite these elusive beings that shifted behind serried rows of tree trunks. For the first couple of hours each day, Munio would hardly shut up, but after that they found the contemplative silence comforting. The only utterances then were instructions to guide them along certain well-trodden routes, or over difficult terrain.

Metal constructs, gargantuan rusted skeletons, their foundations buried deep in the earth, leaned towards the sky. Blood-tinged sunlight filtered through their even-latticed configurement, and the travellers' path took them directly underneath, between the thick shadows. Vegetation had not fully reclaimed these relics, the first exposed structures he'd witnessed in a long time.

People talked of such remains being found off the southern coast, but they had long since formed artificial reefs, and become almost living things once again, contributing to the natural cycles. Rumours intimated there were also abandoned cities to be found, civilizations completely lost to the ocean. Before him now was a sense of history on Earth so compelling that he felt as though he himself barely existed at all.

Stranger, though, was how last night he'd experienced weird dreams of fur-covered creatures – with wings – swooping down to stare at him; and when he lurched awake to see what the hell they were, there was only the eternal calm of the night sky above him. It had happened for two nights in a row now, as they sheltered among ancient ruins. Their ghostly presence disturbed him.

*

On the third day they joined old pathways that would die away suddenly into the overgrowth. They'd cut their way through two small, dead communities, then along open tracks between desolate logging camps, or scarred and ragged open-cast minescapes. Rika and Eir both seemed eager to understand the Empire's diverse territories better, and questioned why these communities were all abandoned.

Randur told them just what the Empire signified out here.

'When the Imperial armies claimed this island hundreds of years ago they declared they'd impose infrastructure and order. They sent the local tribes packing – unless they were considered *civilized*, which, roughly translated, meant abandoning their old ways for those of Villjamur. Quite a few were also forced into slavery.'

'I heard of prisoners committing serious atrocities against soldiers who merely asked them to work . . .' Rika said, defensively.

'Did you ever question, my lady, the source of your information? They were indigenous races who didn't want foreign soldiers disrupting their communities. Empire folk claimed it'd ensure great wealth for everyone. Well, that great wealth was sucked off to the trading cities, primarily Villjamur and Villiren. And even then it mostly fell into the hands of the few people who controlled the forges, especially those manufacturing weapons of war. They made a fat pile of cash, and more war always meant more business. They relied upon constant warfare, in fact. In the real histories, ones that weren't rewritten by Empire-employed scholars, the people of Folke were heavily repressed and their will broken through season after season of starvation. A few local rebellions brought more military here, and then, a few decades back, once the population had submitted completely, the formerly booming markets changed – or the Council collapsed them. Different metals were now required, and these original mining communities were killed off. Just like that. And large numbers of people were forced to leave the island. So that's why you'll see ghost towns all across this island, and maybe it's the same on other islands, too, I don't know.'

Munio remained utterly silent, already knowing this potted history.

'And the people out here ... are they angry with the Empire?' Rika asked.

'Probably just bitter these days, more than anything. But what can they do? They've no control over their own lives. But what annoys me, you know, was back in Villjamur no one had a clue about what was going on here. They just heard the party line about the fringe world from the Council, and never thought to ask questions. The news recovered was exaggerated or incorrect. They assumed that anyone who tried to protest or resist the oppression was simply encouraging evil. Those who objected to Imperial ways were branded terrorists.'

'If you hate the Empire so much,' Rika said, 'why are you now helping me?'

'Because Eir wants to help you, and if that's what she wants, so be it.' He looked across at his love, but she didn't know what to say to that. He'd already sacrificed a lot for her. It was a dangerous way of thinking – and he knew it – but his love was all he had right now. 'Besides, you personally have played little role in history, and you yourself know how tricky people in the Council can be.'

'I believe I can change things,' Rika said. 'Once I'm back in Villjamur, back in power.'

'Best thing you can do, if you ask me, is decentralize that power. Just give the people back the land that was theirs.'

Rika looked thoughtful, and they continued in silence.

*

Down faded paths suffocated by ferns, along steep hillsides with rocks jutting from them like black broken bones. Snow staggered in waves across this hiemal forest.

Near dusk on the fifth day, they decided to take refuge in the ruins of what appeared to have once been a hunting lodge. Constructed alongside a sheer cliff face, it was crowded with spindly ulex plants, and leaned outwards as if the rocks behind had become animated and were pushing it forward. Coloured pebbles were mixed in amongst the masonry, the windows were all long since shattered, and the door was broken – but at least it was shelter.

A storm came, sudden and rough, ripping up the landscape like a wild thing. They lit a fire in the old hearth using sulphur and lime, and Eir, without much idea of what she was doing, began to cook three hares Munio had caught earlier. That was despite Randur's nervous suggestion that he should continue to look after culinary matters. Rika sat down cross-legged in a corner, soon in deep contemplation. While the old swordmaster scrutinized a map, Randur boarded up the broken windows as best he could, with some fragments of wood. It felt good to be doing this – making some progress, settling in. Jokes shuttled back and forth rapidly between himself and Munio, as they slowly rebuilt their relationship.

They lit lanterns. Inside there were remnants of ornaments, paintings, furniture, riding and hunting implements, but closer examination showed they had all been purposely damaged, leaving Randur wondering at the cause of this destruction.

'What d'you suppose happened here then?' Randur lifted a tin plate to examine the decay in the half-light. 'There are even teeth marks in the metalwork.'

'Someone must have been pretty hungry,' Eir suggested. 'Will our horses be all right, left outside in this weather?'

'They'll be fine,' Randur said. 'They've some shelter out back, and I've fed them amply. How's our progress so far, Munio?'

'Good,' the old man said, his face unreadable. 'Right on schedule.'

'You sure it's the most direct path?'

Munio turned and glared at him. 'We must not stray from this route if we ever want to get there, let alone stay alive. Or do you still not trust this old mind?'

'I trust you.'

'Good. Now, do we have any wine left?'

'You drank the last of it last night.'

Munio grunted, and began studying the map again. He had been very diligent in making sure their progress went according to his schedule, but where this sudden burst of efficiency had come from, Randur hadn't a clue. Perhaps it was because all the wine had gone, and this was Munio's natural state – sober and angry and driven.

Eir brought over the cooked meat, her gold necklace glittering in the candlelight as she leant across the table. The food was burnt on the outside and undercooked inside. 'Just another minute back on the fire and we're ready,' he said to encourage her – and also so he wouldn't spend the rest of the night vomiting out into the storm.

Rika finished off her meditation, and engaged with Munio in ascertaining their route. She followed a thick line with her finger and asked, 'Is this a road used by the military? I would rather we kept away from anywhere the army might be.'

Munio shook his head, staring down at the charts. 'We have no choice except to cross it, but there are no soldiers in this section of the island. The road was mainly used for transporting ore.'

With a cautious pride, Eir brought the food from the fire again. 'I think the wind has died a bit, Rand. Would you like to check to see if the storm's eased and look at the horses?'

Randur sighed. *Would you like to...?* was, it seemed, a common question in these close relationships – something he was so far unused to – and the actual answer was of course, *No, I would not like to. I have just spent the last half-hour blocking out any thoughts of the bastard storm. I would rather stay warm and dry, thank you very much.*

'Yes, dear,' he offered meekly, then shuffled through to the next room and over to the front door.

He kicked away two thick logs helping to secure it and unhooked the door. In the dim lighting of the glade stood several figures, glancing about. His heart flipped. He closed the door carefully, so it wouldn't make a noise. Taking a peep through a gap in the wood, he could discern several people with ... pure white skin? What on earth were they – albinos?

Another look: men and women, naked, very slender. They were clearly visible against the backdrop of the dark forest, but when they moved against drifts of snow, they were utterly camouflaged. Their movements seemed jerky. Behind them, the trees stirred loudly in the breeze.

He beckoned Munio immediately and gestured for the swordmaster to take a look. Crouching to see clearly, Munio gave a start of surprise when he saw them.

'Ghosts?' he gasped.

More came, ten in all now, and they began pointing and gesturing in hand signs like tribesmen out on a hunt, ready to kill – that was no reassuring omen.

'Ghosts, my arse,' Randur grunted. 'Ghosts don't communicate like that.'

'And when, dear boy, have you ever seen a ghost do anything?'

'Good point,' he conceded.

There was a gentle sound over to one side, out of sight, then one of the horses was led forward into the open by two of the white-skinned newcomers. They gathered around the horse – primitive weapons in hand, crude spears and bows, axes crafted from stone – and suddenly the animal shuddered violently, staggered, and collapsed, blood spurting from the artery in its neck. With savagery, the alien people set out about severing the animal's head from its body, their own skins reddening slickly.

Light was fast deserting the sky.

'Shit, what should we do?' Randur hissed, panicking. Defending their shack against those unknown beings seemed a daunting prospect, to say the least, but he was prepared to go out and fight. Without horses for transportation they would soon die out here in the wilds.

Munio eyed him harshly until he ventured a response. 'We're heavily outnumbered. And the four of us could just about fit on three horses . . .'

'So your solution, O great swordfighter, is to sit here and do nothing while they eat all our transport. And then maybe us for dessert.'

'You want to get us killed, Kapp—'

'Stop calling me that! I'm Randur now. And I'm not going to just sit around and do nothing.'

Randur stomped into the other room to inform the sisters of what was happening. Eir hurriedly tied up her bootlaces, then picked up her blade. Rika's face maintained the same calm demeanour as always.

He said to her: 'You fancy helping us this time?'

She shook her head. 'I'm sorry, Randur. It's just not my way.'

Smiling to himself, he nodded his understanding. Soon he

was standing by the door with the other two, ready for combat. Randur opened it and the white-skins immediately, simultaneously, turned to face him. Some of them had dark stains around their mouths where they had gorged themselves on raw horse flesh. Their heads tilted and twitched unnervingly.

'Now what?' Eir whispered. 'It's so hard to see them in this light.'

'The young lady has a point,' Munio said. 'You didn't think that through, did you? Rushing into combat, as always . . .'

'Shut up.' *He's just as bad as Denlin was . . .*

The figures came closer, then fanned out, weapons ready, forming a rough semicircle around the door of the hunting lodge. As they loomed nearer Randur could see them more clearly. They possessed absolutely no pigmentation, and their prominent veins were a clear network visible beneath the pallid surface. Their eyes possessed some disturbing quality that made them actually glow blue. They were humanoid, and frighteningly so in some ways – their movements and their mannerisms and their interactions. A figure in the centre with long colourless hair tried addressing them in a guttural and esoteric language. It sounded like the casting of a spell.

'That horse was ours!' Randur shouted, not quite sure what else to say. He pointed his hand to indicate the remains of the horse.

Tips of trees rattled in the wind. He held out his sword and aimed it at the spokesman. 'Leave us. Just go.'

The figure, now clearly a woman, took several phenomenally slow but light steps forward as if the terrain provided an awkward surface to move on. When she was only an armspan away from Randur, she spoke to him directly, although again he couldn't comprehend any of the arcane sounds uttered. Those blue eyes seemed as if powered by relics. Red trickles streaked her chin and neck like she was salivating the dead horse's blood. Her stare totally captivated him, whether because she was so utterly alien to him, or because there was some deep mental power keeping him transfixed, he couldn't tell.

Randur wrenched his gaze towards Eir, then back again. He did not know what to do next. There was a deep tension filling the air, as if millennia of time had been breached.

'Who *are* you?' he breathed.

The white woman raised her axe and suddenly Randur found himself on the defensive, whipping his blade through her extended wrist. A scream worse than that of any banshee ripped apart the evening air and stilled the weather. The others began to crowd in with their weapons.

As they surged on the three defenders, Randur waded into the melee. His opponents were not strong, almost flouncing away before him, but somehow these creatures always managed to block out his line of attack and push his sword away.

A pause in the combat, a sudden gasp.

Randur turned to see Rika emerging from the doorway with a crude torch in one hand, a vision that imposed itself upon his awareness like the appearance of some holy apparition.

At the sight of the flames, the figures scattered manically, though dragging with them the horse's corpse.

Randur looked round to Munio, and then to Rika, and ... Where was Eir?

A muffled scream from the edge of the forest.

'Fuck, they've got her. Rika, make yourself useful and bring along that torch.'

*

Clustered together, they sprinted along a path parallel to the limestone cliff, with the forest to their right. The snow-covered terrain was utterly aphotic, their vision restricted to several paces in front under the light of the torch. There were faint tracks that the white beings had left behind them, punctuated frequently with drops of blood which Randur hoped originated from the hunks of horse flesh.

Eventually they caught up with a figure lying face-down in the snow. It wasn't Eir, Randur saw with a stab of relief. This was the spokeswoman whose hand he had severed. Lingering over her corpse, they realized she must have bled to death there in the darkness.

They moved on, the tracks accumulating, indicating that the intruders came along this path often. It sloped upwards, to the left, towards the cliff face.

And into the rock caves.

'The hell am I going in there,' Munio muttered.

'Fuck yourself then.' Randur continued forward with Rika, leaving his old tutor outside in the dark. He didn't care what was waiting for him – he would get Eir back, or else die trying.

A few moments later, a cry, 'Wait!'

Eventually Munio caught up, but was breathless because of the additional sprint. He panted, 'I can't have you lot all killing yourselves.'

Rika led the way to the entrance, while Randur gripped his blade in anticipation, switching his mind into that lethal zone, ready to be as savage as was needed. Torchlight picked out stalagmites and stalactites, so it seemed that everywhere they looked they were staring into the jaws of some rock beast. Would they ever find Eir in this maze? The surfaces had been weathered so intensely they looked wrinkled with age. In places the stone sagged. They passed mirror pools and zones drenched with bat excrement. The path itself was smooth from years of use, and Randur reckoned that the white-skinned race might not be merely hiding down here, but actually lived here – which would explain the lack of pigmentation in their skins.

Eventually the same path narrowed, before expanding into a larger cavern. Despite the absence of light they noted several exits on the opposite side.

'Down there, look.' Rika was pointing to a pool of water.

A pile of metallic objects was barely visible, a motionless form lying alongside. Randur's heart missed a few beats. They edged their way down cautiously, after detecting an ancient stairway smoothed out of the rock.

'Eir!' Randur called out, the echo of his voice strangely prolonged.

She lay flat on her back at the foot of the stairway, rubbing one hand over her face.

He sprinted to her side and skidded on to his knees. No blood, no wounds, nothing to denote she'd been suffering any pain. 'How do you feel?' he gasped.

'I'm fine. My head's a little sore, as is my neck, but I'm fine.' He helped her sit up and she buried her head in his shoulder. She was shaking and he did his best to comfort her.

Munio nodded at the sight, and stepped this way and that to check for any sign of the white folk. Randur, too, wondered where they'd gone, then he glanced upwards. 'Bohr . . .' he breathed, and Eir squirmed away from him to follow his gaze.

The torchlight reflected off an array of surfaces, gold, silver, copper, brass – hundreds of coins and ornaments, bangles and rings and necklaces. The hoard was vast, extending like a money-beach. Sloping downwards, it descended into a deep pool which bore evidence of rust, the centuries of decay evident.

Randur lifted Eir up in his arms, and they slowly skirted the rim of the treasure, sifting through it with their feet, totally in awe.

Munio crouched, with a groan, to examine some of the coins in more detail, asking for Rika to lower the torch. 'Some of these . . . they're positively ancient. Long before Emperors

Gulion and Haldun. Look, this even has Goltang's image! Well I never ... I've never seen such ... such wealth,' he muttered.

'My necklace,' Eir whispered, exploring her skin with one hand. 'It's gone. They must have stolen it.'

'They might have even taken you just for your necklace,' Randur suggested. 'These people, it looks like they've been bringing all these trinkets down here for hundreds of years, and without anyone knowing about them.'

'Millennia!' Munio examined a piece under the light of Rika's torch. 'This here is from the Azimuth era.'

Randur noted how the old man was slyly filling his pockets with some of the trinkets, but thought better than to query it.

This seemed unreal, for an entire community to lead little more than a magpie existence, obsessed with anything that glittered. How long ago must they have fallen away from the surface world, evolving to become those ghosts who had butchered the horse?

'Look at these markings on the walls.' Rika brought the light nearer to an area of pale stone that had been noticeably smoothed away. Rock-script bled across it. 'These are deliberate markings, symbols or equations. I've never studied the subject in any detail, but I believe this could be the Máthema language.'

The jagged lines were painted in startlingly bright pigments, yellow and red, the workings of a culture tens of thousands of years old. The notion was absurd, because the writing seemed so fresh.

'Vectors,' Rika whispered. 'Geometric patterns, algebra. Integration ... And yet the graffiti scribbled around it all seem like ...'

'The scrawls of madmen,' Randur mumbled, studying the ragged scripts. Vaguely, one set of symbols spelled out:

$$H \, \Sigma P \, \sqrt{\int}$$

To Randur it resembled 'HELP US' and he was hardly surprised they had gone mad because of all the mathematics . . .

'So is this what eventually happened to that great civilization, then?' Eir suggested. 'I always thought it was crop failure that wiped them out. Surely they couldn't just simply vanish underground while chasing treasure.'

There was a noise nearby, an inhalation of breath, and Randur peered towards the dark exits beyond. Sets of orbs began faintly glowing blue, two, four, then an almost exponential rate of appearance.

'They won't come at us – not with that torch.' Randur glanced to Rika, as if to ask *How long will it last?*

'I've plenty of sulphur and lime, and matches if it runs out,' she said. 'We're quite safe.'

They returned their gaze to the hoard and the script, independently investigating their discoveries. For some time they patrolled the area to investigate.

There was a weird and distant howl, like a fractured incantation. The group glanced at each other and readied themselves for a fight, but nothing followed. A tension persisted in the air, though, as if someone had triggered a relic. Sounds began to act abnormally, voices hanging disturbingly in the gloom. Reverberations of their footsteps became suddenly muted.

Then there was the *clink-clink-clink* of metal.

Coins skimmed back and forth across the floor, rolling over each other, rupturing the surface of the water. Of their own accord, the countless metallic discs began to aggregate and spool, to form a figure.

They massed, stacked and banked up, forming a torso and arms and legs, which then pushed themselves up from the mirror-pool. Resting on top of a vague metal head was a semi-shattered rust-crown.

A coin golem?

The four scrambled back up the stairway as the metal entity

strode out of the pool, its legs and feet buckling rustily as it gained control of its own movements. Randur hovered at the rear, now feeling utterly useless, because it would take much more than a couple of sword strokes to bring this bastard down. Stretching upwards, the thing's head nearly scraped the roof of the cavern, sending individual discs slipping away from it like drops of water.

It began to lumber after them, vast and awkward, and making a hell of a racket.

They ran.

'Stick together and aim for narrow passageways!' Randur shouted. 'I doubt it can fit through many of them.'

'Nor do I,' Munio called back.

Light from the torch dipped as they entered pockets of stale air, retracing their route. The occasional enforced darkness made for an unlikely escape. The path narrowed, opened up again. Randur desperately wanted to pause to check on the state of the golem following them. He could still hear the rattle of metal against stone as its body clipped the outcrops of rock, spilling metal-flesh each time. It was in pursuit, but what he wanted to see was how much of it was left.

The air became fresher and colder as the outside world beckoned them again.

A burst of the glade, the stars above, the glow of snow – and they bundled out, breathlessly slipping and sliding down the slope. Behind them, the coin golem was nowhere to be seen.

Randur felt his heart slapping inside him, and he crouched on his hands and knees until he regained his composure.

'Next time,' Munio growled, 'don't let's go getting any stupid ideas about following things into dark places, right?'

'We had to rescue Eir,' Randur reminded him. 'Anyway, I wanted to know who they were.'

'I'll tell you one thing,' Eir panted, 'I'll be glad not to come across any money again in a hurry.'

As the two of them embraced, Randur peered over her shoulder, into the darkness.

She whispered into his ear, 'Thank you for coming to get me.'

'You're our main cook now,' he replied. 'Can't have you dying on us.'

Twenty-Nine

It was called ballooning, and it was how spiders would colonize new territory.

By the open window of Voland's upstairs study, it shuddered and jutted into its new state, organs and segments unfolding in the small, candlelit room. It watched its shadow, double, triple in size against the wall.

The thing bloomed.

Under its abdomen, four glands drooled out the tougher silk it needed. It could secrete silk from its mouth also, a freak biological error that had somehow occurred, but the toughest material came from underneath. The texture began to solidify, then it quickly spun it, flattened it, elongated it, then globulated it. The spider crawled next to the window, draped those masses of silk outside, manipulated it in the air, till soon the wind caught it, began to fill it and, as this gossamer balloon became five times its size, it was hauled out into the skies above Villiren.

In this form it could not feel the bite of ice-tainted air, and so drifted along with a sense of freedom and comfort. Despite the clear skies, the twin moons were concealed by the bulk of the planet, leaving the creature with the advantage of the night. Tugging at silk strands it tilted the balloon this way and that, sensed changes in the currents above and below and took advantage as and when it pleased. Even around midnight, the city was unsurprisingly alive, so it had to choose its routes carefully so that the taller buildings obscured its passage overhead – not an easy job in Villiren, especially towards the southern section of the city. From up here, the movement of all those people registered visually as minute vibrations, minuscule alterations within hundreds of microclimates.

The spider floated above the border between Scarhouse and Althing, the Citadel almost behind. Knowing that the most proficient military gathered there, it did not want to risk being seen by a skilled archer, brought down in a nest of fine swordsmen. Over the Shanties, behind the old harbour of Port Nostalgia housing retired dockworkers and miners. The side along the coast would be particularly quiet, away from the main hubbub, and with a couple of its legs it began to pull at the threads so as to diminish the volume of the balloon.

Descending onto a small, flat roof, the gossamer collapsed to one side like a deflated corpse. It would need to re-inflate it for the return journey, but for now it untangled itself then scuttled over to the edge of the roof, peering at the movement of people down on the street.

Observing. Waiting.

Voland needed good-quality meat, enough to feed a few families for a little while longer, enough to keep the price of food a little lower. It was never a question of morality – Voland being an intellectual – they were merely serving the greater good. It could always rely on him, having endowed it as his arachnid-construct, injecting it with gifts at which it could only marvel.

There: four men in military uniform, all with bottles in their hands, shambling along an isolated alleyway, leaning in and out of varying shadows of the night, sometimes laughing, ultimately oblivious.

The creature waited for a fiacre to move by, then spat out a strand of thin webbing for a swift descent into the cobbled street below. There, it watched the men from a new perspective, moving away between rows of buildings that loomed high and featureless and continuous. A trilobite ran across its path, waist high and with antennae sifting the air, and when registering its presence the little creature emitted a high-pitched noise. With one hook-shaped foot the spider stamped down on it with a mild, clattering implosion.

One of the soldiers heard the sound, and turned and screamed and drew his sword and quickly the others did likewise. They advanced towards it, a tight line. Then three of them stood still, while one edged forward. The spider spat silk in his face and, as he drew his hands upwards, it spewed its quietus, knocking him askew with one leg. Six legs spread wide, it leapt forward over the other men and shoved them onto the ground with their weapons collapsing around them. Like a leaking wound, the spider oozed silk onto their pain-stricken faces, till soon their desperate movements diminished to a helpless twitching. Then nothing.

So simple, so quick.

It gathered up the first victim, then lined them all up, and for a moment it did nothing but simply watch them, and sense for any reactions.

There were none.

As it was seeing to their transportation, by hauling the bodies around the corner, another figure in similar uniform came by. Savagely it lashed out at the newcomer with its jaws, ripping his torso down the middle. Blood surged across the cobbles as it nudged the corpse behind some piles of waste food.

The spider lugged the bodies one by one up to the roof, then considered the problem of carrying this extra weight. It spent a while spinning more balloons, then bound them together, like giant frogspawn.

Deep night drew across Villiren. Clouds gathered momentum, overpowering starlight. The sound of the tide lapping the harbour walls and up against Port Nostalgia. Gentle sparks of snow drifted down, bringing with them a strange sense of calm.

And as the spider ascended, it sensed that in one of the side streets below, some hybrid human wrapped in black was coughing and retching into a gutter, a silent scream on his lips. But it did not have the time to ascertain what it might be.

*

Brynd kicked the sword away and sent it skittering across the cobbles past Nelum's feet. His lieutenant looked up startled, but at the moment Brynd didn't care. A distance had grown between them anyway, a barrier caused by red-hot secrets and speculations.

Right now, Brynd's concern was for what was happening out on the streets of Villiren. Already his day was ruined. Dawn was some minutes away, the horizon barely any lighter than the cityscape, and here he was, witnessing a scene where yet more soldiers had vanished. Those swords lying on the ground were imperial blades all right, the runework was there for all to see.

The man who had summoned them was a rubicund, elderly type, clothed in thick layers of ragged cloth, with a manic look in his eyes as if he was possessed.

'Just here, right here, yes,' the man muttered, rubbing his hands over and over again. 'I's asleep at first, in the refuse – nice and warm it is there – and then when I hear screams and such, and afterwards I get up and ... like I said, at the end I wanted to be getting away from that one over there.' His outstretched hand was directed towards a slender man standing hunched against the wall, his collar turned up, emitting tendrils of smoke from a roll-up, and there was something distinctly civilized about his appearance.

'He responsible?' Brynd asked.

'Ha! Not him, like, but he can vouch for me.'

Brynd glanced at Nelum and they both stepped over to the stranger.

'You have a name?' Brynd demanded.

Dressed entirely in black and with traces of musk about

263

him, the man regarded Brynd with an almost alien detachment. Although vaguely familiar, his pale face looked distinctly unhealthy, and there was something febrile about his mannerisms.

'Dannan,' he replied.

Suddenly the name rang a bell, and Brynd relaxed. 'You're the leader of a gang, aren't you? I didn't recognize you out here, my apologies. Could you tell me what the hell happened here?'

'Spider,' Dannan announced, then went on to describe the creature in terse whispers. This was a different man from the coxcomb gang leader he had seen across a table. Illness seemed to plague him now. 'Twice as tall as a man at least.'

Brynd could hardly believe what he was hearing. 'Why were you here – some gang business?'

'I was merely enjoying the night. Felt that something was going to happen, is all. Happens to me sometimes.'

'And you, what, just came here to watch this performance? I don't understand why.'

With a disturbing smile, the man nodded. 'I can always sense death, but can do nothing about it.' And he gestured with a wave of his hand towards the corner where he had vomited.

The old man edged into the conversation, though hunching fearfully away from Dannan. 'BanHe, this one – likes death, so the word on the street goes. You have your witch women in Villjamur, doncha? Well this is a male one.'

Brynd was used to the eccentricities on the streets of Villjamur, but back in his home city it was easy to comprehend which were merely wild stories.

Out here, he didn't know what to believe.

*

Eventually the rumel investigator arrived, his hat tipped aslant across his eyes. He was clutching a pastry and, with his mouth half-full he mumbled, 'I got your damn message. You realize what time it is?'

'Four more,' Brynd announced. That message had been sent ages ago, and yet the investigator had stopped off at a bakery to fill his gut even more. 'Four soldiers gone tonight, and these two men here are actual witnesses.'

Information was exchanged between them until Jeryd was fully briefed. He then examined the scene, noted the remnants of a giant trilobite, the discarded swords, the precise location. Now and then he'd nod as if what he was seeing confirmed some hunch. At one point he took a blade from his boot, and scraped some residue off the cobbles. As he returned he grumbled, 'Spider, eh?' The rumel suddenly seemed on edge.

'That's what *they* claim,' Brynd admitted. 'But I'm doubtful something of such a size could remain concealed in a city as populous as this. Someone would be bound to spot something sooner or later.'

'Don't be so sure. You can stay hidden very easily, when you don't want to be seen.' Jeryd held out his blade from which drooped strands of some substance.

Brynd was astounded. 'Looks consistent with what these witnesses have claimed.'

'Doesn't it just,' Jeryd observed. 'And, yeah, I've seen this before, smeared across various rooftops. I was wondering what could produce such a substance, and now with two witnesses claiming to have seen a giant . . . arachnid—'

'Bigger than giant, like!' the old man protested. 'Monstrous!'

'I'll fucking second that,' the so-called banHe cooed. There was an androgynous air to the way he inhaled his roll-up.

'Well, issues of scale aside,' Jeryd continued nervously, 'we have at least got ourselves something to go on.'

'Please share that with us, investigator,' Brynd encouraged him sarcastically.

'It isn't an exact science, this job.' Jeryd wiped his brow. 'Some days you find yourself just chasing your tail – if you have one, that is – and you end up getting nowhere. This might easily be one of those days. But I've seen this substance more than once and I'll tell you this: it's nothing natural. If these guys say you got a ... giant spider picking people off, I'm inclined to believe them.' A pause as he screwed up his face. 'Even this banHe guy – met a lot of his female kin in Villjamur. Good sorts, when you dust away the weirdness, so you can rely on what he says.'

'Oh, I'm sooo fucking thankful,' piped the banHe, reminding Brynd fondly of Kym, a man he knew in Villjamur.

'What do you suggest,' Nelum added, 'in terms of making progress? I have to say, it is rather a shame this spider thing isn't our ally. I once read of how silk was used for treating battle wounds, in the past. It doesn't cause any allergic reactions, being quite inert.'

'Tell you one thing,' Jeryd said, 'if any soldier lived long enough to set eyes on whatever the hell produced this' – he indicated the excessive gossamer strands – 'then he'd probably be damn well frightened to death on the spot. I know I would...'

Nelum persisted, 'Still, if it saves lives—'

'At the moment it's not saving anything,' Brynd interrupted. 'It's taking soldiers from the street, valuable men we need in combat.'

'But the real question is, *why*?' Nelum observed.

'Indeed,' Jeryd added. 'Could do with more of your sort in the Inquisition. So, why is this abnormally large creature specifically hunting down soldiers? Do you think it might have anything to do with the aliens that are invading?'

'I've no idea.' Brynd found he was dealing with too much that he knew too little about these days. 'They could be indeed, because we're not really that certain of our enemy.

But it's not just soldiers that have gone missing. Civilians, too.'

'A fact we must remember,' Jeryd confirmed. 'This isn't specifically an attack on the military. And you have soldiers out on street patrol regularly, yet they've not seen anything like this before, right?'

None of his men patrolling the city had reported anything. Perhaps they feared they would be considered insane. Brynd shook his head in frustration.

'Then it looks like we got ourselves one bastard-cunning killer on the loose,' Jeryd grumbled.

People began moving through the streets as the community gradually woke up, carts rumbling towards the iren, fiacres carrying passengers across the city. Those passers-by wearing masks turned to face the small group with fake and comical expressions.

The rumel investigator set off along the nearby streets a little, pacing back and forth.

Five minutes later Brynd heard Jeryd shouting his rank.

The Night Guard contingent ran to see what the matter was. Jeryd was crouching by a pile of waste, gesturing at the base of the nearby wall.

A mutilated man lay crumpled in cold blood. Rats and trilobites had been picking at his corpse, but what was still evident was that something had cleaved him open with ferocious force. The Dragoon's uniform, ripped to shreds, was all Brynd needed to see.

*

Jeryd liked Doctor Machaon a great deal more than Doctor Tarr, who still resided back in a dark corner of Villjamur. He'd only met the latter a few times, but had become more than depressed at listening to his ruminations about death. Doctor Machaon, on the other hand, seemed positively joyous at the case now lying before him. Around forty years old, with rubicund cheeks and a belly that made even Jeryd feel trim, the investigator took to him instantly.

'Such exotic wounds!' Machaon crowed. 'Quite a savage end for this poor fellow.'

Machaon's workroom was to be found in the Ancient Quarter, not too near the bistros for temptation to disturb his work. The Onyx Wings were in full view from the west-facing window. An array of coloured lanterns and flambeaus lit up the room even further. Charts sprawled across the walls, bottles were ready to burst off all the shelves. There was a tray full of chisels and enterotomes and saws and cutters, and in the centre of the room was a table on which the body of the victim had been placed. A lamp hung above it.

Machaon had already flexed the corpse's joints and searched for abrasions or bruising on the skin. He explained that he was now looking for lividity, and jotted something down in a notebook lying open to one side.

'I'm convinced this one's a murder,' Jeryd told him, pressing the doctor for an opinion rather than waxing lyrical about the nature of the wounds.

Machaon opened a small jar and sprinkled some blue powder onto a white plate. Then he took a sample of blood from a major vein and squirted it on the powder, still humming to himself. 'And you are most correct in that, Investigator Jeryd. Most correct. But in all my years as a physician, I cannot recall seeing a wound such as this.'

Jeryd waited for Machaon to continue with the postmortem, soon oblivious to his presence in the room.

'Doctor, do you know what caused it?' Jeryd pressed again.
Go on, say it.

A spider.

'I would suggest ... judging by the way the torso has been severed, the width of the initial bite, exposing his organs thusly ... and accounting for what rodents and trilobites have done to it overnight ... this was nothing human. Nothing

268

rumel either. Nothing caused by a weapon such as a sword or axe.'

'Don't tell me, some kind of *monster*?' Jeryd offered sarcastically.

'That is my best guess, indeed!' Machaon exclaimed.

Shit, Jeryd thought. He seemed to be having the worst of luck in trying to hunt down killers these days. 'Do you have anything I can work with? Any possible descriptions of the perpetrator?'

Machaon sauntered around the body, leaning to and fro to examine some further detail, while his observations emerged only as a mumbled incantation on his lips. Jeryd was growing impatient.

'It was caused by a species of animal, that much is certain. This was not created with teeth, at least I don't believe – nothing was mauled here. The line of severance seems to run from top to bottom, which, judging by the distribution of the incision, indicates a large beast striking downwards. At a guess I'd say it stood much taller than a human. Or a rumel.' He gestured to the huge ripping gash above the ribcage, and the collapsed bones underneath. 'Yet it's far too messy for a hand-held weapon – at a guess, we cannot be certain. That scarring is not indicative of a cultist relic, although some of them are incredibly complex, so it's tough to say. All in all I would wager that these wounds were caused by some creature unknown to us. I hear rumours of a new race having attacked our neighbouring islands. Do you think it might signify something along those lines, investigator?'

Jeryd had heard the commander discuss the Okun, yet *they* were only slightly taller than the average man. And two witnesses had mentioned something else.

A spider?

Jeryd knew it. Didn't want to believe it, but he knew it. He was not at all delighted about this avenue he would have to explore. Just the thought of it brought a surge of fear rushing to his head, started his heart racing. How could it be that he ended up chasing the kind of creature that terrified him more than any other?

'Investigator . . . are you all right?' Machaon interrupted his thoughts. 'You seem a bit unsteady.'

'I'm fine,' Jeryd grunted. 'It's been another early start for me, that's all.'

THIRTY

One of the hybrids had died in his absence, leaving Voland dismayed. He hunched over the corpse, a cat-like thing with a massive spiralling shell on its back, studying it carefully under the light of the lantern. It would only have managed to waddle, unable to cope with the bony weight of the exoskeleton. Two little brown paws now lay perfectly still, though even when it was still alive these were ineffective. With a pencil, he prodded it. There was no sign of wounding, no emission of blood. It was probably due to heart failure, he surmised – the stress of being alive had been far too much for it. Hybrids didn't always work out, didn't always live for very long.

Leaning back with a sigh, he vowed to bury it soon. He covered it with a cloth, gripped the lantern, and rose to his feet.

Upstairs now, old boy.

His chair was one of those battered old leather things, the kind that you didn't care if you spilt something on, intended solely for the business of relaxing. Which is what he wanted to do now. He'd had a hard day working and he just wanted to relax.

Cressets provided a warm light in his makeshift study. There were a few books here and there, scattered rugs and artwork on the green-painted walls. The room was rather pleasant, despite the odour that rose from below whenever the weather was bad.

He tossed his top hat on a side table, alongside a cup of whisky, then reclined into his chair with a sigh. He slid off his shoes and socks, and began to massage his sore feet.

'Oh not again,' he muttered aloud: the outer layer of epidermis was peeling heavily. Only one of his appendages was a human foot – the other had been claimed from a mega-magnus beetle he'd bought off a cultist trading from Ysla. After recovering from severe frostbite caught on an expedition twenty-something years ago, he was forced to utilize his skills in multi-taxa surgery on mending himself. Such procedures being a bit of a lottery, he had attempted the job with several different mammalian appendages until he had found sufficient benefit from the inert properties of a coleoptera. It had been painful and near-impossible to operate on himself, but with the help of his Phonoi friends he had succeeded in grafting the beetle foot onto the stump that remained of his leg.

He leant over to fetch a brush from under the table and began to remove the loose flakes of shell-skin. The result was a sound like raining toenails on his carpet.

A black cat suddenly darted out from under the chair and turned to regard Voland with utter contempt for his habits. Voland merely chuckled as the feline padded indignantly from the room.

Eventually he finished the task, rubbed his weaker, human foot for comfort, then settled into his whisky. On the table was an envelope from the portreeve, Lutto's embossed insignia bold even in this half-light.

So, then, who might it be this time?

He opened it and set the enclosed document on his lap. Names and addresses drifted towards his vision.

Deltrun, Shanties district, Third Street West. Bacunin, Scarhouse, causes organized trouble for Ferryby's, sleeps in the flat above the Workers' Union headquarters. Bukharin, causes trouble for Coumby's, Ancient Quarter, apartment three of the Tauride complex. Plekhanof, Fourth Street, Scarhouse, next to a non-protected iren. Sedova, his wife, same address.

Random script filled the bottom of the page, notes scrawled by the portreeve himself. These were to be 'donations' to the cause, with the addition of 'May they be of greater benefit than they are now'. He wondered who these extra people might be, their role in the city's affairs, and why the portreeve had flagged them for attention.

His name was whispered through the air: 'Voland . . .'

Doctor Voland looked up from his chair as the spider came through the hatch in the ceiling.

'You're back.' He rose casually, as if a guest had entered for dinner.

'Yes.' The voice came as a slur of wind whenever it inhabited this state. 'I have . . . two more.'

'Grand! Where have you left them?'

'Down below, in the first section of the abattoir.'

'Grand.'

The transformation then occurred in front of him: the spider contorted, bulged a bit . . . then juddered into her natural shape. Voland walked over to a cupboard, drew out one of his monogrammed dressing gowns, and handed it to her.

Nanzi said, 'Thank you,' and he noted with delight, as he always did, how she retained the two huge spider legs, those arachnid tendons that joined awkwardly but efficiently with her human hips. It was a wonder she could walk at all sometimes, a wonder due to his own craftsmanship.

He beamed. 'Would you like a hot bath?' Voland suggested. 'The firegrain's been working particularly well this evening.'

'If it's no trouble.'

'It isn't. Not for you, my sweet.'

That soft smile of hers – one that he had fallen in love with long before he had revealed to her his affections – enhanced her natural charisma. She was many years his junior, but this age difference, among other things, generated in him the strong urge to protect her. Voland would have done anything to make Nanzi feel properly cared for.

*

Voland had first found Nanzi five years ago, both her legs smashed up under fallen masonry in the town of Juul, on the other side of Y'iren. It was a quiet place, with an ambience that came from a calm sea, the pungent odour of the fishing boats enhancing his love of that remote town.

Nanzi was lying there helplessly beside the harbour, constant drizzle pooling around her, a flower in her hand that she was taking to her mother, she explained, through gasps of pain. How could he have not fallen for her? A few nearby fishermen and dock labourers had helped him lift the masonry from the wall collapsed through neglect.

They examined her shattered legs as her screams erupted in quiet explosions.

But he then told her he could help.

Voland was a legend among the medical underground, and had even trained with the great Doctor Tarr in Villjamur for several years, before their ethical differences came to light. But what Tarr never possessed was Voland's ability to use *other* forces in this ordinary world.

Voland was not a cultist by any means: his feeling for relics was one of distrust. People seemed to look back at those ancient cultures with a longing, a sense that things had been superior to what they currently were; but Voland had more than once witnessed cultists manipulating these remnants of ancient technology for purely nefarious means. To him there was nothing great about such misdeeds, nothing great about such abuse of technology, and as a result he had decided to keep his eyes firmly on developing the future. It was still the way he saw the world.

In his youth he had tended to the dying needs of a girl

from the Order of Natura, a lone worker and a collector of insects, she claimed. As she bled to death on his operating table, she had confided her wish was that someone would continue her projects – perhaps even this enigmatic young doctor who was struggling to patch her up. She died, however, and as requested he had investigated her belongings.

By scrutinizing her journal, he had very quickly learned the arts of the cultist.

His research became assiduous. He soon ascertained how he could enhance and graft insect parts onto living people. It was an inexact science. When purple light sparked and webbed, joining two organic surfaces in unnatural combinations, he did not know how it was done, only that it happened. And it was real.

His skills were at a peak when he had discovered Nanzi at the harbour. He had warned her of the dangers, the vagueness of the science he practised. She simply stared at the stumps that were once her legs, and accepted his offer.

And where she was broken, he had rebuilt her.

Blood had leaked everywhere at first, pooling in worrying quantities on the floor, so Voland calculated he would lose her, there on his operating table. For sixteen hours he worked on her, first extracting the flattened remnants of her legs with surgical precision, then attaching, generating and lengthening the ones originally taken from a spider. Two separate operations were needed before the joining of these new limbs. Sixteen more hours were needed to make sure the tissue connected satisfactorily, the tendons and bone intersected correctly, and that she would not ultimately reject them. With help from the Phonoi, he had applied his system thoroughly and diligently and lovingly.

In the milky light of dawn he had waited until she awoke. Long moments of time, those were, his arm propped against the wall as the warmth of a new day began stirring something primeval within him.

Yet exhaustion overwhelmed him; as if his entire soul had been put into reconstructing her.

A sadness crept across his face, then more concern, but ... gradually her fingers began to move! Thanks to the power of that ancient race: the Dawnir, a people thought to possess far greater technology than was now known. He was left in awe of what he had done with their help, through this connection of minds effected through tens of thousands of years.

As Nanzi regained consciousness, she had begun to cry.

At first she remained febrile, and wept for days simply because of the pain. Voland was horrified. He had thought he had enhanced her mobility, but what a fool he was to assume she would be smiling from the off. How naive could he have been? While she slowly recovered, he cleared the operating chamber of all traces of blood, mucus, skin, fibrous tissue, hair, and slowly scrubbed the place raw until he felt himself purge the anger within himself.

Surprises followed, eventually. As the pain subsided, there was silence. No clear indicator of her mood, but it seemed something more primitive had now taken control of her emotions. As he quizzed her daily, he feared that she might repudiate his work on her, but she did not. Whoever she had been before the transformation, it appeared she soon forgot. He never really did know exactly who she was before her accident, her family, or where she grew up. It was probable he would never learn.

When she first morphed into a dazzlingly huge spider, it nearly scared him to death. And then she rapidly became at one with her new self, and Voland grew used to her coughing silk from time to time, the occasional and uncontrolled shape-shifting. Even stranger, he felt a strong attraction towards her, partly a parental emotion due to the effort he had put into creating her new form, but something more. *A bond*. A genuine person existed beyond her unique exterior. She cared for him, too, perhaps out of a debt of gratitude but he didn't care. Normal rules for attraction did not apply here. A new psychology emerged from this relationship.

Did he feel as though he owned her? Wasn't that what many people incorrectly felt in their relationships? He did not. He loved her as his equal. She was not a form of capital to him, not merely some proof of his skills. His greatest fear had been that she might not mentally accept her physical state, but she assured him she was not scarred at all, had not been vitiated, and never for one moment considered things that way. No, she was a rebuild, a new woman. Her expression softened when she discussed how proud she was of her present form. She said she adored her new abilities, adored Voland for giving them to her. Her kisses peppered his cheeks. Her old life was immolated so as to allow her to love herself fully.

She might not be all woman – but she was no freak either. She insisted she was more content with who she was now, much more than ever before. So Voland had slept well thereafter, knowing his work was complete.

*

Nanzi entered the bedroom wearing a towel around her waist. It had been a long night and she now awaited Voland's attention. He looked up from having thrown two extra logs on the fire, in the hope of injecting some more heat into the cold stone walls.

'My dear . . .' Voland took her hands in his. She was beautiful, this slender young woman, with her black hair shiny from dampness. Her breasts were small and delicate, the firelight making something defined from the neat angles of her face. 'That was quite a catch you made tonight. You are certainly a wondrous young lady.'

Nanzi always seemed to like such words, some extra confirmation from him, never really tiring of his compliments.

Hands clutching his wrists, she led him to the bed and began to undress him, first his shirt, then his breeches falling to the floor. They kissed eagerly while she stroked his beetle-foot.

A flick of his hand removed her towel, and her modifications were now revealed: two long spider legs attached by fibrous tissue buried deep in her waist. He looked at her lustfully.

He lay down on the sheets as she kissed his chest, her emotions exposed raw in the air, her passions focused solely on his pleasure. His penis stiffened and she took him in her mouth, then, after a while, moved forwards to straddle him, with those two great black legs manoeuvring her torso with stunning flexibility. The hairs on her limbs were sparse, tough as a brush, as he glided his hands up them. She took him inside, naturally now, though it had been surprising the first time – surprising that there was anywhere in which to be taken, after the complications of the surgery. The stickiness enhanced his pleasure, she could tell, but it was Nanzi who came very quickly, a shuddering internal reaction, as silk leaked out of her. He didn't last any longer, releasing himself into her with short gasps.

Their fluids coalesced, which often made a mess. He reached down to pick up her fallen towel to clean them up.

A tender smile crossed her face, as she crawled up next to him, hand resting on his stomach. They lay there, in the warmth of the fire, their intimacy growing even in such silences. Unspoken conversations. He was vaguely aware that female spiders in their natural habitats were known to kill the male after mating, but fortunately she had not yet shown any sign of such intent.

Still, if I must die some way . . .

Tomorrow he would see to the corpses she had brought him. For now, he lit himself a cigarillo, and enquired further about her day.

'Fine,' she said. 'That investigator, he amuses me. He always wants to lecture me, but it isn't arrogant. It's rather endearing in fact.'

'You choose not to kill him then?' Voland tapped his cigarillo into an ashtray resting on the side table, while nearby the fire crackled, wood splitting under the flames.

'No, I believe he knows little about the missing persons. I suppose I *could* kill him but . . .' There was tension in her voice. 'But I really think he's of some use, for the moment. All the same, one of the bodies I fetched in a while ago was a soldier, which may have raised a few questions.'

She looked at him again, clearly suspecting that he was unhappy with this selection, fearing it would draw unwarranted attention.

'It's quite all right.' Voland was indeed a little concerned, but didn't want her to know that. 'Please, go on.'

'Well, his commander, a Night Guard from Villjamur, has asked Investigator Jeryd to investigate. I feel if I remain close to him, I can keep an eye on things. Several eyes in fact.'

A smile each, a shared joke.

'I can also gain information of military movements and Imperial missives,' she said, 'if it would prove useful. If there is a war about to begin, I may know about it early. I doubt I will have such access if the investigator is dead.'

'Is there any further news on the military front, incidentally?' He wanted to be informed as soon as any combat began, then they might have to take their leave of the city.

'No. The soldiers have occupied much of Port Nostalgia and Althing, so they'll have a front line for defence of the Citadel. All those who've been displaced were moved to apartments further back along the Wastelands. They're requesting citizens to fight, too, so more and more are joining up every day. Still not the street gangs, though, which worries them – they need experienced fighters. This is the sort of information I can get – so maintaining the access really is useful.'

'Are you sure, my love, that you're not simply looking for reasons to keep him alive?' Voland asked. Inhaling from his cigarillo, he got up and put on his dressing gown – the one she had made him from her very own gossamer – and peeled back the curtains to gaze out at the city. A shaft of moonlight sliced across his face. He turned to face her continuing silence.

Nanzi's expression was filled with woe. 'He is rather endearing, I will admit. He actually wants to do good – and there are too few people within the Inquisition, too few people in this entire city, who want to put some good back into things.' She spoke with a keenness, a fresh energy. 'Because of who he is, he can allow me into very privileged places. Besides, I can follow his investigations closely, and I will know the instant things turn sour.'

'All these extra soldiers pulled in means', he announced in a measured tone, 'that there are many more mouths to feed.'

'You wish for me to go out again tonight? I was beginning to think that the presence of so many soldiers might make things more awkward.'

'To obviate any risks, why not fly over to Scarhouse and Shanties, to see if there are any ... *strays* like there were the other night. But that can wait; the wind is too strong tonight, and we are settled here nicely.'

'And about Jeryd?'

'Do not dispose of him just yet, not if he still offers us access to information. I'd much rather a chap like that is kept alive, where he can be of use to us – but I'd advise you stay very close to him, and continue to shadow what he does. That way, he'll suspect you less . . .' He came back into the bed.

'I understand.' Nanzi snuggled up against his chest, the warmth of the fire adding to another perfect moment between them. He could feel her spider-hairs bristling against his legs.

'I love the smell of tobacco on your moustache. I feel strangely safe right here.'

Voland smiled and breathed deeply. How lucky he was to

be in love with a woman like Nanzi. So caring and delicate and smart. He would do absolutely anything for her.

*

The next morning, Nanzi left him again for a day's work with the Inquisition. Voland didn't mind her choice of career, realizing she wanted to do her bit for the greater good. He could understand her motivation – here was a young lady who saw the bigger picture, and there was something to be said for that. It was why she so clearly understood that keeping the city fed was essential – also part of the bigger picture. How many people had they kept alive by now? Hundreds at least would have starved if it wasn't for her nocturnal activities.

Garbed in his long-sleeved undershirt, a white shirt, black breeches, and a leather apron, Voland strolled down to his abattoir, lighting wall-mounted flambeaus along the way. There could be no heating system here like in much of the rest of the city; it would make the meat reek as it went off.

As far as private workspaces went, this was a large area, perhaps fifty strides wide. Before Voland had moved in, it was utilized for housing livestock – that was before the meat supplies ran out as the encroaching ice crippled surrounding smallholdings, followed by the larger, industrial farms who were not supported by cultists. That had meant the abattoir was a cheap property to purchase.

It had been designed for animals to enter at one end then flow around narrow, curving passages, so they could never see what lay ahead of them or be able to turn around. Those complex lanes now stood empty, with only the echo of a smell to remind him of some poor animal shambling here dumbly towards its fate.

There had been a separate area for slaughtering the beasts. During exsanguination, channels and gullies had carried excess blood into external drains, which in turn exited via a natural slope into the sea. Pullers were fixed to the wall for removing the hides. There were areas for collecting solid waste, which would be taken to the pig farmers south of the city, and a couple of large cauldrons for plunging carcasses to make the skin easier to remove. The coldest room of all was separate and deep, well away from the external walls, so that any bodies stored for a day or two might not rot too quickly.

Nanzi's latest haul lay waiting on the entrance table in the first room he entered. No sooner had he stepped into its cube of darkness than the Phonoi appeared. The Phonoi were his reward for a successful operation on the daughter of a land-owner on Blortath. That place being near the cultists' island, Ysla, Voland assumed they were based on some relic. The father had been a traveller and explorer, but never once said that the Phonoi were anything to do with the ancient tech-nology. He had said folklore suggested they were simple spirits, from another time entirely, perhaps even another dimension. They would serve the owner of the lead box in which they travelled, now Voland, and upon release they would do whatever he wished of them, as if interpreting his thoughts. But he preferred to keep them free, surfing the air currents, in case anyone should venture down here and dis-cover his activities. He could only imagine what damage they would do to intruders.

'Good morning, Doctor Voland,' they now said. The shapes swirled like the constituents in a drink being mixed, never really taking form unless they needed to.

'Good morning,' another cooed.

'How are you?'

'Grand, thank you,' Voland replied.

'Wonderful!' they said.

'Lovely!'

'A lovely morning, too!'

Voland said, 'I haven't looked outside yet. Is it snowing?'

'No, doctor, no. The skies, they are clear today. It is as if the ice age didn't even want to be here.'

There was some wisdom in that. Voland, ever a practical man, could not accept the ice age – a strange phenomenon, and one that didn't sit right with him. Sometimes there would be a warm current of air that felt more natural, as if that was what the weather should have been. Then it was beaten away by chill force.

'Would you help me', Voland enquired, 'with the latest two? Nanzi brought them in last night.'

'Of course, Doctor Voland, of course!' The Phonoi assumed vague definition against the darkness of the room, only a fraction of light penetrating from outside, but it caught their form, their fabric. Now like wraith-like children, they swooped down on the corpses, a man and a woman, unwrapped them from Nanzi's silk, then transported them, so that a less keen eye might think they floated across the room of their own accord.

As they accelerated around the innermost room, the Phonoi's energy heated the cauldron, flames rapidly bringing the water to the boil. The two corpses were dropped in, momentarily, then hauled out again while Voland selected knives from the wall. They were both hung up from the ceiling, and Voland began his work of removing their skin, extracting the organs and offal, then choosing the finest cuts of meat. The most dangerous incision was the first, through the chest and downwards, because if you were not careful there was a danger of the blade slipping into a vital artery in your own thigh. With such an injury, many a man had bled to death on an abattoir floor. Attentively, he set to work.

Two hours later, Voland had stored enough meat to feed an entire street for the week to come, off-cuts and steaks and offal all placed into separate containers. Once he had scrubbed the chamber and spruced himself up, he set out towards the iren. There, he would provide the traders with something they could sell cheaply. *For the people.* All via that young Malum character, of course; he was the main buyer, had contacts all over the city, methods of ensuring that this meat was sold to the needy. Voland would have felt better if he didn't know about Malum's other dealings. Drugs, protection from so-called tribal raids and other gangs, widespread theft, unnecessary violence. Distant rooftop executions. It was indeed very uncivilized, but all Voland could do was think about feeding the poorer sort, and maybe helping them to live for longer.

He himself was doing a *good* thing.

THIRTY-ONE

Venturing through the thick shafts of betula bark, they rode into a vast clearing. Ruins were scattered over in one corner, shattered and snow-crested fists of granite, remains from a time he had no understanding of. Two decayed totems were carved out of this age-blighted stone, their giant, open-mouthed faces forever staring up at the sky. Birds perched on top of them, scrutinizing the travellers' progress underneath.

Beyond this growth of secondary vegetation there was yet more snow, with ferns or tufts of grass emerging. Their route through the forest had been shaded from the colder winds, so this was a significantly more bearable section of the journey, especially whenever the sunlight burst down, illuminating the intensity of the colours all around. It was about a hundred paces to the other end of this clearing where a sinister stillness lingered. It was if they were being perpetually watched. *Maybe these were totems that have seen sacrifice in a previous era*, Randur thought. *Maybe we're being followed by ghosts...*

He urged the sisters forward, while Munio lagged behind, forever glancing around himself.

'Perhaps we should remain here for a while,' Munio called out, searching for the sun. The skies had cleared momentarily, and the swordmaster was scanning the elements to interpret time and direction. 'It's about midday, and we're well on course. Let us rest a little while. You young things set too speedy a pace for old Munio.'

'I could still go on for a bit,' Randur replied. 'Ladies?'

Eir nodded assent, silent and unreadable. She slid off the horse she shared with her sister and clasped the hilt of her sword. She seemed to be holding on to the blade as if that was all she had left. Every day she practised swordplay, every day she improved. Randur was impressed with how much she'd changed since leaving Villjamur. If only he could have something else to focus on other than worrying about her protection. His mind was falling apart without the distraction of other people and the busy city.

'I'm fine,' Rika declared, although she seemed spectacularly fragile. She wasn't well-built by any means, and how she managed to cope out here in these harsh conditions was beyond him. *Probably retreating into whatever castle she's constructed in her head with all that spiritual-discipline crap of hers.*

'I'm too old!' Munio grunted theatrically as he sat down on a fallen tree. There was something unusual about his face as he peered between the trees, towards the sun, then back.

'What's wrong?' Randur asked.

'Nothing, young Kapp.'

Randur had been feeling paranoid for a while, and the old man's anxious gaze did nothing to lighten this mood. A sudden rush of noise from within the trees, and Randur spun immediately, drawing his sabre. Nothing was visible but the vacant dampness of the forest, layers of dark brown and green, and the patches of snow.

'Munio?' Randur glanced around again. Munio remained seated, his face pressed into his hands.

Breaking twigs.

The clunk of metal.

An arrow shaft thumped into the nearest tree, forcing Rika to jump back, startled.

'Jamur Rika, Jamur Eir,' the voice boomed across the clearing. 'This is Sergeant Howls of the Eleventh Dragoons.

A hundred soldiers of the Regiment of Foot surround you. Please, cooperate with us, and let's be on our way.'

'Oh fuck,' Randur grunted. *Imperial soldiers. How could they have tracked us out here?* Eir gripped the hilt of her sword, ready to fight till the end, while Rika stood quiet and resigned.

Soldiers faded in through the forest foliage, cracking back small branches.

A moment later, a lean and stubbled soldier approached. He appeared to be in his forties, with close-cropped dark hair dappled grey. Standing over six foot, his face was every bit that of an experienced veteran, pockmarked and scarred, and with eyes that said he had no time for messing around. 'Munio?' he said to the swordmaster. 'You're free to go, of course. One of the privates will see about your reward.'

'Uh, sarge?'

'Yes, Felch?' The soldier turned impatiently to one of his comrades, a significantly younger and more cautious character.

'Spot of trouble on that front. He'll have to take credit notes because we, uh, forgot to bring all the money from the barracks.'

'For pity's sake, just deal with it, someone,' Howls muttered despondently.

Munio wouldn't make eye contact, wouldn't let Randur see his face. The old man held his face firmly lowered in his hands.

The realization dawned on Randur. 'You fucker. You hand us over, for what?' Randur made as if to strike him before one of the soldiers stepped in to restrain him, pinning his arms behind his back. Randur strained to break free, his muscles stinging with pain. 'How much were our lives worth to you, you wanker?'

His wrists were clamped in manacles, as were Rika's, while Eir was soon stripped of her sword.

'You said a man can change, young Kapp,' Munio mumbled,

his gaze still to the ground. 'You can never completely change who you are. I will take my place in this world as a bastard, willingly, and for that I can . . . I can only apologize.'

'Money', Howls interjected, 'is a great leveller, but you three are too young to understand that just yet. Right then, from here you'll be taken to Villjamur to face charges. I think you'll know what's likely – you'll be slaughtered on the outer wall of the city – and Urtica has asked to perform the task himself this time. I believe, his words were "This is personal", which means we must keep you alive for the time being.'

'You realize', Randur muttered, 'that we're innocent in all of this.'

'Of course you are,' Howls replied. A smile. 'Go into any gaol and they will say the same thing.'

Just then a bass groan seemed to deconstruct the air around them.

Suddenly a man – or something resembling one – landed in their midst, collapsing down to one knee to break his fall. His impact with the ground could be felt by all. The figure remained there for a moment longer, head down as if in prayer, a dark cloak enveloping him.

Lithely, he stood up, clearly taller than any soldier there. Seven feet at least, he had long black hair, and his skin was a pale blue, his cheeks so sunken they seemed stuck to the bone. As he scanned his surroundings his eyes resembled two lumps of charcoal. He turned to reveal that he was dressed in exotic military clothing, a metallic X binding him across the chest. Casually, the new arrival withdrew two sabres from over his shoulder, fat blades that were twice as long as any Randur had ever seen, let alone used.

Soldiers all around unsheathed theirs in response.

'You are Jamur military?' this apparition asked, a grating tone that was almost painful to listen to.

'Uh, technically, it's Urtican military now—'

'Very well. It matters little.' The speech was slow, as if the intruder was practising the Jamur language from scratch.

'True. A different wax seal on our orders, mainly.'

'Quiet, Felch.'

'Sorry, sarge.'

'We've no business with you, whoever you are,' Sergeant Howls grunted, advancing slowly towards the stranger.

'Leave these individuals – the females. Be on your way. No harm will find you.'

'Impossible.' Howls scowled. 'We have orders from Emperor Urtica himself to return these prisoners to Villjamur.'

'If that is the case,' the stranger appeared to be in deep thought, 'then I will have to eliminate you.'

Randur was bemused by the creature's arrogance. *Who the hell is this thing, trying to save us?* Not that he was complaining, assessing the size of the bugger. *Rather have him on my side in a scrap . . .*

'You,' Howls sneered, 'against a hundred Imperial soldiers?'

'It seems unfair. Yes. But I have warned you. Do not say that I have not given you a chance to *submit* to my will.'

'Fuck this,' Howls grunted, then gave a series of quick, sharp orders to his men.

A flurry of activity from the soldiers as they moved effortlessly, with a programmed discipline, along the perimeter of the clearing. Their ranks soon totally obscured the blue-skinned figure, all except for its head. Dozens of arrows began snapping through the air, and Randur could see the edge of the immense blade the stranger had brought with him as its swing-arc became a silver blur.

Everything seemed to happen slowly.

A staccato pinging of metal rang out, and a first line of ten soldiers surged towards the stranger – before they fell rapidly, their bodies ripped and broken. Randur had never heard so many men screaming at once. They moved forwards, they died. This stranger was a deadly presence.

The creature's blade flashed horizontally, severing two heads. Soldiers on the opposite flank paused in terror.

Blood flecked the snow ever more densely, as further men collapsed, some even dying as they sought retreat, their backs carved open, their spines severed. Without discipline, they now attacked in twos and threes, but gained little ground on the creature, the reach of its blades being so great.

Randur watched in horrified awe.

Screams eventually faded. It didn't take much to realize what was going to happen. Randur almost willed the next two men to flee, but, with both weapons gripped in one hand, the creature picked up one of the soldiers by the throat with the other, crushing his windpipe with one fist, while he skewered his blades into the stomach of the second. The man dropped lifeless to the ground, the other fell apart in two separate sections.

Several soldiers could be seen retreating into the darkness of the forest, and then there fell a perfect silence, not even allowing the sound of bird-call. Randur peered around for some sign of Munio, but the coward had already made his escape. Munio Porthamis had always been – and perhaps would eternally be – a fucker.

Randur's heart throbbed as the blue-skinned man turned to face them. With precise steps that showed no regard for the varying depth of snow, the large figure advanced towards them. *Don't say anything stupid, Rand. Not now – not ever.*

Their rescuer paused before them, Randur seeing its features clearly for the first time. Its skin was the same shade as purpling dusk, and the eyes lacked pupils so it was difficult to know who it was looking at. There was a gesture made towards the two girls, and Eir stepped in front of her sister.

It said: 'You are heirs to the Jamur lineage?'

They nodded.

'Very well. It has taken me far too long to track you down since you fled the city. I am Artemisia, an agent of the Truwisa.' They stared blankly at him. 'My words mean nothing to you?'

The women shook their heads, and all Randur could do was stare at the blood drenching the stranger's clothing. Underneath the blood, glimmered material like silver chain-mail, yet it was clearly some type of embroidered fabric. Deep cuts severed the material at the sleeves, and there was a gash across the creature's chin and several scars across the cheeks and forehead, but whatever it was it gave no signs of being in pain, and it seemed perfectly at ease amid the human wreckage.

'At least it is not my own blood,' the being grunted, following Randur's gaze. 'Or yours, for that matter.'

'True,' Randur admitted. 'It's just that . . . you know, we're, uh, not quite sure what to think of some man just falling out of the sky.'

'I am female . . . And maybe it is best if you do not think of anything for the moment. Now, let us move further into the clearing.'

'Perhaps', Randur suggested, 'you could help get rid of these chains first?' The creature leaned over, and with an effortless tug pulled the metal apart.

'Very kind,' Randur said, stunned at the display of strength.

They stepped across the fresh graveyard, where limbs lay ripped and broken all about them, a glade of the dead. Rika could not bear to lower her gaze.

'I have been following you ever since Villjamur,' Artemisia repeated. 'All in all, this escape of yours has upset my plans greatly. Had you remained inside your little city then the task would have remained simple. As it is, I have had to follow your trail. It has not been easy.'

'Sorry we inconvenienced you . . .' Randur offered bitterly. 'Spot of bother with the business of trying not to die—'

'You talk too much, Earthlander.'

'There's no point in trying to silence him,' Eir muttered.

Randur grunted. 'Look, very nice of you to help us out, uh, Artemisia? But . . . any chance of an explanation?'

'I do the questioning around here, Randur Estevu – if that is still the name you go by.'

'How do you know my name? And how did you know they were from the Jamur family?' He nodded towards the sisters.

'I often wonder,' Artemisia replied, 'how it is you people know so little. I employ a network of sub-agents and lower-rank emissaries from your world – even from Villjamur – although they know not who they ultimately serve.' She pointed them to the spot in the clearing where she had first appeared, and turned her face skyward.

Randur stepped alongside, and followed her line of sight. 'I don't see anything.'

Suddenly something flickered into being up there, a hulking dark shape immediately beneath the clouds. The three humans were soon staring, dumbstruck. How could anything so big just *hover* there without falling?

Eir finally broke the silence, as she spluttered, 'What . . . what is that?'

'*Exmachina*,' Artemisia growled. 'A home, of sorts, for the present moment.'

Eir turned to Randur, to see if he knew what Artemisia was talking about, then shrugged. Rika seemed to be completely in awe of this female giant, which was strange, since she was seldom disconcerted by anything.

Randur studied further the freakish object in the sky. It had the appearance of a small moon, assuming an inverse colour to the sky beyond. As it approached it took on the form of some fat longship, incomprehensibly large, extending widely across the sky. A floating island. Its presence was intimidating and he was becoming genuinely frightened.

Still some distance away, something unravelled down from

it to eventually reach the ground by Artemisia's feet. Then another rope followed.

Suddenly the big woman twisted round: there'd been a disturbance in the distance that provoked her. Her head became perfectly still, and she held a big hand out to request silence. Faintly, somewhere, Randur thought he could hear the sound of a pipe. He reached down to pick up a sabre discarded in the recent combat.

Artemisia frowned at him. 'That won't do you much good.'

'You anticipating much of a threat?'

'One could say that, Randur Estevu. There have been certain forces tracking me ever since I've stepped into this blasted world. How they have managed it, I do not know.'

What is she on about, stepping into this world? Randur wondered, sure he could now see something flicker between a couple of tree trunks. He tensed. 'What's after you?'

'Satyr,' Artemisia whispered. 'Do not move for your own safety.' She edged over to the rim of the clearing. There, in the shadows, stood a bearded man that appeared to have animal legs. Two horns extruded from his skull, and his angular features displayed signs of laughter.

Artemisia unsheathed one of those massive blades and stepped after it, but in an instant it had escaped back through the foliage, bursting into the deep forest beyond.

She returned to the hanging rope, and there was a sudden urgency to her manner. 'A minor inconvenience, but it worries me. It isn't after you, it is after me, so we must evacuate immediately. You must hold on to this.' She indicated the rope. 'The fibre will adhere to your skin, so you will not slip off.'

'What, you don't expect us to go up there, do you? Wind's strong enough to blow your arse off, I bet. Surely there's another way of getting to ... wherever the hell you want us to go? Can't you suggest something else?'

Artemisia glared at him, eyes burning. Her body was still

smeared with the blood of a hundred men. 'Why?' she grunted. 'Do you even have a choice?'

'Good point, that.' Randur shrugged.

There wasn't much else going for them, really. They'd narrowly escaped being carted back to Villjamur: a depressing enough fact. Now this killer had fallen from the skies only to slap soldiers about the forest clearing, and now she had established herself as the one giving the orders. Eir nestled alongside Randur as he took hold of the rope, his heart thumping. When he gripped it, there was a faint glow as his skin touched the fibres, some weird adhesive power making itself evident. She followed his lead, locking her hands in place, and the rope also writhed to fix a loop around their feet. *I don't want to do this . . . we've no idea what's up there.*

'Aren't you scared?' he whispered.

Eir regarded him coolly. 'We don't have to automatically fear everything we don't understand.'

'Empress, you shall—'

'Come with you, yes, of course.' Rika stepped forward with compliance, took hold of the second rope, and placed an arm around Artemisia's back, hooking her hand on to the base of her armour.

Eir gave Randur a glance to say, *What's that all about?*

'Perhaps she reckons she's some sort of goddess,' he whispered, not entirely sure that wasn't the case. The only thing she'd ever shown much interest in was her periodic Jorsalir mutterings. It was ironic how she'd always moan – *Oh can't you function without all this killing?* – and here she was, happily cuddling up to a seven-foot death machine.

Within seconds they were being hauled upwards.

Drifting far above the tree canopy, they watched it grow smaller, the clearing in the forest below them chequered white with snow and red with blood. Winds assaulted them, as the full panorama was revealed.

The latest bank of clouds had rolled away, heading across

the island to the south, so a rare glimpse of hazy sunlight covered the forested landscape, showing them peaks and ridges, and towering plateaus streaked on their flanks with run-off.

Vertigo soon kicked in, and Randur felt queasy, yet his fingers would not budge from the rope. They were in fact utterly safe, but such reassurance only seemed to work on an intellectual level. Eir handled their ascent calmly, which was annoying. 'Are you OK?' he mumbled.

'Of course. What a wonderful view!' she replied. 'Your island is a beautiful place, Randur.'

Behind him, Artemisia and Rika swung in close embrace, the blood from the warrior-woman now staining Rika's outer garments. The material flapped in the breeze, along with Rika's hair, but she herself remained still, her gaze focusing on Artemisia.

Something shot down from above, a streak of darkness so fast he hardly spotted it. Artemisia called out something in an incomprehensible, guttural language. Whatever it was darted up again, and began to fly around them in wide circles. It had a small furry body, with a paler face and veinous webbed wings.

'Eir, is that ... erm, a monkey with wings?'

After a moment's observation she replied, 'I've only ever seen one in a book ... a monkey that is. But it certainly looks like one.'

The creature swooped up behind them, then away again, so that Randur could not get a proper look. And then he was distracted by the sight immediately overhead. 'Oh hell, never mind it, Eir.'

They were heading for the same hulking shape they'd seen from the ground: an immense structure, on whose underside clustered dozens more of the flying creatures. It was a ship of some kind, rather like a floating island thousands of paces wide, and of similar length. Its underside was jagged, with hunks of wood and metal jutting out, and the closer they got, the more he thought he could see through certain sections, to a light glowing within. Randur gaped in awe, as their ropes carried them directly towards the centre of the massive ship.

THIRTY-TWO

Doctor Voland was delighted with quality of the latest harvest. Soldiers provided good meat, and with so many flooding the city, another few of them dead would make little difference.

Nanzi had done him proud, and deserved to rest for a bit longer. It was her day off, and he would cook for her when she awoke. The routine of working at the Inquisition by day and her evenings stalking the street tired her out. Sometimes she would stay asleep for a whole day.

So, that meant four bodies from two nights ago, and a further couple from last night – and he had not even finished with the previous batch yet. It was a grand number to work on, and would fetch a pretty price on the streets.

There was meat enough here to feed dozens and dozens of families, and in hard times, even the most obscure cuts would be consumed. Here, in the dim lighting of his abattoir, he had one body laid out on a workbench while the other three were suspended from thick hooks pierced through their necks. Skin was easier to peel off once the body had been rapidly boiled. It came off just like that and, once the obvious externals had been removed, the human body looked much like that of any other creature. Voland begun removing some of the internal organs, storing them on a metal tray to one side.

He supposed, if he was honest with himself, it did feel a little odd to be doing this to another human, but he had long since felt estranged from his kind. A loner, someone on the outside of society. He simply could not relate much to other people, and for the last decade he had barely conversed with anyone other than tradesmen he did business with. He felt disillusioned with the world, and no more so than here in Villiren. Money seemed to dictate everything, vices flourishing at the expense of any dignity. You didn't need to look hard to find the people who suffered as a consequence, the homeless, the prostitutes, those performing the most menial jobs in appalling conditions, such as the miners in the surrounding pits. In Villiren, people seemed to barely exist at all, and they were all of them slaves to the Empire. It was just those shiny little metal coins that appeased them for the time being, enough to put some food in their mouths, beer in their guts, to stop them complaining too vehemently. And they were kept so far distant from the decision-making that affected them all.

No, he could not stand much in this world, and could not relate to Jamur life – *Urtican* life, he reminded himself. He himself was as much a victim in all of this, being reduced to the status of some cog in the Empire's system, churning out these cuts of meat to help others survive. People had to make a living, didn't they? It was work that few others would have the stomach for. Besides, it kept the citizens from running out of food, kept prices from rising too high for the poor to survive. It was honourable work and benefited the world at large.

The Phonoi sprang to life from nowhere. 'Good morning, doctor!' they whispered urgently as they formed striating mists.

'Can we help you any more?' one cooed.

'Shall we unhook the next one?'

'Are you feeling well, doctor?'

Voland smiled at the little devils. 'Grand, thanks. I'm still working on this one, but you could bring the next alongside if you'd like.'

'Anything for you, doctor!' The mists turned more cohesive, ghosting upwards into the murky light. A body seemed to slide upwards and unhook itself of its own accord, and the Phonoi drifted down to lay it carefully across the other side of the workbench. They suffused out of focus again, and left him to his business.

*

Malum was bleary-eyed but determined to focus on the day ahead. Loitering in a snowy side street next to the old slaughterhouse, the collar on his surtout turned up, he was delivering the monthly payment due to that lonely old freak, Doctor Voland. He wanted to give the personal touch, since there was always another gang looking to get in on the distribution – only last month he'd had to kneecap a man and a woman.

He was shocked to see members of a rival gang, the Lord Cromis, waiting outside the back of the abattoir. *This isn't their patch, the cunts.* They had come all the way from Jackknife Gata – a district that was a corpse, the other end of town. So why the fuck were they here? Voland was a good contract to have, and the Bloods consistently made a large profit with very little effort. Some said garuda, some even said hybrid-rumel, but where Voland was really getting the meat from, Malum didn't know, and he didn't care. All he knew was that the eccentric man delivered on time, at a reasonable price. In this city, people with such qualities were miraculous.

JC and Duka were already waiting for him. Both men were well insulated in jumpers and gloves, and attached to their hips were their sheathed messer blades.

'Thought you was bringing the money,' JC slurred from under his mask, shifting from foot to foot to generate a little warmth.

Malum patted his surtout, under which was concealed a small bag of Sota coins. 'See the fuckers from the Cromis have shown their faces.'

299

'They've been there a while.' Duka wiped his exposed face as if to make himself more alert. He was clearly expecting a fight.

There were three of them, from what he could see, skulking under the red-brick entrance to an abandoned store. No: there were three men huddled in the shadow, and another, a prodigious garuda, dressed in smart clothing, was leaning against the outside wall, wings tucked neatly behind it. Flecks of snow skimmed across the smouldering tip of its roll-up.

Malum made sure his mask was secured properly. 'We should just ignore them,' he announced, but as soon as he spoke the four of them sauntered towards him. Led by the bird-figure, there was a pugnacious purpose to their stride.

The garuda hand-signed something to a skinhead on one side of it, and the man spoke on its behalf. 'We want a slice of this. We know what you're up to, where you're getting the meat from. The *madam* says we want in.'

'What?' Malum hadn't expected the garuda to be female. 'You want to join us?'

The garuda squawked something unintelligible and straightened her coat. Malum noticed that it was made from padua-soy, and perfectly tailored to accommodate her wings. On closer inspection, those appendages appeared to be disabled in some way, looking ragged and ineffectual. The garuda shook hand signals to her henchmen.

The skinhead said: 'We request to relieve you of this contract.'

Malum was filling with rage. 'You dare to challenge *me*?' he shouted. 'Me! You have any idea who the fuck I am?'

'Just the leader of a few men,' the skinhead grunted, 'is all you are.'

Malum shook his knife loose from his sleeve, and JC and Duka followed suit, unsheathing their blades and standing to either side, making three against four. In these precious

300

seconds he weighed things up in glances, in inferred movements.

JC and Duka moved forward into a crouch, blades ready in one hand. The garuda loitered behind the opposing group, with barely an expression on its face. Malum slipped a smaller knife from his boot and whipped it over JC's shoulder at the skinhead, while he wasn't looking. It struck the man under his collarbone.

While he was clutching it, stunned, JC rushed forward, but the wounded man moved in reflexively and stabbed him in the shoulder. Ignoring the pain, JC moved in, parried then sliced the man's throat. Blood spurted across the snow as the man slumped, gasping, on his side.

The rest was done with professionalism: a stand-off and then a slow circling. Malum knew that as your opposition moved, you had to be quicker, to pre-empt it. The men from the Cromis gang appeared very young, and inexperienced.

JC recovered. He and Duka finished off their opponents in less than a minute, working similar moves: arms pulled forward, punches to the torso, then one to the neck, a blade in the back of the knee to ensure the opponent wouldn't walk again. JC and Duka left the others alive, but barely able to speak.

The reactions of the Lord Cromis men were inert and inexact. There were breathless moments when Malum thought the garuda herself would intervene, but she remained languid, and he waited for her to move.

The garuda shook off her coat, cast it aside, stood up tall and spread her broken wings. Her brown plumage was speckled with white. Malum called his men aside, as was etiquette, and she descended upon him like he was her personal prey.

As his fangs grew prominent, her talons ripped left then right across his surtout, golden coins falling softly on to the snow. Rage surged, something within him taking control. She leaped onto him, her wings juddering. He rolled aside then kicked her away. JC made to throw his knife, but Malum waved him off impatiently; he always had to prove his value. As she lay on her side, he stuck a boot into her back where the wings joined. Her painful screech rattled the chilly air.

She lashed out with an arm, but he was too quick, lurched backwards, forwards and managed to bite into her. Another deafening screech and she shook her bitten arm free. Then, as she regained her footing, he slammed his boot into the side of her knee, buckling her askew on a broken leg. She lay on her back as he ripped his messer through her chest, blood pooling on the snow. Her thick beak opened, but there was only silence.

She was still alive and still in pain, as he bit into her wounds and ripped chunks of offal from her chest cavity, unable to control the monster within him. The garuda shuddered and spasmed, then stilled. Finally, he stopped. A thick trail of gore dripped down his mouth as the intensity of the moment ebbed away.

He climbed off her, collected his scattered coins and began to wipe the remains of the leader of the Lord Cromis gang from his face. As was the tribal way, he grabbed a lump of flesh from inside her and shook it at the two surviving men, who huddled against the wall, terrified. 'See this, you fucks!' Malum shouted. 'Don't interfere with us, understand?' He flung the remnants at them and marched away to rejoin JC and Duka, who were both busy nursing their injuries.

Malum ordered, 'Give me a hand with this. And JC – sort out your fucking drinking. You're slow. You'll not always have me to cover your back.'

The Bloods wrapped up the carcass in her own clothing. JC dragged it through the thick snow to the back door of the abattoir. Malum knocked several times.

Voland answered eventually with a startled expression. 'Good morning, gentlemen,' he said, noting the bird-woman.

Malum nodded in greeting. 'Here's another body. You want it?'

'Er, grand, grand.' Voland rubbed the back of his head in confusion, and stepped to one side, gesturing towards the darkness. 'Can you take her in and leave her over in the corner? The new stock is all ready for you to collect.'

'Nice one.' At least he knew now that Voland's sources were as despicable as he'd guessed. Malum turned awkwardly and smiled at his men, who were now muttering in bemusement. 'What, I'm going to ask for some coin for her, all right? Money's money, after all. That's what this city's all about.'

Duka chuckled as JC lumbered inside under the garuda corpse, nearly dropping his mask. A black cat scampered out through the doorway and padded into the street. Feathers scraped against the doorway, fell loose, were blown out into the snow, where the cat went skipping after them.

*

Well, that was strange . . .

From a safe distance, Jeryd had watched the garuda get taken out by the masked men. The black cat sauntered up to him, a stray feather in its jaws, and regarded him as if it could perceive his thoughts. Jeryd leant down to scratch the creature's head, which it permitted before losing interest in him entirely.

Jeryd regarded the closed door. He knew better by now than to get involved in the affairs of gangs without any backup. Many an Inquisition officer had been eradicated while misinterpreting folly for bravery. Because he'd been over-worked and feeling stressed, it was several days since Malum had provided him with this address, a bleak and featureless building in a district full of the like, and he still wasn't sure what he might discover from this Voland character – though the incident in the Peep Show had left him utterly haunted.

Further along, some street beggars hunched under a door-way, warming their hands over a small pit-fire, laughing and exchanging extreme comments. One of them hurled a racist obscenity at him, so he moved along the grubby street, not wanting to create a scene. A group of kids were playing around a patch of ice, slip-sliding in sudden horizontal lurches.

So, what did any of this activity have to do with dodgy meat? He shouldn't have been here anyway. Investigating food was not what the Inquisition paid him for. He should have been investigating the murders, looking into the mystery that was taking people from the streets. But curiosity was getting the better of him. Besides, he worked harder than any of his colleagues back in the Inquisition – so he was entitled to a bit of free time.

Walking back to the building, he scrutinized its brickwork. On the black metal door was scratched some graffiti.

Rumel Fuck Off – Human's Only

Nice, Jeryd thought bitterly, particularly unimpressed by the misplaced apostrophe.

He put his ear to the door but heard nothing beyond. He moved along the side of the building, around the corner on to a busier thoroughfare where skinny horses trailed carts full of mouldy vegetables. A trilobite carrying tools stood patiently between a couple of labourers working on a collapsed wall adjoining one of the most questionable-looking taverns Jeryd had ever seen. It was called Knights of Villiren, and seemed in worse condition than even the Garuda's Head back in Villjamur. Jeryd checked along the rear of the abattoir, but located no other means of entry.

He returned to the corner, and lingered there, glancing back at the only door. After a few moments there was a clang as it opened, and out stepped the gang members, counting coins in their hands. Laughing in satisfaction, they vanished past the beggars, who couldn't look them in the eye. Even the kids took to their heels.

Jeryd strolled tentatively towards the open door, hoping to steal a glance at what might be inside. Suddenly he slipped on an ice patch and cursed, 'Bollocks'. He fell on his arse and skidded several feet, before clattering into a wall.

On turning over on the ground he found Nanzi staring down at him. A gust of wind struck the scene, sending litter cascading along the street, and he noticed, under the hem of her long flapping skirt, that her legs seemed abnormally . . . hairy.

'Investigator Jeryd, what are you doing here?' she demanded, pressing down her skirt against the breeze.

'Making a tit of myself, currently,' he grumbled, as he clambered to his feet, brushing himself down. His rump hurt after that tumble, and now his hands were bloody freezing. *What the hell's wrong with this girl's legs? Has she had a brush with some incompetent cultist?*

'I mean,' she said, 'what are you doing out this way?'

'I got lost. I was looking for the address given to me by Malum.'

'Do you want me to help you? You've not told me much about this particular case.'

He blew warm air into his cupped hands, unable to stop thinking about her legs. 'What're you doing out here yourself?'

'I pass along here on my way to work, and was just heading there now. Are you going to the office too?'

'I can always check that joint some other time,' he said. 'I know vaguely where it is now, at least. Come on, let's get back to HQ. There are probably a whole load of reports to read through, and it's not as though anyone else is going to deal with them.'

*

Later that night Nanzi and Voland made love again in the tenderest of ways. She needed this release after a stressful day at work. There had been an assault involving a beautiful young woman, and Nanzi had spent most of the afternoon calming her down and taking the details. None of the others in the Inquisition seemed to realize how traumatic the experience must have been to the girl.

It was so difficult for her to balance helping the community during the day, with helping Voland at night in her alternative guise. Day and night, she barely ever stopped helping people out. But Voland had rebuilt her and she felt in debt to him – time working for him was important. Certainly it helped that he was a perfect gentleman. On the other hand she also loved working for the Inquisition. That was a job in which she could feel herself a woman who had achieved something. Though it was a male-dominated profession, her efforts over the last couple of years had seen her reach the lofty position of investigator aide. Jeryd was charming enough, if a bit slow – and would he ever stop eating? She found him vaguely endearing, but he was now becoming too much of a risk, and so, lying there semi-naked, she told her lover about her fears.

Voland smoked a cigarillo as he contemplated her problem. 'You wish to be rid of him now?'

'I can't be sure,' she said. 'I really just don't know. He is such a bumbler at times – and not a *particularly* good investigator – but he tries hard, and I do learn from him.'

'Perhaps it may be best for both our sakes to dispose of him.'

Nanzi said nothing, but Voland guessed that she wasn't keen. 'We could both be arrested and executed. There is no overly useful information coming from the commander of the Night Guard. I say it's time we rid ourselves of this Investigator Jeryd.'

She nodded and laid her head on Voland's chest. She then drew one of her spider limbs across his pink human leg, smiling softly at the contrast in colour and texture. It pained her to even think of it – has she had grown attached to the old rumel. He was a nice person – a good person – but one thing that Voland had taught her was practicality. Emotions could ravage her, in her human state, so that her logical thinking suffered. As a spider, the deed should be more simple. Her animal instincts would take over, and it would become a job, just like any other. Sometimes she wished she could always enjoy the strength of will of her transformed state – with no weakness of purpose, no reliance on others.

'OK. I'll kill him. I'll have to do it soon, though.'

THIRTY-THREE

'A golem show!' Marysa exclaimed. Her expression of joy was worth a thousand times the effort needed to get the tickets. She held his hands in hers, and somehow managed to shake the day from him, the way she always did.

'Yeah.' Jeryd was a little coy, for some reason. He wasn't the greatest romantic in the world and he knew it. No matter how old he became, he reacted just the same as when he was a kid doing this sort of thing for the first time. It was such an awkward business. 'I thought we could do with getting out, and I know how much you liked them back in Villjamur. So you'd better throw some fancy rags on, because the Great Iucounu starts in an hour or so.'

'Great, I'll go and change quickly.'

'Hurry now, or I'm going without you.' Jeryd contentedly watched her rush out of the room: surprising his partner was one of his great pleasures. As he listened to the familiar sounds of her getting ready, he sighed contentedly, and turned to look out of the window. It was snowing – no surprise there – but at least the street cleaners had left their path to the theatre fairly unobstructed. There was snow still along the tops of walls, or gathering on rooftops, places where the cultists couldn't easily do their work. To Villiren, snow was still a soft white plague. Storm lanterns hung at street intersections, their soft orange glow caught in the glistening cobbles. A part of him considered that tonight might even qualify as romantic.

To be honest he needed a night of escape like this, for his own sanity. Otherwise, thoughts of the improbable spider killer dominated his mindspace. The case took up his entire day, from questioning relatives about the disappearance of a loved one, to piecing together individual incidents in the hope of establishing a general pattern. And on top of that, as always, was the bloody administration. He wondered what the Inquisition would be like if it wasn't for paperwork.

Could he even match the wits and abilities of this spider, a being so unlike him, something so abnormal that it managed to resuscitate his worst childhood fears? No one else in the Inquisition seemed to care about the case. He had had words about his suspicions with one or two of the senior officers, but he could tell from their expressions that they would be leaving him to deal with it alone. And that was fine – he was used to taking the weight of the world on his shoulders without thanks, but it made for a stressful existence. One of the guys at work had kindly bought him a bottle of whisky, said he'd been working too late and would soon appreciate its company. He merely left it unopened in his bottom drawer, because that was a dangerous road ahead.

Eventually Marysa came downstairs and bounded into the living room, just like old times. A blink of the eye and they might have been kids again – *where did all that time go?* She wore her classic-fit green gown, with the brooch he'd bought her fifty years back, presented to her on one of the bridges of Villjamur as an anniversary present. Her white hair was tied back elegantly and she wore his favourite perfume.

'Shall we?' He offered her his arm.

*

Nanzi loitered on the rooftop, observing people shuffling along the streets below with monotonous strides, one after the other, their heads bowed and hunched under the snowfall. Skies had clouded over. Many of the lanterns kept being taken by thieves looking for scrap metal, leaving a darkness in which

Nanzi, in her arachnid form, could feel comfortable. Snow had amassed along the guttering, obscuring her view, so the spider poked one leg over the top to clear some space for her to scrutinize the scene fully.

She was halfway between the theatre and Jeryd's house. Her target had announced proudly to Nanzi earlier that day where he would be going tonight for his wife's surprise, providing the spider with the perfect opportunity to be rid of him.

Every couple that walked by, she homed in on and scrutinized patiently, sensing to see if any one of them was Jeryd. In the mass she sensed joy, misery, excitement, awkwardness – a whole host of states of being, which came to her in alterations of air chemistry.

Down to the left: Jeryd and Marysa. Arm in arm, he smiling, her laughing at something he had said. After a kid narrowly missed Jeryd with a snowball, he scooped up some loose snow from a wall and arced one back.

Cautious now of being spotted, Nanzi withdrew her legs, and watched them cautiously. The couple drifted further along, and Nanzi propelled her body across the roof tiles with the agility of a ballet dancer, all the time studying their progress. The lights of the city proved hypnotic, reaching her in languid pulses of heat, and chemicals from street vendors smeared the air, but she kept herself as focused as possible, tap-tapping from tile to tile, spitting fresh silk to support herself, so that she didn't slip and plummet to the ground.

Streets became people-thick, the golem show pulling in quite a crowd.

Then she lost them, Jeryd and Marysa, in a throng of bodies by the entrance to the old theatre. Her animalistic instincts took over: she must find him, she must kill him.

Up to the roof of the theatre eventually, up and up to a giddy height. The precarious structure seemed to rattle in this wind. Scuttling back and forth, she examined the surface for a few loose tiles, then managed to remove enough to squeeze her bulbous form into the building itself.

And down into the darkness.

*

Lights out. A dignified ripple of applause.

Three rows from the back, on the right side of a red-upholstered auditorium, Jeryd was getting vaguely interested as a golemist lumbered onstage in a flamboyant white shirt. His face resembled a sack of potatoes and he was laughing merrily to himself. A small white pterodette of some kind, all spindly and barbed, shambled along by his feet.

What a damn humiliation for a cultist, Jeryd thought, *to be reduced to mere entertainment. Does he get teased by the others?*

The man blew kisses to the crowd and Marysa excitedly clutched Jeryd's hand. This was all a little cheesy, and Jeryd couldn't tell if she liked these shows ironically or genuinely, but at least she seemed happy enough. Certain things seemed to reduce her to a sweet young girl again, so he simply smiled then focused on the man up onstage.

As they usually did, the golemist placed several waist-high, pot-bellied statues about the torch-lit stage, before stepping back into the shadows at the centre rear, the white creature tottering after him to stand by his feet.

A guitarist began throwing some chords, minor thirds mainly and, after a few predictable flashes of magic, the stone statues became liquid and motile. One by one, they began gyrating in a hypnotic rhythm.

*

With so many people, the air chemistry completely altered, and individuals began losing their individuality. Nanzi ripped her way through the various floor levels and dropped down onto the ceiling of the auditorium proper. No – right above the stage now, looking down on all the rigging and apparatus of theatre. Ropes spiralled down to the limelight, and a red curtain sagged sadly like an age-collapsed face. Analysing the

311

audience, Nanzi eventually located Jeryd and Marysa near the back, safely away from the majority. Although a large crowd, the theatre could have accommodated hundreds more. The auditorium walls – dry and stable – looked excellent surfaces to crawl upon.

Nanzi scampered across. Her legs pinged along the little metal railings above the stage. The figure on the stage briefly glanced up as she darted into the shadows beyond.

*

Well this is certainly nothing new, Jeryd reflected. *The performers in Villjamur do this sort of thing ten times better than this fool. How much did I pay for these damn tickets? 'Great' Iucounu my arse.*

Something flickered above him, to one side, but it was too dark to perceive what it was. Perhaps he was looking for any excuse not to watch this poor excuse for a show.

Back on stage, the statues flopped about like some poor creatures dying of hunger, while the 'Great' Iucounu glanced up from his semi-bow almost apologetically. In Villjamur you saw these things flying around amidst the audience for the finale – so what would this loser achieve? Jeryd shook his head and sighed. Someone nearby booed, and he would have joined in, if it hadn't been for his wife watching so sympathetically.

*

With precise steps, Nanzi navigated past the vast portraits lining the wall – and she would have to be careful, because Jeryd had scanned in her direction once already. She noticed that she was too close to the people in the nearby rows so she banked up higher, thirty feet up, and now on to the ceiling, observing the auditorium upside down. She then moved to a position directly above the target couple. There, she spat webbing. Satisfied it would take her weight, she began to descend, as careful as possible that others wouldn't—

*

– a scream: a blood-curdling scream and Jeryd turned round, peering left and right, then to the rows in front and the talentless goon up onstage but there was nothing . . . and then it happened so quickly, the *thing* looming above him – *a fucking spider*, just standing there, doing nothing – and he remembered screaming 'Please no!' and his heart hammering, and the tenseness and tightness returning inside, and he didn't want it to *touch* him—

Suddenly Marysa hauled him aside, a blade in her hand, and shoved him beneath the row of cushioned seats. As the silent screams rattled around inside his head, he placed his arms over his face and peeped from behind them at his wife. She was slicing, this way and that, at the massive limbs of the creature darting with phenomenal grace, rolling and ducking under the blows it tried to deliver in return. But he had to turn away and cover his eyes. The seating nearby was ripped apart and Jeryd began to shiver, and the images blurred, and the sound of screaming faded, and he . . .

*

'Jeryd . . .'

His wife's voice, soothing.

Water splashed across his face, not so soothing.

He rubbed himself dry, peering about him now, alert and on edge. 'What the hell happened?'

'You fainted,' Marysa declared embarrassingly.

'Nice one, mate,' someone commented, and a man laughed in the crowd of theatregoers staring down at him.

Jeryd was lying on a pile of coats on the floor of the foyer, with its fancy flambeaus and elegant decor in the background.

'Well, I realize that,' he muttered. 'I mean, what the hell happened before?'

'A massive spider just dropped down and tried to attack us but I managed to fight it off with my messer.' She held it up for a moment, a sharp weapon with a wooden handle, before slipping it back into her boot. 'It's a good thing I went to all those Berja classes.' Her expression showed that she was feeling proud of herself. 'The thing nearly had you at one point – it kind of hovered over you as if it couldn't decide whether or not to kill you. I don't think it *wanted* to – if that makes any sense. How bizarre! Anyway, it wasn't just me that helped you – there were one or two men from one of the gangs, I think, and they fired crossbow bolts at it until it cowered away somewhere up in the darkness.'

'I didn't know you carried a blade.'

She suddenly looked coy. 'I was awarded it in my class, by the master.'

Jeryd grinned awkwardly, and pushed himself upright with great unsteadiness. Then it dawned on him: *the spider*. The one he was tracking – it was after him, too.

A spider. After him.

Fuck.

'Marysa, we have to go,' he said urgently, and she helped him off the pile of coats before guiding him through the parting crowds.

The image of the creature made him breathe heavily once again and Marysa hugged him. He couldn't believe how she was now the *tough one*.

'Marysa, we have to go somewhere safe. I think . . . I think this spider is out to get me.'

*

As they made their way home, he explained the danger they faced. He told her that they had to move houses again, just in case. He suggested two good hotels. Throughout the night they packed their essential belongings and moved out.

It was now abundantly clear to Jeryd that he would have to get the spider or the spider would get him. If he was honest, neither of these options radiated charm – although remaining alive was certainly preferable. So he would have to confront his deepest fears and snare a spider much bigger than himself.

If you looked hard enough, there seemed to be no end of

places a colossal arachnid could hide. Every niche in a stone facade, every section of old guttering offered the potential for paranoia. It made choosing their new abode more complex.

A bloody spider.

In all his decades of working for the Inquisition back in Villjamur, Jeryd had never come up against anything quite so simultaneously ridiculous and frightening, but he had also learned in recent times to go with what seemed unlikely – because in this wide-flung Empire, nothing was impossible.

They'd found a hotel still open, which was all bad carpets and unfashionable curtains, but Jeryd was incensed to have to pay over the odds for a room. Empty corridors and vacant rooms were to be found everywhere, because of the war, but the night receptionist insisted that they did not barter. *Damn rip-off city . . .*

'There had better be a bloody good breakfast as part of this price,' Jeryd muttered as he slapped coin after coin on the counter.

THIRTY-FOUR

The following morning, after a restless night's sleep, Jeryd decided to walk along the harbour of Port Nostalgia, maybe clear his head a little, try to regain some perspective. A calm day seemed promised: the cloud layered pale and high, and for once there was no wind, so a pungent aroma lingered, of seaweed and fish and organic detritus abandoned on the boats. This peace was interrupted only by soldier-calls or the hammering of boards being nailed across windows. Troops had been stationed on hastily constructed wooden watchtowers up on the hills to either side of the city, and garudas sailed constantly through the skies on patrol. It was a watched city.

He had recently discovered the harbour to be one of his favourite spots in Villiren, despite the military presence. Soldiers had brought a sense of fatalism to the place, that there was only an ending in sight. Still, here he could stare out to sea and lose all concept of time. With nowhere to run, all he could do was look back to the past. Memories flooded and ebbed.

A few of the local bistros were doing a roaring trade, serving so many off-duty soldiers, and Jeryd decided that some tea might be a good way to continue the morning, perhaps to jolt his mind alert.

Traders were making their way to the irens further in the city, rumel and humans pulling carts, huddled in layered clothing, their breath like smoke in the morning light. Four trilobites were following a rumel stevedore down a side street. Jeryd could smell bread baking somewhere frustratingly distant.

Further up along the street, he spotted three elderly types in dark cloaks behaving rather oddly. They were crouching over some bizarre object, and something about their mannerisms suggested immediately to Jeryd that they were cultists. All wore different shades of tweed cloth, the kind he hadn't seen in a long time. One was a tall woman, the other two were men as short as Jeryd himself. Listening hard, he distinguished the words 'Amber' and 'Teuthology'.

'Sele of Jamur,' he announced, approaching, and they turned sharply to regard him. 'What have we got going on here?'

'Ah, good morning, indeed, sir,' the woman replied. 'Just a spot of research.' Grey-haired and thin, she possessed well-proportioned features, laughter lines suggesting amiability, and her blue eyes were intense and warm. A wonderful perfume lingered around her.

Of the other two, one man had a thick grey moustache and wore a flat cap over his wide, chubby face while the other was completely bald and it seemed he wasn't one for wasting words.

'Anything we at the Inquisition ought to be aware of?' Jeryd asked.

'Oh, um, no,' the woman said. 'That is, I mean to say, nothing of a questionable nature. We're simply cultists, looking into something unusual. We're not even local, sir.'

'Cultists ... say, maybe I could use a bit of your wisdom. Could I buy you all a drink?'

The man with the moustache grinned. 'Aye. I ain't never turned down a drink yet, and I'm seventy-two!'

*

Jeryd took them to a decent bistro in the better part of Port Nostalgia. The morning rush of traders had finished, leaving just a young soldier writing at a table by the counter. Two old ladies hovered indecisively over the menu. Behind them, a wood stove burned generously.

The cultists shuffled in a line towards a booth at the back, where the tables looked antique judging by their baronial and gothic carvings. Jeryd removed his hat and gazed out of the window. In the street below, a ragged family struggled past, hauling loads of bulky items. Jeryd had seen many such families being moved on by the army for the sake of their own protection, but it must still be demoralizing to be forced out of your own home.

A boy wearing an oddly feminine mask took their various orders for tea. Jeryd also contemplated the pastries offered, then wondered about their contents and declined. Introductions were exchanged: the blue-eyed woman was called Bellis, the chubby man with the moustache Abaris, and the bald man Ramon. He'd met some strange types in his time, but there was something distinctly eerie about Ramon. It didn't help that his left eye was blue, the right brown.

A couple of minutes later, the drinks were brought to the table.

'Now then, there's not too many rumel coming to Villiren these days,' Bellis declared. There was an air of refinement about her, yet overwritten by occasional uncouthness, and Jeryd immediately liked her for this; though he didn't quite know what to make of it when, with a flourish, she whipped out a hip flask and splashed some of the contents into her tea. 'Sherry?' she offered.

Jeryd shook his head.

'Yes, as I was saying, do you find, sir, any hostility to your being here?' She slurped her drink like it was the first she'd tasted in days.

'You get a little animosity, but I just shrug it off. You got a bit in Villjamur, too, where I'm from, but it was a rather repressive city. Women were treated even worse than us

318

rumel, so it never bothered me once you see how corrupt male human society can be. Nah, I suppose I've been around far too long to let that sort of thing get to me.'

'A veteran of sorts, then?' Bellis chuckled.

'Seen over two hundred summers, actually,' Jeryd commented dryly. 'You start to see life with a little more clarity once you're past your hundred and fiftieth year.'

'Hear that, Abaris,' she nudged her companion exuberantly. 'We're just children compared with him. Children!'

Abaris brushed his grey moustache, with a smile. Even Ramon, still silent, seemed to show something in his stark expression.

'So what are you all doing in this city?' Jeryd enquired.

Bellis told their story, with constant interruptions and corrections from Abaris. Ramon never said a word throughout, and now and then he and Abaris would share the odd glance. They belonged to the Order of the Grey Hairs, just the three of them, an unofficial and relatively new sect of cultists. They had been sick and tired of the younger men and women belonging to their previous orders, sick of the suggestion that their age meant they were out of touch. The younger ones were so competitive, so determined to prove their worth – often killing themselves through indulging in reckless experiments that went wrong. Five years ago, they had left Villjamur to search out some of the more esoteric folklore of the Boreal Archipelago. Age had brought them unparalleled experience and wisdom and they were constantly drawn to the unknown and the unlikely.

'And it's just the three of you?' Jeryd wondered about the fact that a woman would travel with these two men everywhere. Were they related? Was one of them her partner and, if so, how did the third one feel about this arrangement?

She suddenly guffawed outrageously, her jangling voice attracting way too much attention for his liking. 'I know what you must be thinking, investigator – here we are, all free single adults. We are none of us together in any respect, other than to pursue our chosen business.'

Jeryd reckoned that didn't seem right, but he decided to ignore that suspicion for now. 'And why come to Villiren with the threat of war? Plenty of other, safer places to be.'

'We might ask the same of you, sir,' Abaris remarked, pushing up the brim of his flat cap.

'I'll give you that,' Jeryd conceded. 'Suffice to say I've poked my nose in too many awkward situations before. Unlikely though it seems, for me this place might be safest.'

Abaris laughed, seeming to like the element of the rogue in Jeryd. 'Well, we're here looking for something. Just like we always does. Only thing is, it ain't proving quite that easy to find, let alone raise—'

Bellis interrupted. 'Abaris, you old sod, remember the investigator is a busy man! And, so, what can we do for Investigator Jeryd? You couldn't have brought us here just to listen to us waffling about our personal histories.'

Jeryd paused for a moment, contemplating why they did not want him to know what they were up to. 'I've come across a very interesting case and realize that I might need a little help with something rather beyond my means. How would I go about eliminating an . . . an . . . unusually large spider? And where the hell could it have come from?'

'Depends how large we're talking,' Bellis said. 'What, an armspan or so?'

'Twice the height of an average man, at least.' Jeryd let that statement hang in the air. The old cultists looked impressed at that, conveying their surprise in their swift glances to each other.

Jeryd went on to tell them about the disappearances, the silk webbing found around the city, the few witness statements. He did not yet reveal his fear but, as he related the events, he found himself becoming increasingly determined to overcome his phobia. The recent confirmation that something solid existed, no matter how outlandish its nature, gave him something to focus on.

'Good healthy citizens are being abducted off the streets,' Jeryd concluded, 'and I'm the only one in the Inquisition who seems to give a damn.'

'Well, slap me silly,' Abaris said.

Ramon, sipping his drink, nodded sagely, never saying a thing.

'Quite the predicament, sir,' Bellis admitted. She reached for her hip flask and tipped her head back to guzzle what was left. She then stifled a belch, and eyed him as if to see what he made of her. Jeryd would have admitted to meeting classier ladies . . .

'There are any number of possible origins,' Bellis declared. 'A hybrid, perhaps. Growth enhancements. It could even have evolved naturally and been imported from some collection of islands off the map! Though what possible competitive advantage its size would provide seems questionable. As for helping you, I'm sure we can think of something useful. You wish to destroy the creature, or simply ensnare it?'

'I'd like to trap it first, then examine it, where it came from, what it's doing here.' He was starting to perspire. Even thinking about the giant spider sent a chill through his body.

'I quite agree,' Bellis declared. 'Something so wonderfully alien ought to be investigated more thoroughly than would be possible just by a post-mortem, no?'

'We're being rather optimistic in even assuming it can possibly be caught. I've no idea where it nests, no idea where it takes its victims. Ideally, I'd like to track it back to its, what's it called, its lair, just to see if there are even any survivors. So, do you really think you can help?'

Bellis grinned amiably. 'Let's have a while to think about it. But I suspect we can rustle something up, right, lads?'

'You charge for your business?' Jeryd asked.

'Good heavens! We're not like all those other cultists. We

do not prostitute the power of relics, no. One cannot assign a mere monetary value to such things, sir.'

Refreshing, Jeryd thought, *to find such an attitude anywhere in the Empire*. 'I'd be owing you a big favour. Is there anything I can offer in return?'

The cultists made eye contact with each other, then Abaris stroked his chin and said, 'Maps?' He paused, then explained: 'We could do with a decent map of Villiren. You being in the Inquisition, like, you might find us something decent and all.'

'Maps I can do,' Jeryd confirmed. 'I've assembled quite a collection while identifying where all these people disappeared. Feels like I know the damn city better through lines on paper than in real life.'

'In many ways, that's all it is,' Bellis said. 'But less theory. Sir, we will get you your spider-trap. Let's meet again here in three days, at the same time.'

But he still had his secret shame to confess, and wondered if they might help him. 'Bellis, there's actually something else. It's uh, a little private . . .'

*

'And it's just that, the touching that concerns you most?'

Jeryd nodded, embarrassed. It wasn't easy to admit this, let alone talk about it. There was an awkwardness from merely opening this region of his mind. The fact that she was a woman helped.

'Just the thought of it touching me and immediately I can't cope. It's their quickness and unpredictability. I don't know what they're going to do. I sound ridiculous. Some bloody Inquisition officer I am – to be terrified of spiders.'

Bellis clutched Jeryd's hand in her own, and he noticed how hers felt. 'Dear, dear man, it's a more common reaction than you think. Why, I've seen great men from the military cower when talking in front of a group of people. I've seen tribal barbarians refuse to venture out on certain evenings due to astrological phenomena. Fear – to such a degree – is often down to something that we experienced in our upbringing – but we cultists also believe many phobias simply derive from an instinct of self-preservation, a primitive echo from our evolution. Perhaps some of your own distant forebears were once poisoned by those creatures!' With a confident smile, Bellis turned to look around the empty bistro.

The day was unwinding itself, and most of the customers had gone, including her two companions. Outside, it was getting dark, and they silently watched a street trader pitch his cart in front of the window, only to be moved on by army personnel. There was a distinct calm about the place – providing an ideal place to debate Jeryd's secret fears.

Bellis produced a glass orb from her bag, heavy enough to require two hands as she placed it on the table.

'Look at this marvel.' She gestured with open palms, and stared at the object with such glee that he felt an expectation for him to be impressed.

'A relic?' Jeryd enquired.

Although it was transparent, he could see how pulses of coloured light flickered beneath the surface, like miniature flashes of lightning.

'We're too predictable at times,' Bellis said shaking her head. 'A relic for this, a relic for that – well, I guess we just get used to dealing with life in such a prescriptive way. Anyway, we call this one *flaraor fold* – which is literally translated as "the false world".'

'Looks like a crystal sphere to me,' Jeryd mumbled, still peering down at it.

'Well, yes, it is that too,' Bellis cackled, and her laughter could almost cut through the glass.

'What's this thing do then?'

'Look closer. What you see won't be real, and if you want to be rid of your fears, then just touch it. Go on.'

Jeryd yielded, and moved his left hand towards the—

s
u
r
f
a
c
e

and suddenly, shooting through insanely bright storm clouds, he was elsewhere.

Warmth? The surroundings took shape, and he found that he was in a re-creation of his former house in Villjamur – in his cluttered bedroom, in fact – but everything was so bright, too bright. Milky light poured in through the windows, from a hazy, too-yellow sun outside, but then it faded into something more like the real world once his eyes adjusted.

Bellis's voice came to him, from a distance or inside his head or both, he couldn't work out.

—*Remember, this is only a controlled vision, a re-created world – it isn't real!*

—*What do I do? Jeryd asked.*

—*Wander about, or sit down and relax. Enjoy it!*

—*Easy for you to say.*

Jeryd slouched on the familiar bedsheets, crisp and clean, and there was a tang of Marysa's perfume in the air, a glass of whisky on one side. He was pleased to discover that he was imagining some of his favourite things.

—*Comfortable?*

—*I guess so.*

—*Something will happen now, and you must realize that it is only an image. I will control it.*

—*Right . . .*

An image shuddered into being. Jeryd froze. There it was, on the floor by the foot of his bed, enclosed in a glass box: a spider the size of his fist. The same feelings besieged him: he felt it again in his heart, not merely in his chest; an overwhelming tightness, as if his very life was trapped. A total shortness of breath. He squeezed his eyes shut.

—*Just keep looking at it, right? It can't harm you, silly Jeryd. It can't go anywhere – and it is not real. It is just an image.*

—*I know, but...*

—*No buts! Focus, if you want to be rid of your fear.*

Opening his eyes with a sigh, he then regarded the spider. Though not very big, it seemed to be staring up at him, taunting him. Jeryd's tail was frozen still, and he could feel his pulse beating in his throat.

Bellis gave him instructions from afar, and Jeryd obeyed her reluctantly. Sometimes her words seemed slurred as if he couldn't hear them clearly, but he could tell they were formed inside his head. She commanded Jeryd to walk around the room. She asked him to look down into the glass box. She instructed him to put his hand up against the side of the box. She urged him to perform a whole series of actions that seemed to go on forever, frustrating in execution, and even foolish at times. Again, her words working inside his skull. Childhood memories flickered into his consciousness once or twice: his mother standing terrified on a chair in the kitchen as a big spider scuttled across the room, his father shambling in drunk to swat it with a book.

Jeryd did what he was told and was surprised to find that by the end he was not experiencing the same degree of paralysis as before. It helped, of course, to know that it wasn't real, that it was an image imprisoned in a false world. All through the ritual, Bellis continued explaining her secret theories about the nature of fear – things, she said, that he would forget as soon as he was removed from this setting, yet would remain lodged deep inside his mind. Jeryd didn't know what to make of any of it and suddenly—

J
e
r
y
d

was back in the same cafe, clutching the box as if it was for real with the spider right up against his face – and there was now minimal panic, no quiver or heart murmurs, and he was totally astounded. Bellis merely sat there sipping her cup of tea, with a satisfied grin on her face. 'The mind', she announced, 'is a powerful thing. Fear is just a mental state, but it can make people behave quite oddly.'

A girl with a mop passed their table, and suddenly shrieked. 'Get that bloody creature out of here. This instant, d'you hear me? Get it out!'

She began to wave the mop in their faces till they slid their chairs back in haste. Bellis scooped up her orb, and the box suddenly vanished. The two of them hurried out of the bistro.

'See what I mean?' Bellis chuckled dryly, once they were safely outside.

As the snow drifted down around them, Jeryd had to laugh too.

THIRTY-FIVE

'I can't stay, Malum. I'm sorry. No matter how much money you throw at me, I want to go.' Beami was standing with her back to the window, daylight hazing around her, a few bags heaped at her feet. Her emotions were evident in her pained expression.

A morning snowstorm rattled outside, as the city was becoming smothered yet again with white. Now and then people would walk by the window behind her, but they seemed completely unreal. He was utterly detached from this moment. Surely this was no way to start the day, was it, with the smell of bacon hanging in the air being ruined for him by his wife walking out.

'Fine.' Malum glanced down at the table, clutching his mask, playing with the red ribbons. Seething.

'I'm sorry.' Beami picked up her bags and began moving towards the door for the final time. 'I haven't taken much. I've got so many precious relics but I can't carry too many of them. It might be easier for me to fetch the rest when there's only one of us in the house ... Malum, I really am sorry.'

'Fuck you are,' he breathed, unable to face her – this woman daring to stand up to him.

Beami closed the front door gently behind her, leaving him alone amidst a remarkable stillness.

Her departure from his life was as simple as that.

Shortly after she left, he put on his mask again in an effort to contain the emotions that overwhelmed him.

*

When you can have anything you want, it's the things you don't have that will get to you.

A trilobite lurched awkwardly into his path, so Malum kicked it. The creature screeched, collapsed awkwardly into a bank of snow, then eventually scampered away towards the docks, antennae bristling in the air. Malum was feeling bellicose, and in no mood to step around anyone or anything, let alone a giant fucking insect. He had spent much of that day in the company of expensive whores who were under his protection. He had ordered them to kiss and fondle each other, wearing corsets and thigh-length boots, while he watched, waiting for something to happen inside himself. But nothing did. Later he had taken out his aggression on minor gangs that had borrowed heavily from him and couldn't repay the interest. He killed two other young men, used them for their blood, then afterwards he berated himself in the darkness of his room, smashing his fist against the wall.

Now he needed help.

She lived at the other side of the Ancient Quarter, the witch, some distance away from the Onyx Wings, in a street that was perhaps the very oldest in the original city. A chilling sea mist had rolled in for the evening, smothering the streets, allowing every corner even more anonymity. Flares of torchlight punctured it occasionally, providing enough guidance for him, though he knew the route by instinct – after all, he had been born and brought up around here. Up ahead someone had abandoned a box of wasted biolumes, their impotent glow revealing only their inevitable death.

The witch had helped him with so many things. After he had been bitten, and he discovered he could not bear to be in sunlight any more, his reaction was one of a violent allergy – but the witch had concocted one of her treatments and healed him, so that he could face sunlight again, and maintain a normal existence.

He found her door, a squat panel of wood set in a damp corner, lichen and moss caking the surrounding stonework, and he knocked twice and stood waiting, his hands buried deep in his pockets. The door opened with a creak, showing it was darker inside than out.

'Sycoraxe,' he greeted her.

The old woman stood there hunched in her shawls, holding a thick wooden staff with a lizard's face carved on the top. Her hair was white and straggly, her face broad yet clearly undernourished. Two blue eyes examined him with ferocity from amid sagging flesh.

'Another potion this time?'

'I'm after something more potent.'

Sycoraxe grunted and let him in, leading him through the cold darkness of her hallway and into the kitchen.

'She left me. The bitch has left me.' He explained his predicament, and the witch watched him, just like she always did, saying nothing, reading between his words for any extra meaning.

'Take off your mask. I'll return presently.' Sycoraxe set off through the house, shifting back and forth, humming to herself between rooms. All the while he sat in a chair feeling miserable.

Eventually she returned, carrying an open book in her hands. She gaped at its pages as she spoke to him. 'You wish for her to be *deleted*, I take it?'

He pondered for a moment about the chances of renewal, about rebuilding something. He couldn't have this sort of thing happen to him, couldn't let the lads find out, because he'd then be a joke to them, wouldn't he, a man whose wife *fucked off*.

'Of course I bloody do,' he mumbled finally.

'You can't do this yourself?'

'I don't know where she's gone.'

'As you wish,' she replied. 'I have a little something I've been working on for some time, but never found an opportunity to use it. I'll need some of her belongings, of course. Particularly, get some of those execrable relics, if you can.'

'Fuck are you going to do?'

'Just fetch some of her belongings, and one or two things of your own, while you're at it.'

*

Malum skulked off into the night, wondering what the hell Sycoraxe was planning. More than once he had called upon her to find her busy with some unnatural thing contorting in spasms, but he had known better than to ask about it. She was a legend throughout the underground, a being from another time entirely, and her name was whispered with fear.

No doubt she would be overjoyed to have this opportunity to try out some new-fangled evil.

He hacked his way through chill winds, reaching his home through a dank sea mist. Beami hadn't yet taken much, not that he knew precisely what had gone – just a sense of something missing from the house. The bedroom first, where he gathered a pair of her breeches, and a long skirt she hadn't worn since the ice had taken a firm grip. He then proceeded downstairs, still drunk with frustration, into her workroom. Oddly, he couldn't remember the last time he had actually been there. This had always been *her* space. Papers lined the walls, drenched in esoteric scribblings and sketches. Charts of territories that were, on closer inspection, layers of the known world in other dimensions. Detailed anatomical diagrams of a rumel body. Equations with symbols he could barely identify let alone understand

Just get some of her shit and go.

There was a relic standing nearby, some cone-like piece of equipment with wires leaking from the top end. At first he touched it with reverence, as if it was some cherished and holy item ... or as if it might explode in his hands. But it didn't, it simply remained cold and inert, and so he picked it up and left.

*

'Good. Very good.' Sycoraxe turned the item this way and that, before spitting on the ground to indicate her distaste.

He observed her, half amused, half curious. She reeked of strange incense.

'I may need two or three hours to prepare for the operation,' she said. 'I would meanwhile prefer it if you didn't watch.'

'You want me to go, I'll go.'

'You can stay if you wish. Your mind is exceedingly vexed tonight. You might do something rash that could jeopardize your followers, or your own life.'

You hag! I'm more than capable of looking after myself. 'Your concern for my well-being brings a tear to my eye.'

*

He had fallen asleep, but remembered weeping before he had drifted off. Through bleary eyes he watched Sycoraxe close the door behind her, a macabre smile on her lips, flecks of blood splashed on her cheeks.

'I have finished my preparations,' she announced. 'Three hours it has taken me. Three hours! And during that time, my books and theories have proven correct.'

'What d'you mean?' he eyed her with caution. Faintly, he heard a growl coming from somewhere. In triplicate? It was too dark to fathom much of what was going on.

'Come, let me show you what has been created.'

It took an effort to pick himself off the chair and follow her upstairs. He felt he was still involved in some weird nightmare as she pushed open the door to her workspace.

Smoke burst out, and some smell he couldn't place, then a strong musk followed a deeply animal aroma. The rumbles grew intense, then he saw the eyes first, three pairs of them.

331

Dirty yellow, they were focused right on him. A momentary fear paralysed any movement.

'What . . . the fuck . . . is this?'

'Cerberus, that's what it is. Three heads denoting the past, present and future. You look concerned.'

Too right I am. The creature stood slightly taller than himself, with a shiny fur coat and jaws that looked capable of shattering stone. There was something almost human about each head, and when he squinted, he could make out anthropoid features shifting beneath the flesh of the skull as if trying painfully to push free. The three necks were pulled taut, tendons flaring with a deep aggression. They acted independently of one another, as if three creatures were inhabiting a single entity, then suddenly they would become as one, something completely at accord with its own evil.

'What does it . . . do?' A vague question, and one more concerned with his own safety than its true purpose.

'It knows her scent. It knows yours, too. It will hunt her through the streets of this city and fetch her back. When it does so, it will consume her.'

'As in . . . eat?'

'There are souls trapped within it. When it takes hers, it will join them, and thus any traces of her influence on your mind will be erased. Her soul will go to the hell realm, or so I believe.'

Cerberus lumbered up to him, each of its three heads shifting independently. Muscles rippled beneath its fur, strongly noticeable even in this dreary light. Malum could smell the creature's rank breath and pondered at the cause of that. A head came looming down towards him, till it was almost up against his face, baring its canine jaws. But Malum stood firm, not wanting to give ground despite the threat, almost wanting to growl back. The other two heads began to sniff at him, analysing his scent as if to confirm something they already knew.

'I'm not scared of you,' Malum breathed. He narrowed his eyes, and could sense that the old crone was eager with anticipation. 'How does it know who to kill? Will it go around ripping to pieces every person it encounters in the streets?'

'No more than you would do.'

'I select my targets,' he snapped, returning his gaze to Cerberus. 'I'm no random killing machine.'

'Hmm. Well, in answer to your question, it already knows her scent.'

'Then send it off, and let's get this business over with.'

Sycoraxe hobbled up to the creature and breathed something into Cerberus's nearest ear. She then led it downstairs and Malum followed, watching it descend with its awkward gait.

The mass of black paused in the street as snow spiralled about it. Both moons glowed diffusely beneath a thin layer of cloud hanging low in the west, but above the city itself there hovered the remnants of a sudden blizzard. Cressets and oil lamps glowed from inside neighbouring houses. Cerberus was kicking plumes of snow around, curious and disturbingly ludic, then with a word from Sycoraxe's mouth it ceased, and came to attention.

She uttered another order, and the gargantuan beast lumbered off into the night.

*

'Are you happy now?'

'Yes, of course I am,' Beami replied. 'Relieved too, and happier once I collect the rest of my things. I suspect I'll miss him for a while.'

'Really?'

'It's from habit more than anything else, I guess. Any new routine makes me feel unsettled. I know instinctively I've made the right decision; it doesn't stop me from feeling like a shit.'

Lupus seemed to half expect some thanks from her, and

tried to probe her mind further. 'Do you reckon that my staying here, you know, in Villiren, helped things along?'

'I'd taken other lovers after you,' Beami interrupted, and the sudden disappointment in his eyes forced her to continue quickly. *Men and their egos* . . . 'They just helped me through when I needed a little help. When I wanted to feel something, before I met him. This isn't only about you. It never was – much as I adore you. It is about getting away from . . . him. I suppose I could have gone and stayed with Zizi or someone, but I wanted to make a clean break.'

'I'm fine with that, really,' Lupus replied.

He had helped move her into a safe apartment half a mile from the Ancient Quarter, near one of the major stairwells that led down to the escape tunnels, ever concerned for her safety during any forthcoming fighting. It was a plain room, with unattractive furniture, but at least it was her own. He had asked her if she wanted to invite some of her friends from the Symbolist, in fact was hoping to meet them himself, but she declined, preferring something altogether calmer tonight. So while she unpacked he purchased coloured lanterns and cheap food and made a fire. He rustled up a traditional slave dish from the ore-mining days, and they were able to make a night of things. She drank beer from the bottle faster than he could, like they used to.

Later, after several quick alcohol-tinged kisses, they lay on the bed feeling quite separated from everyday life, listening to the sounds of the city nearby, louder than her old home, more sporadic, more unsettling. She didn't like living near two bordellos situated on the south side of the street. He couldn't resist some cheap jokes, and within the minute her hands were moving down towards his breeches.

*

Later, she joined Lupus in peering out of the window. It overlooked one of the rare crooked streets that curved away from the Ancient Quarter. The original gothic architectures had been preserved and were well lit by torches and storm lanterns. Two teenagers wearing garish masks shuffled by drunkenly, their arms around each other, and they walked right past the man sheltering in a doorway without giving him a second glance. Their raucous laughter could be heard echoing from a nearby alleyway.

Suddenly something lumbered briefly across the periphery of his vision.

Beami must have noticed his reaction because she said, 'What's wrong?'

He glanced instinctively over to his compound bow resting in the corner, then to the quiverful of arrows slung from her bedpost.

'There's something out there,' he said, trying to see where it had gone. 'There it is again, something black and bulky, a sharp contrast against the snow.'

'It's probably nothing, I wouldn't worry.'

There was a scream, followed by 'Oh no . . . no please *shit* no—'

'The homeless man's gone.'

There was a noise she couldn't place, like a dog growling.

'Would Malum have come after us?' he asked nervously.

'Possibly.'

'Look down there.' Lupus pointed to where the snow was stained by flecks of blood.

'Maybe this area is rougher than we thought,' Beami said uneasily.

He moved to the bed, slung the quiver over his shoulder, picked up his bow, then checked there was still a backup knife in his boot. He handed his short-sword to Beami. Wordlessly she accepted it and nodded, before turning to the corner, to her leather satchel full of relics.

There was an immense thud.

'The door of the building,' Beami gasped.

'Whatever it is, it's trying to get in,' Lupus confirmed. 'Shit.'

335

The door was struck again, and she heard it give way.

Beami pulled out a set of *Logi* chains from her satchel, and began to swirl the ultra-light metal artefact around until it began to emit light, and soon she was carving out shapes that separated from nothingness, bordered with a bright lilac light at first, but then becoming more solid.

A lumbering noise approaching up the stairs.

Lupus nocked an arrow and aimed it at the doorway, stepping instinctively in front of Beami.

Oh, please. Men!

Something threw its full weight against the door, making the wood shudder, and immediately it tried again, sending a thick splinter to cough back and rattle around their feet. Through the gap exposed, something with fur could be seen moving.

Lupus loosed an arrow.

It screamed – no, howled. He nocked another, fired, nocked again, fired and eventually whatever it was moved away, leaving a deep silence.

Then the door burst completely as the creature came exploding through it, and three grotesque heads were biting at everything, saliva slopping to the floor in pools. Blood seeped from the arrow wounds, but they didn't seem to impede the thing's movements.

'Get out of the way,' Beami ordered, but Lupus ignored her.

He drew his blade and assumed a fighting stance, crouching and ready, relaxing back his vision to concentrate on all three heads, and when two of them attacked simultaneously he sliced his weapon horizontally, cutting one in the cheek, then ducked beneath the other set of jaws and punched one of the creature's throats. It reeled back, winded.

Using the *Logi*, Beami whipped and cracked three bright liquid-lines out to one side of Lupus, where they slapped into the monster repeatedly, leaving a staggered row of burning light-scars in its hide.

The floorboards almost buckled as it collapsed on them, dust motes drifting around it. There was now an overwhelming stillness.

'I think I'm going to lose my deposit on this place,' Beami said eventually.

Lupus stared breathlessly at his lover, at the thin metal rods in each of her hands, and the two trailing chains that had now lost their light. 'What the hell did you do to it?'

'These things shoot concentrated energy, distilled elements – a bit like lightning. I just stunned the brute, that's all.'

'Couldn't you put enough *whatever* energy in it to kill the damn thing?'

'No, it came after us specifically, so I wanted to get a better look at it. You can slash its throats afterwards if you want. Anyway, do it outside. I've only just got everything unpacked here and I'm pissed off that I already need to clean up.'

Together they extended the heap of fallen body out till it nearly covered the length of the room. The light-line wounds were still glowing, between the parted fur, and there was a stench of burnt flesh as if it had been branded with a red-hot iron. This was clearly some form of dog, although Beami observed that no cultist had produced this. It was too perfect a specimen – cultists could only splice, creating awkward and macabre hybrids. She felt sorry for it, realizing it wasn't its fault that it had been sent here to hunt them down. The thing began to regain consciousness slowly, and Lupus was forced to kill it.

With all three of its throats slit, it bled slowly to death.

*

And in a distant, unremarkable house, far from the scene of the carnage, an old woman sat staring at her runes, screeching a torrent of abuse against the beast's destroyers.

'Fat lot of good your magic is, if the damn thing's dead,' Malum complained.

'She is evil, with her relics!'

'I suppose I'll get the lads to hunt her down after all, if there's no quicker option.'

'How will you know where to find her? Magic is the best—'

'You've tried and failed, so leave this to my lot.'

'You didn't see what I saw, through its eyes!'

'And what, dare I ask, did you see?' As if it could possibly be anything either natural or sane.

'Another man. A soldier. You have seen him, maybe? One of the Night Guard.'

He stormed out of the room. Fuck this, it was bad enough being abandoned by your wife, but to find she was running around with another man . . . He had never felt so humiliated. They both had to die, immediately.

He grabbed the relic he'd given to the witch, determined to sell all Beami's crap in the market tomorrow.

'He looks like a wolf!' the witch wailed after him, as he strode out into the cold. Her words followed him down the street, either as an echo, or in his head, he couldn't tell which.

But on his way back, he did something unexpected. With the relic – that extension of Beami – in his hands, he meandered along the lanes where he had once gone walking with her. He headed past the boarded-up stores where he had bought her presents, past bars and bistros where they had shared intimate conversations. Whenever one of his gang members approached, he ignored them, keeping his head down and his hands in his pockets, and tried to identify the moment where he had let things reach the point of no return.

Most of all he was bothered at why he had become so concerned over someone else. How was it that he, a leader of men, a half-vampyr, who could get anything he wanted, now found himself with his wife walking out of his life, and with only emptiness in her place?

Tonight he was a hollow man.

THIRTY-SIX

Jeryd drank tea, chatted with the waitress as she came to the end of her shift, but mostly he made some ephemeral notes that quickly became doodles. He watched her talking to another old rumel, and wondered if this was all she ever had to do, and if it got boring.

He sat waiting at a table by the window of the bistro, biding his time and thinking about all the things he had seen so far in this intense city.

The street door opened, a little bell rang, and Jeryd peeked up, still fractionally on edge. *As if a giant spider would come waltzing in through the front door . . .*

Bellis, Abaris and Ramon strolled in. 'Come along with us, Jeryd,' Bellis called out. 'Tonight, we converse in higher places.'

'Don't you fancy a drink?'

Bellis patted the inside of her tweeds. 'My own supply. But something warming first, to help it along my system, would be delightful.'

*

Up on the flat roof, Jeryd handed over his gift of maps one by one in the darkness, so Ramon and Abaris had to tilt them this way and that to catch some of the dim light from one of the street lamps below. They whispered swift and private matters, which merely heightened Jeryd's curiosity as to what hell they were up to in this city. After some curt discussion, each map was pocketed.

The completion of the exchange prompted Bellis into motion, and she bounded forward keenly to produce her relic. 'Now then, what we have here is a wonderful device designed to attract spiders.'

'That it?' If Jeryd was being honest, it didn't look like much, merely a narrow obsidian rod with a glowing bulb at the top. It seemed even less impressive given that the weather had turned even more sour, and he was freezing.

'Of course it is, you silly man,' Bellis added. 'Its structure is made from tektites, a mineral originating from another world – ha, we always say that, don't we? – since it's found mostly in meteorites, but whatever the stuff contains, it has tested superbly in sucking up dozens of our little arachnid friends. We've augmented – you know the word? – augmented the frequencies of the inner circuitry and so, according to the theory, we should have this giant arachnid of yours bagged in no time.'

'And when it gets here?' Jeryd enquired.

'Ah yes, the boys have been working on that. Ramon?'

The sinister-looking bald man leaned down to pick up a small bag. From it he retrieved a small brass tripod, which he then lowered to the rooftop, several feet away.

'Best move back,' Abaris warned, arms wide, steering them back another several feet at least. He pulled an ordinary stick from his pocket, and threw it in the direction of the tripod.

The relic remained inert, not reacting.

'It wasn't actually meant to do anything because it was too small,' Bellis whispered to Jeryd. 'Now, watch this.'

Ramon moved towards the relic, hands held behind his back. As soon as he was within two feet, light stuttered into being, aggregating into the glowing bars of a cage. Light continued to spit and stutter, and Ramon was totally imprisoned within it. Grinning, he made a flamboyant bow so that the light reflected off his bald head.

'So you see,' Bellis explained, 'when your spider arrives, it will be catered for very well indeed.'

'You lot really are a bunch of wise old geniuses, you realize,' Jeryd said.

'It takes one individual of wisdom to notice another,' Bellis declared.

'Nah, I've done nothing yet,' Jeryd protested. 'I won't consider myself as having achieved a single thing until that monster is locked away.' He waited as the cage was deactivated, the light collapsing into blackness, and there was a noticeable *absence*, some void left by the relic's trickery, even the faint smell of burning. Jeryd was mightily impressed.

'Let's give it a go then,' Bellis said, and the others set up the two devices next to each other on the rooftop. And they waited, shivering, in the cold winds.

Jeryd regarded the cityscape in anticipation, wondering how his own deepest fears would manifest after his experiences with Bellis's orb.

*

Nanzi felt something deep within, a summoning in her very core. She shuddered, leapt up from her bed, glanced furtively around the room. The black cat peeked up in surprise from the foot of the bed.

'Is everything all right, my love?' Voland asked, glancing up from his book as he lay beside her.

'I don't feel all that well. I might make a drink and take some fresh air outside.'

'Would you like me to get it for you?'

'No, I'll go.' She pushed aside the sheets and clambered off the bed. Her spider appendages rooted out her skirt and boots, and within the minute she was heading downstairs. At the front door, she rested her hand on the frame, staring across the street, hoping to find something. The darkened buildings were defined by starlight, while a couple of tramps huddled by a small pit fire.

What was this strange sensation that had seduced her out here? It was like a thirst. All her emotions had condensed. A need for some long-lost lover. A lament for a dead friend. But this was rare – this was calling for her ... *other* state. She felt intoxicated by her urges and, within the minute, she began to collapse inwards, then fold out again into her spider form.

With one limb she pulled the door shut, then crawled up along the surface of the wall to the roof of the abattoir. There, she could read the world in a different manner, decipher these gentle vibrations of activity. The city always appeared thronging to her in this form, but some way in the distance she could sense something so alluring, so delicious, so essential that she could not prevent herself from scuttling as quickly as she could across the deserted nightscape.

*

Jeryd watched in slack-jawed awe as hundreds of tiny spiders bled from the city's architecture.

Out of habit he felt the need to jump on something to avoid them, but there was no way of escape up here. And this time ... he felt no fear.

Black streams of arachnids centred on the Grey Hairs' relic, countless trickles and trails of tiny legs and bulbous torsos. As he gazed across the nearby rooftops he could see their massed progress gliding across the slick slate-crowned buildings, and they were coming from all directions. By now Jeryd had retreated well out of the way for fear of being smothered by them, but he did not feel anything like as petrified as he used to be.

Jeryd's nerves jittered from simply being present in this intensely surreal scene, from being surrounded by what seemed like all of the spiders in the Boreal Archipelago. Creatures that normally inhabited the dead regions of the city were gathering in one place – but he did not tremble, and felt only a fraction of that familiar tightness in his heart. All the time, though, he kept a lookout for the one monster, stealing glances between the buildings and wherever the moonlight failed to penetrate.

He untucked a blade from his boot and clutched it uncertainly; of what possible use could it be against this immense arachnid abomination? The Grey Hairs, by contrast, seemed thoroughly relaxed, as they slouched about in casual postures. Bellis turned to focus on him now and then with her hands resting on her hips. Jeryd simply nodded the answer for her unspoken question, *Are you all right?*

Ramon was sitting at the edge of the roof, while Abaris seemed preoccupied with the workings of some other relic. It was as if they found themselves in crazy situations like this every day of their lives.

Bellis suddenly called out, 'Good heavens, I think it's coming!'

Jeryd clambered to her side, his vision following the direction she was pointing in. About forty feet away, to the east, a large shape could be seen lumbering closer, moving with a fluid gait across and down in between the architecture, now and then spitting out a slick gossamer rope of silk to aid its progress.

'Bloody hell,' Jeryd breathed. This was all right in theory, but now the thing was actually on its way, he had no idea how to cope with it.

'Aye, I'll second that,' Abaris murmured, now beside them.

They watched it come closer, accruing in size all the time. People peering out of windows began to scream, and in the streets below others avoided its path. It almost seemed drunk, staggering in and out of vision with ragged movements. The creature was mammoth, each leg probably longer than Jeryd himself, yet it hauled its bulk onto the stone parapet of their rooftop with a series of precise clicks, as thousands of its miniature kin swarmed around and underneath.

With its myriad eyes, the monster observed the glow of the relic tentatively, but it simply could not resist its allure; a distilled, love-hate tension generated between them. It could not counter this enchantment. Very slowly, it edged closer, lowering its bulbous black head, and levering its thorax and abdomen forward. Then it stretched out its two front legs like a dog, tilting back up on the four hind ones.

There, it quivered ecstatically.

Light suddenly snapped itself free from the relic, lashing up to form a huge cage and trapped the spider within. The creature threw itself at the bars of light only to be stung savagely into retreat. It lunged repeatedly at its light-restraints, all the while emitting high-pitched screeches. Back and forth, the stinging inflicted by the bars was clearly audible, and after several attempts, the spider cowered into submission, its body rising and falling in spasms.

'Splendid!' Bellis declared, clapping her hands. 'It was that simple, eh, Jeryd?' The glow of the lure relic ceased, the torrent of smaller spiders hesitated, then began to move of their own volition, suddenly a million individuals once again. For a moment they milled about uncertainly, and it seemed an age until they had located tiny exits in the surrounding buildings.

Approaching the cage, Jeryd stood and gawked at the beast contained within. He'd expected to be far more frightened than he now felt. Was this the thing that was snatching people off the streets? What the hell kind of case was he dealing with here? He was long used to dealing with monsters of the human or rumel kind, but this . . . this was something else completely.

The three Grey Hair cultists approached from behind and studied the monstrosity alongside him. Bellis had even begun making sketches in a notebook, while the others inspected it from all angles, Abaris muttering anatomical features and cladistic theory out loud.

It seemed to possess innumerable eyes, all of them reflecting the light radiated by the cage. All staring back at him. Examining him. And whether or not this was his paranoia, he couldn't tell, but it certainly seemed as if the giant spider knew exactly who Jeryd was.

*

Voland leapt out of bed as he heard the Phonoi make a screech downstairs.

Where was Nanzi? In a panic, and sensing something wasn't right, he scampered around the room hurriedly dressing himself. He darted away from the bedroom, still bleary-eyed, and called out for her. There was no reply. He stumbled downstairs.

There was no sign of her throughout the entire house in fact, so he hastened even deeper through the darkness, feeling his way along the walls to the abattoir with its familiar stench of death. He was met only with silence.

'Nanzi?!' he shouted urgently. 'Nanzi, are you there?'

'She's not here,' one of the Phonoi replied. It quivered in and out of ghost-form, first the face of a screaming child, then an old woman, then blackness.

'Sorry, sir,' another chimed. 'We know she's out. We sense her . . .'

'She's right across the city.'

'We sense she's trapped somewhere.'

In the stillness of the room the Phonoi began to glow uniformly. They shifted through the air, as they always did, drifting about in sharp bursts only to skim away into nothing at all. He wished they would stay still so he could establish some clear answers.

'Where is she?' Voland pleaded.

'Trapped is all we know,' the Phonoi declared. 'We simply feel it.'

'I need to get to her,' Voland ordered. 'Help me, please.'

'Anything for Doctor Voland,' they called out soothingly. 'Yes, anything at all.'

After a brief silence, a number of them took form and

became one mass, then began to circle the room in rapid motion. They tightened their circuit around Voland, a strangling wind that settled underneath him, and around his waist. He felt a sudden lightness, and realized he was being lifted into the air then moved backward along the route he had taken to the slaughterhouse.

'She'll need clothes when she transforms . . .' Voland began.

They whisked him upstairs in a flurry, let him stuff a few of her garments into a satchel, then down again. It was dizzying.

Ahead of him a door burst back, and as he flew out suddenly into the streets of the city, people pointed and stared. The Phonoi tilted him upright, like he was walking on air, and he held on to his hat as they rose higher, heading to the west, above the snow-slick rooftops of Villiren, noticing the little street fires and torches and flashes of magic, the movement of customers to and from taverns, the patrols of soldiers . . . all becoming smaller with the distance.

He flew towards his lover.

*

Jeryd turned and pointed. 'Over there, in the distance above the rooftops.' Something was moving across the horizon, a figure with a faint white glow blurring its outline. It dipped back and forth, then moved steadily. Bats scattered from the crevices along its route, making their escape in erratic paths.

'What on earth do you suppose that is?' Bellis asked.

'It wears a top hat.' Abaris was peering through a small telescope. 'Blimey. Those are Phonoi around it, I'll wager.'

'Bugger, I hope not,' Bellis whispered. 'You sure, Abaris?'

'Aye, for sure,' the man replied, moving the brass tube in gentle pursuit of the moving figure. 'Quite an intensity of them, I'd say. They're helping him to fly.'

'What the hell are Phonoi?' Jeryd had moved with the Grey Hairs away from the cage, towards the edge of the rooftop, infected by Bellis's sudden nervousness.

'Spirit wraiths,' Bellis explained. 'Those blighters were once prisoners – murderers to be precise – who had their lives *quite literally* sucked out of them by means of ancient technologies. At a very creepy and unsavoury point in our history, I'd say.'

'I'm not sure I've a clue what you're on about,' Jeryd sighed.

'The process was intended to separate people's minds from their bodies, but it failed to produce any real results, so at the time led to the belief that mind and body were in fact one. Instead, it was the prisoners' ... essence, for want of a less technical word, that was ripped from them, and distilled neatly into portable devices. That stolen essence is what comprises the Phonoi, making each of them a spirit of murder. And, pardon my language, but they're bloody nasty to deal with close up.'

And I used to think those nights in Villjamur were full of freak shows, Jeryd thought. *This place is twice as bad.*

'So we shall deal with this from afar!' Bellis immediately scurried back to her satchel, and began rummaging around inside. The figure was coming closer now, still hovering on that white wind. The Grey Hairs advised Jeryd to shuffle back towards the cage for his own safety. He was neither reluctant nor eager to do so, feeling so utterly out of place amid such weirdness. There were clearly things in this world of greater mystery than he knew how to deal with.

The old cultists took up position on the edge of the roof, each of them gripping an identical metal tube in one hand. Abaris seemed to pull a strip of material off his tube, amber dust from it caught up in the wind. They conferred. They clashed their relics like tankards in a bar. Suddenly something sparked up into the sky above, like a firework, carving the air with a scream, which faded as their missile penetrated the cloud base.

Thunder rolled in the sky, or something like it, and then came a glow that highlighted the dense layers of cumulus.

Well, I never ... Jeryd thought, as if he could witness any more surprises tonight.

Swooping down from out of the clouds came a titanic skeletal form of a garuda, constructed entirely from a purple light. Only the edges of this being glowed; in the gaps where the meat should be, there was nothing.

It swooped down directly above their heads, then arced majestically towards the oncoming figure. Jeryd noticed how Abaris and Ramon were both grinding their relics this way and that, in the same manner, as if operating a kite.

As the electric garuda sailed down, forcing a current of wind, the figure spotted it and began heading away instantly, towards the east, no longer towards them, all the time chased by its relic-inspired pursuer. The hunt was fast and intense, their weird shapes skimming just above the tops of houses, ripping up roof tiles and stirring street detritus in their wake.

It was all over before the first minute was out.

The garuda opened a skeletal framework of jaws and consumed the figure whole, then turned slowly in a graceful arc back towards the rooftop where Abaris and Ramon were cheering loudly like a couple of kids playing games. They guided the apparition gently down towards the cage, murmuring brief orders and directions.

Jeryd edged backwards in alarm, wary of this construct. As it merged with the bars of light, the figure that had been pursuing them was deposited alongside the spider, his top hat falling to the floor beside him.

'Oh, well done, boys!' Bellis cried.

It was only then that the spider began to change shape, at first lurching and convulsing, then its limbs bending and contracting out of context.

You are absolutely bloody joking, Jeryd thought. *That's impossible . . .*

It contorted into his Inquisition aide, Nanzi, who was now naked, and upon seeing this, the man with the top hat immediately produced a satchel with some clothing in it. She

348

hastily covered herself up, and then huddled alongside him. He placed his arm around her protectively.

The cultists and Jeryd stood in awed silence observing their catch.

'We've a fine brace tonight, then. Shame we couldn't trap the Phonoi, still, it's a fairly good haul even for us old things,' Bellis declared. Then, after a deep frown: 'I say, Jeryd, do you suppose these two know each other?'

'I'm not sure about that,' he replied, eyeing them still. 'But would you believe that girl is meant to be my assistant?'

*

Back in the lazaret adjoining the Inquisition headquarters, deep in the night with all the investigators and aides and administrative staff safely at home, and with Aharis and Ramon 'recalibrating' their equipment, whatever the hell that meant, Jeryd and Bellis contemplated Nanzi and the man in the top hat. After restricting the initial cage in size, they had forced the pair to walk the streets surrounded by their light-prison, while passers-by gawked in awe. Jeryd brought them back to the quarantine section, afraid of what diseases these culprits might carry.

With them safely behind bars, Jeryd lit a flambeau fixed to the wall, and their faces glowed softly from the corner of the room. A deep chill persisted, but he lit no fire for their comfort.

For some time he merely watched them. His mind was overflowing with questions. But where to start?

'What *are* you?' he demanded finally.

Her head was down, her hair in front of her face.

'What were you *doing*? You claim to be some honourable girl, and yet ... And yet ...'

Jeryd sat down on a stool with a sigh, his energy drained utterly by the scenes he had witnessed earlier. There was always a strange sensation of emptiness when he brought in a

349

perpetrator after such a difficult case. The search for them filled up some hole in his life, so once they had been brought in, there was just a void. He devoted such a degree of mindspace to each individual criminal, carrying their activities around in his head. 'Why didn't you kill me, Nanzi, when you had the chance?'

She looked up at him meekly as if to speak, but after the man whispered something to her, she immediately focused again on the floor.

'I'm guessing,' Bellis suggested to Jeryd, 'that you must have provided her with some sort of essential information. Hmm. Was there any specific Inquisition stuff that only you had access to?'

After a moment, Jeryd mumbled, 'The commander, maybe. She was with me some of the times when he would give me military updates.' Did she want details of patrols? The movements of soldiers around the city so she could plan her next killing? Maybe to know when to be ready to flee?

'But she tried to kill me earlier, in the theatre . . .' None of this was making sense. Perhaps she . . . this *thing* actually did care for him enough to let him live for a while. Jeryd turned to the man with the top hat. It was just possible that this fellow had some control over matters. 'Hey, you there, what's your name?'

'My name is Doctor Voland.' The words were spoken crisply, and he held himself with great dignity. So at last some answers might be forthcoming.

Voland: the same name Malum had given him. The same man who made weird specimens, and dealt in questionable meat. Jeryd would get to that later – the essentials first. 'Is Nanzi here your wife?'

'She is my *partner*,' Voland insisted.

'So that's why you came to rescue her, right?'

No reply.

After a moment's consideration, Jeryd stood up and approached the bars to study him closely. He was a distinguished-looking gentleman, much older than Nanzi. His clothing was also finely tailored, and there was an air of mild arrogance about his manners. Although at the moment he appeared glum, in another situation he might electrify a room with his persona.

Jeryd asked, 'What's your business in Villiren?'

No reply.

'Why did you come out to the rooftops tonight?'

No reply.

'What do you know about selling bad meat?'

He looked up at that, but gave no reply.

Jeryd turned to Bellis with a nod.

'Right you are, investigator,' she responded. The cultist pulled out the device that activated the imprisoning bars of light, this time separating the prisoners by bisecting their cage. Voland at once took renewed interest, his face expressing his concern for his lover. He prodded the intervening bars, but wrenched his hands away as soon as he touched whatever electric diablerie they contained. Nanzi had said nothing all this time, simply staring into the distance. One of her knees was raised so he could see the black, coarse-haired appendage that was one of her legs. *She can't even look at me*, Jeryd thought. He didn't know what to make of her now – though he was getting used to being betrayed by those closest to him. How could such a quiet, determined young woman be a killer? It made no sense. It was not in her essential nature to be so.

'Leave her alone,' Voland cautioned, looking from her to Jeryd, and back again.

'You're not in a position to give orders,' Jeryd declared. 'Talk, or her cell gets smaller than yours, by a considerable amount.'

Voland sighed deeply and Jeryd knew that he would provide

answers soon enough. He might be proud and determined, but he seemed to be too much in love with Nanzi to have her suffer any further.

'All right,' he conceded. 'But please refrain from harming her.'

'Harm her?' Jeryd asked. 'We've reason to believe her responsible for the murder of dozens of innocent civilians, as well as military personnel.'

For a while, Jeryd could hear nothing but his own feet as he walked back and forth through the room. 'First thing I want to know is how does Nanzi change her shape from this one to . . . that creature? I've heard how certain members of the underworld haven't been too happy with your shoddy work in creating hybrids.'

'That's absolutely outrageous.'

Jeryd smiled. 'You admit to constructing hybrids then? Did *you* make Nanzi into a monster?'

'It's a difficult art . . .' Dejectedly, Voland went on to relate the couple's history, about the collapsed wall on the harbour, and her damaged legs and his talents as a surgeon. He confirmed that Nanzi possessed this innate ability to change physical state between that of a spider and that of a human being – aside from her new legs, which remained arachnid.

'Touching,' Jeryd added sarcastically. 'So, tell me, where do you live?'

Voland gave the address of the building that Jeryd had been loitering outside only recently, the one into which the dead garuda had been taken.

Jeryd rested an arm on the bars as he leaned towards his captives. The wall of purple light gave off a deep warmth and a faint hum. 'We have witnesses stating that Nanzi, in her other form, has committed the murder of military personnel. We also have reason to believe that she has been responsible for numerous other deaths. What do you want to say on the matter?'

Voland peered at her, through the light, then back towards Jeryd. He merely gave a brief nod, and pressed his fingers to his eyes as if to prevent himself from becoming overly emotional.

'How much control do you have over her?' Jeryd asked.

'I don't know what you mean?' Voland replied.

'Did you force her to serve you in some way?'

Nanzi suddenly spoke up for the first time. 'I did what I did because I loved him, and I did it for myself, because it was the right thing to do. We work as a team.'

'So you confess, then?' Jeryd offered, unmoved, unflinching.

There was venom in her eyes, as if the satanic creature she once was had resurfaced. Jeryd was glad of the bars between them, and suddenly he realized the meaning in her last words. 'You were a team? You worked together? What on earth were you both doing, just killing all these people for sport?'

No reply.

'We'll have your residence searched immediately, you realize. Whatever you're hiding there, we'll find it. We'll dig up every last piece of information and, if we don't find enough, the next procedure is to commence torture.'

As if to hammer her point home, Bellis made the light-bars flare even hotter, and Jeryd could see the resignation in the man's eyes. He didn't want anything bad to happen to Nanzi.

What Voland told him next stunned him. 'We've nothing to lose, not now anyway. So, to business. I am working on a high-level contract from Villjamur.'

'What kind of service is required?'

'I'm a specialist surgeon,' he replied proudly. 'I don't just make hybrids for the underworld. Although my current work now is highly specialized – and commercialized, if you will. You may have noticed that there is an abundance of food in Villiren, which seems odd given the desperate times we live in.'

'You work on providing food?'

'Indeed, and there is an ample meat supply – essential during the ice age, and also a period of war. I am responsible for that supply – or rather, Nanzi and myself are.'

Jeryd had a bad feeling about this conversation. He thought back to the garuda he had witnessed being carried into the abattoir building. 'Garuda meat?' *Is that why it smelled off?*

'On occasion, yes, but mainly human or rumel meat. Good, lean chunks of it, distributed though the markets. To feed the people, and nourish our city. Our culture does the same to animals, so what difference does it make regarding humans?'

Was the man lying just to show off?

Jeryd turned to catch the expression of shock on Bellis's face. 'How can this even be possible?' she managed to say, but Jeryd had already put together the picture in his head.

'Quite simple, really,' he offered. 'Nanzi here ventures out at night in her other form. She drags citizens from the streets, leaving no evidence – hence they're considered missing persons, and not murder victims. Then she brings the corpses back to Voland. He performs whatever sick rituals he needs. They then sell the cuts of meat to the gangs, who in turn sell it on to the traders. In essence, the city is now full of unwitting cannibals.'

'And we once suspected you weren't all that bright.' Voland was clearly getting some pleasure from listening to this explanation. The man pushed himself up to his feet, flicked back his sleeves and approached Jeryd, till the two stood almost face to face. There was some sinister elegance about the man, some deep connection with thoughts that were too sickening for Jeryd to contemplate.

'Why did you kill soldiers? You knew they're helping the city.'

'They provided good meat that would feed numerous families.'

'Where did you draw the line? Women, children?'

'We never took children,' Voland declared with pride.

'Couldn't look into their innocent little faces? Too much guilt?' Jeryd suggested.

'No, too little meat,' Voland replied. 'There was no point.'

Scumbag . . . 'This high-level contract you mentioned, is it in any way connected to Emperor Urtica?'

'You know him, then! He's an old school chum, from back in Villjamur. Never thought he'd rise so high in the Council, let alone become Emperor.'

'You're not one of his cult, are you?'

'I know of no cult. He merely wanted his people here fed, and this is such a simple solution, isn't it? For me, it's an interesting little job, and it keeps the money rolling in – certainly a more interesting challenge than making trophy beasts for the gangs. In a free-market economy such as ours, dear investigator, everything has a price. All those deaths . . . well, they're merely the externalitics of the market. Would you rather have people starving?'

How free do you think the market is, in an Empire like ours that cripples one endeavour and props up another? Jeryd thought. *Bohr, how can anyone even begin to justify any of this?*

'Is it just Urtica you're working for?'

After a moment's reflection, staring into the darkness and absent-mindedly rubbing his arm, Voland declared, 'Might as well drag the rest along with us: our Portreeve Lutto knew about it, for a start.' A grin slid up one side of his face.

Jeryd composed himself from the shock, turned away, then methodically paced the room in a soundless rage. He was not at all surprised to learn that Urtica was at the root of this evil. Even from afar, the Emperor seemed able to disgust him with his sick machinations, his secret dealings, his whispered words and cult worship. In this Empire, the innocent were considered merely numbers and statistics, overlooked in a relentless drive for expansion and the centralization of power. But Lutto too? Would Jeryd even be able to report this connection, and risk being hunted down by the portreeve's henchmen?

355

He glanced at Nanzi, who still sat hunched on the floor, knees drawn up to her chin, utterly silent.

'Do you eat the killings yourself?' Jeryd asked Voland.

'Oh heavens, no,' Voland laughed. 'I'm a strict vegetarian. To me, all meat involves killing.'

'How many citizens have you killed in total?' Jeryd demanded. 'All those people who have disappeared off the city streets – are they *all* down to you?'

'Quite probably,' Voland replied coolly. 'Although I'm sure quite a few may have gone missing for other reasons. I couldn't really put a number on them since we've been operating for some time. I wouldn't be surprised if it was a couple of thousand. It's been the devil's own work . . .'

The doctor seemed totally detached from his activities. In his own head, the man must clearly rationalize the impossible and the immoral, to the point where he considered he was actually doing something commendable.

'You sick, sick bastards,' Jeryd declared. 'You don't regret any of this carnage, do you?'

'Why should I regret it?' Voland replied. 'I've been keeping people alive and healthy enough to face a war. One must always look at the bigger picture, investigator.'

In all his decades of working for the Inquisition, Jeryd had never encountered such large-scale horror. Thousands dead and distributed along the food chain: Villiren had unknowingly become a city of cannibals. He might have even eaten such meat himself.

Jeryd indicated for Bellis to disconnect the intervening light-bars separating the captives. After a tentative movement, as they contemplated the removal of the barrier, the pair of them embraced for all to see in the chilling darkness of the cell.

Jeryd left the room with Bellis, too depressed to speak to her at first.

Having made sure the cell door was locked firmly, with as many security measures as possible, they made their way along the corridor heading back to Jeryd's office. There he lit a fire before the two of them slumped into chairs in contemplative silence.

Bellis spoke first. 'Well now, you've caught them, at least.'

Jeryd exhaled deeply. 'I'm a lousy investigator, and I just have to face the fact.'

'How d'you mean?'

'I took far too long to put all the pieces in place. I'm inept. How could I not consider Nanzi being involved...' Jeryd shook his head. 'I'm struggling at this job, even though I try hard. I'm too old maybe. I guess reality catches up with you eventually.'

'Nonsense, you miserable sod. The killers are caught, that's all that matters. So what will you do with that pair of freaks?'

'I'll have to search their dwellings and see if there's any further evidence. We've already got witnesses to Nanzi's transformation, and their own confession, so it should be quite a straightforward case that'll result in their execution according to Empire laws. That's if we can manage to convince our superiors – they claimed the portreeve is in on this racket, too.'

Bellis nodded. 'We don't know that for certain since we only have their word for it.'

'True,' Jeryd murmured. 'And thanks for helping me. It was you who did all this – brought them in so easily, and helped me get over my own fears. You're a remarkable woman, and I realize there's very little in this for you...'

'Little in it?' Bellis said. 'You *are* silly! I do things because I choose to, helping others because I'm not thinking of myself all the time.'

'That why you're here in Villiren, to help others?'

'More or less,' Bellis admitted cryptically.

'You're never going to tell me, are you?'

'Next time we have drinks, perhaps I'll tell you then.' Bellis gave him a distant smile.

Jeryd realized then that, if anything emerged from all of tonight's debacle, he had at least made a friend, and that you could never be too old for that sort of thing.

'And what's the situation with Ramon and Abaris then? Always giving each other funny looks.'

'Oh, those old queens,' Bellis said lovingly, 'they're such wonderful cultists. Never give me a dull moment. Their actual speciality is necromancy believe it or not, but despite that there is more life and wisdom in what they do and say than I get from nearly anyone I've met. I don't like to say too much about them – you know, with the laws and such, primitive as our culture is. But you seem the sort who wouldn't make an issue of it.'

'Well, I'm not too stuck in my ways, despite being an old-timer. But I notice Ramon never says anything,' Jeryd added.

'No. The old fellow received some kind of energy overdose once from a relic. Robbed him of his voice and, oddly, his hair. But Abaris adores him and speaks for him often, since they know each other so well. I've seen Ramon only need to look at Abaris in a particular way and Abaris can instantly interpret it.'

They both looked up at the sound of an explosion outside – somewhere deep in the city. The floor shook just moments before a second explosion.

'What the hell was that?' Jeryd exclaimed.

THIRTY-SEVEN

The *Exmachina* was a city ship, Artemisia had declared proudly, powered by two immense metal plates reacting to the Earth's hidden forces. Artemisia further described it as a 'magnetic barge', although this made things little clearer. Randur had no comprehension of much of what Artemisia explained, or the true functions of the ship.

He remained simply in awe.

There were city decks below, situated where would have been the hold and bulkhead of a normal ship, three levels containing streets and eclectic wooden buildings impossibly crammed in. And they were all empty. No people wandering in and out of the darkness, a ghost city of lanterns remaining unlit, passageways crowded by dust. Bold and intricate arches adorned many of the buildings down there, some billeted and others possessing fine interlacing motifs but in designs that were beautiful, completely alien to the new arrivals. Small and ragged rips in the hull permitted sunlight, although these gaps were being repaired at a constant rate by the Hanuman – the term Artemisia used to describe the winged monkeys. For the time being, this warrior woman was living alone on here, she told them, with only the Hanuman for company, moving through the skies in search of the travellers. She spoke philosophically about her lonely quest.

They were all now seated on the main deck – there were no benches to be found anywhere. There was no mast, no sails rippling tightly, just raised wooden platforms that stretched endlessly, and isolated cabins scattered across the ship's width seemingly without thought or purpose. There were shrubs and plants and vines sprouting everywhere, and lichen swarmed around the rim of the ship, clinging on the few vertical planes where nothing else could exist. It might just have seemed possible that this vegetation was holding the entire structure together.

Randur enquired about the ship's origins.

'It is able to slice through from my own world to any other dimension,' Artemisia revealed. 'That is a word you use, is it not? My terminology may well exceed your range.'

'You mean from your world to ours?' Eir suggested. 'Then, yes, I suppose that's still the word we might choose, although it has other uses in our language. Come to mention it, how is it that you can speak our language, if you do not come from our *dimension*?'

'I speak most known languages, give or take a few dialects. Your own is enforced within your Empire, which certainly makes things easier for me.'

'Artemisia,' Rika breathed the name as if she felt honoured to be in her company, 'tell us why you're here. Are you ... Jorsalir? Are you even one of the Dawnir? I feel I already know you, perhaps from a description in some text I've studied. There was someone in Villjamur who was said to be that ancient, but he looked nothing like you.'

'I know nothing about this fraud you mention. He could have been one of any number of types. Where I come from, there is no shortage of variants.' Artemisia gave a macabre chuckle, removed her swords and placed them on the deck. She sat down cross-legged next to them, and almost instinctively Rika moved closer to the bulky figure.

Randur kept wondering why the former Empress was behaving in so strangely intimate a manner.

The expression on Artemisia's face suggested what she was

about to say was not easy for her. 'You need to know that my own people have been fighting a war for hundreds of epic cycles. In fact, ever since we were liberated by Frater Mercury.'

'Who's that?' Randur asked.

'It was he who gave us our freedom – our whole existence is thanks to him. But we abuse such freedoms through long millennia of violence. Only now have our internal wars infringed upon your dimension. The last ten cycles have seen our enemy find methods of entering other dimensions, although they have not yet set foot in this one. How may I put this simply: they wish to repopulate this primitive world with inhabitants from their own, and carve out a new society. All of our races wish to come here, in fact, because our own dimension is scheduled to end long before this one will. The temperatures for us are very hostile, the sun something we have no experience of. The invasion has already come to your lands to the west of this archipelago, while in the east, beyond your cartographical awareness, cities greater than Villjamur are already burning, with millions being slaughtered in their own homes. Cities are being systematically cleared in preparation. You have a word called "genocide", I believe?'

Randur took a deep breath, trying to absorb this staggering information.

'I had hoped to find you in Villjamur, Jamur Rika, to make my discussions with you somewhat simpler, but you went on the run instead.'

No one said anything for a while. A melancholic atmosphere took over the group as they attempted to comprehend just what this warrior woman was telling them. Randur simply didn't know what to make of it. He had thought he knew a lot about the world, but clearly not. In a few sentences their entire existence had been so casually undermined – if this being was to be believed.

Artemisia continued. 'I have therefore had to track you down – not a simple task given your current weather patterns

– which has meanwhile allowed their brood to not only wipe out an island but also move to assault one of your major urban settlements. Personally, I care not about dead humans, however my superiors, what you call the Dawnir, feel somewhat indebted to their creators.'

Eir suddenly then realized. 'We created *them*, the Dawnir? We created the gods?'

Randur thought he had never heard anything so ridiculous, but stole a glance at Rika, who had devoted so many years to worshipping Astrid, the female embodiment of the Dawnir that humans had now apparently created. Still, they only had the word of this murderess to go on. 'How can we trust anything *you* say on this?' he snarled.

A thunderous sigh from Artemisia. 'I guarded you, even when you didn't know it. I watched those Empire warriors closing in on you – I had located you by the time you had departed that rural abode, but I already knew the old one had sent signals for those men to intercept you. You, Randur, even saw one of the Hanuman while you were dozing by the fire – they were watching over you. You were all quite safe, even when Jamur Eir was snatched and taken into the caves by Ancients of your own world. They were harmless creatures and their construct would not have significantly harmed you.'

Randur felt shame at having been spied upon without his knowledge, but shrugged it off. As if hearing their name mentioned, one of the Hanuman darted overhead, followed by another. Artemisia barked something at them in an unnatural tongue, before the creatures calmed down, descending in a flutter to settle at the far end of the deck.

'I simply do not believe this assertion that we created our own gods,' Eir said suddenly.

Artemisia sighed. 'Time is vast. The Truwisans – people of Truwisa, or Dawnir as your culture corrupted the name – are crafted from your ancient technologies. We were made from your *imagination*. This was all before you diminished yourselves to this primitive way of living after the wars of your culture, your rebellion against such change. One human guided our creation – Frater Mercury – and our liberation was with the guidance of him, too. He is now a god to us. So we ancient creatures – my ancestors, I mean – had been cultured to perfection, before they took over your world. Then they were forced to abandon it.'

'What, just like that?'

'There were ... complications. Technology had become so intimidating, so it is said, and much of your kind rebelled against Frater Mercury and his creations. Given the bloodshed, it became prudent for us to sidestep into another realm of existence – and we departed from the very location where Villjamur now sits. So now I have come here seeking to bargain with the most powerful leader in these islands, and the fact that you are no longer the ruler of this Empire, Jamur Rika, causes me a predicament. *You* are the one my superiors instructed me to find. It is by your permission that landscapes can be altered. It was with you alone that we were supposed to form an alliance, so that we could move ourselves from our world in a well-ordered and peaceful manner.'

'Peaceful?' Randur snapped. 'You didn't seem particularly peace-loving just a while ago.'

'In my superiors' eyes, I am considered violent,' Artemisia admitted. 'Why else do you think they keep me away from my homeworld as often as possible?'

'Why not just negotiate with Urtica?' Randur sneered. 'He's the one in power now, so you should be talking to him.'

'He suffers from some kind of ... instability, so it is believed. It is clear that he is not one for us to debate with. He would not understand our ways, which makes our task substantially more complex, and, furthermore, he is not a man with a peaceful nature. As I said, the repopulation must be conducted harmoniously. Besides, my instructions were to find you, Jamur Rika.'

'Couldn't you just come back at any point in time and repopulate?'

'You say that as if there was any room for debate in the matter. There are a handful of time-paths available. This is the path of least resistance – because you are still so primitive, and the land remains reasonably hospitable. Remember, we come not to fight.' She turned to the two women. 'Jamur Rika, I feel, has a more pacifist nature than other leaders. To introduce our alien culture into yours successfully, it is essential that the process is holistic and integrated. Otherwise, this entire world of yours collapses too.'

'Can't you put a stop to any of this endless violence, in both our worlds?' Rika interrupted.

Randur realized then that Rika was ready to believe everything this death-machine was saying to them.

'On these islands,' Rika continued, 'across *my* Empire, peace would always be preferable, then your lives would not be wasted.'

Artemisia laughed bitterly, then simply shook her head. Randur imagined he saw the distant millennia reflected in her oddly glowing eyes. Here was a woman absolutely tired of what she was. 'You say *peace* as if it were an offering of wine.'

Rika took hold of her gaze for a moment.

*

Artemisia left them alone for a while, and the three sat in a contemplative silence. Dusk approached, and the two moons progressed alongside each other, skimming the blood-coloured cloud-base.

'It might all be lies,' Randur said eventually. It irritated him, this sudden revelatory burst of new knowledge.

No one responded to him at first.

Eir said, 'Unlikely though, isn't it? I mean, just look around you. And don't stare at me like that. Whenever you don't understand something, you simply become irate. It's perfectly all right to not understand this.'

Calming himself, Randur glanced up to watch the Hanuman flapping about eccentrically as silhouettes. Artemisia rejoined them eventually, carrying what he took to be a telescope. For a moment she focused on the horizon.

'The two moons look beautiful from here,' Rika offered.

'You think *both* of them are moons?' Artemisia seemed surprised, and pocketed the device. 'That does amuse me.'

Not more crap. Randur was now feeling overwhelmed by unwanted information. His entire concept of the world had been shattered by these conversations. He almost didn't want to know the truth, preferring the sanctuary of innocence or ignorance.

They talked of nothing significant for the rest of the evening, instead taking shelter below deck. Artemisia remained intimidating, but she conducted herself with grace, and saw that they were well looked after. Food had been left for them on a large platter, fruits and vegetables he'd never seen, olives and figs, and there was also bread and watered wine.

They huddled together in a small cabin panelled with dark wood, on a bed covered in opulent cushions. Around the edge of the room were placed long chests whose flat lids were painted with various scenes presumably from this other culture. A tripod stood next to the bed, and coloured lanterns hung from the roof. Gemstones were set into the wood furniture – lapis lazuli and jasper and quartz.

The three of them ate on the bed in silence. Randur kept thinking about the things that Artemisia had saying, about their world not being how they had thought it to be.

*

After night had fallen, Eir and Randur took a walk above deck. It was surprisingly warm, as if the ship was emitting its own heat from within. Initially, the smell of smoke prompted thoughts of wood fires, but they couldn't see any. Eventually Eir pointed out that all the Hanuman were smoking roll-ups, similar to those used back in Villjamur.

Randur thought it absurd.

'Little addicts, are they not?' Artemisia had appeared silently behind them, her hands clasped behind her back. She approached alongside. Even without factoring in her size, Artemisia would have seemed intimidating, yet dignified – a killer yes, but a regal one. Now wearing a simple black tunic, her pale-blue flesh was exposed and her muscles frighteningly well-defined.

'How come they all smoke?' Eir asked.

'It is their payment.' Artemisia spoke proudly, a notice-ably different tone from earlier. 'They work in exchange for tobacco, to which they are addicted, and therefore they become addicted to working for me.'

'Isn't that like slavery?' Eir suggested.

'It is no different to working for money, like your races do,' Artemisia replied.

'What do they do, on this ship?' Randur asked, strolling up to one perched on the edge of the rail so precariously, he wondered if it might fall off. He began stroking its fur, and the winged monkey regarded him coolly, taking another puff of its roll-up. It wore an expression of deepest satisfaction.

'Mainly they do repairs on the *Exmachina* for me,' Artemisia said, 'since they can easily access all the way underneath. They run errands about the ship, and they scout better than any-thing else I've known, providing they fly on solo missions. They're prone to arrogance and infighting among their tribes.'

There were so many questions Randur wanted to ask, but it didn't seem urgent. It occurred to him that he felt immensely secure on this ship – being on the run had driven him into a sense of paranoia. A gust of wind came on board, disturbing the peaceful ambience. Artemisia glanced up in irritation, and only then did he think it odd that the wind hadn't really been present before. His first thought was of some cultist trickery, then he realized that this woman and her ship might be beyond all that.

Rika strolled across the deck, a dark gown rippling softly against her body, once again every bit the Empress. Her demeanour was like a premonition, a return to something more ancient and established. Artemisia responded with something that might be mistaken for an emotion, though what, he couldn't say.

Rika had noticed them survey her clothing. 'I found it in one of the cupboards. It doesn't fit perfectly, but it's surprisingly warm.'

'It is an example of what the few humans might wear, where I come from,' Artemisia said.

'You have *humans* in your world?' Eir asked, but received no response.

Rika's glance towards Artemisia was wide-eyed and approval-seeking. Randur knew this because Eir had often done the same to him. So Rika sought attention from this being but, according to Eir, Rika had not once in her life shown such interest in anything other than the Jorsalir church.

'Lady Rika,' Randur said boldly, 'you look at this woman like she's a god.'

'Perhaps she is,' Rika whispered, speaking to herself more than anyone else.

'She said that we – we as a race, as a species – *we* created *them*, in another earlier time,' Eir observed.

'Let us not steer into teleology,' Artemisia said. 'Has all my earlier information been absorbed?'

'It's just too much to believe in without seeing confirmation for ourselves,' Eir said.

'Agreed,' Randur said. 'You have evidence for all this, I take it? Something we can just, uh, see?'

'Amusing that you assume merely seeing will confirm reality. If one sees a stump of a tree in a field at dusk, it may resemble the form of another human, and your fears may creep in, but it is still a tree. One should question what is being seen, at all times.'

Artemisia moved away, assimilating into the darkness. The remaining three stared at each other and then Randur gave a shrug, pushing back a lock of his black hair, and turned his attention to the Hanuman once again. A moment later, the creatures squawked and flapped off to one side, out of sight.

Randur needed to know what they would be doing next. This lack of purpose and clarity was unsettling.

Suddenly Artemisia strode back towards them, carrying a massive metal container in one hand, displaying her immense strength. In her other hand she held two ends of some metallic rope, which trailed away to a part of the ship he couldn't see. She dumped the container on the deck and declared, 'Come over, if you wish to see.'

The three of them knelt by the side of the tub, which was about four feet wide, and peered into the shallow pool of water it contained. Carefully, Artemisia draped the two pieces of metal rope into the water. Numerous sparks began skidding across the surface. A sizzling sound came and faded, and before long images with the consistency of a reflection began to form in the water.

'This is in my world,' Artemisia declared, standing a distance away as if she couldn't look at it herself.

An apocalyptic landscape.

Structures that Randur could barely identify: metallic and ivory alien architectures.

Lumbering creatures engaged in abstract warfare which was barely possible to imagine.

Skies suffocating from smoke? No, there was merely a sun scarcely as potent as a moon.

Races similar to Artemisia's, many humanoid, some like rumel, others possessing a square spine that revolved as they walked.

Occasionally the flash of explosions.

Swarming numbers of inhabitants.

'Who's fighting who exactly?' Randur asked.

'The enemy is led by the Akhaioí – your own mythology calls them Pithicus – who possess potent military might. I have served on these battlefields and tried to combat their finest warriors. They are constantly attacking us – we, perhaps, who are the last free culture. I cannot remember for how long, precisely, but we estimate this current set of campaigns began all of ten thousand years ago. At this current stage, the Akhaioí lay siege to our greatest city, Truwisa, having seized the outlying beaches long ago. Our two cultures have been engaged in combat for so long it feels as if we are wedged in some epic cycle, destined never to end, apart from when the earth dies, and even then . . .'

'Enough,' Randur said, pulling back. It hurt him mentally to contemplate the phenomena he'd seen. 'Why don't you just invade our world like the other lot? What's a few more deaths to someone from your world?' He indicated the vision in the water, which was now stuttering out of shape, losing its clarity. Soon it had become simply water again.

'Because, Randur Estevu, if we wiped many species from this world, it would create an unstable system, which would inevitably lead to our own collapse. Your human cultures have done so again and again, wiping out biological systems that were depended upon. Among all things, we Dawnir cannot be accused of thinking about the short term.' Something flickered across her expression, a smile perhaps, or something darker.

'If I could be Empress again,' Rika said, 'would you wish me to help?'

'It is, perhaps, the only option I can see. We need you – or an equally trustworthy leader – to mobilize your people effectively.'

'I feel . . . it is the right thing to do.' It was as if the very presence of this woman had intoxicated Rika. A true seduction by the gods. There was something about Rika's manner, a glimmer in her eye now, which indicated she had regained her determination. Perhaps she felt this stranger was still a deity, and would do anything requested by her.

'Hang on,' Randur said. 'What's to say you're not representing evil, in all of this? How can we trust you over the other lot, the Pith-wotsits?'

'The Pithicus, the Akhaioí. And to answer your question, you're still alive aren't you? That should be sufficient indication. And, remember, across the outermost islands – our enemy, are they not wiping out your people?'

'I've not seen it.'

'There were intelligence reports, Randur,' Rika offered. 'Indeed there has already been genocide on Tineag'l. That's why the Night Guard were dispatched to the north – it wasn't a simple military mission. They were to investigate what could have destroyed the settlements.'

'Good,' Artemisia finished. 'It is settled. Let us rest for tonight. You have, I feel, witnessed enough for the moment. Please, absorb what I have said. I will get a couple of the Hanuman to guide you two to some comfortable quarters. In the meantime, Jamur Rika, I invite you to my bedchambers to discuss the future.' It was said so matter-of-factly, but Randur couldn't help but think she had designs on Rika in some way, although he hoped she was sensible enough not to be swayed by such attentions.

'Yes,' Rika said, 'it would be an honour.'

'Rika!' Eir exclaimed.

'Easy.' Randur held her arm, and whispered a reminder of just how many soldiers Artemisia had killed.

'Eir, I will be perfectly fine,' Rika said.

Artemisia and Rika strolled away from them, leaving Eir seething. Randur held her but she shrugged him off.

He raised his hands in despair and muttered, 'She's a grown lass. Dammit, she's older than you, and Empress, and can do what she wants.'

'Not now!' Eir snapped.

Two Hanuman fluttered down to his feet and began screeching something, and with little hands they waved emphatically for them to follow.

*

Through the night and through the walls, the groans of a woman filtered in gently. Eir lay there awake, trying to discern if it was Rika's voice. A candle flickered in the bedchamber, casting a warm light across its wood panelling. There was a constant dull hum somewhere below.

'Get to sleep,' Randur mumbled into the pillow.

'It's her,' Eir said. 'She's doing *something* to her. It sounds like they're having . . . you know. Sex.'

'Least someone's enjoying themselves.'

She slapped his back and he grunted. 'Not Rika. She's never done anything like that. And, anyway, Artemisia isn't even human. It's wrong, and it sounds as if Rika's in pain. What if she's torturing her?'

Nothing was to be heard for a moment. Then Rika's voice penetrated the night like a muted banshee, then a moan that was sensual and deep. Eir made to get up but Randur placed a restraining arm across her, then leaned nearer, squinting in the candlelight. 'Eir, it doesn't sound like torture. If it's sex, then yeah, I'm surprised too, but I'm sure Rika knows what she's doing. The fact that Rika is not yet dead suggests that Artemisia doesn't hate the lass. And if they've developed some form of bond – then I reckon that it bodes well for all of us. Look at us – we were betrayed by that arsehole Munio. We were about to be dragged off and at some point executed, and then this . . . whatever she is, fell out of the sky and saved us. She needs us alive – or at least Rika. So as long as we're on her side, we're safe.'

'Maybe you're right.'

'I'm always right.'

'What about Munio?'

371

'Well, nearly always.'

She softened at the sight of his face. He was trying to smile, but by now she'd learnt to see beyond his bravado. She turned over and attempted to sleep, but the noises her sister was making continued to disturb her.

Dozing off, Randur wondered, too, *What is Artemisia doing to her?*

*

Morning, and red sunrays spilled across the ship's deck. A wind buffeted them, and the massive ship groaned under the elemental forces, yet the vessel maintained its stability. Hanuman drifted around the ship, a flock of oversized gulls silhouetted against the sun. Randur really wanted one for a pet, he decided. They seemed pretty nifty, couldn't do any harm, so he would ask Artemisia for one, at some point.

'Where're the others?' he asked.

Eir hadn't slept well at all, and had kept him awake for half the night. She was now leaning against the railing, peering down across the cloud-base.

Joining her, he still couldn't believe what they were standing on – a city-ship that apparently floated along, using sources of energy he couldn't get his head around. The texture of the clouds looked unusual from this angle, the inverse ripples carpeting the distance. Only by seeing all this did he realize just how far he'd come since he had first left Folke for Villjamur.

'I don't know,' she yawned.

The ship was easier to see at this hour, and he was astounded by how extensively moss and lichen blanketed the deck. The platform itself seemed so long that Randur could barely see the end of it.

'Good morning.'

The face was hers, Rika's, but the voice was utterly different. Her clothing had changed also. Dressed like a man, in khaki breeches, a black shirt and boots, she looked like an assassin more than an empress. She strode purposefully towards them, Artemisia some distance behind. Everything about Rika's posture and her manner told Randur that this was someone reinvented, but he was surprised to see it happen so quickly, so thoroughly. Was that a blade hanging from her belt? Leather straps ran diagonally across her shoulder, and he stole a glance to see if there was a sword nestling behind, but there was nothing. Why was she dressed like this? What had happened to this formerly passive woman?

The transformation disarmed him.

Eir moved nearer to her sister and seemed uncertain how to begin. 'What happened last night? We heard—?'

'I was absolutely fine,' Rika replied sternly.

'You look different.'

'I am different.'

Eir sighed and shifted back by Randur's side. He placed a hand on her shoulder but she shrugged him away. Rika regarded them both as if they were merely a part of the ship.

Artemisia reached them, unchanged, as if she never could be any different. Her skin looked lighter now, but the ridges of muscle in her arms were still clearly defined.

'We're heading for Villiren immediately,' Rika declared.

'Still to see the commander?' Randur asked.

'Yes. Artemisia has offered to aid us in combat, so while I'm there I'll persuade the Night Guard to give me their allegiance. Once they're made aware of the situation, we're certain they will comply. From there we can build a platform to seize back the Imperial throne from Urtica – by force, if we must. That man will suffer for what he's done to us.'

Seize it by force, Randur thought. *Make him suffer. These surely aren't her own words?*

'The allegiance of the Night Guard lies with the Empire,' Eir observed. 'Not you, personally.'

'Then their allegiance will change.'

Randur was impressed with Rika's tone, her firmness. Her

manner suggested things might be done with a little more zest at last.

'And just what *can* Artemisia do?' Eir turned to face the pale-blue woman. Randur wished she wouldn't behave so petulantly in front of the killer, not that Artemisia seemed to care much.

'I will turn whatever fighting there is in favour of the defenders,' Artemisia said. 'My presence alone will probably cause quite a stir. I believe, also, that I can set the *Exmachina* on course to disable the gateways through which they've infiltrated. I might lose the ship temporarily, but I can salvage enough equipment for me to return home.'

'Why didn't you just stop them coming through earlier?' Eir said.

'It is not a permanent solution. My disabling of the gates will not last that long. The Akhaioí will open them within . . . weeks perhaps. The technology they use is sophisticated enough. It's rather like drilling a borehole through existence.'

Randur didn't understand the concepts or the philosophy, and being made to feel ignorant merely angered him. 'Let me get this right,' he said. 'We go to Villiren – if it's still there and we're not too late – and join a war in which we'll most likely perish.'

'Worry not. Rika will come to no harm under my guidance.' Artemisia placed a hand on Rika's shoulder. 'And we will aid the Jamur dynasty, as part of our deal.'

Eir looked disgusted. 'What did this thing do to you?'

'*She* did nothing,' Rika replied coolly.

'Last night – I heard you.'

'I don't know what you're talking about, sister.'

'Look, I think we're all wondering, did she fuck you last night?' Randur interrupted. Everyone turned to glower at him, and he could sense their collective rage. He held his hands up, apologetically, knowing that he had been a tad too blunt.

Artemisia towered in front of him, then pushed her way

past. A dozen Hanuman spiralled above their heads, and she communicated to them in that guttural language. Then she turned to regard the group of humans, but only Randur was paying her any attention. Eir and Rika stood gazing at each other, the fracture between them painfully clear.

Artemisia announced, 'We leave immediately.'

THIRTY-EIGHT

They scoured the streets house by house after nightfall, the Bloods, searching for vacant properties or rented accommodation where a Night Guard soldier and a cultist woman might have taken shelter, and all the while a snowstorm was gusting bitterly around them, never settling.

Malum had requested for his gang to embrace their more feral nature. His anger had connected with some deeper, weirder aspect of his vampyrism. They were masked and fuming and filled with purpose. They swaggered. They strutted and hollered out names to women heading home from the bars. They brandished hand-signals to intimidate the other gangs, who were hanging back in the shadows: *Come fight us, you cowards. Fuck the Dog Gata Devils.* There were stand-offs and mock scraps, name-callings and a sense of belonging. This was a subtle, directionless conflict.

Malum, wearing his surtout and mask and heavy gloves, flashed his blades in the eyes of the hesitant until they whimpered their responses to him.

'No, we ain't seen nothing.'

'Please, we're just two old sisters.'

'Fuck you doin' at this time of night? Oh, it's you, Malum – I didn't mean to be rude, I . . .'

He found out where all the slum landlords were located, those who had enjoyed licence from the portreeve to rip off the poor, who possessed no housing rights, and were without provision of firegrain for nights at a time. He beat them up because they were of little help to him, and maybe because they deserved it. One guy Malum decided he particularly despised was even chosen as a blood donor. In the man's new-built Scarhouse mansion Malum's gang gleefully ripped into him, punching their teeth into all his major veins and arteries. Malum took a glass from the man's own drinks cabinet, filled it with fresh blood, before raising it in a toast to his victim's good health.

*

Fifty gang members in all sifted through the likeliest streets and districts. They kicked down doors, surprising couples who were rutting like animals; disturbed three old cultists who projected a net of energy into the doorway to block their entry; outraged a disgruntled rumel belonging to the Inquisition who was wearing some terrible-coloured breeches.

The first real clue he got was from a lonely fat tenement owner he caught entertaining himself with a porno golem – Malum vaguely wondered if it might have been supplied by himself: 'Yeah, they was here, the floor below, about two nights ago, though mainly the woman 'cos the fella keeps slipping off back to the barracks, like. But they only stayed a night.'

'Where'd they go?'

The man shrugged and meekly pulled the sheets across to try to hide the writhing pink golem as it fell off his bed, its overly made-up lips constantly mouthing coy surprise, touching its clay breasts. 'I heard them mention a hotel two streets west, I think, but didn't catch the name.'

*

They progressed with their usual clamour, retreating only from encounters with the routine patrols of soldiers, nor did they venture too near the docks, where regiments were well established, thinking trouble from the military men would cause too much distraction from their simple purpose: to find and kill Beami and her lover. Was it all a waste of time? Malum didn't much care – he possessed all the money and resources he needed.

Ten of his men were searching a neighbourhood a mile away from the Ancient Quarter when, on the back of a tip-off, they finally found them.

Malum waited and focused, then spotted her silhouette appear in a mid-floor window of one of the more expensive hotels in the city, one set in a complex of vast gothic towers stalled in mid-construction. Her familiar shape was distinct against the soft light of coloured lanterns, as her hands reached for her hair, and presently a man was working his way around her body. It all seemed so oddly intimate, so detached, and all the while he had been haunted by the memory of her face. He wanted to kill them, to prevent them having what he himself couldn't give her. It was now a primeval competitive instinct, to prevent another man intruding on what he felt was his personal territory.

He sent one of his gang for reinforcements, waited a while, then he motioned for the rest of the boys to go in.

*

After bursting through the front door they ran through the reception rooms filled with trashy decor. Then they kicked ornaments aside and headed up the stairs to reach the upper floors. Then, Malum glanced down the stairwell to see twenty more of his gang arrive.

Everyone inhabited the shadows. Beami was already waiting out in the long corridor, her lover standing behind, framed by the dim light coming through the open door. He was indeed a soldier in the Night Guard, this new man of hers, standing still with an arrow aimed towards them. He didn't look much, at first, just younger, more slender, a lean face, and Malum didn't know what to make of the fact that she had chosen to leave him for this guy.

'What do you want, Malum?' Beami demanded.

378

'For you to die.' Malum's hand moved instinctively to his messer blade and he began to bare his fangs, but suddenly his urge to appear normal took over once again, and he let his rage subside into a blend of feelings that he couldn't identify. He was a mess.

Beami said, 'Can't we talk?'

'That's all we ever did.'

'No,' she corrected, 'that's what we *never* did.'

He glanced around at the reaction of his men, catching one or two raised eyebrows and uncertain expressions appearing on their faces. Well, now, this was awkward, to be unmade, to have his marital life laid bare in front of the guys. What next must he endure?

Suddenly Duka tried to throw a knife from behind but the soldier released his arrow in the same heartbeat. Duka screamed, the offending hand now a ruined, bloody mess, and the knife fell uselessly to the floor.

This soldier was a damn good bowman, that was for sure.

'Leave us be,' the Night Guard growled.

'Fuck we will,' Malum snarled back. A few of his men shuffled forward, pirated relics brandished in their grasp.

Tre, a young blond rookie, began to transform a brass cylinder and set it glowing.

Malum could just about make out the anger flaring on her face as Beami made a circular gesture, and lines of luminescence began to form, air tightening in strands to create an undulating wave of purple light.

'You dare to use your fucking relics on *me*?' she sneered, as if the years of disgust and pain had suddenly accumulated, gathering momentum, ready to be unleashed within the next moment.

Tre darted forwards and hurled his relic and, slow and surreal, the device exploded into tiny electric nails. Beami raised her hand to command her light-lines, then raked her arm down, whipping air. The nails collapsed around her, clattering to the floor or against the wall behind her and the soldier, leaving a near-perfect circle of remaining wall that was not ruined. Her strands of light remained afloat. Tre stared dumbly as the Night Guard's next arrow thumped through his thigh, pinning him to the floor. He screamed and ripped off his mask and clawed at his leg.

'Don't try that stuff with me, Malum,' Beami snapped. 'I don't know how you've managed to get your hands on those things.'

'I've got contacts,' he growled. He was getting really pissed off with her. She should be dead by now, her body stiffening in a shallow grave alongside her new lover.

'Why don't you just leave us alone?' she snapped.

Two of the Bloods fired off their crossbows: swift bolts were caught in the strips of light and hung there. It was difficult to see properly in the darkness, but Malum crouched by the wall and prepared to take out the soldier himself. The Night Guard soldier continued to bury his arrows in members of the Bloods with a frightening efficiency, and Malum wondered how he could see so well in this light.

Beami dispersed her electric strands in wide arcs, filling the corridor from wall to wall, and she gradually shifted this barrier of light forward so that Malum's men could only retreat—

– Suddenly an explosion: one of the outside walls shattered, filling their confined space with masonry dust, while a sharp blast of winter air blew inside. Everyone stopped, and began whispering urgently in confusion.

'Fuck was that?' someone coughed.

Shouts drifted up to them from the street below, men giving orders, a woman screaming—

– A whistle, then a dull explosion.

Malum scrambled backwards through the rubble, stepping over the bloodied limbs of two of his fallen men, and looked out through the broken wall on the city facing the coast. All over it there were soldiers, moving like a plague of rats infesting Villiren, their footsteps clumping in unison across the streets. A bell began to toll, deep and resounding, bringing the city to a standstill.

'What's going on, Malum?' someone asked.

He had no idea. Several of his gang stood by his side, staring in shock at what had happened, and only then did he register the fact that something had struck the outside of the hotel. It seemed absurd something could hit a building at this height.

By his feet, a man was buried under the shattered wall, his mouth opening and closing but no words were generated, and on realizing this very fact, the man's face creased up in agony.

Strange, Malum thought.

Another whistle, another explosion, somewhere down to the right: a two-storey row of cheap flats coughed up dust and smoke. There came more screams, and soon further alarm bells were tolling.

Malum scrambled back into the damaged corridor, noting the absence of Beami and her soldier-lover. He kicked in the door to find their room abandoned.

The damn woman had escaped him.

*

Beami and Lupus sprinted at full-tilt past bewildered citizens. His quiver strapped tight to his back and bow still in hand, he was now speaking to her with great urgency. The bell was calling him back to the Citadel.

The war was beginning.

Something hit a building somewhere above their heads and stonework crashed a full forty feet behind them.

What the fuck caused that? Was it a missile of some description?

Beami turned and noticed a ruined cafe ahead, still smouldering from the heat of an explosion. People milled around outside, children crying, men shouting muddled orders, and shattered glass was crunched into the thin layer of snow. As they watched, three men and a woman were being hauled from the rubble to safety. Beami and Lupus approached these survivors to see if they needed any further help, but when they tried to respond, no sounds came forth. They faced each other aghast, pointed to their throats and gave a silent scream.

All three had been muted.

Beami gazed up at the sound of another whistle: a missile was heading through the air directly at a ruptured firegrain pipe, where it impacted to send a thin stream of liquid fire deep into the sky, lighting up the cityscape. They ducked instinctively as bits of stone clattered down. Silence, briefly, then the tolling bells recommenced. Lupus whistled for a fiacre to take the voiceless injured somewhere for treatment.

The lovers sped to the Citadel.

*

Brynd listened to the reports that flooded in regarding those caught up in areas where the missiles had impacted, that many could no longer speak. Their voices had been completely purged. A name for the device had been quickly created by witnesses: mute bombs.

A squadron of five garudas had been sent flying off to investigate precisely where the bombs were coming from. How could any regular commander plan a retaliation against such weird technology? Brynd had never even heard of missiles being fired over such distances, and to such a devastating effect. This suggested a level of warfare beyond the scope of the Empire's armies – a concept altogether unthinkable in any previous campaign.

Brynd immediately sent a missive requesting the help of the cultist Blavat, knowing full well he would soon need whatever relics and skills or advice she could supply. Messengers were then dispatched to round up any other cultists available in the city, offering a high reward for their skills.

There was not yet any direct invasion, no Okun had crossed

the water, and there had been no landings further along the coast. Large-scale casualties seemed inevitable, though the orders from Villjamur were clear:

Minimize the death toll, but make sure the city does not give way – it is too important a trading centre for the Empire. If you do lose the city you must build up forces to retake it, and fight for it until the last man stands.

Which wasn't very helpful, of course. Brynd officially militarized the front lines of the city, ordering Port Nostalgia and the Shanties to be cleared of any remaining civilians who were not prepared to fight. Those who joined up were issued with basic weaponry by the Regiment of Foot, and civilian militias were formed according to pre-prepared schedules, with appointed commanders selected from the lower regiments of the Imperial forces.

All approaching routes to the newly militarized zone were shut down by the Ninth and Seventeenth Dragoons. The escape tunnels out of the city were checked for roof falls after the explosions. Deep underground settlements, a mile south of the southern wastelands, were directed to be populated by those wishing to flee – he could not have them dying in the tundra above. Over the centuries much had been made of these ancient mining excavations, and the military had recently opened up the more stable shafts to provide shelter.

With a deep sigh, Brynd stepped onto one of the observation platforms of the Citadel, where members of the Night Guard had gathered behind the battlements to examine the intermittent flashes from far off. The mute bombs had come in ones and twos at first, then accumulated, but by now had all but ceased. He had estimated around fifty explosions in all, and wondered how many citizens had been silenced. Anticipation and concern was clear to see from the expressions on the soldiers' faces. Now and then Nelum had given him disapproving glances, but Brynd, as always, buried his problems as deep as he could. This was not the time to be thinking about the issue of his lieutenant.

Lupus and that woman had joined them ten minutes earlier, bringing a vital, first-hand report on the mute bombs. When he first arrived, Brynd had been angry because he had brought Beami – then she explained she was a cultist, and soon persuaded Brynd that she could be of use.

Criers were dispatched into the city to repeat the message: every man and woman will be needed in the coming conflict. Even a child if he or she can hold a sword well enough.

Because he had no idea what else might be coming.

THIRTY-NINE

Investigator Jeryd moved through the streets at his usual sluggish pace until he came across a building reduced to rubble. Glass and wood and shattered stone were scattered across the cobbles, and trails of smoke drifted across Villiren. A unit of soldiers was still searching through the wreckage for survivors, even though it seemed that they had probably found them all during the night. Onlookers stood by idly, staring at the gap now yawning in what had once been a row of merchant stores. Jeryd flashed his Inquisition medallion to shove past them and get a better view. The sight dug up memories from Villjamur, when his own house had been destroyed in an attempt to kill him. From first-hand, he knew that this was no mere spectacle, but that people's lives had exploded across the melancholy scene.

One of the sergeants on duty informed him that something now dubbed a mute bomb caused the destruction, just one of dozens that had rained across the city in a short-lived assault the night before. Over fifty civilians had died, and another two hundred and twenty were found permanently silenced by some component in the bombs, which the cultists were currently studying in order to find a cure.

Jeryd moved away from the scene in disbelief. What was happening to this world? For decades he had known only relatively predictable offences – murder, theft, violence – but in the last year he had witnessed a huge increase in malevolence. It was as if the ice was bringing with it some kind of insanity.

Head down and his hands in his pockets, he stormed on towards the house of Doctor Voland. Before leaving headquarters the previous night, Jeryd had written up a full report and left it on the desk of his superiors, with the strict instructions that Voland and Nanzi should not be released pending their trial. He had underlined the words twice:

Highly dangerous.

For a couple to work together in this way was something rarely encountered. Jeryd didn't know what to make of Nanzi or her bizarre abilities. He was mildly disgusted to have been duped by her all this time, but he was getting used to it, getting used to the crap he had to deal with every day, and he felt glad he could put some distance between them. He accepted she was a 'blend', which helped him get his head around her being a killer. But Voland . . . he was something else entirely.

The man was a beast builder. He must have a clear sense of purpose and an ice-cool conscience to accept a contract to slaughter so many people in order to feed others.

Jeryd passed beggars and children skidding on ice as he followed the route he remembered, until he finally came to the house. He was prepared to prise the door open with a crowbar if necessary, but it was unlocked – obviously due to the killer's hasty exit to save his partner. He headed inside and drew back the curtains. He was searching for hard evidence, something beyond the word of Voland and Nanzi.

Over to one side, Jeryd found a lantern, and lit it.

Fine decoration, antique furniture, superior paintings on the walls embellished a well-stocked library. Everything tidy, with bottles of spirits neatly lined up alongside crystal glasses. The end of a cigar in an ashtray. A taxonomy book lying open.

Nothing to denote a psychopathic killer. But then what personal items would do so exactly?

Jeryd moved from room to room, as he sifted through the couple's existence, the lantern casting aggressive shadows across the polished furniture.

A pencil sketch of the two of them by a harbour was wedged in the corner of a mirror standing on the dresser. A tribal fertility ornament lay on a side table. In their plush bedroom, with audacious drapes and a decorative mirror above the bed, he found some erotic lingerie, which made Jeryd contemplate the ways in which Nanzi gave Voland his kicks.

Another of the rooms clearly acted as a study of sorts. Notebooks lined the shelves, detailing biogeography and evolution and cladistics. Complex cross-sections of species he didn't know smothered the papers littering a desk. Diagrammatic representations of what looked like some weird form of fusion surgery could be seen on the walls. On another desk lay a wooden display case containing a neat array of pin-raised insects, with a scalpel and mount to the side.

A small book nearby was labelled 'Voland's Journal', and contained sheets of lined paper containing names and addresses. Jeryd picked it up and several other pieces of paper fluttered to the floor. At once he recognized the portreeve's handwriting, and he scrutinized them further. Labour activists and union leaders, these were the men who had disappeared. Voland was telling the truth then – this was the documentation that would prove Lutto had been intending to get rid of union leaders so that he could make working conditions as vile as possible, and in order to maximize profits for the private companies. He flicked through the journal, but found nothing relating to crimes per se, merely scientific ramblings on physiognomy or etymology.

So then, another conspiracy that goes right to the top ... Just how much corruption makes this realm what it is? I'm too old for this. I can't fight an Empire like this one.

But who could he tell about this discovery? Jeryd didn't know anyone in Villiren well enough to trust them.

He pocketed the journal and the loose pages, and wondered what he might do with them.

Then he went down further steps, carrying the lantern towards the basement where a strange metallic smell lingered. He found a wall-hung cresset and lit it, more for peace of mind than for anything else. It was damn eerie down here, so the more light the better. Along the constricted path, winding around a corner, and there was now a change in the way the air moved, signifying to Jeryd that he had arrived in a vast chamber.

Light was lost to the corners, so he found a coloured lantern and some matches to light it. Metal implements hung from the walls, and there was a dripping sound from the far end.

Suddenly he spotted several dark figures lined up against the wall to his right. He moved tentatively in their direction, before raising a hand to his mouth in shock. His tail became perfectly still.

Seven corpses were suspended with hooks driven through their throats, their tongues hanging out uselessly. They were naked and bruised, and streaked with dried blood. One was even skinless, the muscles and veins exposed horrifically. On the body at the far end, a rip in the throat caused by the weight of the body dragging on it suggested that it had been hanging there for some time.

Further along on a workbench stood two massive metal trays that reminded him of those he'd seen at Doctor Tarr's mortuary back in Villjamur. He wasn't surprised to find them full of internal organs, which he assumed could only be human. As he moved the lantern over them, they glistened slickly, confirming they were relatively fresh. An inert eyeball stared up at him and he drew back with a shudder.

None of this was set out as if to aid a crime investigation, however, with Jeryd being called in to look at some remains. These cadavers were destined for the dinner plates of ordinary people across Villiren, and it was possibly the most despicable activity he had ever witnessed. He was standing inside a human meat factory.

The smell was overpowering and he turned away, to prevent himself from gagging. Reluctantly, with a handkerchief over his mouth, he began jotting down notes and making sketches, detailing every horror on display.

*

In the dim light of the obsidian chamber, Commander Brynd Lathraea faced Jeryd across the table with a despairing smile. A small tray of refreshments had been brought to them, and Jeryd eyed the food suspiciously. 'No thank you ... I'm, uh, on a diet.' *I don't trust anything now that I haven't seen being prepared.*

He had just informed the commander about the fate of the missing people, and what it probably meant about the missing Night Guard soldier, revealing every detail and nuance about the case.

'I find this all rather difficult to believe,' Brynd murmured.

And who could blame him? Jeryd spoke of the confessions. He showed the commander Voland's journal, then his own notebook, tilting it sideways and pointing out the corpses and the various implements he had sketched.

'Human flesh, distributed through the city? And, you suspect this was all at Urtica's request?'

'I do,' Jeryd confirmed. He revealed the incident concerning the refugees back in Villjamur, where Urtica had arranged for large numbers of refugees to be eliminated; that because Jeryd had delved too deep into those affairs, he had had to flee to Villiren.

'So, anyway, Voland basically admitted that he had a contract with Urtica. The guy is entirely honest about his own participation in the events. And it's not just that – it seems the portreeve knew about it also, even supplying the names of political enemies he wanted eliminated, to make his life easier.'

The albino seemed to contemplate this information for some time, and Jeryd could have sworn the man's eyes burned even redder than before.

'I myself am having trouble contacting the portreeve at the moment,' Brynd finally said. 'No one seems to be able to find him. Those close to him suggest he's already fled the city because of the bombs. It matters little, anyhow – I've taken measures ensuring full military control of Villiren. As for following up the allegations of corruption, unfortunately they will have to wait.'

'So it goes.'

'And, Nanzi, your aide – the girl who came in here all this time. You really had no idea?'.

'She's an utter psychopath. You know the two of them genuinely think they're doing a good thing, right? They actually think this helps the city. Keeps everyone else alive. She helps the population with her work at the Inquisition, and in her head it's the same thing as feeding them.'

'A perverse logic,' Brynd admitted.

An interruption to their meeting – a messenger entered the room to whisper into his superior's ear, then left with urgency. Jeryd tried to read the commander's expression, without success – this man did not give much away.

Brynd gave a sad smile. 'I believe, investigator, that a more forceful attack on Villiren is imminent.'

'You reckon you can save the city?'

Brynd located some deep place inside himself and stared into it. 'Let me explain something to you: the portreeve has nurtured a terrible culture here. I'm not sure of his methods, but I've never witnessed more drug use, or known of more brothels. Thieves openly help themselves to goods on the stalls, people pay to watch violent acts in underground theatres. Lutto says that citizens are, on average, wealthier and healthier.'

'I'd suggest those figures are skewed,' Jeryd interrupted. 'From what I've seen, the people on the streets have very little, while the gang members and dodgy traders continue to piss all their wealth up against a wall.'

'The gangs control everything here, investigator,' the commander said, 'and the portreeve rewards them by leaving them to bask in their pleasures and vices, and to sell such lifestyles to the citizens.'

'Barely any crime seems to get reported,' Jeryd agreed.

The commander smiled, as if he had been leading Jeryd to say it was so. 'And what does that indicate to you?'

Jeryd thought about this. 'That most of the people in the city are criminals anyway, or at least condone this culture.'

'So contemplate your question once again, on whether or not I can save Villiren.'

'The city', Jeryd concluded, 'has already fallen.'

'Yet we must press on, out of duty. If you have anyone you love, now's probably the time to get them down to the tunnels and away to safety. I expect you yourself will still be able to fight?'

Those words hit him like a low punch in the stomach. The situation had till now been on the periphery of his conscience – that he might actually have to fight – and being so concerned with the missing persons he had almost forgotten about the possibility.

'I'm ready for anything,' Jeryd lied.

FORTY

Malum's life hadn't always been as screwed up as it was now, though even as a kid he'd had it tough – his father walked out on his mother before he even really knew the man. There were a lot of young men in the Bloods in a similar position. Maybe that's why such a band of men had formed in the first place, through looking to each other for some kind of guidance. It was why he had once tried so hard to be a good father . . .

He'd been walking across Villiren for hours now, and he still didn't know for sure how far he'd travelled. The streets were empty at this time of day, pre-dawn, and it was only then that he realized he'd been awake all night. A sea fog blanketed the city, the lines of the streets and the few tall buildings hidden indefinitely.

He badly missed Beami – who'd have thought it? For the first time in his life he had been humbled and, like a fat blade, the experience had sliced him open. He wasn't someone who was used to brooding about his wounds.

With the impending conflict likely to wipe out the city, he had probably lost any chance of finding her again. He wanted to tell her he was sorry, to remind her that he wasn't always so malevolent – because he had to face it, that's what he was at times: a man who manufactured evil. But he'd not had an easy life, what with his upbringing and . . .

Here it was at last, the street he'd once lived on. Not with

Beami, no – but with his first love, deep in his youth, the girl he had spent forever trying to forget.

Back before he had been bitten.

He could not bring himself to think of her name ... it was so long ago anyway.

And there was the house, which had once stood on the very edge of the Wasteland district. Now it was an integral part of the city, as if symbolizing how Villiren had grown too far beyond his own life. The house he was staring at was just a crumbling, terraced cottage with pieces of marbles pressed into the masonry so that it glittered with different colours in the right kind of light. They were all like that, round here. Its door was painted a different colour now and it was inhabited by a different family.

But, once, this was home.

When someone has no future, he realized, *they look in the other direction*. The ghosts of his past emerged out of the fog, and he removed his mask to confront them, face to face.

*

This is where it ends.

He is as yet unbitten, a twenty-one-year-old father. Styl is there, his son of two years, laughing up at him. The little guy's got the same colour hair and eyes as himself, the same smile. Crafted from the same wood, this one, people have told him. Malum has huge hopes for him, and wants to give him a future he can be proud of. Styl says he wants to be Emperor one day, and he speaks with such a spirit that you might think that it is really a possibility.

Hope: it is one of the reasons Malum works so hard at his small trading company. In a business inherited from his uncle, he distributes wares of all kinds around the city, and even dabbles in the ore market now and then. His wife is cooking breakfast in the morning sunlight, which streams through the kitchen window. She is intensely blonde, with full lips, a chatterbox who's very sensitive to everything he says, and he loves her. Malum relieves her of the spatula, tells her she should go and relax in the warm bath. He kisses her on the collarbone, on her neck, then she heads upstairs, smiling at both of them.

Later in the day they're walking as a family towards the commercial districts, looking to buy food for an evening meal with his business partner.

A unit of Empire military is coming down from the Citadel, apparently on its way to tackle a tribal uprising beyond the city limits, somewhere in Wych-Forest. Nothing serious, just a few hundred of them wanting revenge for the Empire's confiscation of their ancestral lands. Malum crouches down next to Styl, stares at the streams of uniformed men on horseback along the rain-slick streets. Armour and weapons glint in the sunlight during this display of duty and courage.

Someone lets off a firework in celebration.

Suddenly several startled horses lurch, startled and mad, seeking escape from the commands of their riders. Some of them break free, and begin galloping towards the crowd. Malum remembers being knocked sideways, remembers his son screaming and then the sight of Styl's face being crushed by hooves.

A spreading pool of blood.

A woman crying.

Anxious faces blurred through his tears.

Once the uproar has died down, he can barely bring himself to look at the devastating aftermath, at the pitiful remains of his son, and all he and his wife can do is collapse on the cobbles and wail.

The next evening he finds his wife has bled to death in the bath. Her wrists were slashed so crudely he knows she must have taken a long, painful time to die.

That is where it began.

*

Malum flicked a stone at one of the windows of the house, and it pinged off harmlessly. Was it any wonder he hated the military? He would never fight alongside them, no matter what the argument, no matter how much the Night Guard pleaded with him.

He had never risen above that day his life was smashed, where his dearest hopes had died. Eventually, after the witch had helped him, in his new-found bitterness, he turned his young trading empire into a criminal enterprise, channelling his anger.

His cadre had built up around him. They became his family and, eventually, they shared his blood. They stood by him without question, would carve open any enemy on his behalf.

After you see your son killed in such a way, and you find your wife dead from despair, you don't care about much else other than doing whatever you can to capture whatever satisfaction you can from the world.

*

The city was beginning another day.

Traders headed to the irens rolling their carts along by hand. Citizens were moving about their routines, some in masks, bustling about, getting on with their own lives. Bitterly, he noticed a unit of Dragoons trotting past the end of the street. He looked up at the house one last time and then turned to disappear into the fog, wishing that he might be lost forever in its mass.

FORTY-ONE

Few people were blessed or cursed enough to have their own moment in life, a window of time in which they were the centre of the world and everything revolved around them. Tonight Brynd had a whole city waiting on his every word and, no matter what he said, there would be bodies littering the streets on a scale no one would comprehend.

The mute bombs had changed the texture of the city, the spirit, the geography. Now thousands of people were gathering around the barracks and the Citadel demanding action and protection. Portreeve Lutto had vanished completely. Villiren was Brynd's to control.

With the Night Guard lined up behind him, Brynd addressed the citizens of Villiren at regular intervals for half a day, from a platform high up on the Citadel walls, one that offered too much grandeur for his liking. The crowd huddled below, or amid the thick stone arches and pillars. His throat was raw from repeating his message into the cold wind:

'There is no need for you to panic,' he lied.

'But what do we do?' came the reply. 'Tell us what to do.'

Years of yielding to the will of the portreeve had left these people with no self-sufficiency. He issued instructions for those unwilling to fight to head underground, into the escape tunnels. 'We are to roll the city out past the Wasteland district and into the wilderness, establishing temporary villages beyond Wych-Forest, the other side of the Spoil Tower and

Vanr Tundra, or sheltering in disused mining networks. We have ensured basic supplies to cater for this temporary solution. The military stationed on the perimeter of the city are now being brought in, unit by unit, tens of thousands of soldiers, most of the Empire's available resources. We will ensure the stability of the city within.'

Out of this city of several hundred thousand residents, the citizen militias just managed to match the official military presence. There were forty thousand extra people willing to fight, and a total force of, he estimated, eighty thousand. Over the past few weeks, Brynd had ensured the blacksmiths were developing enough weaponry for them. Citizens only now signing up were attached to their own regiments based on the streets they lived in, neighbourhood comrades, with military personnel to guide them through their basic training. Sadly, hardly any of the gangs had opted to join, and none of them were the most violent sort, the few thousand truly skilled civilian fighters in the Bloods or the Screams.

Ten cultists had enlisted, which surprised Brynd because they rarely cared for anything other than their own arcane practices. He herded them in a room together with Blavat to try to discover what might explain the nature of the bombs, then to develop useful technology to help them fight the enemy as equals. He was quickly impressed with Beami, who had taken charge of the group, and a meeting was organized for the morning, so that they could brief him on their findings. She warned him that he might not understand the sheer complexity of techniques on offer. Miffed by the usual arrogance of these people, he decided he would never properly understand what cultists got up to anyway.

That same evening Brynd leaned against the ice-cold battlement, and necked a shot of vodka for warmth, to relax. And with one eye fixed on the horizon in case ... just in case. In this bleak weather, there wasn't much to see.

Just what was the enemy's motivation? Assuming these

Okun had come from somewhere not part of the Boreal Archipelago, why had they needed to invade and wipe out the population of Tineag'l?

*

A key piece of information came to Brynd, just after dawn.

Marine vehicles of an unknown variety had been spotted by garuda surveillance. They were not longships, and were thought not to be constructed of wood. No sails or visible crew either, merely a dull humming sound as they thundered their way across the narrow channel towards the city. Garudas confirmed that the vessels were moving slowly, even pausing mid-crossing so that more of them could gather. They massed like a school of titan sharks, twenty by the beginning of the missives, then fifty by mid-morning. But they had not yet reached the city, and that was the main thing. It meant he still had time.

Brynd ordered his elite troops to assemble within the hour, and dispatched messengers and criers to all the northerly districts of the city.

Bells tolled across Villiren.

FORTY-TWO

Randur stood on the deck, wincing into the light. To his surprise, he did this a lot, staring into the red sun. There were vague comforts to be discovered in deep contemplation, and up here he felt he had found time to slow himself down and grow up a little. How his life had turned so bizarre and out of context, he didn't know, and he vowed to seek out a quieter existence in future. All he needed was a place by the coast, maybe a decent local tavern in which to lose the years. *Enough of the constant pressure; maybe those people in that tavern back on Folke weren't so wrong in their attitude after all.*

Under the dying rays of the sun, the *Exmachina* continued drifting above the cloud base, heading towards the mountains soaring up through it from the southern coast of Y'iren. They pierced the cumulus, icebergs in the sky.

Then Randur noticed something different from the panorama: one of the taller peaks appeared to be peeling fragments from its highest ridge. Vast clumps of earth were breaking off and hanging in the sky alongside. And some impossible force was keeping them afloat.

'Artemisia,' Randur called out to the empty deck.

A moment later, a hatch burst open and the woman-warrior came up to him. He didn't even need to say anything. She tilted the end of her telescope and sighed. 'This is something to cause concern,' she decided, then dashed back along the deck.

A moment later there was frenzied activity in the skies above the ship as the Hanuman fluttered manically, unbuckling their excitement, and the *Exmachina* began to slow its pace and veer off-course.

Eir and Rika joined him, and gripped the railing as the ship's motion readjusted. 'What's going on?' Eir said.

Randur pointed to the huge unfalling clumps of land.

'What is that?' Eir whispered. She had a way of showing her apprehension by rubbing her arm above her elbow, as if she felt cold.

The wind accelerated because of the change of direction, sending his hair in tendrils across his face. 'Whatever it is has sent Artemisia legging it, which doesn't bode well.'

Artemisia returned with an armful of items.

'Keep these on and you'll be fine.' She offered some masks of red mesh that fitted over their mouths, crafted from no material he knew of, and they dutifully secured them. Randur discovered that his breathing was just as easy.

The looming peaks sailed towards the ship, and small dark objects could be seen above and below, skittering and darting about in ragged patterns of flight.

'What are those things?' Randur asked, his voice slightly muffled by the mask.

'Those vessels, they are called Giasty – literally earth cities, although little lives there. The structures you will see on them are, in fact, largely constructed of human bones, which should, I hope, give an indication of how they view your species. Human bone is valued as a building resource in our world. And those things you see flying about are called Mogilal – they are quite a menace. And, I fear, they have been waiting for us.'

'Are they the creatures you are fighting?' Randur asked.

'My world is, yes.' She unsheathed her blades with a zing, and Randur took a step back as their arc whipped past his face. If Artemisia herself was anything to go by, these other creatures would probably be violent.

'Should we be doing anything to help?' Randur glanced towards the girls, whose gaze was locked on the drifting island. He drew his own sword, and Eir, alert to his gesture, followed suit, but the dismissive glance from Artemisia suggested that such weapons would be of little use.

A fizz across the sky, a high-pitched whistle, and something slapped into the ship below. Artemisia hastily put on her own mask, fabricated from the same red mesh. She seemed to wait for . . .

Two deep thuds, then stillness.

Another object streaked across on an upward trajectory, visible white trails carving up the sky . . . towards the ship, above the ship, then the Hanuman clustered around it and screeched, and something exploded in a smoke-plume. Bits of flesh began to litter the deck.

Artemisia began shouting orders in some unknown language, waving her swords at the Hanuman who seemed utterly stunned by what was going on. A flock of them clustered as one mass, and waited overhead. The next projectile they dealt with better: slowing it significantly, then gently steering it away from the ship till it dropped over the side.

The warrior turned to the three humans. 'Do not move. Do not inhale when they explode. Do not remove your masks or you will not be able to speak afterwards.'

They nodded in silent affirmation as Artemisia took several big strides towards the centre of the deck. The sun was nearly below the clouds, extending the woman's shadow bold and long.

Time after time the Hanuman steered the projectiles away from the ship and into harmless oblivion, and occasionally there were explosions from down below, well out of sight.

Both blades drawn, Artemisia waited like a prophet as the Hanuman circled in the air above. Her hair stirred in the wind.

The land masses came close enough so that Randur could perceive settlements on them, weird esoteric homesteads and other structures that cluttered up the rockscape. They seemed too bizarre to be real.

A smaller fragment of land peeled away from this one, then drifted like a bubble towards the *Exmachina*. A shadowy figure stood on top of it.

Across the intervening sky. Then alongside.

The figure banked alongside the large vessel and hopped aboard with a thud as it touched the deck. As tall as Artemisia, white-skinned and gold-armoured, the thing took three steps forward and Artemisia backed away cautiously, enticing it further into the centre.

Then it happened strangely:

The combatants slowed and juddered in and out of time and location, flickered from one part of the deck to another, appearing each time in different fight poses as if racing and grappling with each other through incomprehensible zones of space, a fight spiralling through dimensions that were impossible.

The third pose: blades locked at the far end of the ship, silhouetted against the red sky.

Flicker.

The fourth: amidships, two strokes from the stranger and both connected with the deck; and Artemisia severed its arm, blood pooling all round.

Flicker, the fifth pose: now nearby, her victim screeched as she jumped and kicked out at its chest, sending it sprawling on to its spine. She marched closer and, with its other arm, the intruder raked its sword horizontally. The edge sliced through Artemisia's thigh.

Rika gasped in concern, and Eir had to hold her back.

Artemisia buckled on one knee, dropping her blade, then the two began to grapple hand to hand. Pinning the enemy's free arm, Artemisia brought up her remaining sword then stabbed it through the chest, the tip of the metal splintering the deck beneath.

After a moment of violent but silent juddering, the enemy fell still.

Artemisia pushed herself upright, panting, wiping blood from her brow, and gestured with her weapon at the corpse.

'Earthlanders, come. I shall show you one of those we fight.'

Randur and the girls moved tentatively over to her side and for a moment they watched the warrior rip some material from her clothing then wrap it around her wound.

The body looked inglorious in its wreckage: yet this was something once noble, with a slender face almost human in its features, and something almost deer-like about its bodily form. A muscular white body was encased in golden armour, into which was carved all sorts of intricate designs, making it look too precious for use in combat.

'It is one of the Pithicus – using your mythological term – who with others make up the nations of the Akhaioí. Another race invented by your early ancestors. These people command a wealth of forces, including the race which has breached into your world, their expendable foot soldiers – the Cirrips. Though no doubt your people would have given it another name by now. These Akhaioí deem themselves superior to other species, and I am surprised to find that they have come through already. Normally the Cirrips do all their fighting in the early stages.'

'This creature seems so elegant,' Randur remarked. 'Clearly these things were wrought to look good.'

'Do not be deceived by their beauty. These are people who, if granted victory, would see you wiped out in order to repopulate with their own kind. I have seen so many of their like, and fought . . . thousands of them. Be warned, the human and rumel races will come to an end if the Akhaioí lay siege to your dimension, like they do to our last city. Our people are becoming too few to protect you all.'

'What do they want here?' Rika enquired.

'The same as we all do. To survive. Is that not what species seek? We may appear vastly esoteric to people of your culture, but I can assure you of this: when faced with the end of our existence, we are desperate and humble. The difference between ourselves and our enemy is that they wish to clear the land totally first, and then to use your bones as material to build their habitations. We simply wish to live alongside you, or quietly on our own in some distant corner. I repeat, this is why I have been sent to find you.'

'How the hell can *one woman* achieve anything? I mean to say, you're pretty sharp with a sword, but against whole armies?'

Artemisia seemed unconcerned by this query. 'I may be able to disconnect their sentience – which is how they, your new enemy, communicate. The doorway through which they entered is a massive chain of communication utilizing various primitive signals transmitted through the air. Without this link, they become *significantly* less skilled as fighters. The rest, admittedly, may be up to your own armies. I am not a god, but I can still utilize this ship's science.'

Randur began, 'We have cultists—'

'Your cultists', Artemisia interrupted, 'are constantly flapping about the Archipelago as if they actually know something. I can tell you this much: they know *nothing*.'

FORTY-THREE

Under pressure from the soon-expected sea landing, the meeting of the cultists with the commander was brisk and volatile, with an explosion of demands and requests for help.

As they discussed detail, Beami watched him, the albino, brooding over every statement in agonizing slowness, his elegant fingers tapping on the table as if to deepen any silences. She wished she possessed a relic for freezing time in order to get things done more quickly in real time. Commander Lathraea was proving unhelpful, as she had expected. The army were to have total control. The army would dictate everything.

The army this. The army that.

The other cultists in this emergency unit were seven men and one other woman. Originally congregated from various minor orders, two of which she'd never even heard of, they were all keen if not completely proficient.

Two of the men were middle-aged, one with grey hair and the other with none, and she felt immediately that they were powerful, despite their seeming unwillingness to take the threat of war all that seriously. They gave their names – well, one of them did: Abaris and Ramon.

Ramon had a look of psychopathic intensity about him, the kind of glint in his bright eyes that suggested he could be friendly one moment, but would have no trouble in slitting your throat the next. Stocky, with perspiration glistening on his bald head, he stank of stale sex and bad magic. His colleague, Abaris, chubby and moustached, was the only one of the pair who would ever speak. Only in the silences did she notice how Ramon had one blue eye, one brown.

Abaris made a minimal yet bold claim. 'We might', he said, 'be able to do things with the dead.'

He marched his fingers across the tabletop as if to suggest their intentions.

Necromancy . . . Is that what they do?

And how exactly would that be of any help? Beami had never heard of these people, but the more macabre cultists did tend to isolate themselves.

'Which is fine,' she replied to the weirdly light-hearted figure of Abaris, 'but what about making the enemy dead in the first place?'

'Lass, we'll require a measure of time before we can go into action. And then . . .'

Ramon did nothing but grin, yet she noticed the creases in his face, evidence of years of almost blissful anguish. The two of them frightened her with their deep serenity. They possessed a kind of confidence that overwhelmed her.

The conversation lurched back and forth between the commander and the cultists. She did not want her kind to be treated merely as weapons. They were people who thought and reacted carefully and could use relics to a devastating effect – if they were allowed a little freedom.

Messengers frequently interrupted them with updates on the invasion fleet heading towards the city. Every new one of them left the room feeling darker, as if a death in the family had been announced. And how many thousands of those would there soon be? The increasing stress was obvious on the albino's face. Frequently he would rise from his chair and circle the room as if no one else was present, and occasionally he'd catch the eye of Ramon, who would smile back at him in a macabre fashion.

As Beami peered out of the window trying to see where the enemy were currently, her vision drifted over the docks and the front line of fortifications, the makeshift barricades and the archers stationed in windows and other vantage points. Would they really be enough?

*

An idea came to mind and Beami announced it to the room.

Abaris clapped his hands. 'Lass, that's proper genius, that is. Me and Ramon will wait for you to finish up, before we can make our immediate contribution.' Ramon's head began to rock back and forth, his eyes firmly closed as if he was contacting someone outside the room via some ethereal means. Abaris adjusted his tweed robe and leaned in to await a further reaction from the room.

A murmur of approval rippled towards her.

The albino slumped forward in his chair, resting his chin on his hands, and he stared at her. He didn't seem particularly unenlightened in his attitude towards her, but did he really believe she was capable, this mere *woman*? She had been used to receiving that response throughout her life, and had learned to suppress her frustrations. Brynd said, 'We could defend the docks with our forces stationed on the quayside to prevent the enemy getting into the city.'

'Let them just come ashore, then I can rid you of many more than your army could ever hope to do in one attack.' Beami couldn't wait any longer. If she was going to aid his defence of the city she had to do it immediately. 'Leave it to me, please. I only need half an hour. Send the order to call the soldiers back from the front line and make them stand two streets away from the waterfront instead. They'll be safe there, and meanwhile I can focus on the—'

'One hour and the invasion fleet will be arriving here by that very same entry point into the city,' Brynd snapped.

'Exactly,' she smiled. 'So trust me.'

With a rush of emotions she fled the room, hearing him

say, 'You have just one chance to earn that trust, do you hear me?'

*

She burst out through the fog, this cultist on a lively mare, heading out through the back of the Citadel. Gathered civilian foot soldiers looked up half astonished at her thundering through their mass.

Out into the city, her route took her the long way round, due to the military blockades and the thousands of troops readied for engagement. Under the shadow of the Onyx Wings, along the fringe of Althing, the Shanties, and straight towards Port Nostalgia, with a bag of modified *Brenna*-based relics slung across one shoulder, and suddenly Lupus was riding behind her, on a muscular black mare, still in his Night Guard uniform, a bow strapped across his back.

'Why're you following me?' she shouted.

'Commander's orders. He doesn't quite trust you, I'm afraid.'

'Well, he should,' she replied.

'Beami, wait a moment.'

She sought to curb her horse and was surprised at how quick its response was. 'What?'

'Have you ever killed anyone before?'

She shook her head. Only then did she realize what she was taking on.

'You want to prove things to a world of men, I know,' Lupus said, his voice carefully controlled. He was on army time now. 'But listen, when you kill, your heart will start to beat incredibly fast and you'll feel a rush of emotions like you've never felt before. Your throat might seize. Take deep breaths to calm yourself and take control of your body else your muscles might seize. Think only of the relics, that might help.'

They galloped through deserted streets, abandoned neighbourhoods, rubble and detritus. Hooves reverberated loudly on cobbles. The mood of the place seemed to foreshadow a forthcoming apocalypse, but only a few streets away life flared: files of men and women lined up behind stout barricades, with their cheap weapons, and charged by a hope laced with fear.

Eventually Beami slowed down, and she moved the bag of relics in front of her.

Lupus pulled in alongside her. 'Where are we heading exactly?'

'Western side of Port Nostalgia,' she replied, 'and then we're moving through to the east, and at some point we'll need to cut a line back to the front of the Citadel. We won't have long so please, Lupus, you'll have to hold back because of the sheer scale of this experiment.'

She undid her necklace, the silver tribal symbol he'd given her all those years ago. 'Look after this for the moment.'

Without emotion, he took it and placed it safely in his pocket. He made a silent but important gesture, edging his horse slightly behind hers once again. Drawing his bow over his shoulder, he glanced from side to side. 'At least let me cover your back.'

'Thank you,' she whispered.

Beami primed the relics and stared up as the snow began falling, bold flakes that saturated the grey sky. She nudged her horse forward into the open Port Nostalgia district – surprised at how this unfamiliar mount seemed to react as if it already knew her thoughts. Now to the harbour front itself, where four ships of the invading fleet had already breached the harbour walls and were parting the vessel-crowded port with ease.

Fishing boats capitulated in their path, buckling under the impact, a series of tiny wooden explosions.

'You'd better hurry,' Lupus advised her.

Beami observed the terrace of coloured buildings, noting their vacant facades. Thankfully there was no one stationed in the windows, no sword points or arrow tips sticking out from behind the barricades.

The commander had done what she asked.

She dismounted and hauled out the first of the amplified *Digr-Brenna* relics. She had modified several of them so they could sit on spikes, and with a small mallet pounded one into a gap between the cobbles.

Lupus loitered close by, watching intently.

'Please, Lupus, keep clear. I'll be all right on my own. It'll get dangerous very soon. Please, go now – and take my horse with you.'

His understanding was instant, and nothing seemed to demonstrate his respect for her more than when he silently turned his horse away.

'I'll be at the east end of the harbour, waiting.' A smile and he was gone.

No time for emotion, not now. *Deep breaths.*

She wedged another device in a gap, where it leant at an angle, but remained upright. Another twenty paces, another relic, and so on; all the time she had to endure the fearsome racket of the enemy ships crunching their way towards the shore.

For ten minutes, Beami continued at her task, her cloak billowing around her. She dared not stop to examine the hulk of metal now towering immediately before the shoreline.

There, that was the last of them.

She took several more deep breaths – and fled.

As she ran she heard the ship doors opening, the sound of them lowering to strike the stone quay, then the clanking of footsteps across a metal bridge. Things crawled out from inside, unnatural creatures with shells. Whatever they were, they were armed and came skittering across the quay towards her, towards the city, pouring out of the boats as if they'd sprung some vile kind of leak.

Deep breaths, remember.

There were shouts and cries from within the city, people beginning to react to this sight. An arrow whipped through the air from somewhere deeper in the city, and she prayed that the soldiers would not come forward to meet the invaders in combat, not yet.

Patience.

She crouched to plant the detonation device as one of the creatures scuttled forward, now only twenty feet away from her. With her heartbeats slamming in her mouth, she waited for as many of these *things* as possible to descend onto the harbour front. A subtle twist of her hand, and she set off her chain of devices.

A web of purple light shot out across the quayside. In an instant the harbour front ripped into the sky.

Cobbles exploded upwards all along its length and the aliens began to scream, unnatural and piercing, suffering under such an almighty display of her cultist power.

Deep breaths.

A brutal hail of stone fragments slammed down around her, and she ran further along the street to take shelter in a doorway. Ripped body parts and portions of exoskeleton clattered along behind her, coating the road with blood. A rumel head, severed by the blast, spun towards her and finally fell still, eyeing her reproachfully.

Suddenly she could sense the underpinning cohesion of the ground begin to fall apart, and she realized that she needed to escape. Dashing through successive street junctions, her cloak flapping around, she kept glancing back, but none of the unnatural invaders seemed about to catch her.

She turned to witness the next phase of her handiwork while nestling in the shelter of a narrow alleyway.

A terraced row of housing shook and leaned over in a surreal fashion, then fell forwards as if the buildings themselves were drunk, smothering any enemy left standing from the first assault.

Masonry dust and smoke obscured the scene, and when it partially cleared it revealed that hundreds of the creatures had been massacred – with no cost to civilian life. Beami felt an adrenalin rush at having for a moment halted the invasion, so she did not quite understand why she was crying and shaking.

Lupus burst through the smoke, still on horseback, and in silence he hauled her up behind him. She clasped her hands around his waist, and with her cheek pressed up against his back they rode off to the sanctuary of the Citadel, through gathering numbers of soldiers shifting forward to form a line of defence.

Out of the corner of her eye she caught a glimpse of Abaris and Ramon sauntering slowly back the way she had come.

Into the Citadel and towards one of the broad arches surrounding the quadrangle. Lupus dismounted, helped her down, handed his horse over to a comrade. He lowered her onto a chair in a side room and wrapped her carefully in a blanket.

Beami was febrile and tears drenched her face, though she had stopped crying now.

'Beami, I'm stunned by what you did,' he whispered, his tone full of admiration.

But his words, like all other sounds, seemed so thick and distant.

*

As they strolled along the street, crowds of soldiers brushing past them, Abaris clasped the hand of his long-term lover, Ramon.

'We are at war now, my dear,' Abaris informed him. Above the helmeted heads of soldiers from the Regiment of Foot, he could see the metal hulls of the invading fleet. 'Are you ready to work your hoodoo?'

Ramon reached under his vast black cloak to where, fastened on his left hip, were two animation relics he had designed himself. They were like hand-held metal dream-

412

catchers, each consisting of a brass circular rim about a handspan across, filled with fine webbing and decorative muscovite mica. They were called *Eigi*, and one in each hand would suffice for these numbers. Abaris looked for a vantage point, and gestured to Ramon that they should climb the external steps of a three-storey whitewashed building just up ahead.

They proceeded slowly through the mass of soldiers, and then upwards, to the flat roof, where they enjoyed a spectacular view of the potential battleground. Extending out among the roofs either side of them were dozens of archers garbed in the green and brown uniform of the Dragoons, and they were firing remorselessly downwards. Now and then a runner would come by to dump a fully stocked quiver beside them, collecting the empty ones for refilling.

The rows of houses just in front had collapsed where that marvellous Beami woman had been at work. *Most impressive*, Abaris concluded, *to be able to have such an impact. Such a wonderful use of cultism with* Brenna-*based devices to disassemble the natural world*. He was not one for that side of their business, but could appreciate a well-devised relic when he saw one.

Below, the battle surged, violently loud. In thick trails of metal-covered flesh, the Empire's regiments pooled into the streets heaped with rubble and debris from earlier. The two forces clashed awkwardly over such terrain. The grey ships – constructed from no element Abaris knew of – loomed vast and smooth and featureless. The so-called Okun came clambering out of the large holds, but struggled to achieve mass due to the destruction all around. And Abaris noted there were rumel following – red-skinned warriors with black armour, stepping more cautiously over the pulp of the dead.

The dead . . .

Foot soldiers piled in, thick rows of bodies that seemed too close together to manoeuvre – and the front lines were downed, men ripped apart by sabre or shredded by claw. More filled in behind – this was like a well of the future dead. At the rear came several lines of Dragoons on horseback, equipped with lances and maces – an odd tactic to use them so early, Abaris thought. They soon found themselves at the front, and fared fractionally better, the animals trampling down Okun, maces smashing the shells and cracking them open. Troop movements were fluid. Horses began to fall in that horrific silent manner. Abaris seemed so detached from it all up here, viewing the theatre of war from this distance. Dying screams and bellowed commands blurred into incoherency. People were dying without any context. Both cultists were familiar enough with death, but on this scale, it was something else, and they had to wait long enough for there to be sufficient numbers of dead to make what they intended to do worthwhile.

'Let us begin, dear,' Abaris declared, and Ramon held up the two *Eigi*.

Abaris reached beneath his cloak to retrieve the chargers, and slotted them into the handles of the devices Ramon was carrying. He took one of the relics himself.

Side by side, catching bemused glances from nearby archers, Abaris and Ramon watched as a soft light descended down to the carnage. Soldiers fought on, and in peripheral glances he could see someone's arm being severed; another's organs strewn up against a wall; a severed female head impaled on a shattered window frame.

And in the mass of the enemy pouring onto the streets, there was utter disarray. Rumel shouted in incomprehensible tongues, suggesting to Abaris that they were commanding other creatures. There was a noticeable alteration in the enemy's mood.

It took a while for the pieces to aggregate, but they did, as they always would ... Limbs began to coalesce. Arms to feet to flanks of thigh, ribcages woven around organs, fragments of tibia and humerus and femur melding. A slick and glistening thing began to rise up behind the invaders, and glared around with two eyes made from skulls. Its silhouette was that of a single giant, but this was not one creature, it was dozens.

The amalgamated flesh of the dead had become alive once more.

It scooped up more of the carcasses of soldiers, and pasted them to its body, lathering on the blood. Hunched yet taller than any of the surrounding buildings, it lumbered slowly along the streets, Abaris and Ramon controlling it through strings of light. They sensed its abilities, perfected its movements, tentatively exploring what it could and could not do. As it shambled in a line towards them, the cultists shifted further along the rooftop to maintain a panoramic view.

A massive macabre marionette.

The thrill of it was shared by both the necromancers, as they exchanged knowing glances, not needing to voice their own awe.

They put it into action.

The monstrosity bent down awkwardly and swiped away red-skinned rumel soldiers then, one by one, gripped the Okun in its massive surrogate fist and forcefully imploded them. Victims perished, their oozing remnants offering it material for augmenting its growth on this plane of existence.

As it swung its arms they ripped off the parapets of buildings, sent roof tiles skidding into enemy lines amid a shower of masonry. Then it marched into the invaders with apparent glee.

Okun forces began to focus on their attacker, and relentlessly hacked into its composite flesh, angling swords and axes and claws at its feet.

But this thing already belonged to the dead.

It bent over and pulled a few dozen apart like bits of bread, then discarded them in a surge of blood that was pouring down towards the harbour. It leant back, wobbling on its flesh-jelly legs, then stood upright as if admiring its own devastation.

The battle lines became staggered and blurred, and neither

invaders nor defenders were certain what this presence now meant. An increasing anxiousness hung over the scene.

A commanding officer ordered a retreat for the Dragoons, and the Imperial soldiers pulled back, maintaining a neat and efficient front line as they withdrew through the awkward, winding thoroughfares at this end of the city. All streets that the enemy might pass through remained blockaded and well defended. Archers hung from the windows ready to pick off those who attempted to follow, but the enemy had thinned out considerably.

The first onslaught having been halted, the cultists turned their puppet on to those remaining, crushing them or swiping them into the harbour. The seawater behind turned red.

No cheering, no cause for celebration.

Next stage: soldiers ran forward to retrieve the wounded. Stretchers were soon lined up and were carried back into the city.

It began to snow heavily.

Abaris released his control and let the monster come to a halt. Abaris did not realize just how excited he had become, his chest heaving in and out, his head perspiring.

Through the bleak vista beyond, another wave of invading ships loomed, at least twenty to Abaris's eyes. He felt a vague disconnection from the scene. Even someone such as he, who was used to dealing with death, experienced dread at what might happen to this city.

Something ripped through the air and a building behind him exploded, coughing rubble on to the street. Ramon turned to see where it came from. Another explosion followed, originating from somewhere Abaris couldn't see. One of the archers screamed. He turned quickly and heard a shrill whistle, then the roof on which he was standing rattled and shook, and began to collapse. As he held on to Ramon, they descended into the rubble.

*

Brynd watched the monstrous apparition fall slowly to one side, like a drunk keeling over at the end of a night. Whatever the thing was, it was no longer able to help them, but he was thankful to have had it on their side. The Night Guard were standing in a line along an observation platform of the Citadel watching the carnage in the snow. Some of them were eager to be deployed, but Brynd would only allow them to ride into combat when the first lines of defence were broken fully.

It was essential for him to retain an overview of the situation. Surveillance from garudas had confirmed that there were no enemy ships heading towards the settlements further along the coast. It meant that this was a blistering assault on the largest mass of population; and that, in itself, suggested their plan was to neutralize the place. Since there had been no attacks on supply routes feeding the city, they clearly did not anticipate a long-term siege. All-out annihilation was the enemy's intention.

Brynd's new plan was to force the Empire's front lines as close to the invaders as was physically possible. He would smother them to prevent them from firing any more bombs, because it would mean too many casualties of their own – that was, if they had much in the way of morality.

Finally, a wave of garudas flew in from the east, carrying cultist-designed *Brenna* explosives, as he had instructed earlier. Ten avian soldiers entered the airspace above Villiren, and Brynd could see them modifying their flight paths to avoid dropping the devices on their own people.

They rushed towards Port Nostalgia and released the relics, and the explosions could be felt even up in the Citadel. The city rocked ten times, yet none of the garudas were shot down, retreating safely to the skies in the west.

Brynd's hopes that their efforts would be lasting began to collapse when he counted at least another twenty-five enemy vessels approaching the harbour.

FORTY-FOUR

Investigator Jeryd was packing his belongings in their decrepit, dusty little hotel room. He and Marysa had spent a few good nights in safety here, and Jeryd had become strangely attached to the place, although he was aware such emotions were misplaced.

The blasts of explosions came and went in the distance, far enough away to not yet seem real, and occasionally there was the sound of a troop of soldiers or civilian militia trudging by under his window.

He could leave carrying only one small shoulder bag, and wondered where it might be stored when the time came to fight. Would there be rooms for those who weren't in the traditional army? Would they all be expected to sleep in a dormitory? Would they be able to sleep at all? He assumed that this sort of thing would be well planned – Commander Lathraea seemed like a guy who knew what he was doing.

Jeryd checked his crossbow and slung it on the bed along with a bundle of bolts. He checked his various knives and placed them in his boots. He wore only a tight-fitting tunic, and folded his Inquisition robe on the bed. Would he even need it again after all this? One minute he was busy chasing criminals, the next ... The change in circumstances had all happened so quickly.

Marysa joined him. He looked longingly at this woman he

had loved for decades with such an emotion he felt a lump in his throat.

'I want to go with you.' Marysa clasped both his hands in hers.

'No.' Jeryd shook his head slowly, closing his eyes to block out her gaze. 'It was me who dragged you all the way out here, into this mess. I want you to have a chance of getting away at least.'

'But I can fight – I saved you, for pity's sake!'

'Marysa, I know you're probably tougher than me after all your training. I thought we'd discussed this.'

That conversation had lasted for hours. They talked about her being more use in the escape tunnels, helping lead people out of the city. Jeryd said there'd be people who needed protecting from rapists and thieves, and that it was unfair that all the best fighters would be remaining above ground. There would be men and women and children who needed protecting from each other, and not even the major gangs had offered their services in any way.

He gave Marysa his spare Inquisition medallion as a badge, an object that might be more use to her than him. She sighed and focused on him with those big black eyes – so much was happening in that gaze, so many conversations from the past returning. He kissed her fondly, smelled her hair. It was funny that these would be the things he missed the most, the details he barely remembered in everyday life. He was more afraid of being without Marysa than he was of dying.

A painful goodbye.

Still with a faint hope that they'd see each other again very soon, they made arrangements for meeting after the end of the war, suggesting where they could meet at what hour of any given day. Past the Onyx Wings and the bone archways, by one of their favourite bistros. Or if the city was to fall they would meet at one of the villages further out, a couple of points on a map which he'd scribbled down for her.

Marysa went off first, leaving an overwhelming sense of emptiness, and the hotel room seemed to pause in time.

*

Jeryd put on his hat and marched through the streets. All around him people wrapped in warm layers were shifting through the narrow lanes, their expressions full of melancholy. Aside from the wailing of those who had already lost loved ones, the busy city was eerily quiet. He could almost breathe the tension. Another explosion came, and the massed confusion of battle could be heard in the distance – but closer than before.

Villiren wasn't his city to protect, so why was he even here? He was doing this for the common good, he realized, a duty that seemed written in his heart. The same sense of morality that had kept him in the Inquisition for so many decades. Private gain didn't matter. If everyone acted solely on private interests, there'd be no citizen militia, no lifeboat teams around the coast, no soup kitchens for the starving. Jeryd had to laugh at himself. *Investigator Rumex Jeryd: now aspiring philosopher.*

*

At some point near the Althing district Jeryd realized that he was caught up in the flotsam of new recruits for the citizen militia, men and women and children, with heads lowered against the driving snow, some with expressions of determination, others with a sad disconnection. The flow was moving towards the older buildings surrounding the Citadel, gaining in numbers and intensity. The streets lost consistency here, curving and twisting, a few blocked by the rubble, which was being carted off by soldiers to form defensive barriers. Row upon row of mounted Dragoons waited for engagement, shifting in their saddles, totally emotionless, consummate professionals.

Dozens of men in uniform stood about with hand-held boards taking names, patient and calm, directing people towards the Ancient Quarter. Citizens shuffled off wherever they were told to. There were a fair number of rumel too. Jeryd was asked to stand in line with the rest, silent as a queue waiting for the executioner's block.

The young soldier eyed him cautiously, noted his details, said very little.

'Something wrong with us rumel, sergeant?' Jeryd enquired. 'I've noticed there's a bad attitude towards us in this city.'

The young soldier regarded him coolly, unspoken narrative racing behind his human eyes. 'There appear to be a lot of rumel soldiers fighting among the enemy forces. So we have to be cautious, is all – security checks and the likes. I'm afraid I'll need to ask you some questions about your background—'

Fuming, Jeryd pulled out his medallion. 'This thing may convince you I'm fighting on your side, just like I've been doing for the last hundred and eighty fucking years.' Jeryd was aware that an expectant crowd had begun to form around them.

'All right.' The man palmed the air dismissively. 'We just have to follow rules.'

If things were this bad now, how much worse would they get as this invasion progressed? The rumel were a minority group here, and he could do without being considered sinister. As his indignation abated, he realized this young soldier was merely following orders. Perhaps a quiet word with Commander Lathraea was called for.

His instructions directed him to a different line from the others. Apparently his position in the Inquisition had made him a valuable asset: he would be rewarded with command of his own unit. Very quickly he discovered he was joining a group of other rumel, and they nodded an acknowledgement as he greeted them. There were maybe fifty in all, moving forward to an armament point. On finally arriving where he was supposed to be, Jeryd found a Night Guard officer calling out instructions in a vast chamber piled high with weapons.

Jeryd showed him his medallion, for what it was worth any more, and this time was shown no discourtesy for being a rumel.

Investigator Jeryd now Lieutenant Jeryd – platoon leader of Rumel Irregulars One. Three of the others he recognized from the Inquisition headquarters in Villiren, but there were at least thirty other men and women under his command. All were armed with basic crossbows and cultist-developed munitions, and he learned that because of their tough skins, they would be required for sniping and guerrilla operations in exposed positions, or for holding blockades after nightfall. They were fitted out with crude uniforms and white sashes featuring the seven-pointed star of the Jamur Empire, then Jeryd was briefed on what was required of him.

It all happened so quickly, this business of going to war – Commander Lathraea suddenly appeared, the crowd peeling back to let him through as if they were frightened of this pale-skinned ghostly vision.

'Investigator, a word please.'

'Surely I'm lieutenant now,' Jeryd joked. 'What can I do for you?'

*

They took two stout horses and rode back towards the Inquisition headquarters, thankful that the snow had momentarily ceased.

Jeryd asked the question of why the troops were giving the rumel a hard time. But the commander coolly stated that the enemy consisted of a number of rumel troops, albeit of a different nature, and that they must check none infiltrated the Imperial lines by stealth. Once they arrived, Jeryd led him to the arch-inquisitor of Villiren, an ancient grey-skinned rumel who seemed barely able to stand. In a dust-polluted, wood-panelled chamber, littered with legal texts, two assistants helped the antiquated rumel into his chair, then left them alone. They sat down facing the desk.

Brynd didn't waste any time: 'Sir, as you may know, we have now imposed military law over much of the city.'

The arch-inquisitor wheezed softly and nodded. 'You wish to make a point of it, so as to make matters easier. I quite understand.'

Brynd offered a rare smile. 'Indeed. I believe you have two prisoners in custody, awaiting trial for execution – the Doctor Voland case.'

'Investigator Jeryd was truly assiduous in that matter and has done this institution proud.'

Compliments did not sit well with Jeryd, but he gave a coy smile anyway.

'I don't doubt that, sir,' Brynd continued. 'But I come to you with a strange request, and it's possibly one you may not like.'

'Go on . . .'

'I am led to believe that these two individuals are rather unique. But given the nature of our current military engagements, I may have a use for them.'

'A use?' Jeryd spluttered incredulously. 'They're fit for nothing.'

'On the contrary,' Brynd declared. 'I wish them to be released immediately.'

Jeryd almost spat his tea across the table. 'Are you insane? Why the hell would you want to release that serial killer and . . . that monster?'

FORTY-FIVE

Nanzi, in her spider form, lumbered awkwardly over the rubble, deep into the city and deeper into the night.

With the clear sky, a chill set in, calm and suffocating. Fighting had come to a halt as the sun faded, and there were now only swift conversations in the dark, strategies being passed mouth to mouth. Or on papers carried via messengers, as their horses bolted into the distance. Swords remained unsheathed. Bows remained in position, rumel archers sniping from their high vantage points, waiting it out in the cold. Men and women of the Dragoons or Regiments of Foot stood alert by crude blockades.

Yet none of them would have been able to stop her.

And she had to do what she was ordered now – because otherwise Voland would die and she couldn't let that happen. How could these people not appreciate the good work they'd done together?

The first location: just behind Port Nostalgia. A heap of the dead lined the landscape, and she could sense the chemical secretions of human and rumel and alien corpses. Mounds of unidentifiable flesh littered street corners and alleys, armour and weapons lay shattered and idle. Buildings, too, had become corpses, crippled by whatever technology these new beings had brought with them.

But in between all this morbid mess there were fallen soldiers still alive, who still breathed this foul and rank air.

Centring her vision, she crawled tentatively around a smear of decayed matter towards them. They screamed, either because of their wounds or the pain of seeing her, she didn't know which, but she had received her instructions and she sought out their wounds and dribbled silk into them, sealing the wider abrasions. Some fainted at the sheer sight of her, others regarded her with a total absence of emotion. Nanzi picked them up two at a time, in custom-woven slings, and hauled them back towards the fiacres waiting on standby a hundred yards beyond the front line. Two women on horseback were posted beside the vehicles, and they watched Nanzi warily as she crept towards them, absolutely terrified she might do something to harm them.

'We know what you are,' said one of them, waving a dagger in her direction. 'We've heard what you've done. Don't care if you're helping us now, you're still a bloody monster. Just hurry up so we don't have to look at you for too long.'

From there, the newly recovered injured were sped towards a makeshift military hospital underneath the Citadel, leaving Nanzi alone in the darkness.

*

Voland sighed as yet another consignment came in. Cries of anguish echoed in his head. A small team of men and women lifted the casualties gently from the fiacres. When another delivery appeared, Voland wondered if it would ever end.

How can I repair so many of them?

He rolled up his shirtsleeves further and tried to adjust the detonator-collar he wore, which Brynd had commissioned from a cultist. At first, Voland was livid at the indignity of having to wear such an object, but was warned if he did not do as instructed, the device would explode and shatter his neck, killing him instantly.

Staying alive, for now, seemed the preferable option.

Voland had been offered something near freedom in exchange for the benefit of his skills. He would have done almost anything to get out of the darkness of his cell, to get Nanzi out too. It was not an opportunity to refuse.

He had taken only two hours' sleep, meanwhile, while other doctors came and took over, eyeing him with caution, and noting the device on his neck. Occasionally a soldier would come to check on him as he worked. Some of the other nursing staff whispered behind his back, more than once he heard the word 'butcher' being uttered, and all the time he wondered if this was how the great Doctor Voland would spend his final days.

Eight rows of bedrolls were lined up before him, spreading far into the cavernous darkness. Lanterns hung from the ceiling and cressets threw light from the walls. Two other medical professionals, both female, and neither as proficient as himself, attended to the patients, their shadows falling across the injured like some stark premonition of death. A dozen or so volunteers also moved back and forth between the lines, seeing to their basic needs or following the doctor's direct commands.

Casualties were laid out according to the severity of their injuries. From broken or dislocated limbs, lacerations, abrasions, punctured lungs, up to severe haemorrhaging, the wounded soldiers were admitted and distributed according to probability of their survival. Minor injuries were confined to the far end of the chamber, while Voland's duties involved the almost-dead. It seemed futile at first, temporarily patching up wounds that were simply too severe, too brutal; they continued to arrive at a steady rate. He smiled at the sweet thought of Nanzi whenever he came across one whose wounds had been treated with her silk.

Nanzi herself would stagger back into the makeshift hospital in between her missions. In her human form, of course, she came to check on how effective the silk was at sealing wounds. The substance acted as a coagulant, was quite inert with regards to the human body, and she had undoubtedly saved many lives.

'But they look at me and say vile things,' she mumbled into his shoulder, trying not to cry. 'They really hate us. They hate me, the things they say . . .'

He knew it must be worse for her, being so rare and precious a design, and people always feared what they did not understand.

FORTY-SIX

The invasion force ate further into the city, and Brynd despaired. Four hundred yards deep, huge enclaves of Villiren were being thieved from them. All the way from the seemingly distant rubble of Port Nostalgia, right into the heart of the city, and they now occupied streets in the Shanties and way down the western flank of the Wastelands.

In a few hours, Brynd estimated that over a thousand lives would vanish.

The Seventh Dragoons were now a shattered force, and the remnants filtered in among the troops of the Second and Fourth. The Regiments of Foot had felt the brunt of the attacks, losing ten thousand warriors so far. Garudas reported simply that more of the enemy were coming, via ship, but ultimately through the gates.

As night settled across the city, a strange calm could be felt. It seemed as if this new race and their red-skinned rumel allies did not want to operate without daylight. He knew already how the captive Okun had been sensitive to changes in light, so perhaps they were somehow dependent upon the sun.

Reports from the city:

Soldiers stood now in silence, under a cold, star-filled sky, waiting and watching the edges of buildings for movement, just in case. But darkness also meant respite, a chance to rebuild on both sides. It was also a chance to release the souls of the dead, and pyres sprouted everywhere, bright and morose blossoms, offering the stench of burning flesh to the sky.

But at some point in the night Brynd accepted that the Imperial front line would fall back further the next day. More of the invasion fleet would arrive – they seemed endless – and of the garudas dispatched with relics, only a few might return. He still knew so little about the enemy, about their strategies and their weaknesses.

And people were whispering throughout the city that the elite force was needed.

He summoned Nelum to the obsidian room, where they conversed in the half-light. 'Lieutenant Valore, I believe we require a second level of augmentation,' Brynd suggested. 'The cultists believe it will enable us to be an indestructible force. Your thoughts on the risk?'

'Would we simply become stronger, with greater prowess, or would such a level of artificial enhancement kill us?' the lieutenant enquired. 'I argue that we fight initially without this second reinforcement, to see how we fare, but for the cultists to prepare the enhancements just in case. Power isn't everything. Integrity and *good morality* goes a long way.'

*

A clear day for once, and the fighting resumed as the first red rays of the sun hit the city. More warships came, breaking a path through the sea, bringing with them the same kind of hell. Brynd issued tactical briefings to the Night Guard as noise spilled up from below the Citadel, which shuddered as they looked down from their crenellated sanctuary. Within a few minutes of the recommencement of combat, two key defence positions were lost near Scarhouse. Scouts later told him how rumel had poured into the district in great numbers, slaughtering every soldier in their path. Then they trampled over the dead to kill yet more.

In instant retaliation, Brynd summoned the garudas.

*

Erupting out of the morning sky, they soared over the northern streets of the city, then showered their replenished munitions on the main advancing units of the invaders, exploding flesh and rubble with equal intensity.

Enemy forces staggered back under the flash-flames that ripped through the narrow lanes till only a few Okun survived. Had there been an endless supply of *Brenna* relics to deploy in this way, Brynd might have had some cause for optimism. But the reality left him as morose in spirit as ever. And worse still, the mute bombs launched from the ships cramming into the harbour kept picking off the garudas in mid-flight, so that they tumbled towards the streets, exploding in a shower of feathers and flesh across the rooftops.

*

More industrious weapons were released. There was enough sheer bulk of the enemy now that the Empire's forces deemed it appropriate to utilize catapults. Normally reserved for sieges, the Ninth and Tenth Regiments of Foot deployed trebuchets and mangonels from behind their front lines. On the Citadel Brynd watched these great constructs, the length of five horses, being wheeled into position, like slow-moving beasts, their tops breaching the rooftops.

Soon they were busy launching colossal chunks of broken masonry at the mass of invaders. Boulder-sized debris also shattered the surrounding buildings, disabling the progress of the enemy and making their ability to reinforce key positions more difficult. They were fast destroying much of the city, Brynd realized, but this had to be done to save the rest of it.

The last sight that Brynd witnessed, before he departed the Citadel, was of rumel and Okun corpses being slung back towards the enemy.

But he then gave an order for these machines of war to hold fire.

Now was the hour of the Night Guard.

*

They lined up, twenty elite fighters, garbed in shadowy darkness. All were mounted on black horses that stood motionless despite the commotion going on around them. Brynd withdrew his sabre and watched faint flickers of cultist technology skim and shimmer across its metal surface. Well armed, and well protected by contoured body armour, they headed east along the wide boulevards, past onlookers from the civilian militia. Brynd felt the heavy weight of expectation, as smoke began to blow back from the *Brenna* bombs.

Only minutes from the front line.

He was disturbed by the numbers of civilians that had stayed put here – refusing to abandon their homes right in the warzone – and had not evacuated themselves through the tunnels as instructed. A woman in rags ran screaming towards the soldiers, and gripped Nelum's feet. She screamed for them to stop the fighting, shrieked that four of her sons had died in the first wave of attacks. Brynd nodded to his lieutenant, who pushed her gently away, and she collapsed to the floor sobbing, as the Night Guard continued past.

This war would be an endless, thankless task.

He took a deep breath and felt the thunder in his heart. To Brynd, these minutes seemed like the longest in his life.

Some missile collapsed the corner of a building about fifty yards away, and rubble clattered across the plaza. Frustratingly, at any given point, Brynd couldn't see what was firing the mute bombs.

Suddenly, another one connected with a nearby store, but the expected explosion didn't follow. And stranger still was how it fell to the ground – so slowly, and almost changing shape.

A nearby Dragoon moved his horse over to investigate. Brynd ordered for Lupus to ride with him in pursuit of the soldier.

The terrain was littered with minor debris and large chunks of masonry, so they dismounted, and hitched their horses to a railing outside a decimated tavern, then marched across the plaza. Old men and women, unable to fight, were loitering in doorways, and some residents prised apart their boarded-up windows to see what was going on outside.

Brynd and Lupus halted next to the bomb.

'What do you think it is, sir?' The young Dragoon stepped back, clearly nervous at the presence of the commander.

The fallen object was writhing back and forth in the snow, with tiny arms flailing. About the size of a human baby, its skin was grey and blighted with scale, and its grim, gargoyle-like face was peering back up at them.

It was a living creature.

Suddenly its legs fizzed into flame and it emitted a high-pitched, manic laugh.

'Get away!' Brynd shouted.

The other two soldiers dived instinctively to one side, while Brynd managed to cover his mouth with his cloak. Just then there was a scream and the ground trembled under a deep explosion, and fragments of stone rattled across the plaza.

Brynd looked up to assess the damage, and felt a small shard of glass had cut his knee. He brushed aside the injury and realized Lupus was standing right next to him, looking stunned. They went back to where the creature had detonated, and saw that the Dragoon was dead. His arms and much of his upper torso had been blown away, and his face was unrecognizable – a consequence, perhaps, of possessing no augmentations.

Brynd staggered away from the corpse, brushing cold sweat from his forehead.

'The hell was that thing?' Lupus muttered, still dazed.

'You held your breath, then.' Brynd adjusted his belt and straightened his sabre. 'I think it was . . . well, some outlandish grey reptile. A living bomb? Sounds ridiculous. I don't under-stand how it could just explode.'

'Maybe with those wings, it flew at high speed.'

'That would certainly explain why we can't see where it was launched from.'

'It didn't seem to mind killing itself,' Lupus observed. 'In fact, we both saw it laughing just before it detonated, so perhaps it's not sophisticated technology, just some species we don't yet understand. Which, to my mind, makes our military objectives seem a lot more attainable.'

Brynd nodded at this rare heartening thought.

The other Night Guard soldiers arrived, and Nelum slid off his horse to assess the scene.

Brynd related to the others what had happened.

'Suicide bombs?' Nelum muttered, examining the ground, the corpse, Lupus. 'How can such beings exist?'

'It's not that many stages removed from dying for your own nation, is it?' Lupus observed. 'In fact – the motivation is the same.'

'No, I don't agree!' Nelum snapped. 'It is execrable if you ask me. There is no dignity in it, no honour.'

'We'll have time to assess such things later,' Brynd interrupted, noting the expression on Nelum's face. 'Now, to the front line.'

*

As the Night Guard pushed on towards the front line, commands were issued along the ranks to allow the legendary regiment through. Men in Jamur uniforms were carried back, dead or dying, and Brynd told himself not to look.

They stationed themselves behind the Sixth Dragoons, the best part of a hundred men blocking this main thoroughfare leading west into the Scarhouse district. Featureless walls towered on either side, sandstone structures, and here the street was about sixty paces wide.

As the noise level increased, reports were passed to him: so far, an estimated nine or ten thousand Imperial soldiers had been killed. This figure shocked Brynd, as there had never been so many casualties in living memory, especially so early into a conflict. The city had become a trauma factory.

Jamur longbow archers were stationed on rooftops, firing deep towards the harbour and into Scarhouse, while closer to the front there were men with shorter bows, sniper units to pick out individuals from amidst the throng. Many of them glanced down and saluted the Night Guard as they deployed. Brynd knew that the very presence of his warriors brought momentary hope to those around them.

A line of soldiers moved forward, their armour rattling as they shifted into line. This was a time to face the facts. There was only a unit of the Regiment of Foot in front of the Sixth Dragoons, and that formed the line of battle. Buildings had collapsed three streets across to either side, leaving only this gaping avenue into which the aggression of both sides was funnelled.

Brynd gave his unit the orders to secure helms and armour and, through the slits of his visor, he watched the men in front begin to move.

*

Beami stood at a window overlooking an empty street, a visual echo in her mind of the last time she had seen Lupus. In a wood-panelled room behind her, three other cultists were examining their aggregated relics, deciding how they could best be used. A fire raged in the corner, and one of the others told her to close the window to keep the warmth in. She did as she was asked, reluctantly.

What will become of Lupus? she wondered. *Is he already dead?*

The thought of him going to war left her quite numb, even though at the very start she had been involved in the fighting. And now it was Lupus's turn to prove himself. Beami was so happy that they had rediscovered their love, even if only for such a short time. They had shared only the briefest of goodbyes at the Citadel gates, very aware of the other soldiers present, but in her mind it had seemed he would certainly return shortly.

Only now . . . now she wasn't so sure.

'Are you going to help us or what?' one of the cultists called out to her, distracting her from gloomy thoughts.

She moved back to the table with its heap of technology, and focused her attention instead on finding a way to help the city.

*

A row of soldiers moved forward.

They watched as the Sixth Dragoons surged forward in organized lines, closing the gap quickly, then their horses went ramming into a unit of Okun positioned at the far end of the street, leaving nothing in front of the Night Guard now except cobbles and blood and snow.

Brynd looked on grimly as the ranks of Dragoons fought within the narrow urban spaces. Horses were speared, ripped open by the claws of the Okun, riders tumbling on to the ground. They rejoined the fray, on foot, only to be hacked apart again. And all the time, arrows continued raining from above, selectively picking off the enemy.

Soldier after soldier fell. The collapse of their unit was rapid, yet a small core of them burst through the opposite ranks, vanishing out of sight, and all Brynd could do was hope for their survival.

There was a brief pause, as the depleted enemy ranks drew up together. Not a single Jamur soldier stood between them and the Night Guard.

A line of rumel, garbed in dull-grey armour, hesitated at the far end of the street as if they could smell cultist trickery on the Imperial weapons. As Okun joined them, they combined into one line with an alarming symmetry, as if they were separate components from one alien entity.

Brynd wondered at the sentience that united them while the enemy staggered forward, with swords raised, every move in sync.

The Night Guard waited, then Brynd delivered some short, sharp commands, his words reverberating among the empty buildings.

They rode straight for the enemy, eating up the intervening distance, first a hundred yards, sixty, thirty, twenty, Brynd kept speeding towards them, constantly thinking *Don't look at the dead, don't look at the dead*. They barged into the enemy lines, their horses rearing up and savagely trampling the first row of rumel. Bodies crumpled under the impact; heads exploded on the cobbles, then Brynd slipped off sideways from his saddle, as his horse collapsed on the blood-slick streets. The animal struggled to its feet, skidding desperately on the ice, then bolted away to safety.

Other Night Guard had merged into the mass of bodies and relentless screams filled his ears, and then something scraped against Brynd's arm, ripping his uniform, drawing blood. Confident in his augmentations, Brynd stepped aside and lashed out again and again, striking left and right, reacting solely on instinct, while thinking *Fuck I can barely see a thing*.

Okun armour split like eggshells as his blade impacted, and he cleaved an arm here an arm there. Grotesque faces flashed in and out of focus, but there were also rumel almost identical to the ones of the world he was so familiar with, and suddenly this alien army became distressingly real. He recognized the fear in them, too, and the sudden hopelessness, but he parried and chopped-spun-blocked his way through.

A pause to try to assess the scene: whereupon he called out for various tactical routines. In response, his soldiers filed in around him on horseback, pushing forwards, and sweeping past. They continued the slaughter, feeding his body the adrenalin he needed. His relic-doctored sword sliced so easily through armour. A blade in, blood out, then rip the creature's spine. Something turned, a weapon narrowly missed his head. He ripped into it, wrenched sideways, spilling offal on to his arm.

By now he could feel his face covered with sweat and blood.

Don't look at the dead.

A street packed with bodies, grunts, metal clanging on stone. Exhaustion.

The constant blur of motion removed any coherency from the scene, but very quickly he saw that he was at the rear of the skirmish. Most importantly, up ahead the Night Guard was forcing the enemy line back efficiently and quickly. They were decimating the columns of the foe.

Air support arrived suddenly, and began attacking the invading forces further back with *Brenna* relics. Intense fireballs rolled towards him from the explosions ignited between the distant buildings, flames billowing and licking their way upwards. And nearest the drop zone he could see the churning silhouettes of enemy soldiers.

Snipers based on rooftops continued their onslaught relentlessly till hundreds of red-skinned rumel and Okun lay dead on the ground, and any still showing signs of life were picked off one by one.

Combat edged away. The density of enemy bodies decreased. The Night Guard finally halted and moved aside. Barricades were instantly hauled into place, ordinary soldiers sprinting forward into position.

A calm settled over the scene. This storm had passed, and Brynd collapsed breathless to his knees on the freezing street. Feeling totally disconnected from the reality of what had just occurred, he flipped up the visor of his helmet.

After a moment's respite he was able to assess the damage to his unit – amounting to just a single casualty. The dead man was Brox, only thirty years old; his neck was savagely gashed and his body had been trampled.

The street looked as if it had been spliced straight out of hell and into Villiren. Body segments and discarded armour littered the place. Walls in the distance were charred with flame damage. One of the Dragoons had descended into shock, and was huddling shivering against a wall; blood was splashed against pale stonework behind him.

There were several injuries to his soldiers, but the rest of his team had survived. The lighter wounds were already beginning to heal before his eyes and the medics could soon see to the others. Every one of them should be ready to fight again soon. He eyed sadly the remains of four of the black horses, then gave the orders for them to be added to the nearest funeral pyre.

In the uncanny silence, a battle line had been redrawn. The mission considered a success, the Night Guard withdrew back into the city.

*

Evening arrived, and the battle front had held firm exactly where his elite troop had left. Brynd's eyes reflected the flames of a funeral pyre as he watched it carry the soul of Brox to the heavens. One of his regiment had just informed him that the mood of the city had been lifted, that people were now feeling optimistic.

Brynd wasn't so confident himself, but now decided the enemy were not totally alien; he had raised hopes of perhaps negotiating with them. Prisoners would need to be taken from their ranks, and somehow used as bait for opening channels of communication.

Still, neither side seemed to engage in activity during the night, which was fine with Brynd because they certainly wouldn't be able to defend the city efficiently in darkness.

After retreating into the Citadel, he was alarmed to learn that yet more ships had been sighted cutting south through the waters. Was there no end to this offensive? And what the hell did they want with the city in the first place?

In the obsidian chamber, arranged around the vast table, the Night Guard held a council of war. They ate hastily provided food and someone had brought in ale, though none of them touched a drop. There were lingering silences as they nursed their bruises from earlier, all the while mourning a comrade.

Smoke, as usual, commented about the plight of the horses. Syn seemed to relish the opportunity to fight against new techniques. Brug spoke diligently about the enemy's weaknesses.

'How long can we last?' Nelum asked. 'What happens if we're eradicated? They all seem to fight as one coherent, slick organism, as if they can communicate telepathically with each other. What can be done against such a level of organization? If we fall, the city's doomed.'

'Not necessarily,' Lupus argued. 'The Dragoons have held the front since earlier.'

Then the idea of further augmentation was again mooted, and in principle everyone seemed eager to seek advantage. Towards the end of their discussion, a new report came through that civilians had been recently rounded up by the enemy and were being kept in a fishing warehouse behind the Shanties. No one knew if they were to be slaughtered, or would be taken from the city as hostages. At least a hundred had been snatched so far.

FORTY-SEVEN

Just after sunset, there had been a minor skirmish: two rumel enemy scouts were constantly checking the state of a deserted plaza, a tentative step to sense the depth and breadth of Imperial lines.

But the red-skinned rumel didn't realize they were already being watched by the Rumel Irregulars One. They crouched by the bomb-wrecked ruins of what was once a bakery, making a final inspection before darkness fully descended.

Right, that's as close as you're coming, you bastards.

From his hiding place behind a thick barricade of rubble, Jeryd leaned over and signalled the order to fire. In relative silence: crossbow bolts were suddenly let loose, skimming across the cobbles, shattering the window of an overturned fiacre, then hammering into the two scouts. One target was struck in the arm, the other clipped in the thigh before both fell to one side, raising shields as they dived for cover. Once safely out of sight, the two rumel sprinted to safety, pissing Jeryd off immensely. He had wanted at least one prisoner, so they could extract further information. Or even just to see what they were made of . . .

He couldn't decide how he felt about the presence of these differently coloured rumel. Seeing them changed the texture of his world. It unsettled him, having to contemplate how his own race might have a history bigger than he'd previously thought.

*

Dusk became darkness, into his third night of the war now.

Bored shitless, Jeryd leant on the barricade, pointing his crossbow into the darkness beyond. Nothing had moved for some time. Moonlight skidded off the surface of shining cobbles at this point where Althing, Saltwater and Scarhouse converged.

His orders were to hold this position and should an attack seem imminent overnight, to relay an immediate warning to the Citadel. Such communication might make the difference between the city staying in Jamur hands or falling to the invaders.

'It's fucking freezing out here, and not so much as a rat has farted tonight,' he grumbled to Corporal Bags of Rumel Irregulars One.

'Aye, sir,' the young brownskin rumel replied. 'Better that than fighting, yeah?'

'Guess you're right,' Jeryd conceded.

The son of a fellow Inquisition officer, Bags himself was a barber who seemed to know half the residents in Villiren. And when it came to those he didn't know about, Bags would tap the side of his broad nose and scamper off to have a word with some contact or other, returning shortly afterwards with the necessary background information, and occasionally a little scandal.

Jeryd liked that quality, and had drawn the lad to his side quickly. He had to admit, it felt good to be around so many other rumel again – if only they could have met under different circumstances.

Suddenly, a scuffle broke out in his own ranks, and being the senior officer, he made his way across to investigate. Despite the new sword being so unfamiliar and heavy, constantly getting in his way, he did well to maintain his dignity as he approached.

'What the hell d'you think you're doing?' Jeryd called out to them across the street.

A rumel soldier was engaged in a brawl with a couple of humans. By the time others arrived to break it up, the young rumel had a broken nose and was bleeding heavily.

'What do you think you're doing? There's already a war on, without us fighting amongst ourselves.'

One of the humans, brushing himself down, yelled back. 'You rumel, you're the ones that's invading. You're the fucking enemy. We always knew there was something wrong with you lot and now look. A load of you hanging about with weapons. Fuck should anyone trust you?'

Bags stood by Jeryd's side, levelling a crossbow, but Jeryd eased him away. 'Get back, lad. That's just what they want.'

He turned back to the humans. 'We are defending Villiren, by order of the Empire. We are on *your* damn side, and you come here trying to harm us. As if this city hasn't seen enough death already.'

'Fuck you, rumel,' the human snarled and made offensive gestures, then ran off into the darkness. *If things are this bad here, how bad will they be in the tunnels with Marysa? Bohr, I hope she's all right.*

*

An elderly man tripped and fell, dropping his bags on the muddy floor. Marysa helped him to his feet then his family came to thank her. Soon they were lost again among all the others.

Slowly, they all shifted through tunnels lit occasionally by storm lanterns or torches. It was like some lower region of hell. Now and again there was a sound like thunder overhead, though the only clouds down here were those of fear and misery. *To think, this was considered the safer option*, she thought. *I wonder how Jeryd is coping with the storm above.*

As they shuffled forward monotonously, occasionally the network of tunnels would open out into a vast cavern, where the remains of some ancient settlement was in the process of decay. Towers and spires rose a good forty feet high, examples of perfect symmetry, punctuated by windows only visible now as bold shadows. In the light from the lanterns carried by Villiren's fleeing populace, these structures seemed both eerie and awe-inspiring.

Stunned and delighted, she recognized some of the architectural embellishments as characteristic of Máthema, therefore tens of thousands of years old. Never in all her years of archaeological study had she seen anything quite like this. Down here there was no rough weather to wear them down, which must explain their good condition.

If only I could remain here for a while . . .

Progress had been fine until the city's notorious gangs had arrived on the scene. Sauntering along in their hundreds, and pausing to fight with their rivals, they had become a constant obstruction. Marysa was disgusted that these fit and healthy men – and women – chose to flee their city rather than give help to the armies up above. Hoods hauled over their heads, garish masks to hide behind, they pushed their way ahead with no respect for others. They flaunted their weapons simply for the fun of scaring people, who were already frightened enough.

Up ahead of Marysa, a woman began wailing hysterically.

As she approached through the murk she could see a blonde woman huddled on the floor, cradling a young child in her arms.

Just then a man in a sinister red mask approached and crouched down to speak to the distraught mother. Marysa paused, feeling self-conscious about watching the pair, as people flowed around them with their carts and luggage.

Is he going to harm her?

'What happened?' the man asked.

The woman was silent for a while, refusing to speak. There was fear in her eyes, as if she recognized him, and after the man asked again she replied, 'My boy gets ill and we don't have any food and . . . now he's dead.'

'How old was he?' red mask asked softly.

'Two years in only six more days. We was going to have a nice time, just me and him. His father left . . .' She began to sob again, hugging her dead son to her chest, and rocking back and forth as if to soothe the corpse into an even deeper state of rest.

The man stood up, glancing briefly at Marysa and the others who had stopped to watch. A man behind grumbled at them to get out of the way.

Red mask's gang had now assembled, a sizeable outlaw regiment waiting for their commander to speak. They wore feral masks. Metal glinted beneath their well-made cloaks. Many of them looked young, under twenty at least.

'We're going back,' the man decided.

'Boss?'

The man spoke firmly, did not even raise his voice. 'We are going back.' He lifted up his mask to reveal handsome features, which surprised her. 'Give this poor woman some damn money and a decent cart and one of you – I don't care who – make sure she gets out to safety.'

'Why are we going back up there?' demanded the redhead. 'We do that, we all get killed.'

The boss grabbed the man's collar and lifted him up onto his toes. 'See the dead kid? How many more of those d'you think there'll be if people like us don't do something? I've changed my mind. Put word out, to round up affiliated gangs. Tell them, one of us goes down, we all go down together – that's what we're all about.' He dropped the fellow, shoved his way back through the other men. They looked at each other, shrugging. No one knew what to make of this change of plan.

'What difference can *we* make?' the redhead called out after him, but it wasn't any use.

The man in the red mask had vanished.

*

444

If they were going to do it at all, they would have to do it his way.

A hub of fifty or so Bloods soon became an aggregate of dozens: hundreds of masked fighters from the various gangs who, somewhere along the lines, had stopped caring only about themselves. Or maybe many of them had begun to understand just what it meant if they didn't have a home, if they didn't have others to intimidate, if they didn't have rackets to engage in.

They now listened only to Malum, and their own leaders backed down. It was futile even for them to oppose this acrimonious band. Reluctantly the military had handed over weapons and armour, realizing that this change of heart was in everyone's best interest. And, anyway, it wasn't *their* city, this wasn't their turf. It had always belonged to the gangs of Villiren and Malum wanted to keep things that way.

He was distantly aware of just how powerful he had become, but even that didn't matter at all. He was a shattered man, and didn't give a fuck if he got killed. People afraid of dying usually possessed something worth losing. It was possible that many of the other Bloods felt the same – all they had ever had was the gang anyway. They would do anything for him now.

He didn't know how it happened, but ever since he had seen all these people underground, especially since he had seen the children with their haunted faces and tenuous futures, he had managed to focus his anger on the things that were invading his city.

The Okun and those red-skinned rumel.

Dirty relics and illegal blades and outlawed poisons, the gangs began to use every nefarious piece of equipment they could get their hands on. Archaic systems were established, a no-leader culture despite their reverence for Malum, and as a result they became surprisingly well organized, a rough but self-sufficient fighting unit, with no need for Imperial direction. Some of the more primitive, barbarous types were in their element, able to indulge finally in killing as much as they could. There was something strangely poetic about the freedom they now operated with.

While the Okun possessed an instinct for knowing exactly what was coming, the red rumel made easier targets. Unlike their allies, they didn't fight as one, so their small patrols were easily hunted down by the feral gangsters.

Malum himself was armed only with his messer blade and crossbow, and sauntered behind a group of gang members until they had cornered their enemy against some old factory wall, then he'd push his way to the front, fangs protruding, to watch the fear in those black eyes as crossbow bolts thudded into them at any attempt to escape.

Finally, he would slit their throats and thrust his maw forward to drink their blood.

*

On the third night after the gangs had become embroiled in the fighting, some insane genius released from their cells all the cultist-bred monstrosities, the ones used for arena combat, and his followers rode them through the narrow streets to plough straight into large clusters of the invaders. The enemy's synchronicity didn't deter the hybrids in the least. Unable to register any kind of fear, and bred without susceptibility to pain, these monsters did not suffer from any hesitancy.

Creatures many feet tall, endowed with multiple limbs, thick hides glistening with scales, advanced, all teeth and violence, to bombard the sturdy ranks of the rumel and Okun. They tore through whatever streets they cared to, sectors that had already seen days of fighting. They killed late into the night.

As Malum and his colleagues looked on from afar, tenement blocks were now being appropriated in the name of the gangs, and it wasn't long before it was mooted that some of these buildings were no longer Imperial territory.

And by the next day they'd be designated as autonomous zones – pirate territory. The first such enclave lay in the heart of Saltwater, offering a fine view over much of the fighting, and during the next day it expanded into former enemy territory in Scarhouse. Such reoccupation of the invaded city – including the Shanties, Althing, Scarhouse, and the Wasteland – could potentially stretch for miles along the coastline.

This new realm would have no emperor.

FORTY-EIGHT

Some distance from the front line of fighting, Nelum again found Priest Pias in the Jorsalir church. This holy place was redolent with incense and history. Breathing it all in, it brought him great solace to be away from the pressures of war. It was somewhere he might find a moment of blessed silence.

A few days of combat had passed, but he found the priest still there, lighting candles in front of the opulent tapestries hanging at the far end of the church, whispering verses to himself.

The old man peered over his shoulder as he heard Nelum's boots scuffing on the marble tiles. 'Ah, my holy soldier,' the priest called out, turning to regard the tapestry once again. 'I am deeply happy to see you have survived – clearly, Bohr smiles favourably upon you.'

Nelum approached the priest and kissed the jewelled ring on his extended hand. Here indeed was a magisterial figure. 'I'm surprised to find you still here. Wouldn't it be prudent for you to leave the city?'

'I find that in such troubled times, I am busier than ever. The shepherd's flock swells in number whenever death is easier to envisage – it has always been the way of things.' He gave a knowing half-smile. 'People need comfort, so I am here to provide it.'

'I can understand that,' Nelum replied.

'I have been hoping you might have news for me on your wayward commanding officer.'

Nelum paused, pondering the right thing to say. Every day he'd looked for the right moment to arise, but there were always too many others around. Even in the obsidian chamber they were rarely left alone together. Nelum had even tampered with Brynd's saddle, loosening the girth so it would slip round during combat, but that hadn't succeeded either. And he had meanwhile suffered his doubts, tested and questioned his motives. He could barely sleep because of the stress. 'It isn't easy, you know, waiting for the best opportunity. Sometimes I can't help thinking it is not the right choice of action.'

The priest nodded, but Nelum could sense some dissatisfaction in his manner. A vague sense of shame washed over him. How could he let down a Jorsalir priest, of all people?

'He's a very effective warrior,' Nelum offered, hoping the priest might review his stance on this matter. 'He's helped kill so many of the enemy so far, and his training and strategies have primed the army to the best of their abilities.'

'That may be so, but should we permit sinners of this kind to go free on the streets to pollute the minds of others? He does not count in the larger scheme of things. You could assume his role very easily ... Walk with me now, for these are not matters for discussion in a public place.'

Under soaring arches, and between stout columns, Nelum followed the priest into a small, musty room near the front of the church. Ancient texts covered in mould and dust lay heaped in piles, and Nelum could see enough from their spines to know that these were rare works indeed – many not even written in Jamur script.

'Is this your study?' Nelum asked.

'Of a sort. We keep all sorts of forgotten books here, and there is a small group of us documenting their significance.'

'Are they not all recorded?'

'Many were lodged in the libraries of various monasteries

and churches across the Archipelago, but because of recent occurrences, we are now being more cautious about whom we entrust with them. Now, please . . .'

Pias gestured to a large wooden chair standing next to a sturdy table. He lit a cresset as Nelum sat down, still feeling vaguely anxious. The sharp features of the elderly priest's face were exaggerated by the light.

The priest wandered over to a set of shelves to retrieve a small, cream-coloured volume. He opened its age-tattered pages while continuing the conversation. 'I'm going to talk to you about something called mantraism, of which you won't remember anything after you leave. I won't patronize you, but enough to say it is one of our most ancient and secret arts.'

'I'm not sure I understand what—'

The old man began chanting, a cycle of words, adopting old tones Nelum had never before heard, and whatever language it was, the words repeated themselves. Occasionally the priest seemed to stop speaking but the sound of his voice amazingly continued. Over and over again the incantation looped, and Pias now spoke on top of it, reading from the book, layering and harmonizing everything he uttered.

And, in the middle of all this, Nelum heard in urgent tones: 'Think how highly you would be regarded for having cleansed this world of such a corrupting influence. Your commander's kind is not natural. Men should lie only with women since it's for *creation*. Anything else . . . No, it cannot be. Lieutenant, try not to think only of this one lifetime, but where your soul will proceed in the next – you will be rewarded for this. So often we think only of this existence, when there are many more to consider. So you will, you must, find an appropriate time, and then you will begin to feel an absolute urge to kill your commander, and thus rid this world of such an abomination . . .'

The flow of words eventually slowed to a halt, leaving an

450

agonizing silence inside Nelum's head. He could remember nothing, could feel nothing, as Priest Pias loomed above him smiling.

'Are you feeling all right?'

'I'm sorry, I must have missed some of what you were saying. The pressures of the war must be getting to me.'

'I do understand. We were merely discussing your commander.'

Brynd. That queer had to die. 'I see.'

*

On his departure, the priest handed him a piece of paper inscribed with an address, saying it would help. Nelum stole off into the night.

He rode his horse to the location indicated, on the eastern fringe of the city, part of the new-build sectors. Satisfyingly it put some more distance between himself and the fighting, but he needed to be quick: people would begin questioning his absence.

Icy sleet tingled on his skin, yet there was a curious warmth to the air, as if the ice age was being repelled by natural elements, and this wasn't meant to be.

His destination turned out to be one of the worst areas of the city.

The crippled and homeless huddled together in the bowels of the district, shelters and squats and makeshift camps. An anarchic repossession of a district constructed only a decade ago, but now worn down by the world. More than once on the way, he could have sworn he saw some unlikely beast, maybe one of the talked-about hybrids with grafted-on wings.

Lonely figures dawdled at street corners, caressing flick knives, but never looked his way. Women caked in too much make-up braved the cold, displaying a little flesh. They cooed and pouted towards him, outraging his deep sense of morality.

A gaunt-faced man with a shaven head and stubble shambled towards Nelum and demanded money. Another figure in a cloak sauntered in from the left, a cock-sure stride denoting this was a routine procedure.

'I've nothing for you.' Nelum dismounted and moved away from his horse towards them.

The cloaked man flicked open a knife and thrust it at him lazily, but Nelum batted his hand away, grabbed his wrist then broke his assailant's arm across his knee. At that point the first thug jumped him with his own blade, drawing a faint line across Nelum's cheek, before staggering away.

The man's expression turned to surprise as he watched Nelum's wound heal before his eyes. He began thrusting his knife aggressively, while Nelum darted this way and that, ducking appropriately. He then palmed the man's forearm, sent the blade spinning from his grip, before he yanked the man's wrist downwards and jabbed a vicious punch to his neck. He collapsed to one knee, clutching his throat.

A few of the whores further up the street laughed awkwardly before sashaying off into the darkness, and Nelum mounted his horse again, then rode away wondering just where on earth the priest had sent him.

*

He arrived eventually at a dilapidated shopfront adorned with a discoloured sign that read 'Cheap Lunches'. Every other building up and down the street looked unlived in, redundant, yet he felt dozens of eyes observing him. Shutters covering windows, a boarded-up door, and Nelum was left wondering how he would get in. He dismounted, tethered up his agitated mount, then went around the back to find a door, on which he knocked loudly.

Eventually a hatch slid back, a pair of eyes regarded him, and someone asked his business.

'The priest sent me,' Nelum explained and, after a few more seconds of staring at those unblinking eyes, he added: 'I'm here to buy some of your wares.'

The hatch closed, then the door creaked open, and Nelum was beckoned into the darkness by an old man wearing scruffy breeches. The place stank of either chemicals or cheap incense, and there was someone playing a piano in a far-off room, a gust of laughter accompanying. The man led him into a small but well-lit room resembling a grocer's shop, with a counter and dozens of vials and bottles teetering on shelves – so much glass sparkling in the lantern light. Dozens of knives hung on one wall like rows of teeth of varying lengths. Ornamental masks lined another. Gemstones rested in boxes beneath the counter, amber, jade, topaz and a hundred varieties he didn't recognize.

Nelum stared at the man and dropped several Sota discs on the counter. He was skinny with sallow skin, and his jaw narrowed dramatically to a point, which in this light made him look like he'd been cross-bred with a rat.

Laughter again from the other room.

'I'm after some of your substances. Toxic substances in particular.'

'Got all sorts here,' the man replied. 'What you after?'

'Respiratory inhibitor,' Nelum said hesitantly, remembering some textbook from his studies. 'Cyanide, possibly?'

The man smiled, eyeing Nelum's clothing, clearly realizing that he was a military man but still not commenting on the fact. This unspoken pact was reassuring. 'That's old school,' he said. 'An amateur's choice. You're a traditionalist, I see.'

'Have you anything better then?'

''Course, lad. People come to me when they need a job doing.'

'Well, I need a job doing *well*. Something to be injected directly into the bloodstream. And it needs to be tough, with no messing around. Distilled so it's strong enough to kill many men.'

'Bloodstream . . . Maybe haemotoxins? No, you might want to consider charged metals, but that can be slow – and usually it's ingested. You want to be able get out quick?'

'I do.'

'Hmm. You considered a blade rather than toxins?'

'That could be messy ... I don't want to be involved in a simple fight, not if I can help it.'

The old man turned and looked at the shelves like he was searching for something in particular. '*Clostridium botulinum*,' he breathed, and turned round with a small knife, holding it reverentially in front of him. He placed it on the countertop.

Nelum was impressed with the filigree of work: it was the most ornate and uncanny knife that Nelum had ever seen, with a marble-like handle and gold edging. Dark substances oozed beneath what appeared to be a transparent surface – no, the blade itself seemed to be constructed from some form of liquid, yet one capable of holding its shape.

'Using this won't be pretty, since *Botulinum* causes extreme paralysis and physical distortion. One of the most toxic substances I deal with. Myth has us believe that people used this to stop themselves from ageing – insane to believe that, but I've heard funnier things about the past ... This is called a botulinum blade. Fabricated from the poison itself.'

'How can I trust that it works?'

'Who knows what they got up to in times gone by – but they was darker folk than in our own day. Now, wait here.' The old man stepped away to the back and Nelum was left with only the sound of laughter eerily drifting somewhere in the distance. He eventually returned with a steel cage, inside which a fat rat scampered aimlessly. Beckoning Nelum closer, he sat the cage down and poked the strange blade between its bars. The rat merely brushed up against the tip of the blade, but instantly it began to shudder, then convulsed, its entire body contorting and blisters forming under the fur. It finally collapsed on its side and Nelum realized it had died, but its body was still reacting violently to the toxin.

'I'll take it,' Nelum declared.

When the old man described a phenomenally high price,

Nelum was forced to reach for a second purse of coins. The blade was wrapped up and boxed and slipped under Nelum's cloak, before he left the broken-down building to find his horse.

*

A knock on his chamber door, and Brynd jolted awake to find he'd fallen asleep across his missives. Zones across his shoulder and neck had become bitingly stiff from the combat.

A messenger shuffled into the room, announcing more bad news. There had been confirmation from the scouts that the enemy were indeed taking prisoners. Over a thousand citizens of all ages were now locked up in a warehouse somewhere in the west of the city, and ships were lining up to transport them to the north.

*

Later that night, Brynd asked Nelum to meet him in the obsidian chamber to discuss a possible mission to the warehouse. Lupus was standing by the far wall, studying maps of the area that the enemy had captured.

The central table seemed increasingly an extension of Brynd himself, so much of his business was now conducted from here. This wasn't soldiering any longer, it was administration.

After explaining the news in detail he rested on his elbows and peered across at his lieutenant. The man seemed more agitated than he'd ever known, and it seemed he had not listened to a word just said. Brynd knew this to be totally out of character for him.

'Part of the Night Guard's duty is protection of the Empire's subjects,' Brynd said, by way of reminder. 'It seems there are many innocent civilians imprisoned and waiting to die, and I believe we must devise a way to get them out of there with minimal loss of military personnel.'

'Agreed.' Nelum frowned at the table. 'I'm sure I can come up with a strategy.'

Brynd wanted to do that himself, but as a gesture to Nelum,

he backed down. 'If you wouldn't mind. So long as absolute stealth is integral to—'

'You think I don't know that?' Nelum snapped.

Ungrateful bastard. 'Lieutenant, you need to show some more respect for your commanding officer.'

A pause, as Nelum searched his mind for the right words. 'I find it difficult, is all. I think the stress of this campaign is getting to me.'

'Getting to *you*?' Brynd stood up suddenly, tipping his chair to one side. 'You think *I'm* not fucking stressed? I know exactly what you mean, lieutenant. But you remain under my command. Is that fucking clear?'

Nelum's eyes betrayed his rage.

'Indeed, commander.'

At that point, Brynd suspected he had lost any future support from his second-in-command. He realized that Lupus was facing them now, wide-eyed and uncertain how to act. 'As you were, private,' Brynd ordered, and Lupus turned silently to face the maps again.

Brynd moved to pick up his chair and brought it calmly to the table. 'The only question is how we do this. I suggest it needs to be a night mission, because although witnesses say the Okun can be active after dark, it seems they prefer not to fight then – and neither do our own forces – but at least we Night Guard are enhanced. Somehow, we'll need to penetrate a zone that lies deep within enemy ground, without being seen.'

'We could use the garudas,' Nelum suggested eventually, and Brynd liked that idea.

*

Hours had passed and still it wasn't the right time – it seemed that he'd never find the right time. Sleep had so far avoided him, as Nelum let his concerns and angst continue to ricochet around inside his head. He pushed himself up, got dressed, picked up the case containing the botulinum blade. He unwrapped the curiosity and held it before him, marvelling at the technology involved.

The two men he shared the room with – Brug and Haal – would be out of the way for the next few hours, wading through the messages and directives in the report.

Which meant Brynd himself should be taking this opportunity to get some sleep.

How dare the albino talk to him like that – in front of Lupus. There was no respect from Brynd, no appreciation of how Nelum's mind liked to work. He wished to shut out all distraction in order to formulate this operation, and all the commander did was offer annoying assistance. Nelum needed no help. *No, if there is ever a time to do it, it's now.*

He pulled up a black hood to keep his face in shadow, then headed outside. Soft footsteps on the flagstones, as he moved along the corridors with the blade ready in his hand. There was hardly anyone else up at this hour, and he felt himself more on edge than he'd ever known. His senses were sharpened by his desire not to get caught, every sound alerted his gaze, every flicker of light ahead challenged him.

Four doors along on the right was Brynd's room – the commander preferring to sleep apart from the rest of the men. If this had not been a time of war, there would have been night sentinels stationed along the corridor, but now every single soldier needed to be fresh to fight.

Nelum took a breath to steady his nerves, and listened for any sound of movement inside. His grip on the door handle was so gentle, almost caressing it open, without a sound.

He slunk inside.

There, at the far end of the room, lay a man breathing to the rhythm of his dreams. The milky light of the moons filtered through a tiny round window high up on the wall and, as his eyes rapidly adjusted, Nelum could make out clearly the form of the commander on the bed.

A pale face turned slightly, and the words were whispered suddenly: 'I wondered how long.'

The chink of metal unsheathing, and Nelum moved fast. Brynd must have kept a blade ready by his pillow.

They fought desperately in the dark. In an instant they were locked together, gripping each other's wrists, muscles stinging, then Nelum felt two sharp blows connecting with his ribcage before he managed to headbutt Brynd away, with a heavy grunt.

After their separation there was a pause, as each of them waited for the other to strike.

Nelum lunged again, his blade skilfully slicing back and forth, forcing Brynd to topple forwards. Nelum kicked his opponent's legs under him, but Brynd gripped Nelum's ankle then raked a knife across his shins. Nelum managed to twist himself away but the agonizing pain had him writhing on the floor as the commander began to retaliate.

Nelum managed to grab and deflect Brynd's wrist, sending the commander's knife skimming across the floor. He then kneed Brynd in the stomach. The albino grunted, forced himself upright in an instant. He aimed a punch at Nelum's cheek – something cracked – and now it was Nelum's turn to feel pain. Brynd slammed a sideways kick across his knees, bringing him buckling back to the floor again.

Brynd punched down on to his neck.

Nelum's breath escaped him rapidly. He gasped for air, holding the toxic blade up uselessly. Then, as he reached for his damaged throat, the knife in his hand slipped . . .

*

Brynd watched Nelum's face flicker like a stroke victim's, then it contorted dramatically. His limbs collapsed into abnormal postures, and he began juddering movements. He arced his spine and tried to scream, but only gasps and saliva emerged. The muscles on his face began to twitch hideously, as his skin bubbled and blistered. Then after what seemed far too long, Nelum fell still.

458

Brynd struggled to one side and lit a candle. Some strange blade made of alien technology was partially lodged in Nelum's chest.

Dear Bohr . . . What is in that knife?

Nelum's skin had turned a vibrant red, his body so deformed that Brynd could barely recognize him. For a moment, Brynd's breathing came in short, sharp gasps.

Why did you have to come after me, Nelum? Just because of your damn beliefs and prejudice? They had been comrades for years – close enough to know each other's quirks. How could Nelum have planned to kill him, after all they'd both been through?

Brynd slumped back against the bed and pressed his face into his palms.

FORTY-NINE

Brynd now had to wake up his unit in the middle of the night. Bleary-eyed and half asleep they shuffled to the obsidian room, where in near-darkness he told them of the murderous attempt on him, and the outcome. Their reaction was a stunned silence.

Did they believe him? Would they think he had killed Nelum because of their recently expressed differences?

'Why would Nelum attack you?' Tiendi asked. Only the woman dared speak.

'You tell me,' Brynd suggested, scanning the rest of them for signs of insubordination, for subtle expressions indicating anyone else out to get him. If he wasn't careful, he could become completely paranoid. 'He just came into my room with a weapon when he thought I was asleep.'

Brynd had already requested two of his men to help him carry in the body, carefully wrapped up in bed sheets. It now lay on the table, and Brynd pulled the sheets aside to reveal the corpse.

'Fucking hell,' someone gasped.

'Shit.'

The bubbling beneath the dead man's skin had worsened, leaving little to identify him except his uniform. His arms were bent out of shape, one of his legs so swollen that it had split his breeches open.

'What could have caused such a reaction, commander?' Lupus asked.

'Whatever that blade was made from.' Brynd gestured to the weapon still in the corpse's chest. 'Probably some hybrid form of poison – which was intended for me. I'm making no assumptions that he was working alone.'

Silently, members of the Night Guard huddled around the body, then some walked away as if trying to distance themselves from this hideous sight. One or two exchanged glances and Brynd examined their movements. Judging by their body language, this was as much a mystery to them as it was to him.

Tiendi persisted, 'I don't get it. Why did he want to kill you?'

Because I'm gay. Because I'm an abomination to his definition of man. Because his beliefs told him to? 'I can only guess he didn't agree with my decisions in some way.'

*

Ice-wet steps descended to the central courtyard of the Citadel. Layers of moss and lichen added to the gloom. Sombre and still shocked, the Night Guard formed a respectful line past which Brynd, Lupus, Brug and Mikill carried a stretcher bearing the silk-wrapped body of Lieutenant Nelum Valore. A few other people had gathered on the viewing platforms, peering down at this black-garbed troop of mourners.

Morning sleet skidded past his face as Brynd helped steer the remains of his old friend – *because that's what he was, doesn't matter what he's done* – towards the funeral pyre. He was acutely aware of the questioning gazes of his regiment. Some of them had not wanted a traitor burned with dignity.

The line of soldiers stamped to attention, bringing their right fists to their chests. Brynd and Lupus steadied the front end of the black-shrouded stretcher bearing Nelum's body, guiding it gently onto the head-high shelf, then stepped back in line with the others. Brynd gave the orders for the pyre to be lit. Someone applied a flaming torch to the base of the pyre and slowly the fire spread till it formed a beacon under the dark sky.

'I hope your chosen gods will treat you well, lieutenant,' Brynd whispered, staring through the shimmer of heat.

Lupus leaned towards him. 'It was good, doing this. That is a good gesture, given what he tried to do.'

'He was still a Night Guard, private. Still, ultimately, a good man.'

*

The best of what the Empire had to offer was lined up in a chamber overlooking the north face of the Citadel. In the distance the sounds of combat drifted ever closer, like an approaching storm. A sense of dread hung in the air, as Brynd watched Blavat the cultist arranging her display of vials on the stone table to one side. He scrutinized all of the little glass containers, already knowing the order in which they'd be selected. Each moment seemed to stretch out in time, as he kept getting tangled up in his own thoughts.

The rest of the unit was morose, standing with arms folded in a contemplative silence. Brynd reminded himself to work on their morale before the mission, since he needed their dedication, especially now.

Lupus volunteered to go first, his partner Beami standing ready to conduct the new augmentations. Lupus removed his shirt and lay down on the plinth, the others waiting and watching mournfully like he was preparing himself to die. Relics were made ready, metallic and crystalline devices lined up, plates attached to his head, then he and his partner shared a final glance before he was injected with extra life. He coughed a loud gasp, clenching his fists then fell to the floor. Beami gently helped him over to the side of the room, where he gripped his gut and rubbed his head.

Everyone stared in anticipation. He seemed completely alive and well and flabbergasted at his new-found senses. He described possession of enhanced qualities that made Brynd excited.

The others followed suit. One after another came Tiendi, Syn, Mikill, Brug, Smoke, Haal, Bondi, and the rest: injection, gasp, collapse, struggle upright, alive.

Then Brynd himself approached the plinth, baring his chest before the cultist. Cold metal penetrated his skin and a surge of technology exploded through his veins –

Like being plunged in ice-water.

Breath fled from his body and he felt his heart beat in a myriad of rhythms. In one instant he felt crippled, then the next, utterly healed. It was only a few seconds before the side-effects were overcome by the new enhancements. Brynd suddenly became quite aware of the changes in his body: the throb of muscle. His sense of smell was more acute, and his vision sharpened by a new quality that he didn't yet know how to control.

*

Twenty minutes later, and Brynd requested an update of the current status of the citizens being held captive. The latest estimation was one thousand five hundred. The Night Guard was gathered around the massive table of the obsidian chamber feeling much darker and more oppressive than it had ever been. He related the data to them.

To Brynd's newly enhanced vision, the outlines of people's expressions appeared so acutely prominent that he could almost read their minds. Eighteen of them left, all in all, and Bohr-knows how many of the enemy. Brynd had to remind them just how much more efficient the Night Guard would prove on an individual basis, and that their extra enhancements might have made them near indestructible. Confidence and psychology were the key.

Brynd described the tactics:

They would now initiate Last Resort Storming. Because the warehouse was deep within enemy territory, a squad of garudas would drop them in, one bird for every soldier. They would swoop into a derelict street, half a mile to the south of their target location, where it had been reported there were minimal defences. Full-scale engagement had to be delayed as long as possible, therefore any interim combat would have to be swift and silent. Cultists could provide them with newly developed *Reykr* relics, a smokescreen tool. They would be armed with a sabre, a dagger, and a crossbow, and in small groups would penetrate in five locations, while garudas would blanket-bomb with *Brenna* three hundred yards north, to cause a distraction.

They would start under cover of darkness, but meanwhile there was still one other person Brynd wanted to speak to before the evening began.

*

He found her waiting as requested, in a dark annexe of the hospital, far enough away from the screams and howls of surgical horror. She was slumped in a chair at a table, a hot beverage beside her.

When he addressed her Nanzi looked up at him meekly, her hands still resting in her lap. Her eyes revealed the trauma of witnessing so many people in terrible pain. How could she ever be a killer, this woman who was little more than a girl?

'Good afternoon, commander,' she murmured expectantly.

Brynd nodded a greeting, then ploughed on. 'With your . . . ability of transformation. What can you do with it precisely? I believe, you can ensnare several victims at a time.'

She expelled a bitter sigh. 'You want me to fight, don't you? You want the big bad monster to go to war on your behalf.'

'In a manner of speaking, yes.' Brynd divulged the details of his operation. 'So you see, I'd like to make use of your skills, to secure certain vantage points that would help us infiltrate where necessary, then use your . . . secretions to hold back the enemy as we advance. And to aid with wounds, as you currently do.'

'I will try,' Nanzi agreed finally, then suddenly broke down in tears.

Brynd felt uncomfortable at this emotional outburst. She was a killer, nothing more, but he couldn't let her see his resentment.

'Look, after this war's over, I promise both you and this Voland chap can leave as free people. You'll have my word.'

She regarded him in wide-eyed incredulity. 'I will do as you say.'

*

Armed and ready, the Night Guard lined up in neat rows in the Citadel quadrangle, while storm-torches flared and receded in the breeze. Brynd paraded up and down, calling out instructions, last-minute strategy. Then, in hand language he signalled to the garudas perched above.

They glided down, each landing behind a member of the Night Guard. They linked straps, binding man and bird together. Brynd gave some brief commands: the garudas spread their massive wings outwards, and the soldiers crouched in unison with the bird-soldiers, an awkward joint posture.

Then everyone leapt skywards.

*

Jeryd had received instructions to hold several streets situated on the western side of the city, which seemed strange because this was practically now the invader's turf. Clearly there was an operation about to take place, something big, but he didn't know what. It was annoying how at times like this, even stray rumours got dissected as if they were encrypted orders.

Reading the entrails of gossip, that's what you're relying on, Jeryd. Why don't you find a primitive tribesman and ask for a shell-reading?

The irregulars had managed to hold on to a street as the

conventional military was pushed back, a professional regiment half slaughtered before his eyes. He felt proud of his rag-tag band of rumel – although they hadn't suffered the brunt of that skirmish, they were holding their ground, so the position didn't fall. Only the Okun had been tricky to deal with – with their daunting oneness of action, and they could somehow relay the irregulars' position to each other so as to avoid their snipers. Which pissed Jeryd off immensely.

And now there was endless waiting, it seemed, and Jeryd didn't know what for. The only clear instruction he'd had recently was to expect a visitor later that night, someone who'd contribute to implementing further orders.

Three hours since that message, and now long into the night. While drinking hot tea, snipers and scouts examined the neighbourhood for movement, when eventually a shrouded figure emerged from a side street. A couple of the lads went to investigate and escorted the newcomer over, cloaked and silent, to stand before their platoon leader.

Jeryd then laughed. 'Nanzi, you murdering bitch. The hell are you doing here?'

'I've been selected to help the Night Guard,' she declared, her tone almost apologetic.

Someone behind him gasped and there followed a moment of stunned silence. The presence nearby of that regiment was profound, and had a profound effect on everyone's morale. Jeryd's curiosity increased exponentially.

'Not in this shape, I imagine.' Jeryd gestured up and down at her human form.

Nanzi shook her head. Jeryd shook his.

'There's more,' she said. 'Because of such low temperatures, they want rumel to guide me into position, and then to oversee the escape of the hostages.'

Jeryd held back his disbelief. 'We've not had any official instructions yet.'

No sooner had he said this than a Dragoon came riding up

to them, and jumped down from his grey. 'Sele of Jamur, Lieutenant Jeryd. Sergeant Vígspár. I have orders for you from the Night Guard.'

As his mount's hooves crunched on the debris, the sergeant confirmed what Nanzi had just said, and Jeryd listened carefully to the well-organized plan.

Vígspár rode away, and Jeryd immediately dispatched platoon members in search of carts to retrieve any injured hostages.

As the moment for action approached, he heard a communal gasp. He looked back to see Nanzi begin her transformation. She began juddering into shape, limbs unfolding, tufts of hair sprouting.

Within a minute she had contorted into the vast shape of the killer spider.

A couple of the rumel in the platoon cowered back some distance and Jeryd shouted at them, 'Get back, *for fucksake*. We're meant to guide this . . . thing into place.'

In the awed silence that followed, Jeryd inspected the dark street once again for movement, all the time waiting for the sound of *Brenna* devices detonating, forcing the enemy into fighting at night, against their will.

Then suddenly it came, a dull booming in the distance, and shortly afterwards, the faint but urgent response of the invaders being pressed into action, their battle cries.

'Right, lads. Let's go,' Jeryd called.

*

Brynd couldn't tell whether his attack of nerves came from being transported by a garuda or the prospect of the mission ahead. His armour was buckled tight, and he had a cultist-enforced hoplon shield and sabre. To one side of him, Lupus had a double-compound bow slung across his shoulder, a quiver full of flu-flus and standard arrows strapped to his back. They were hauled above the cityscape watching the lights of the explosions some distance away, dull thuds followed by

467

yellow flashes. Unmanned garudas flanked those carrying the Night Guard, and instead they carried shields and nets to prevent the mute bombs from intercepting them.

In the distance could be seen a surge of enemy troops away from their target location, at least a thousand enemy rumel, and the sight of their departure brought a pang of relief. As the garudas tilted their wings and began to descend, the change in altitude and pace was distressing. Brynd couldn't help swallowing as the streets rushed vertiginously towards him. As soon as their feet touched to firm stone, his troop untied themselves, and the garudas shot skyward.

Brynd checked all were present, whispered brief orders.

Then they separated.

*

Strap your weapons tightly, Brynd signalled to Lupus, and he nodded his understanding.

Their small troop of four – Brynd, Smoke, Tiendi and Lupus – then slipped along a side street, behind several war-torn buildings, before tearing down the main thoroughfare that led north towards the warehouse.

The streets here were smothered by a thick layer of snow, and since Brynd had warned that footprints could ultimately give them away, they had to work quickly. Smoke and Tiendi arrived next to him as he paused a hundred yards from the broad street on which their target was located. While Smoke seemed to analyse the elements like he always did, Tiendi signalled discreetly for instructions, with her newly learned hand-language.

Wait until clear, Brynd hand-signed back to her.

Lupus unstrapped his bow, extracted three arrows, nocked one into position while the others readied themselves with sabres and crossbows. Perceiving the world in bright shades following their enhancement, there was no one to be seen around this side of the target building. This peaceful ambience disturbed him, although there was no reason for the enemy to know they were coming.

Then something crossed his vision, at the far end of the street: four dogs appeared, and began barking loudly. He willed them to shut up, for their own sake, knowing what would now be expected of him.

Brynd shifted his gaze towards Lupus and signalled *Kill*.

Lupus aimed his bow towards the animals, as suddenly they began to bound towards the soldiers, closing the distance at an alarming pace. The first muzzle appearing in his sight, Lupus fired. Then he loaded-fired, loaded-fired, loaded-fired until all four dogs collapsed into the snow in rapid succession.

Good, Brynd hand-signed, but Lupus didn't seem to think so.

A sign to follow, then they trotted past the corpses, Lupus pausing to recover the arrows.

At the broad intersection, there was nothing now between them and the rear of the warehouse. Glancing further along, Brynd spotted Night Guard huddled ready, their weapons glinting in the moonlight.

We wait for one other, Brynd signalled to them, meaning the monster.

And there she was, right on cue, scrambling over the rooftops towards them, an unnatural sight even in the most unnatural of circumstances. He watched in awe as she dropped herself to street level using some kind of self-produced cable. Brynd whistled three times and the towering creature scuttled next to him. Lupus instinctively raised his shield in front of him.

Brynd signalled to another group, then he jogged to a different position. By now, the Rumel Irregulars had arrived as backup, led by Lieutenant Jeryd. The ex-investigator nodded to him, acknowledging the situation. Brynd found he had to admire this tough old professional. A reassuring line of grey-skinned rumel stretched behind him, various wagons and carts visible among them. As Brynd returned, he gestured to the spider then whistled three times. In decreasing amplitude, the whistles were echoed into the distance.

The Night Guard crossed the intervening street with stealth, in one swift and fluid movement. Backs against the granite warehouse now, whose wall must have been a hundred yards in length. Reeking of marine odours, the place had probably been used as a fish storage facility and just how many hostages could fit inside it was anyone's guess.

A look to the left, the right, up, across and down.

Then along the street the rest of the Night Guard came stepping lightly through the snow.

Brynd had placed an ear against the wall, making the most of his heightened sense of hearing: indistinct shuffling – could have been rats – and a groaning, like some painful lament.

Was that them?

The spider lumbered across his path and skittered up the wall. The soldiers gaped as they watched her climb then flip directly onto the roof.

Another hand signal, a further change in position, this time further along the wall in search of the suspected points of entry. The Rumel Irregulars came through the snow to draw up behind. Jeryd stood at the front with his crossbow at the ready, one hand held out to urge caution. Their silent approach was matched by the eerie calm of the war-torn city at night.

Brynd located a suitable entry point, signalled for them to follow, whistled sharply to those further along the wall. The metal door was slung open, Brynd's small group began to enter. With bow nocked, Lupus was just about to follow the others inside when a small troop of red-skinned rumel came marching into the main street. They didn't notice the remaining Night Guard soldiers in the shadows, and focused instead on the Irregulars, now running towards them, a cacophony of yelling. The enemy began to release arrows and the Irregulars instantly returned fire with crossbows. Two rumel had fallen on each side before Lupus eliminated three of the redskins in rapid succession. They retreated back before it could develop into a close-quarters skirmish.

Brynd signalled for Smoke to deal with the redskins before they could get away and bring reinforcements.

A quick sprint back to investigate the casualties.

Four Irregulars were gathered around Jeryd, who now lay on his back with two arrows in his face and another in his chest.

Fucking hell, you too, Jeryd. After all you've done to help us.

'Shit, the old sod's dead,' someone said, pointing out the obvious.

'He's not just some old sod,' Brynd snapped, 'but an investigator who served the Empire loyally. Make sure he gets put on a decent pyre, you hear, and free his soul with some dignity.'

There was a high-pitched screech as the spider suddenly reappeared. It came bounding through the snow at an unlikely pace, forcing everyone away from the body of the investigator. The creature prodded the corpse with one of its legs. It tried to secrete something to stop the bleeding. How bizarre, Brynd reflected – this was the person who tried to put the creature behind bars.

Smoke rejoined them with a simple nod, confirming that he'd finished off the escaping redskins.

'Good work,' Brynd murmured.

The soldiers trotted across the street, weapons in hand, and all the time Brynd was checking around for any further incidents. Bringing his shield up in front of him, they headed into darkness.

*

Scan the walls, the doors, any signs of ways in or out. Lines of the corridor were evident to Brynd's senses, as was the cold dampness and stench of decay, but he couldn't source where the hostages were being held.

They pressed on for some time, the only noise detectable the footsteps and breathing of his own soldiers. An open space presented itself, a hallway, and after brief analysis he chose another corridor to follow. Lupus held his bow ready, Smoke and Tiendi gripped small crossbows and sabres.

He put his arm out behind to halt the others: there was a distinct change in texture in the light up ahead.

A flicker?

A redskin rumel stood at the far end of the passage, leaning on his sword, talking in alien constructs to someone out of sight. Brynd signalled for Tiendi and Smoke to take out the nearest one, and for Lupus to fire at the one beyond.

Click, click, thud.

The enemy collapsed on each other. Brynd dashed ahead and, by the bodies, gave a quick look around. If their minds had been connected in some way, then others would be arriving soon. He dragged the corpses into shadow where Lupus retrieved his arrow.

They had to be getting close now.

Stepping with extreme caution, they approached a partially closed doorway. Back pressed against the wall, Brynd nudged the door open with the tip of his sword. Three soldiers beyond: all redskins, no Okun. Brynd gave his team the signal then deliberately coughed.

Two of the redskins emerged into the hallway where their throats were slit quickly. Brynd burst into the other room, shield raised, and engaged immediately at close quarters with another. He found it easy to block the sloppy strokes, then he knocked his assailant's arm against the wall. With his sword he ripped open the creature's torso, thrusting upwards to the hilt. Thick blood spilled onto the floor. The creature slumped sideways.

The rest of his unit filed in behind. Brynd hoped the rest of the Night Guard had managed to penetrate this far.

The next door they came to revealed some kind of wash-room, with decrepit plumbing and broken wall tiles. The floor was covered in ice so they had to slide forward on hands and knees to the door leading into the main chamber.

Brynd opened it to reveal a vision of hell.

Immediately before him lay the remains of dozens of humans, and it took him a minute to realize they were mainly children and the elderly. Their corpses littered the floor or were heaped in the corner. Bones were fragmented across the floor, amid pools of blood long congealed. Many of the corpses had been sliced open and the bones partially removed, then left discarded. He wondered why. Were they rejects, the human waste? Ones who had not been loaded on boats and removed from the city?

There was no hope of recovering these bodies until later, so Brynd beckoned the others to move on. He could not blame them for standing there gaping with their jaws slack and eyes wide in disbelief.

We move on, he signed.

Too late? Lupus queried.

No. These are abandoned. Young and old. Probably find citizens still alive further on.

Tiendi was the first to shake herself out of the shock, coming to stand alongside Brynd, expectantly.

Into the next room . . .

Where hundreds of hostages lay slumped on the floor – but still alive.

Suddenly they began stirring. They had already noticed the arrival of the elite troops, more of whom were now appearing through different entrances.

Don't talk, don't talk. Brynd made obvious signs for them to remain quiet, but it was no good. The sounds that would blow their cover rippled through the warehouse, and within a few heartbeats, enemy soldiers began filtering in to the room.

Fuck.

Brynd now shouted the commands for combat focus.

The Night Guard united ranks as best as they could, while Lupus fired repeatedly to distract the enemy, his arrows plunging into the enemy, who were now spilling into the vast warehouse. Arrows and crossbow bolts sparked off the stone walls.

No sooner had a significant cluster of the dreaded Okun burst in, than Nanzi disgorged a thick drool of silk from above. The enemy was instantly halted, unable to navigate the sticky pulp. Lupus began an insane dash, sprinting across the front of their line, firing two arrows at a time into their weak spots as they waded through the viscous substance – and they began to crumple one by one.

Hostages were shouting and screaming by now, making a chaotic situation even worse.

Nanzi dropped to the floor and reared up on her back legs to force the hostages in hysteria towards the rear exits – and towards freedom. She then turned to confront a unit of the redskins, and Brynd ordered Tiendi and Smoke to provide her with backup.

The redskins lined up uncertainly before her, at first not quite sure what to make of this intruder, and suddenly some of their archers buried a dozen shafts in her abdomen and thorax. There was a deafening screech as her legs buckled, and she toppled forwards. Several others rushed forward to hack at her legs. She swiped at them with her razor-sharp limbs, severing their heads and arms in one go.

More came in, driving their blades into her thick black spider-flesh.

She screamed. She wheezed. The texture of the warehouse subtly changed.

As she settled herself down amidst her torture, a horizontal wave of purple light burst from her body and spread across the room.

A deep explosion knocked everyone to the floor, blew the upraised shield from Brynd's arm. He sprawled across the flagstones to retrieve it.

The battle regained momentum as the civilians scrambled to safety, and eventually the Night Guard managed to get themselves into position of forming a wall between the enemy and the hostages. By now about seventy enemy soldiers had arrived, and dozens more were soon filing into the room, many more than Brynd had anticipated, but he didn't reckon they would be too much to handle.

He screamed an order. The Night Guard merged, locked shields above their heads and in front, utilizing the hoplon's shape to form a phalanx formation. Arrows came crashing into them, an inexorable iron rain.

Under this metal shell, they nudged forwards.

*

Voland almost despaired at the sight of another delivery of casualties. Most of the time he felt like he was merely patching up the living dead.

Over the last two days he had slept for maybe eight hours in all. It was a job without gratitude, a life without motivation. As soon as one bed was cleared, another two bodies were waiting to use it. Time and time again, he had tentatively touched the detonator-collar round his neck, but it didn't seem as if it could ever be removed.

A moment of peace, finally, as he seized a few minutes to take a sip of water and contemplate his surroundings. He was in a chamber of the temporary hospital, a lantern-lit hole with a few empty cups, a few bits of stale bread.

Where is she now? he wondered.

The light suddenly blew out and he was left in darkness, uttering a weary sigh. Suddenly a wind caressed, one he was familiar with, like an old friend. Or friends.

'Voland . . .' they chimed.

'. . . we've found you again.'

'We want to help you, but we bring bad news.'

'Bad.'

'Sad.'

'Oh, so sad.'

Voland stood up, discerning the faintest glimmer of their wraith-like wisps. The devil chorus had returned. 'What is it?'

'Nanzi has left us, Voland.'

'Died.'

'We felt it, so sad.'

'Oh, so sad.'

Like an arrow in the heart, it struck home. He sat down, stunned. He tried to process what the Phonoi had just told him as they spun around his head. They were dizzying. He felt sick.

'What happened?'

They told him all.

He crumpled to the floor. All meaning had petered out of his life, nothing making sense any more, and soon confusion turned to frustration turned to rage.

Nanzi. The woman he adored, the woman he had helped to save once already, the woman he had helped to craft: there was as much of him in her as there was in himself.

She's gone . . .

There was a void in his heart so sudden and terrifying, he did not know what to say. In this suffocating darkness he could barely breathe. *She died for those people up there, the riffraff. She had no business with their lives, and she was forced to it against her will because of a crime that should not have been thought a crime. It is their fault she isn't with me any more . . . my Nanzi.*

'We're so sorry, Voland.'

'Please let us help you.'

'You have been so kind to us.'

'We want to make you feel better.'

Sobbing on his knees he managed a 'Thank you'. He then wept openly in front of the Phonoi for some time – he couldn't tell how long. Time had begun to lose any context, and slowly anger began to establish clarity in his thoughts.

When he had finally regained his composure he shuffled his way by touch towards the door. Opening it, he stood in the half-light, looking across a sea of the wounded, the dead-to-be.

It was *their* fault.

FIFTY

Dawn of the fifth morning, Malum was smoking a roll-up, standing at a smashed window, enjoying the contrast of the hot ash he occasionally flicked, and the cold wind. He was watching the Empire's soldiers mount an offensive against the border between Althing and the Ancient Quarter, buffer zones lying just oeast of the city centre. The savage shouts of war seemed so remote, so unreal. Grey clouds whipped across the horizon, over violent white-tipped surf. Smoke from pyres on the outskirts formed horizontal trails blowing down across Villiren.

The floorboards whispered underfoot as JC came up to him. 'Boss, someone to see you.'

On exiting, the man's footsteps crunched over crumbled masonry.

After a silence came a voice: 'Malum . . .'

Beami. He took another drag, exhaled calmly. She didn't really bother him any more.

'How did you find me?'

'It's not difficult for someone like me,' she replied. 'You leave enough of a trail wherever you go.'

'Even with the city in a state like this?' A half-hearted gesture towards the city, but she didn't say anything. The silence provoked him, eventually, to ask, 'Fuck do you want, Beami?'

'I never realized just how much of this you lorded over. I

mean, I knew you had all your business interests and the like, and the odd fight, but all these violent men—'

'Fuck do you want?' Didn't want to look at her, didn't want to let her get the chance to affect him again.

'Won't you take off your mask?'

He considered his answer: 'No.'

'OK. Well, I tried to go back to our house – there was something I left behind, and it's completely empty. Where did you put all our things?'

'*My* things, mostly.'

'Come on . . .'

'The hell does anything I own got to do with you?' Eventually he had to face her, a black hood revealing only the outer angles of her face. The rest of her clothing was dark-coloured and tight-fitting, and something about its condition suggested that she'd seen some action in the war. He didn't know quite what to make of that.

Behind her, in the doorway, stood several of his men, but he motioned for them to go.

'You've every right to hate me,' Beami said.

He did and didn't. Most of all he just didn't care any more, and he told her so.

'Well, that's fine – and I don't feel any anger towards you. I want you to know that.'

'I'm surprised you didn't leave the city.'

'I've been doing my bit for the Empire,' Beami replied. 'I took out several hundred Okun at the moment of invasion.' Then, 'That seems like forever ago now.'

'Impressive,' he mumbled, more jealous of that achievement than he was of her other man.

'Look, Malum, I need a relic that I had to leave behind. Can you tell me where I'll find it? I'll understand if you don't want to cooperate—'

'Probably in the underground vault, where we keep all the gang's hauls.'

'So you didn't destroy it then?'

Silence was all he offered. There was nothing to say other than of course he had fucking loved her, so wouldn't simply get rid of her belongings just like that. But he couldn't bring himself to actually let her know such things, preferring to leave the constructs of his ego intact. His mask ... what was left of his sanity, intact.

'Can you show me where that vault is?' Beami asked. 'I need to know, Malum. It's urgent.'

'No,' he replied, and heard her gasp. 'But someone else can show you.'

'Thank you, Malum. Thank you so much.'

Such a pathetic tone now. 'Whatever. Just don't steal anything that's not yours.' His attempt at a joke.

She ran up to him and hugged him and whispered, 'I'm so sorry for everything.' Then she stepped away, but he could still feel her intense gaze.

'You're a different man now,' she observed. 'You don't care even if you die, do you?'

'Look after yourself, Beami.' Malum chucked the remains of his roll-up out of the broken window. And as she left, she took all that was left of his being human. There was no need to hide from it any more. *Embrace what you are.*

*

The kid couldn't have been more than thirteen or fourteen, with blond hair slicked down in a modern style, his mask a parody of anger. Beami followed him through part of the underground over which Malum had ruled, cast-iron structures that she could barely see. Beami guessed that they now propped up the roof. Nothing human had designed these passageways, she suspected. Walking though elaborate designs, they kept veering off at odd angles, till she thought they must be heading back the way she came. Now and then they'd come to some subterranean settlement, a nexus of decayed shopfronts and bars, broken chairs littering the open spaces, though a few seemed just recently used. Given the war, they became, like the other quarters, mere ghosts of settlement.

This was how Malum genuinely existed. They had always been a spurious cover, his trading contracts, his networking, these important business operations that he couldn't talk about. He had always consorted with devious men, but she'd never fully grasped the extent of his underlife existence.

The boy said little, just grunting occasionally to indicate a change of direction. He held up a torch, forcing shadows across her path. She asked him questions, to get a better understanding of Malum's other life. 'Who are you?' 'Where are you from?' 'How old are you?'

To the one 'Where are your family?' the kid eventually spoke: 'Bloods is my family, woman.'

He carried a short blade in his other hand, clearly afraid at accompanying this cultist. With shifty glances, nervous steps, the boy led her towards the vault.

'What are all these crates?' Wooden boxes were piled haphazardly in the tunnel all around.

'Drugs, sort of. Alcohol. Nothing fancy.' It was the most he had said during their journey.

'Is that a body?' She gestured to one half-open crate that looked like a human arm was hanging out of it.

'Just a golem – you know, for sex and stuff. This is the vault you want.' A cave-like opening barred by a sturdy wooden door. The kid unlocked it and, with surprising strength, pushed it open.

As he stepped aside, he handed her the torch so she could go in first. It was an unremarkable chamber, filled with the contents of their past life together. She wasn't even that old, so how was it possible to have accrued so much junk? Vases, rugs, brass figures, paintings, all these things were infused with memories, but she shoved them aside and searched for the better part of half an hour, while the kid stood sighing and tutting outside.

'You gonna be much longer?' he asked finally.

'Nearly done.'

He had kept all her relics together in a box at the far end, untouched. She'd half expected them to be smashed up out of anger.

As soon as she found the *Brotna* relic, the cone she'd spent days working on, all her tension ebbed away. There was nothing else in the box she needed, so she grabbed it and exited the vault.

''Bout fucking time,' the kid muttered.

*

Night, as Beami placed the relic in her small room at the Citadel. Due to the proximity of the military lines, she'd had to trek the long way around to get there. Everywhere she went, a figure from the Dragoons or Regiment of Foot would redirect her path. The invasion force had penetrated deep, had seized one half of the city, but it was still relatively safe on that side.

There were fewer than ten thousand Imperial soldiers left. A staggering number had died. Exhausted men and women, lined up time and time again to resist the incursion, their faces haunted and determined and frightened. The citizen units were now few and far between, and Beami wondered if most had been slaughtered or were stationed elsewhere. Some streets had become bloodbaths, lined with human and rumel remains, and in one road she came across the bodies of several Dragoons who had been lined up against a wall and decapitated. She forced herself to look upon this carnage, to remember what was happening here.

Safely in the Citadel, as she lay back in a chair by the fire, mentally exhausted, she forced herself to think that Lupus might still be alive somewhere on his secret mission. He was a Night Guard, for Bohr's sake, and one of the best, but that didn't alleviate her fears. She promised herself that the two of them would get out of this mess as soon as possible. For him the priority was his job as a soldier and, if he survived, they would leave together and find peace.

There was a knock at the door and a soldier entered.

Beami bolted up straight. 'Have the Night Guard returned?'

'No miss, not yet,' the young man answered. 'There's a new cultist who's just arrived, and she needs some help in finding someone. The others are all asleep, I'm afraid, so would you mind seeing to her?'

'Who is it?' Beami demanded, her heart sinking.

'She said her name was Bellis, and she's quite old.'

'Tell her I'll be out in a moment.'

*

Out in a dingy corridor, with soldiers rushing past them, Bellis explained carefully who she was and what she wanted. 'I'm looking for the boys, they're called Ramon and Abaris, and it's been so long since I've seen either of them.'

'I remember them.' Beami's voice was soothing. 'They came to offer their services, but I'm afraid they're thought to have passed away in the fighting. They made an incredibly impressive golem of body parts which hampered the invasion ... They really were very brave ...'

'The silly buggers,' Bellis whispered, trying hard not to sob.

Beami came to her side and held her. 'I'm sorry. Were you very close to them?'

'How can I explain that bond of companionship in a world where no one regarded us of any use?' Tears filled her eyes, and she closed them tight.

'Come on,' Beami soothed. 'Let's get you somewhere warm.'

They went back to Beami's room, where Beami poured them each a whisky. 'This might not solve the trauma, but it'll ease the pain. So, tell me, what were you doing here?'

Bellis carefully explained what she and the Grey Hairs were doing in Villiren all this time, what they had been seeking, and how she needed someone's help to raise it. Intrigued, and

483

without hesitation, Beami found herself volunteering her services.

'You do realize that this will be big?' Bellis warned. 'There may well be widespread destruction.'

'If you think it will help sway things in our favour – then it will ultimately save many lives. Though I'm not sure I quite comprehend the scale of it.'

Bellis nodded. 'Then, my dear, I will show you.'

*

Across the city, across the night, the two female cultists slipped quietly past soldiers and blockades and mourners gathered at pyres. They cloaked themselves in darkness as they approached the first location.

There, Bellis produced a crowbar and turned to Beami. 'My back isn't what it used to be. Could you help me with this flagstone.'

She indicated one in particular that had an unusual symbol painted on it, one that Beami wasn't familiar with. Possibly a hex sign? Together they prised it open and shifted the stone to one side ... and underneath, embedded in the soil, lay a relic. Only the top of the orb was visible.

'A *Hefja*,' Bellis explained.

By the way Bellis looked at her, Beami felt that she was expected to understand. She thought the antique word meant 'lift' or 'raise', and suggested this.

'That's absolutely right, in the most literal sense. Pretty and bright – how wondrous!'

Beami understood then how it would work, how they would all work. Bellis had already explained there were a number of such symbols painted around the city, which the Grey Hairs had assiduously identified according to ley lines. 'These locations are precise to within an inch,' Bellis added. 'All of them, once primed, should be enough.'

'How will you know if they're successful,' Beami asked, 'if

you're going to be somewhere else by the time they're all activated?'

'Ten in total, and all we can do is hope for the best. You see, this isn't my first time...' As Bellis smiled her face wrinkled up in delight.

Beami felt inspired by the woman's confidence, and she had to admit it had taken her mind off things, to have this little assignment drag her out into the middle of the city, to prevent her from sitting alone and brooding over Lupus.

She watched Bellis set the device, turning the dials then placing her palm against its exterior surface. As the old woman withdrew it, the ghost of her hand remained visible under the surface of the orb.

'This one is set,' Bellis announced with a sigh of satisfaction. 'Right, let's get right to the next one.'

*

They shifted across several districts of the darkened city, through desolate lanes, stepping over corpse-thick passageways, while somewhere in the distance there were explosions and, shortly after, garudas arced back overhead.

Luckily eight of the ten devices were to be found in what was still Jamur territory, or no-man's-land. Beami helped in lifting the stones, or in shifting corpses away first. To reach the two devices located in enemy-occupied territory, they had to use relics to shift between degrees of time. They shunted back and forth, vibrating between seconds, in order to reach them in real time, at a point just before they'd activated the first ones. It was all about synchronizing, of course.

Beami felt increasingly in awe of Bellis's skills. The old woman possessed more wisdom and talent and imagination than she would have thought possible, and was surprisingly fit and agile. Now and then they'd stop to rest, and the old woman would whip out a hip flask of sherry, a grin appearing on her face as if the burdens of life had been lifted.

Dawn threatened on the horizon, and Beami felt a renewed sense of urgency because, once light arrived, the war would resume in full.

'Don't worry, my dear,' Bellis said. 'We're just about set.'

The final device was back in Deeping, far across the city and safely behind Jamur lines.

'Do you have any idea,' Beami asked, 'what it will do once it's up and active?'

'One can never be quite sure,' Bellis replied, not really answering her question. They scrambled up to a flat roof that offered a perspective across towards the Shanties. The Onyx Wing rose behind them, and behind that the Citadel, allowing them a perfect view of what was about to happen.

'Do the Jamur military know what you're doing?' Beami asked.

'Not one iota.'

'But what if there are citizens out there, getting in the way?'

Bellis's gaze softened, and she sighed audibly. 'Perhaps there's no one there by now. We can only hope that, can't we?'

Before Beami had a chance to say anything more, Bellis produced a smaller orb, the size of an apple, and began to tamper with it, muttering something to herself. 'A-ha! And here we are. Three . . . two . . .'

Villiren groaned.

'. . . one.'

Some of its thoroughfares glowed a pale violet, began vibrating and shuddering back and forth, and further out, towards the Shanties, there was a sudden haze of bright light.

Bellis grabbed Beami's arm and said excitedly, 'Let's just hope it heads the right way!'

The noises of troop movements became more distinct for a moment, then buildings in the distance began to veer and teeter sideways. Dawn birds scattered manically. People surged out on to the streets in hysteria.

Cobbles spat up in a fluid line in three locations. Then something possessing an electrical outline breached the roof-tops, and rose till it gained immense height, thirty, forty, seventy, a hundred feet and then doubled again and again in size until it took clearer form. Tentacles swirled around, crashing through the war-battered architecture.

A giant squid, made entirely from light.

Beami was shocked, truly shocked. Despite having been told, despite having known what was coming from Bellis's explanations, this was far beyond anything she could have contemplated.

As the city delivered itself of this light-formed ghost, the streets themselves giving birth to the monstrosity, Bellis clapped her hands with glee, jumping up and down on the rooftop.

'That *thing*, that cephalopod,' Bellis explained loudly, 'has been trapped beneath Villiren for millennia. The Archipelago is littered with such electrical ghosts, waiting for re-activation so, after some detailed research into electrical teuthology, all I had to do was put the right relics in the right place.'

These charged corpses were just waiting there to be unlocked.

Vast and garish, the squid's tentacles flailed through the air, swirling in the dawn light. It pushed outwards, dragging buildings apart, trampling everything in its hundred-foot-wide path. Screams rose in the distance and, as a cloud dust accrued in its wake, it ploughed right through the enemy-occupied sectors of the city.

And through countless enemy soldiers.

As it slunk into the sea, probably trashing what was left of Port Nostalgia, it would, Bellis hoped, also eradicate the invasion fleet, those grey vessels in which the Okun and the redskin rumel had arrived. Water sloshed to huge heights as the harbour waters banked and surged far inland, and even the larger boats were cast around like toys.

And all the time Beami kept praying that as few of the Imperial forces as possible would be harmed.

*

Brynd glimpsed Lupus releasing an arrow which imploded a skull somewhere in the darkness. He fired again through a gap between the shields as the Night Guard maintained their protective structure despite the onslaught of redskins and Okun. Brynd was breathless and his legs seemed about to buckle because of maintaining this cramped position. Caked in sweat and blood and severed flesh, he rested his hands on his knees and tried desperately to draw in air.

With limited visibility he could not see clearly where the next attacks might come from, so had to remain ultra-alert. Attacked from the front and sides, simultaneously they broke position only briefly to launch savage assaults on their assailants.

Their recent enhancements had so far kept them alive.

Suddenly the entire building began to shake, causing another pause in the combat. It continued to shudder like it had a fever, before a sound like a *Brenna* device exploding. Stone spat inwards at every human and rumel and Okun alike, and then there were shouts of a different and more desperate kind. Holes appeared in the structure, revealing strange lines of bright light outside.

That's when the ceiling collapsed.

FIFTY-ONE

Beami was back at the Citadel by the time the news reached her. Bellis was snoring triumphantly in Beami's bed, while she herself waited anxiously for news of where Lupus and the Night Guard had gone. The more she fretted about it, the more she was convinced something terrible had happened.

A senior commander of the Dragoons began giving orders to a squad of soldiers out in the main quadrangle and it was then she heard something of what happened. The Night Guard were delayed ... perhaps their mission had gone seriously wrong ... although the hostages had been released, every member of the elite unit was still missing in action.

Beami's felt her heart thumping in her throat. *Please, not Lupus ...*

*

After his briefing was completed, Beami stalked some lieutenant of the Eleventh Dragoons, a blond, athletic man with a beard, and tattoos spiralling across his neck. She pursued him for some distance through the corridors before she managed to stop him.

'I need to know where the Night Guard have been sent,' she demanded.

'I'm afraid, miss, that's classified information.' He nonchalantly turned to continue on his way, but Beami grabbed his arm.

'Tell me where the fuck they are, all right, or I'll hit you with an energy so hard . . .'

The soldier snatched his arm back, laughing, so she slapped him with a *Tong* relic, a metal device that clamped itself into his arm like teeth and brought him gasping to his knees. 'Tell me where they were sent.'

As he scrambled about on the floor, half trying to maintain his dignity, half convinced he would die, he spat out the location of the warehouse and what they were supposed to be doing there.

'So much for classified information,' she sneered. 'Thought you guys were trained to withstand torture?'

After she removed the device he said nothing, merely rubbed at his arm and breathed heavily through his nose. His mouth was now clenched tight, but it was too late. She had the information and was on her way to wake up Bellis.

*

With their bags of relics slung across their shoulders, the two women headed back across the warscape. In daylight now, the ruins were clear to see and ordinary and depressing. Beami's heart sank when she realized just how much damage her city had suffered because of the war – war with some enemy she knew nothing about, a conflict that seemed so distant from her previous existence. Her life had little context in all of this.

In the Imperial zones, the citizens did not seem willing to leave. Babies shrieked from doorless buildings and distraught women sobbed openly in the streets. In one plaza, at a table propped up against a whitewashed wall, two old tramps still stubbornly played their game of dice. This was their home, after all, this was all that many people had ever known – their reluctance to abandon it was understandable.

In the contended zones, corpses lay in the snow, in decrepit armour, amid isolated limbs, bloodstains and rotting flesh, and the streets reeked with the taint of death. Where windows once glimmered, black holes seemed like gateways into hell.

Red mist was sprayed across the banks of snow, where people had been slaughtered. Without the street cleaners' regular attention, there was little to stop the weather from reclaiming the city, and it almost seemed the kindest thing to do would be to bury Villiren, to let it suffocate under the elements.

*

A warehouse, that's what she'd been told. With street locations, and grid references discovered from a map, Beami and Bellis crept past the blockades, using relics to bend light around them, to create invisible stairways over ruined buildings. Every trick they knew of, they used. Every step was weighed down with a sense of dread that Lupus had been crushed.

At one point, she defended them both against a couple of Okun who skittered across the rubble so clumsily that she wondered how they could have inflicted so much damage in the first place. She employed whips made of light that fizzed and sizzled across the Okuns' shells, flinging the vile creatures across the desolate street.

'Oh, well done,' Bellis trilled. 'Very good use of energy.'

*

The two women had been walking for miles now, their feet aching and legs growing weary. Fast-moving clouds brought sleet but nothing worse. They'd been moving slowly for at least three hours now, taking occasional stops to sip from bottles of water.

Beami checked the map again, but the further west they moved, the more meaningless the lines on it became. Former streets had reorganized themselves into intermittent chaos. In places navigation became guesswork. Luckily Bellis had been studying the topography of this city for years, and soon felt confident that they were heading in the right direction.

An hour later, they were approaching the area where the warehouse should have been.

'Where is it then?' Beami asked. 'I can't see anything that looks likely.'

'It's just possible that our cephalopod friend managed to destabilize some of the buildings.'

'You mean your fucking squid flattened the warehouse,' Beami snapped.

'Oi!' The voice echoed across the street. A unit of rumel – citizen militia by the look of them – came trotting across the snow-strewn rubble. Two black-skinned men and a brown-skin arrived, a troop behind them, all equipped with cheap armour and swords. 'Ladies, get off the street.' They ushered the women behind a broken terrace of housing, then explained to them who they were and what they were doing.

Beami turned to the Rumel Irregulars. 'What happened to the Night Guard?'

There was an awkwardness to their expressions, a tentativeness about their manner, and Beami had her worst fears confirmed. One of the citizen-soldiers, a young brown-skin by the name of Bags, explained, 'Roof came down, miss, when they were all in there. They'd been clearing the place of civilian hostages – over a thousand – then fuck-knows-what comes flying across the city and heads out to sea. Wasn't the thing itself what knocked it down, more the rumblings, if you see what I mean.'

Swallowing, Beami suppressed her concerns for the moment. 'I need to go inside there.'

'Impossible, miss. We've been looking all around there, but there ain't nothing but rubble.'

'They're Night Guard. They're enhanced soldiers. The collapse may not have killed them all. That means some of our best soldiers might still be alive.'

There followed a swift discussion amongst the Irregulars, whispers and nods. Bags then said, 'We can lead you up to the building, and pick off any of the enemy that are still around while you go in.'

*

As they approached the wreckage of the warehouse, her heart sank. How could even Lupus survive this? Rubble was strewn far and wide, where the structure once stood, chunks of masonry of varying sizes, brick and slate and tile scattered haphazardly. Jagged knuckles of stone jutted skyward.

In this corpse of a building, its broken pieces scattered over hundreds of yards, where could they possibly begin?

'Watch out for any Okun, miss,' Bags called out as his troop disappeared behind the ruins.

'Let's get started,' Beami sighed.

She first deployed the *Brotna*, intending to break up all the stone around them so they could more easily scour the site. She unravelled the tendrils of the large metal cone, then aimed the top of it across the first cluster of rock. As she charged the device, a humming sound could be heard, before a bolt of energy disintegrated the entire mass. Bellis assisted with some extraordinary fork-like implement that expanded to lever up larger segments.

Presently, citizen soldiers began to gather and, once they realized what they were doing, even offered assistance. Where they came from, Beami didn't know, but soon other tools miraculously appeared: lengths of rope, spades, crude pulleys and even a bucket of biolumes for searching under the darker crevices. An uplifting mood descended on the scene: these people wanted to see their best soldiers get out alive, a repayment for their efforts in coming to this city to defend them.

An hour passed. Then another.

Finally, Beami led the way into the centre of the now revealed structure. Everywhere they found broken bodies, and she sighed with relief each time she realized one was not clothed in the familiar black uniform.

*

Everyone took a break, apart from Beami. Exhausted though she was, her body seemed beyond pain. Snow came and went, a brisk wind blew dust into her eyes and mouth. She merely wiped it away and continued. There was only one thing she could focus on. She shamed everyone into working almost as hard.

Dusk approached and Bellis came to tug at Beami's sleeve. 'My dear, you've got to get some rest.'

'Not yet, there's still light enough. Then there's the biolumes to help. You go back to the Citadel if you want to.'

Another hour, a step closer to pitch darkness. She clambered over towards where one of the inner walls jutted up through the rubble, and continued her work there, shredding stone and moving on, shredding stone moving on . . .

A groan? Was that a groan?

'Over here,' Beami called out, her heart racing. She scrambled closer to the source of the sound and, with her bare hands, began hauling smaller hunks of masonry out of the way. Once that was done, she used her relic again.

A Night Guard shield was suddenly exposed.

'Hello,' she called. 'Hello, can you hear me? How badly are you hurt?' Others arrived behind her, excitement rippling around the group.

A voice called back, its Jamur accent precise and clear. 'I think . . . I think some of us . . . Some of us, we're OK.'

She didn't recognize the voice – it certainly wasn't Lupus – but a rush of adrenalin spurred her on. With the help of others, large chunks of stone were lugged away, biolumes were brought forwards. They laboured under night conditions now, ten of them, little conversation except brief instructions. Stretchers were fetched by the Rumel Irregulars, who lined them up close by.

'Keep your eyes closed, all of you who can hear me,' Beami said, before disintegrating more of the masonry with her relic.

A big enough gap now, and she climbed down to reach the trapped soldiers, immediately looking for Lupus, but she couldn't see him.

Beami lifted one of their shields and handed it to a rumel loitering above her. 'Biolumes,' she ordered, and the bucket was passed down. She tipped its contents on the ground where the luminous creatures gave off their eerie light.

Beami called up, 'Someone give me a hand getting this man out.'

A bulky rumel stepped down and took the weight of the soldier. Together they carefully pulled him out by his arms and, as Beami guided his body, she winced at the stump of his ruined leg, too severe for the augmentations to have much effect.

One by one the Night Guard were lifted out of the rubble, their faces bloodied, and there were smashed arms and scars that had begun to heal. One had been hit in the eye with an arrow, one was a female, one was dead – but he was not Lupus. One was the albino, but still no sign of Lupus.

There he is! Lupus lay on his back, his shield half covering his face. His leg was bloodied, and his face was blackened with dust. She moved to his side and peered to see if he was all right.

'So you leave me till last then,' he rasped weakly.

Beami sobbed with relief, and rested her head on his chest. He tried to say more, but clearly could not.

*

Beami had found a surprising new point beyond exhaustion where she felt she could carry on. For nearly three hours she walked by his stretcher as it was carried through the safer streets leading to the Citadel, an arduous route in this pitch-blackness.

The commander of the Night Guard was now reasonably fit enough to guide the line of stretchers down towards the underground hospital, offering to carry his own men where possible. The line headed through the sanctuary of those passageways, and a sense of calm returned to her. Lupus even managed to smile at her now and then.

As they shuffled into the main ward everyone stopped and gawked at the scene in disbelief.

'Dear, Bohr no!' someone exclaimed.

Rows after row of the makeshift beds had been toppled over. Lying on the floor, or in whatever postures they could manage, were hideously deformed patients. No, it was worse than deformed – they had had things grafted on to them, appendages that were from . . . other creatures.

'Fucking hell,' another voice gasped.

'Bring some torches so we can see what's going on in here,' Brynd ordered.

Light arrived. Hundreds of men and women were revealed to possess furred or scaly replacement appendages, limbs ripped from reptiles, or legs transplanted from horses, or heads grafted and grown from invertebrates. The rumel patients had been similarly deformed, grafted with human heads and hands, amassed in stockpiles. They groaned and wept with shock and depression, for as far as you could see. To one side lay the dismembered corpses of the doctors and nurses who had been tending to them, their entrails strewn across their bodies.

And up near the ceiling hovered something like wraiths or ghosts. A trick of the light perhaps?

A soldier came running towards them clutching a note, which he thrust towards Brynd. 'Found it on that guy at the far end of the ward. Hanged himself by his shirt – think he's been dead for some time.'

Brynd read it, shaking his head: 'It's from Doctor Voland and it says simply: "If you manage to survive this war, here's to your happy ending. May it be as happy as mine was. Fuck you all. Sincerely, Voland."'

The noises being transmitted from these people-monsters were alarming. Many of these things tried to lumber towards them, but collapsed almost as soon as they moved, being unused to having spurious limbs. An elderly female, with giant dog-legs for arms, pawed at a soldier before someone pushed her over. One man with a lizard head managed to get close before someone shot the thing with a crossbow.

Brynd ordered everyone to get out of there, and they firmly bolted the door.

Was there no end to the horrors?

FIFTY-TWO

The *Exmachina* droned across the skies. It seemed to be taking forever to reach Villiren. In the distance, the columns of smoke did not provide a good omen.

They must be funeral pyres, he thought. *Bloody hell, how many people can have died?*

The city looked flat – either by design or from war damage, he couldn't tell. It wasn't at all like Villjamur. The sea lay beyond, a darker expanse of grey that merged indiscernibly with the sky.

Eir joined him and surveyed the view. 'Rika's still the same,' she fretted.

It seemed Eir could not let up on how much her sister had changed. Randur kept telling her she was probably now safer under Artemisia's protection than they could manage for her themselves. It made his own life easier, anyway – this was what he wanted to say, but instead he dutifully listened to her complaints.

'Doesn't look good out there,' he observed, trying to change the subject.

'I'm still not sure how we're going to go about this.'

'I'm sure she'll have it all planned.'

'She has schemes for everything, I'd wager,' Eir said. 'I still don't trust her.'

Just then Artemisia strolled up to them, dressed in full battle gear.

'I think the city's seen better days,' Randur said, gesturing over the edge of the ship.

'It probably has. But it stands, which is an achievement. Your military is rather useful, it seems, and this bodes well.'

'So what's the plan?' Randur asked.

'We ourselves shall enter the city, while the *Exmachina* continues onwards. I plan to have it destroy the gateways through which this invasion originated. I guarantee it will disrupt the sentience of the enemy.'

'How?'

'They relay their inter-communications via the gateways and my own dimension.'

Relay their inter-communications? Randur didn't understand the terms, the definitions. 'Which means?'

'They can't talk to each other unless they are communicating through the interface. If it's disrupted, they won't understand each other. Temporarily, that means they will be on equal terms with your own military forces.'

'Can understand that, more or less,' Randur mumbled.

As the ship glided above the city, the devastation below was clear to see. The southern and eastern sections seemed largely unscathed. But as they progressed further most of the city was in ruins. At least the huge fortified Citadel was still standing, he noticed.

*

Plummeting, they fell from the skies about an hour after dawn, the cold wind buffeting and tugging them to extremes. Their descent seemed to last a lifetime, and it was Artemisia who touched down first, the others being more reluctant to let go of the ropes.

As Artemisia stared upwards, Randur followed her gaze.

For a moment the *Exmachina* seemed to adopt a new texture entirely, as if now made up of tiny squares, then it shuddered and shot off in a streak of light towards the north. The sky above was suddenly vacant, but Hanuman fluttered down like ticker tape, drifting and flapping earthwards before perching on what remained of the city's rooftops. A distant thunder was heard. Randur wondered if the ship had already done what Artemisia promised.

The warrior woman unsheathed both massive sabres from over her shoulder and strode into the warzone.

*

Randur had never been to Villiren. He was stunned: the city had been crippled in a way he could not comprehend. Buildings leaned at bizarre angles, many now a haphazard lattice of timbers. Some streets were utterly silent save for the sea breeze rattling through them. Human and rumel remains nestled at the bases of walls, feral dogs or cats picking at the decomposing flesh. Across the accumulating snow, the red spray of death was everywhere. To one side, a rumel woman lay face down and naked, her throat slashed, and a crossbow bolt through the back of her skull. Randur half-expected Eir to show distress at the sight, but she had become hardened of late, and remained impassive.

The small group followed Artemisia through this apocalyptic nightmare, stepping over tiny gutters filled with bloodstained debris and ice. Groups of men with machetes lingered everywhere, whether civilian soldiers or looters, he couldn't tell.

A cacophony of sounds and voices could be heard in the distance.

Eventually they came across a sector of the city packed with Imperial soldiers. A church spire had collapsed down on to its side, now covered in snow, and troops lined up either side of it. Some men at the rear turned towards Artemisia, and tried to stop her from advancing, but she easily brushed them aside. When she drew her sword Rika leapt in-between.

'Who the fuck are you lot?' one soldier demanded.

'I am Jamur Rika,' she replied.

He searched his mind for the correct protocol then gave up and stood back.

Artemisia pressed on through the military lines, which parted as if by her will; she was a good head taller than most of them.

Suddenly, a unit at the front were dispatched, peeling off then disappearing around a corner. In the distance, the sounds of combat continued.

They followed Artemisia as she went after them, preparing to launch herself into the fighting, and found line upon line of soldiers getting mown down as they pushed forward.

Randur could see the enemy for the first time, the Okun and red-skinned rumel, about seventy of them ranged ahead. Every one of them now turned in uniform motion to face Artemisia. There was a brief exchange between them in an alien language, after which there was a profound silence.

Then a deep explosion sounded in the distance, and every-one looked upwards as if seeking an explanation, And then, a few moments later, they felt a back-draught of warm air.

Suddenly the precise coordination of the enemy was visibly reduced to confusion. Their uniform thinking had been dis-rupted, and in frustration, red-skinned rumel in elaborate uniforms paraded up and down the lines, shouting orders, livid at this new state of play.

Artemisia smiled, the first time Randur had noticed a change of expression on her face.

And why is it suddenly getting warmer?

Artemisia darted forward into the thick of the enemy and soon she was engulfed in their mass. Soon he couldn't see much, merely heard grunts and metal connecting with metal, and now and then a piece of severed flesh would flip out from the scrum of bodies.

Eir glanced at him questioningly, but he merely shrugged. Rika stood aloof and watched with a neutral expression – as if she, too, had been infected with Artemisia's impassivity.

Finally, the entire street was littered with dismembered corpses. Artemisia came towards them, glistening with fresh blood. 'Now would be a good time for the Jamur troops to mount a surge,' she declared. 'How many of your soldiers are left?'

'Eight thousand, approximately.' An officer shuffled towards her, a sudden respect evident in his manner.

She loomed over him. 'How many did you begin with?'

'About sixty-five thousand in military service. Civilian casualties are as yet unaccounted for.'

'So be it,' she replied nonchalantly. 'You will find that your enemy has now been disabled significantly. Purge as many as you can, and I shall assist in finishing them off. Meanwhile, someone will take us to your commander.'

FIFTY-THREE

This was the first time in years there had been gang unification, of sorts. Beneath the official war had meanwhile run another. Turf brawls had become all-out combat to splice districts into enclaves of unofficial rule. Autonomous zones had been raided by others, new front lines coming and going by the hour, and it was only this morning that some kind of weird law had been laid down. Verbal treaties exchanged, confirmed with a sly handshake and a nod of the head. Things were made clear.

Malum went looking for the BanHe, but he was dead. Someone accused Malum of killing the creature – it wasn't true. They found what was left of Dannan's body in one of the underground strongholds. The room reeked. It seemed he had exploded from his throat and chest, and men gaped from behind their masks at the mess splattered on the surrounding walls. Someone pointed out that Dannan had died a few days ago, when the death count within the city reached a level where the scream-impotent BanHe had vomited bile for hours at a time, coughing and retching as the body count mounted up. He had crawled down here to try to avoid the escalating pain, and died alone.

Something had now happened that changed everything in the city.

Dark shapes in the sky, out of the sky, then a change in temperature. It was suggested that the enemy were suddenly weakened, that there were now few of them left, and that those remaining were unable to fight as efficiently as before. Malum didn't understand what these specific changes were all about, but he realized the final hunt was on.

Malum marched somewhere near the front of the mob. The Bloods had now aggregated with the other gangs again in a quest for all-out slaughter. They spread rapidly across Villiren like a virus. Somewhere on the way he'd succumbed to his primal instincts, and allowed his fangs to breach permanently. He had become utterly *savage*, and so had the others. Even battle-hardened soldiers looked upon their work with disgust.

Joining in behind the citizen militia, which in turn merged with several Dragoon regiments, more of a vicious mob than a disciplined army, they pushed westwards across the city, thousands of men and hundreds of women scooping up any kind of weapon out of the melting snow. Sunlight peeled back from behind clouds till the slick city glimmered.

Confident and violent, this mob-army came across small clusters of remaining Okun. Cornered in twos or threes, with nowhere to flee, the now seemingly confused invaders burst into the crowd of their assailants only to be hacked down with axe and mace and sword. Citizens took out their frustrations by ripping apart the shells and leaving little but pulp soon mashed into the snow. With confidence that the invasion was being reduced to nothing, and no more ships appearing on the horizon, the gangs took a manic pleasure in their work. They were in the grip of a death fetish.

Surprisingly, the red-skinned rumels were the more difficult to kill – they seemed more skilful in these embers of combat, more cunning in their methods of escape. Some even offered surrender, but no such bargaining was accepted. Tails were ripped off and stuffed into their screaming mouths; they were beaten into a bloody pulp or then stoned to death with rubble. Such savage methods appealed to Malum for some reason, and violence bred violence. Perhaps it was a confirmation of his own reason for existence.

This business continued for most of the day. What surprised Malum was that there was no definite end to this, no clear finale. Everything petered out. The city was too decimated for its people to understand that they had won this conflict. Though maybe 'won' wasn't quite the right word. It had more or less survived.

What next, though? The city needed rebuilding, reconstructing.

About an hour after the final killings, people began ambling around the city, cutting paths through the aftermath. Civilian soldiers sat on the remnants of shattered structures, utterly depleted. Even children began to emerge from hiding, gazing up at the red sun as if they'd never seen it before.

In his meanderings, Malum at one point came across a shattered mask lying on the ground. He took off his own and suddenly wondered why he always hid behind it. What benefit had it given to his life? And, now that the one woman who sustained his sense of normality with the world had walked away, what did he care for hiding any more?

Malum dropped his own mask in the rubble and walked away.

He was what he was, a vampyr, and he would now make himself king of the new city.

*

'But quit the Night Guard? That's your life ... everything.' Beami lay on the bed next to him, her eyes aching with tiredness. 'It's what you do, it's who you are. You're a hero to the people, after you helped save so many lives.'

'This city isn't a place for heroes,' Lupus replied flatly.

All he had done, since they had returned, was stare at the ceiling. So it was over, and that was something. Yet it didn't really feel like an ending.

'There's so much death. That's all there is here. That's all this fucking world brings us, isn't it? You see these creatures invade our land, but that's what the Empire has been doing to other nations for centuries. We tread on them with no regard for their lives, or the way they already fit into the world. I've now seen it from the other side ... I used to have a sense of pride in what I did, but there's no honour in any of this.' He paused, breathing deeply. 'I just want to step outside of it all. With you.'

'If you're sure,' Beami replied thoughtfully. 'You realize that if we ever come back it will be exactly the same moment in time as we leave?.'

'Skilled archers aren't all that useful in the construction business, and that's what this city needs now, builders and craftsmen or nurses. Afterwards, destroy your relic, if you want to. Or just hide it, whatever. I'll take my chances in that other place, and even if we can't communicate with anyone else, so be it. I don't bloody care. We've nothing here. Bring all your equipment, whatever you want, and let's make a new start – away from everything.'

*

Beami balanced the legs of the *Heimr*, twisting the ball at the top. It had been a while since she'd used it, and she felt a sudden inexplicable fear that she'd forgotten how it worked.

They had already gathered their belongings. Lupus didn't have that much, and he mocked Beami for bringing so much. Where was she going to put it all anyway? They had no home to look forward to, so how reckless were they being?

Holding each other tightly, his head on her shoulder, they stood in her desolate chamber in the Citadel. He was much recovered now, and he hugged her more gently than he'd ever done. Every touch was exploratory, as if he was deeply grateful to be holding anyone.

They heaped their possessions in a neat pile around the relic.

'This might be the most ridiculous decision we've ever made,' she observed.

'No, that was when I cleared off to the army. Now I'm leaving the army for you. Think about how we could have saved ourselves so much time and effort.'

She smiled. 'Well, now we've all the time we could want.'

One hand to the relic, one to him, and the *Heimr* began to pulse.

Time suddenly stretched o–u–t—

FIFTY-FOUR

An end.

But could you call it a victory if around a hundred thousand people had died? Was it really called winning when your own army was nearly destroyed?

Overwhelmed with exhaustion, Brynd had been sitting alone in the darkness of the obsidian chamber for hours. His muscles shivered as a spasm of pain flickered through his body, soon to be overridden by whatever trickery the cultists had developed. Sometimes a messenger would enter to update him, when Brynd hunched forward in his chair and stared at the floor as he listened to them. The few surviving garudas were still flying reconnaissance missions along the coast, but for now, it seemed Villiren held firm. Just then, Brug entered the room, and whispered that Haal had haemorrhaged in the hospital, and died.

'When will it stop?' Brynd sighed.

Brug left the room with a vacant expression, leaving Brynd alone again.

A breeze blew through the open window, disturbing his strategy papers and maps. He let them drift to the floor. *No need for maps now.* This city would have new streets, and new lines would need to be drawn. Lutto hadn't been seen for days – the cowardly portreeve had probably fled the city long ago. Reconstruction was Brynd's task for the time being.

Images of horror still burned into his mind's eye: severed flesh, pools of blood, the tide of aliens clamouring over their dead ... He had heard that other soldiers were experiencing fits as the ghosts of terror haunted their skulls. Grown men reduced to tears. There was nothing in the Empire's military manuals to guide them on this point.

A lack of sleep had dulled his reactions, which was why it took him a while to notice the arrival of Jamur Rika, the former Empress. An immense figure beside her loomed over him, but if this was to be his fate, he was too exhausted to challenge it. A clamour of military indignation behind them confirmed that they had forced their way in.

Brynd did a mental roll-call of the muscles in his body, then sat up. He was more interested in the massive, weird-looking stranger beside the ex-Empress. *What is it?* He regarded Rika once again. 'Shouldn't you be dead?'

'Shouldn't you, after all that fighting?' Rika replied.

'Probably,' Brynd said. 'So how can I help you?' Looking from Rika to the presence beside her, he noticed a slender young man with ridiculous hair shuffle in. He was accompanied by Rika's younger sister, who looked considerably hardened since the last time he had seen her. She smiled at him, and he mumbled a greeting.

'Who's this then?' A nod of the head indicated the odd figure. The creature must have been at least seven feet tall, wearing a uniform of some kind he'd never seen before. Its material seemed to be bolted together rather than stitched, and those blades she sported looked superbly crafted.

'I am Artemisia,' the giant figure replied.

And it was what came next that shocked him.

*

Context at last, or at least reasoning and understanding.

Artemisia explained that she was one of the Dawnir, though she didn't look much like Jurro. She boldly declared she was one of the god-race. So began a narration of thousands of years of history, and Brynd was not used to being made to feel so ignorant.

*

Randur and Eir had found a room together, nothing fancy, but at least containing a bed. They lay down alongside each other. Randur was still reeling from what he'd seen today. The world was a dark place, but he still had a life to lead, still wanted to get Eir away from all this.

'It's not yet over, is it?' he whispered.

She stirred beside him. Her fingers brushed his chin. 'I wanted to stay alongside my sister.'

'Do you still?' He paused. 'She's not even the same person.'

But by now Eir was asleep, and he didn't blame her.

*

Later still, seated around a table with Rika's entourage and the female god-thing, Brynd finally composed his thoughts. As commander of the military, he still had a job to do, and forces to command. Whether or not he followed Imperial law, he could see himself writing a history of his own. The weight of decisions burdened him – his mind had already been taken to breaking point because of the war, but now . . . now was a time for rebuilding.

According to orders, he ought to have had Rika arrested, but in present circumstances, that didn't seem to matter so much. Besides, Artemisia had broken the arm of the last guard who had tried to restrain her – so tough measures didn't seem all that prudent while he was still weighing up his options. Besides, he did not trust Urtica.

'Here's what I propose,' Rika announced, placing both hands on the table.

'What *you* propose?' Brynd echoed. 'You're currently a prisoner of the Empire.'

'You already know *me*, commander, so you can rely on my word.' Rika explained the events of their capture, and their journey to Villiren.

'Just tell me what you propose,' Brynd interrupted, 'and I'll tell you if I can trust in it.'

'I want to detach Villiren from the Empire, for the military here to switch allegiance to me. We need to take Villjamur – but then comes the difficult part. We must form an alliance with the alien nations in Artemisia's world, allowing their gradual repopulation within the Boreal Archipelago, living alongside human and rumel. It is only when we accommodate Artemisia's culture that we will have the resources to resist any further attacks. Can you seriously tell me we'd all survive on our own?'

Brynd replayed the horrors of the war through his mind.

'The main gateway through which the Cirrips – what you call the Okun – arrived has been disabled temporarily,' Artemisia added. 'They may repair them soon enough. We have an unspecified amount of time to act.'

'Essentially,' Brynd said, 'you're suggesting our cooperation is your only hope?'

'We are each other's hope,' Rika argued.

'As I have been saying,' Artemisia intervened. 'Let us seek peaceful solutions from now on. Peaceful integration is the only answer.'

This was a head-fuck, all right. Did Brynd even have a choice? 'It could take a while to get things straight,' he said eventually. 'The city's a wreck. The army is depleted. We'll need to rebuild. Yet you just plan to take Villjamur? Do you have any idea how well protected that city is?'

'Once the alliance has been declared,' Artemisia suggested, 'I may well be of assistance in that matter.'

*

When nothing more could be said, they left Brynd alone with his thoughts. Left in solitude, he went over to the window overlooking the city. There were purple-blue skies to the north, something he'd not seen in a long while, and a warm breeze gusted over Villiren – it seemed like an omen of what he'd just learned. Pyre smoke trailed up from distant quarters of the city, and seabirds had returned to scavenge. *You won't find much there.*

Brynd strode out of the obsidian room and went back to his private chamber. The place was still a mess after Nelum's attempt to assassinate him, though at least the bloodstains had been removed. Exhausted, he collapsed on the bed, breathed deeply and pressed his head into his hands.

There was probably no choice, he realized. What Rika suggested made some sense, though pulling apart the Empire which he had served all his life felt instinctively wrong. But these were different times, and the islands faced change whether they liked it or not. If he was to make a beneficial impact on the Boreal Archipelago, it would be by helping in its reconstruction – though he had no idea of the outcome after alien cultures had been introduced. And after the battle raging across Villiren, he felt he could take on anything now.

Shaping cultures, Brynd thought, finally closing his eyes. *This must be what it's like to be a god.*

FIFTY-FIVE

Voices were the first thing to return to the abandoned streets. Conversation, everywhere more conversation, people talking about what had happened, what to do, where had so-and-so gone, have you seen my husband, my son, my daughter? People were coming back to the city, finding their homes no longer there, whole streets and entire districts had vanished.

Marysa stepped carefully through the rubble-littered streets. Cultists had begun a clear-up, and uniformed personnel trotted everywhere, carrying their weapons. Now and then there'd be an alien scream as one of the Okun was found hiding in the darkness, and was slaughtered. Such incidents made the return to their homes more frightening than a relief for the people of Villiren.

She proceeded with purpose, now and then glancing at the map she kept in her pocket, but it was of little use. She was heading past the whalebone archways and the giant Onyx Wings, towards the little bistro that Jeryd and she had agreed would be a good place to meet after the conflict.

A lot of things had happened underground which she now wanted to forget – they didn't actually happen to her, just to others, but that didn't make the experiences any more agreeable. How could people be so cruel to one another in a time of desperation? While the majority felt solidarity, there seemed to be a predatory few who would ruin the lives of others in fulfilling their own selfish needs and desires. Now and then humans would stare at her and shout abuse for here being a rumel, but she couldn't blame them because of the alien red-skins that had been part of the invasion.

People feared only what they did not understand.

*

It was now some time around mid-morning, and she stopped to watch several cultists use a cone-like device to shatter rubble. Even they themselves seemed surprised at the effectiveness of the contraptions. Paths were slowly carved, gaps in the snow-covered city forming, allowing people to pass through. Horses, and other weird beasts, were used to help cart away chunks of salvageable masonry. Already, useful items were being sold by quick-thinking traders. Makeshift irens sprang up, and soldiers and civilians gathered there, queues several people thick. All faces looked so *tired*, as if something had vanished from their existence, and they were now struggling to hold on.

Most of all, she hoped Jeryd was OK.

*

The shadow of the Wings seemed bolder than she could remember. War hadn't visited here, or destroyed buildings, but most were empty. In some cases, boards were already being lifted from the windows. And there was the bistro they had agreed to meet in, seemingly unscarred. She walked towards it, her belongings suddenly heavy across her shoulders.

She waited for him as sunlight skimmed off the cobbles, shading her eyes as she looked up and down the street.

Marysa waited for him. And she waited.

*

The red sun slouched across the sky, as more and more people sauntered past in front of her. She examined their faces eagerly to see if one might be her husband, then eventually she stopped looking, because the routine had become too depressing.

Please let Jeryd be OK.

A massive lump rose in her throat as she fingered the medallion he had given her. She looked up to see that the darkness of evening wasn't far away.

Sighing, Marysa pushed herself back out into the mainstream of the city, back to find somewhere to spend the night. She passed citizens huddling in blankets by the warmth of barrel-drum fires.

As agreed, she would return again tomorrow, to wait for Jeryd.

There was always tomorrow.

THE BOOK *of* TRANSFORMATIONS

by Mark Charan Newton

The next novel in the epic Legends of
the Red Sun series, following on from
Nights of Villjamur and *City of Ruin*.

A new and corrupt Emperor seeks to rebuild the ancient structures of Villjamur to give the people of the city hope in the
face of great upheaval and an oppressing ice age. But when a
stranger called Shalev arrives, empowering a militant underground movement, crime and terror becomes rampant.

The Inquisition is always one step behind, and military
resources are spread thinly across the Empire. So Emperor
Urtica calls upon cultists to help construct a group to eliminate
those involved with the uprising, and calm the populace. But
there's more to The Villjamur Knights than just phenomenal
skill and abilities – each have a secret that, if exposed, could
destroy everything they represent.

Investigator Fulcrom of the Villjamur Inquisition is given
the unenviable task of managing the Knights, but his own
skills are tested when a mysterious priest, who has travelled
from beyond the fringes of the Empire, seeks his help. The
priest's existence threatens the church, and his quest promises
to unravel the fabric of the world.

And in a distant corner of the Empire, the enigmatic cultrist
Dartun Sür steps back into this world, having witnessed horrors

beyond his imagination. Broken, altered, he and the remnants of his order are heading back to Villjamur.

And all eyes turn to the Sanctuary City, for Villjamur's ancient legends are about to be shattered . . .

OUT NOW

ONE

This was no time to be a hero. Under the multicoloured banners of the sanctuary city of Villjamur, under the reign of a new emperor, and amidst a bitter northerly wind reaching far through the knotted streets, something was about to start.

Seven human teenagers sauntered back and forth in front of a gate that permitted access to one of the highest levels of the city.

Sleet was whipping by in the channels between these old stone walls – buildings three or four storeys high, with fat timber frames and decorated with hanging baskets inhabited by little more than limp tundra flowers.

From his horse, Investigator Fulcrom could glean only so much about the movement of the youths: their first walk-by was purely to check out the guard situation, maybe gauge the soldiers' temperament. A little tease. Those kids had done well to get this far, given the current political climate. In their baggy breeches and hooded wax coats, they moved with long, easy strides right past the military installation. They possessed every intention of creating a scene. At least, that was what the guards were meant to think.

But Investigator Fulcrom, a brown-skinned rumel in his younger years, knew better. He'd seen this kind of thing before, from his casual dealings with the underworld – an advantage that these simple guardsmen did not possess. No, these youths were decoys – they didn't have the guts to challenge the guards outright. Sure, they laughed and whistled and threw around tentative insults and crude hand-slang gestures; but this wasn't the real deal, not by a long shot.

So if they're not looking for a fight, what're they up to?

About a dozen armed men and women sporting the crimson and grey colours of the city guard peered on glumly from behind the bars of the massive rust-caked gate. Fulcrom suspected they were probably annoyed to be out in this weather as much as being faced with these young piss-takers.

Another group of kids loitered by the massive, arched door belonging to a disused tavern. *Are these connected with the main display?* In the shadows they chattered and pointed at a piece of parchment nailed to the wood. Fulcrom knew they were looking at the artwork of MythMaker, an unknown figure who would occasionally leave his hand-drawn stories about the city. It was rare to see one of the sketches here – rare, in fact, to see them much at all these days. The parchments were usually left by schools, or in places where children would loiter, and Fulcrom wondered for a brief moment if it may or may not have anything to do with the events about to transpire.

Back to the main show: a second taunting walk-by from the youths still yielded no response from the soldiers.

Cobbled streets weren't as dangerous to traverse these days, not with the cultist water technique imported all the way from Villiren to keep the ice at bay, so the kids strolled safely in a line, right before the assembled military.

A shadow flickered, followed by a sharp ripple of wind: a garuda skimmed the air overhead, making its presence known. Fulcrom tracked the garuda as it flew between the spires that defined Villjamur. A few of the older structures here were latticed with ladders and scaffolding, bearing workmen and cultists as they continued the Emperor's massive programme of regeneration. Either side of Fulcrom, the streets weren't at all packed – merely a few of the usual well-to-do citizens that you found about the fifth level of the city, trudging from store to store. Faded shop facades indicated tools or gemstones or bistros, and not for the first time Fulcrom noticed a couple of those new private soldiers of the Shelby Corporation stationed as guards. Beyond, cobbled lanes arced upwards, winding and twisting like slick-stone veins into the heart of Balmacara, the dark fortress that was the Imperial residence. Suddenly the bird sentry banked upwards, drifting into the haze, then scrambled to a standstill on one of the overhead bridges, where it stared down ominously across the scene.

Fulcrom inched his horse forwards, closing the distance. He should have been at the office by now. He had dozens of high-profile burglaries to be investigating, but he wanted to see how this played out, and his tail swished with anticipation. He was fifty years old – remarkably young by Inquisition standards – but he could tell a ruse when he saw one. *Pity the guards can't ... How useless can they get?*

He would have intervened, but it would be bad etiquette. In the moment's pause he absent-mindedly wiped the excess mud from his boots, then rearranged his crimson robe.

A greater density of people now began to mill about around him, drifting forwards, curious about the show. Women in drab shawls, men hunched in furs and wax raincoats, the dozens soon became a hundred: here was the promise of something to break the monotony of everyday life in Villjamur. Citizens were currently experiencing lockdown conditions – the Council was in its regular session, and virtually no one was allowed near the upper levels, the forbidden zone lying beyond the guarded gate.

The third walk-by now, and all laughter had faded as the youths began aggressively throwing rocks at the guards. The stones pinged off the bars, or slapped against the wall to one side.

'Get the fuck away, brats,' a veteran guard growled. Stubbled and heavily built, he looked like he knew his way around a fight. The man unsheathed his sword with a zing.

One of the youths strutted forwards, took a wide-legged stance and beckoned the guard forward, much to the entertainment of his mates.

There followed a *clank clank clank* of a mechanism; the gate started to lift and the youths inched away, peering at each other, then around the streets.

Fulcrom followed their gazes, but could see nothing out of the ordinary. They were just looking for escape routes.

So where is it? When's it coming?

The guard grabbed the youth who was beckoning him by his collar, slammed him into the ground and pointed the tip of his blade at the kid's throat. In all the commotion, Fulcrom couldn't hear what was being said, just continued to followed the anxious glances of the others. A woman from the crowd screamed for the guard to leave the kid alone.

Suddenly, from two streets away, four figures garbed in dark clothing and riding black horses burst through the bad weather and, with immense speed, approached the gate. The one at the front swung his sword and decapitated the veteran guard – blood spurted across the cobbles, his head flopped uselessly to one side, the kid in his grasp shrieked in disgust. The other youths made their escape.

The four riders, their faces obscured by black scarves, collided with three guards, knocking them aside, then spilled through the gate. Another soldier was trampled, another was driven back into the wall with a scream, and then the others were hurled aside by a violent purple light that burnt at their flesh.

The crowd were in hysterics.

Cultists? Fulcrom pulled up his crossbow, loaded it, and nudged his white mare in an arc across the wide street, trying to make his way through the fleeing masses.

He spotted a gap – and moved in pursuit of the riders, with two city guards moving in to flank him. The winter winds whipped across his face.

*

Like hammers on anvils, hooves pounded on the cobbles.

A trail of seven horses curved upwards through the high-walled streets and galloped through a thronging iren. Screaming people lurched aside while traders cursed as their cheap wares were scattered across the ground. Bones of the unfortunate were crunched into stone, but Fulcrom ignored this and focused on plunging through the horse-made gaps in the crowd, his heart racing. These invaders were quick and skilled and working those horses with purpose. *They know where they're going*, Fulcrom thought. *This has been well planned.*

As the skies above cleared, the sun cast its amber haze across the buildings. The pursuit moved ever upwards, carving through the higher levels of Villjamur, away from the iren, through narrow side streets, under flamboyant balcony gardens, and past lichen-blighted statues. More military riders drifted in alongside Fulcrom, and warning bells resonated in the distance. Fulcrom shouted directions in the hope that the military would follow, but they didn't – they were young and unskilled riders, almost injuring their horses as they pushed them around dangerously tight corners.

Up ahead, one of the insurgents suddenly turned around and, from some handheld device, launched back two purple bolts of energy. Fulcrom yanked his mare out of the way. The soldier to Fulcrom's left had his arm burned; another's horse crumpled under him when her leg was shredded by the light. Fulcrom pushed aside his fear: whoever they were, they needed stopping.

Across another plaza, the chase continued: wealthy women shrieked, and their husbands stood blinking dumbly in the light as their perfect morning was upset by the hubbub.

'Out the fucking way!' Fulcrom yelled, using his tail for

balance now. Leaving the military riders behind, he nearly slipped off his saddle when his horse lurched to the left to avoid colliding with two basket-carrying women. For a moment he thought he had lost the four marauders, until he glimpsed them up ahead. They were moving now at a much slower pace, heading across a thin bridge.

He headed after them holding his breath; this wasn't a pathway meant for horses. It was narrow and crumbling and stretched from one platform to another like some rickety plank. The cityscape spread open below him, the glorious spires and slick slate roofs, the baroque architecture, the massive structures of legend.

If he fell from his horse he would die.

His horse tentatively plodded along to the other side before he nudged it into a gallop again, on to precarious terrain where the cultist water treatments had begun to wear off. By now Fulcrom had worked out where the riders were heading: the Jorsalir Bell Spire. Where the Council was said to be in session.

The criminal gang had dismounted by a row of expensive terraced cottages, which were used for retired military leaders, great whitewashed structures with winter hanging baskets and thatched roofing. Another road sloped up and down along a high viewing platform that overlooked the tundra beyond.

Fulcrom slid off his mare and approached. The figures were hooded, garbed in similar featureless dark outfits.

Fulcrom drew his sword. 'Strangers, state your business.' His voice seemed lost in the city's haze.

'I'd stay away from here if I were you, brother.' Fulcrom couldn't discern who spoke due to the scarves protecting their faces. The accent was bass but curious – definitely affected by some distant island.

The speaker seemed to be at the centre of this group; he didn't turn around.

'What've you got there?' Fulcrom approached closer and

pointed to the sack in which the man who had spoken was rummaging.

The figure turned around and commanded, 'Brother, I have warned you – keep back.'

A thought struck Fulcrom: they had not yet killed him, or tried to, and he knew there was little he could do alone against so many if they tried. *These people want someone to witness this.*

'On behalf of the Inquisition, I demand you halt and show your faces,' Fulcrom ordered. He withdrew his gold, crucible-stamped medallion from beneath his robe.

'And how exactly are you going stop us?' The figure reached into his pocket and flicked an item that landed at Fulcrom's feet, some coin perhaps, but it disappeared instantly. Fulcrom instinctively leapt back, but nothing happened.

As he walked forward he collided with something ... invisible. He spread his hands, testing the unseen force between him and the stranger, who was now laughing behind the scarf.

All Fulcrom could do was watch. Infuriated, he slammed the heel of his fist against the force, but again nothing happened.

'Your name?' Fulcrom demanded. He tried using his sword to strike the shield around him – the physical absence – but it merely bounced off the nothing that was between him and his target.

A moment later and he watched the group run across the bridge in a neat line with sacks tied back over their shoulders, their heads held low. They sauntered across the wide road between the crenellated walls towards the Bell Spire, which looked so high it threatened to puncture the clouds. Guards, stationed there today, approached them, but Fulcrom saw the assailants use the same trick they had on him, a disc to the guards' feet, and then they, too, were caged by an impassable force.

So they weren't killed either – what does this group want everyone else to see?

The group moved towards a huddle of Jorsalir priests, who tottered sheepishly away, and the gang then began to climb one of the walls with frightening agility, probably using relics to aid them. Two garudas flapped in to intercept them, but flashes of purple light punctuated their wings so badly that they plummeted out of the sky.

All Fulcrom could do was watch. He couldn't be certain, but it appeared as if the would-be terrorists were leaving devices all around the base of the thick, conical spire. Frustrated, Fulcrom walked along the edge of his barrier, still prodding it to test for weakness in that direction, but he could only go backwards, and there was no other route to the Bell Spire that way. He rested his hands on the invisible barricade and gazed helplessly across to the brigands, his breath clouding before his eyes.

The figures climbed down from the spire, leaping near the base – and almost floating back to the cobbles. They stepped up on the edge of the crenellations, spread some rigid-looking rain capes and leapt down to drift across the sleet-filled cityscape with the grace of garudas.

A moment later and the base of the Bell Spire exploded; bricks scattered like startled birds, slamming into the surrounding structures and rattling onto roads. A thunderous crack like the wrath of Bohr split the bridge first, sending it buckling in on itself and crumbling down onto the level below. The spire leaned to one side, groaning, and eventually it twisted in upon itself, as masonry dust clouded up around.

The ruins collapsed down across Villjamur. Block and brick slid into this fresh abyss, and people screamed from every direction as dozens of bodies fell from the site of the Jorsalir monastery, and Fulcrom lost sight of them a hundred feet below. For a good minute he stared helplessly, refusing to believe that all he could do was watch. People swarmed down below, in hysterics. He wondered how many councillors had been in that building.

Fulcrom turned to head back the way he came, and the only way he could go, to try to reach the crisis down below, but he noticed many of the nearby banners had been somehow replaced whilst he was facing the devastation. There were no crests here any more, no flowers, no depictions of great creatures, no displays of wealth.

Only black rags rippled in this chilling wind.

EDITOR'S PICKS – EXCLUSIVES – COMPETITIONS
INTERVIEWS – EVENTS – PREVIEWS

SIGN UP

WWW.PANMACMILLAN.COM/TORNEWS

TWITTER.COM/UKTOR

TOR®